Stuart Campbell is a full- now living in Glasgow. He and advisor in the Lothians Health in Mind, an Edinbu He has previously written *Scottish Book Collector*. He *in Love*, an anthology of Robert Louis Stevenson's love poetry, and author of *Boswell's Bus Pass*, a travelogue of modern Scotland following in the footsteps of Dr Samuel Johnson and James Boswell. Stuart Campbell is married to Morag and has four grown-up children.

Also published by Sandstone Press

RLS in Love
Boswell's Bus Pass

JOHN McPAKE
and the
SEA BEGGARS

Stuart Campbell

First published in Great Britain
and the United States of America in 2014
Sandstone Press Ltd
PO Box 5725
One High Street
Dingwall
Ross-shire
IV15 9WJ
Scotland.

www.sandstonepress.com

Editor: Robert Davidson
Copy Editor: Kate Blackadder

The publisher acknowledges support from Creative Scotland towards publication of this volume.

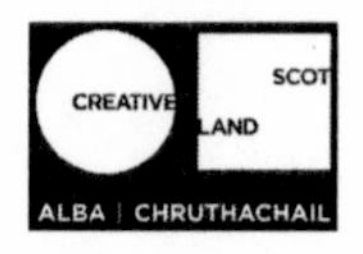

ISBN: 978-1-908737-69-4
ISBNe: 978-1-908737-70-0

Cover design by Mark Ecob
Typeset by Raspberry Creative Type, Edinburgh
Printed and bound by Totem, Poland

People with a diagnosis of psychosis often hear multiple voices. To the hearer the voices are as real as if they were listening to someone standing next to them. The voices, often unpleasant, can have completely different characters.

PART ONE

ONE:
Leith 2014

Unable to sleep, John raised his window and breathed in the chill early morning air. He could just make out Jack lying in the grave with his arms crossed.

Overall, the garden was not proving a great success. After a heavy night's drinking Jack Sprat (he was after all just skin and bones) had taken a spade and started to dig by moonlight. He had thrown earth over his shoulder as if rescuing a smothered relative from a landslip. Despite his slight frame the hole grew ever deeper. He knew a thing or two about graves having been employed as an NVQ assessor to a large firm of funeral directors in a previous life. '2.2: Sides of grave are shored where depth of grave exceeds 1.5 metres or as determined by enterprise policy,' he recited from memory.

Increasingly bored with tending to the needs of the dead, Jack had joined the army and found himself in Bosnia where his previous training proved invaluable. After three months he stormed into a formal regimental meal and harangued the Commander on account of there being no nationally defined professional competencies for mass graves in this part of the world. It was a disgrace and clearly the Commander should have a word with the Serbs. He subsequently left the army and set up home with his new companions, psychosis, trauma, alcohol and several other men with whom he had nothing in common apart from a diagnosis.

'*Alas poor Jack,*' said a rueful voice in John's head.

He looked again at Jack, now sitting bolt upright, saw him lean forward and tug at something on the ground, the edge of the sheet on which he had piled the earth from his excavations. Soon his feet were covered. He then pulled at the sheet on his left, and again a cascade of soil tipped into the grave.

Jack lay back and skilfully tugged at the remaining sheet, dropping earth onto his face. This was the largest deposit, judging by the size of the soil pyramid where Jack's head had been. For a moment his one arm remaining above ground flailed, and then became still, a blind periscope emerging from the freshly dug grave. John ran from his room.

'Some of us are trying to sleep.'

'They always come in the night, fascist bastards.'

The door to the garden was locked. After rattling the handle John remembered Beverley's lecture on safety. The key was behind the Nescafé jar. It took an age to open the door. He tripped on the top step but kept running until he reached the grave. He threw himself onto the mound and tugged at Jack's hand. The excited Voices assailed him. He shook his head like a wet dog to dislodge them but they only got louder.

'*Well done Johnnie Boy! Quite the hero. You'll get a mention in* Psycho Times.'

'*Ask for me tomorrow and you shall find me a grave man.*'

'*Climb in alongside him you loser! Ever considered necrophilia, John?*'

John heaved on Jack's arm until it grabbed him round the neck and pulled his face into the cold earth. The man was stronger than he had realised.

'*Fight!*'

The arm let go and Jack's face emerged from the grave, his face black and hair matted.

'He's turned into a darkie, one of those rastapharoahs! No baby, no cry ...'

Jack sat up and grabbed two handfuls of earth which he crammed into his mouth. He filled his ears, shaped two plugs of clay and forced them into his nostrils.

'Straitjacket, nurse!'

John put his arm round Jack's shivering body and tenderly put his fingers into his mouth like a mother whose child has swallowed a humbug.

'Now put your fingers up his arse! Gay boy! Gay boy!'

'Shut up! I can't hear what John's saying ...'

'He never speaks anyway.'

John helped Jack out of his grave, brushed him down and, with the utmost tenderness, led him back into the house.

TWO:
Flemish Brabant 1572

The three weavers caught their breath on the brow of the hill and stared at the pig roasting on the spit. Strings of saliva dripped from the dogs. The smell of bristle, gristle, flesh and fat was unbearable. Johannes glanced at the fox hanging from his wrist, a bracelet of elongated skin and gaunt flapping skull, a mouthful of meat at best. The pig dribbled its tallow into the flames, its eyes open and its nostrils flared.

Cornelius approached the black-cowled women tending the fire. The nearest, either a child or a dwarf, seized the poker and jabbed it towards his face eager to scour his eyes from their sockets. Her two companions took up positions to either side of her. They stood in a shared silent scream.

'Their tongues have been cut out,' said Balthasar, placing a hand on Cornelius' shoulder.

'Leave them be. They too have suffered.'

'Shit, shit, shit!' said Cornelius, moving away angrily while slapping his chest to beat out the cold and hunger. He wrenched his neck from side to side as if he was in the grip of a huge bear, and his head was the only part of his body he could move. 'Shit. Mother of God!' he added for good measure.

Balthasar, the older man looked at him. 'Have you finished?'

'Almost,' said Cornelius. 'Shit, pish and the pus from the sores of martyrs' wounds. Gabriel's scrotum and eunuchs' foreskins!'

'Did Gabriel have a scrotum?' The two men looked at each other. Cornelius knew that his companions were trying to distract him from his anger.

'But what if they find her?' he continued. 'What if the Spanish catamites suspect something and burn down the barn?' A thin, nervous man in his thirties, he moved quickly from foot to foot as if wary of being attacked by his own shadow.

He sought reassurance in the eyes of Balthasar. The older man had seen it all before. According to village legend he had survived the first massacre by feigning death beneath a heap of dead fighters, lying in urine and biting his lip when cramp grabbed his thighs. The more gullible claimed that he had once laughed in the face of the Grand Inquisitor, tweaked his beard and somehow lived to speak of it. He was, when all was said and done, the talisman, the augur of good fortune who would bring this mission to a successful conclusion.

Balthasar was just tired. He had already exceeded his allotted lifespan, and had no wish to play the hero. His back ached, his scrofula had returned, and at some point on their journey his bowels had turned to stone. He would not tell his companions but secretly harboured grave doubts about their quest. It also occurred to him that Cornelius' young wife, Geertje, was indeed at risk from the foreign soldiers. 'She'll be fine,' he said, 'keep the faith.'

'Come on,' said Johannes eager to move again before his fingers, already stiff in his gloves, froze completely. The pack of dogs dreaming of chase and kill foraged for scent beneath the layer of hard snow, the trace of rabbit, the hint of fox. They had been joined on the hill by every starving cur from the village. Cornelius kicked out at the unwanted beasts catching one in its throat. It yelped away and the others followed. Their own two dogs tucked in beside the men as they moved down the slope towards the frozen lake.

'They're hungry too,' said Johannes.

'I know, I know,' said Balthasar. Despite his strong views on not overfeeding hunting dogs he was no advocate of starvation. 'Keep them lean and mean,' he would say. 'When they find Michel, then they can feast like the beasts of Kings.' He looked up at the cold sky from which the light was seeping away. 'What we need is a star.'

'What?' asked Johannes.

'Well, there are three of us, I'm called Balthasar, we're looking for a child, we need a star.'

'I'm poxed if I'm changing my name to Melchior ... a stupid name. What was the third one called?'

None of them could remember.

'Anyway, we haven't got any myrrh.'

'What is it anyway?'

'It's the sweat from angels' armpits,' suggested Cornelius.

'Angels don't sweat,' said Balthasar.

'It's hard work sticking red hot pokers up devils' arses all day,' said Cornelius, stamping his feet from which all sensation had drained.

'When we find Michel,' said Johannes, 'he will be raised as a weaver, not a carpenter.'

By screwing up his eyes they could see the distant skaters in greater detail. There were couples dancing on the ice, their movements exaggerated by the effort of keeping their balance. They were all older women. Occasionally they embraced each other in a parody of happier times, aping in slow motion the same steps they once shared with young lovers and sweethearts.

Johannes shivered beneath the rough wool of his cloak. He was itching too from whatever species of vermin had taken up residence in the warmer crevices of his body. He stretched his arm down his back but he couldn't reach it.

'What's up with you?' enquired Cornelius as he watched his friend squirming, 'Are you dancing with St Vitus?'

'Is Satan pulling your strings?' asked Balthasar. 'Are you a puppet or a man?'

'A man who will fight the pair of you with one hand, while his other hand keeps trying to find this hell-escaped flea,' said Johannes, who abandoned the unequal struggle. The dogs' breaths mingled in cold shafts.

Halfway down the slope the men paused again. They were tired but mercifully could no longer smell the roasting pig. They gazed down onto the frozen lakes where the black figures, skating, tumbling and mock jousting, had grown larger. The Babel shouts of children were distorted by the distance. Life-sapping cold rose to meet them. Johannes wanted to be back home; he wanted to roll back the seasons and tell Antonia all the things he never had the chance to tell her when she lived. He wanted to lose himself in the rhythm of the loom. Above all else he wanted to find his son.

In the foreground he could make out the figure of a bowed old woman, a black bundle on her back, trudging snail-paced across the bridge that linked the two halves of the hamlet. She was most likely carrying kindling faggots that had been stored for the months when the water, the soil and the blood would freeze. She had picked out the small bodies of hibernating mice, as hard as stone to the touch and tucked them out of harm's way into the adjacent stack. Soon she would be home at her hearth. Her witch's fingers would twitch as she conjured a spark from the tinder, cupped her hands and blew on the minute glowing angel of light to keep it alive, before gently feeding it with crispy splinters of wood.

'That's old Mother Kuiper,' said Balthasar. The others nodded and acknowledged the similarity to the village crone who dispensed gossip and saliva with equal enthusiasm. She spent most waking hours stirring a pot full of rooks, starlings and crows: feathers, bones, lights and gizzards. A sense of loss took hold of the mens' souls.

On the far rim of the pond young boys played with a stone puck and willow sticks. Each was attempting to outdo the other with frantic sweeping movements that sent the puck spinning across the ice in a film of water. Up above, an alien skeletal bird hovered.

Taking their cue from the dogs, Balthasar and Johannes relieved themselves in the snow. It seemed unwise to void so much body heat.

Johannes shivered as the sweat felt cold between his skin and the buckram. Balthasar pointed beyond the frozen ponds and fields towards the forest. Johannes screwed up his eyes and struggled to distinguish between the motes floating in his vision and what just might be a distant knot of men moving in slow motion towards the forest. 'It could be them,' he said. 'We're not far behind.'

A whistle from Balthasar and the dogs stopped foraging, their snouts pointing through a cloud of hot breath. Men and dogs set off down the slope. 'Jesus!' said Cornelius as his boots sank well beyond his knees in the crisp snow.

With great effort they levered themselves forward and downwards. At the edge of the pond the boys, who moments before had been absorbed in spinning their tops, dropped their leather whips and stared awkwardly at the three strangers. Perhaps they too had been visited by dark apostles of the Inquisition, spitting Spanish curses, trying to identify the fattest one who could be roasted just for sport, to loosen the tongues of the others, and send a bleak message of retribution to their families.

Johannes smiled reassuringly at the nearest boy who quickly looked away in case he was the chosen one.

Progress was easier on the ice if you spread your weight evenly. In his youth Johannes could dance on air. One distant frozen St Nicholas Eve he had swept Antonia off her feet and held her aloft like a captured swan. The other villagers clapped and threw their bonnets in the air as he swept her across the ice, his arms tight around her tiny waist.

One of the dogs paddled helplessly and then splayed itself on the melting surface. A young couple wrapped in each other for warmth and love glared at the travellers, and the old woman they had seen from afar, bent under her trussed-up faggots, seemed to be treading water as she dropped her bundle and skidded in her haste to escape.

Beyond the pond the snow that had drifted against the thicket hindered their progress. The dogs vied with each other to find a way through. The disguised wall of thorns tore at the snout of the foremost. He yelped and searched the hedge with sharp-edged breath. The men beat their staves against the thorns until they yielded. The clods of snow became flurries.

'Spanish bastards,' muttered Johannes, aiming blows at a snow-heavy branch as if it was the compliant skull of his enemy, each strike a small revenge for whatever wrong had been visited on Michel.

The realisation that the distant specks were indeed men and not cattle provided the travellers with renewed strength.

Johannes glanced up. The bird was still hovering; it was either a strange mutated angel sent to guide them or a malevolent spirit leading them to inevitable torture on the rack. He heard the crack of bone and sinew. The specks merged into the forest. There were perhaps six of them but it was impossible to tell if one might have been the child roped to his masters, his hands tied as they dragged him for a purpose known only to themselves.

Cornelius took the lead; his movements mimicked those of the dogs, his head rocking from side to side as if trying to detect the merest scent of sweat from their enemies. The wind conspired to sweep away what could have been footprints. The leading hound bounded a few yards to its left, its paws sending up a miasma of snow as it padded and scratched at something lying on the surface.

Johannes patted the dog with one hand and picked up the item with the other. 'It's Michel's lace!' he shouted. 'It's from his boot. His mother always told him to tighten them but he never did. It's his.'

Balthasar and Cornelius inspected the tiny trophy. Balthasar was less certain but understood his friend's need to believe. Breathing fast he nodded at the others and strode towards the forest.

The wind-felled trees lay collapsed on each other in caked nets of branch, foliage and snow. Johannes clambered over a bough which had the girth of a fatted sow and sank to his waist into the pit gouged by the roots when they had burst from the ground. 'Jesus wept!' he shouted as he floundered in the icy water. For the briefest of moments he disappeared beneath the surface. Despite the cold spearing his heart and freezing his brain, one flailing hand was still holding the lace. Balthasar and Cornelius sank to their knees and offered him their staves. They pulled him spluttering from the pit. He lay shocked and choking on the ground. The dogs circled anxiously. Eventually he spoke: 'Caspar!' he spluttered.

'Eh?'

'The third wise man.'

Cornelius uncorked the flagon of genever and pushed it to Johannes' blue lips. 'Get this down you.' Balthasar was briefly minded of the guttering wheezing sound a boar makes when its throat is cut. Johannes spat out the bitter spirit, and beat his fist on the ground in exasperation, all energy sapped by his heavy sodden clothes. They had lost vital minutes. Their quarry must have gained ground and melted further into the forest.

Balthasar glanced back as the last of the cold sun bled into the snow. There was no point rushing headlong into the forest.

Despite the failing light they made their way into the shelter of the trees whose branches had linked arms far above them to hold up the roof of snow. It was a relief to feel the pine needles beneath their feet after the constant battle with the drift. Balthasar could see that Johannes was still shaking and that his teeth were chattering.

'You sound like a devil sent to frighten children.' Seeing that Johannes was in no mood for mirth he changed tack. 'Men, we must rest,' he said. 'May God visit sleep on us and misfortune on our enemy.'

A scream pierced the night. The men jerked into vigilance.

THREE

John wandered into the sitting room and sat down on the stained settee carefully avoiding the vengeful spring that could inflict injury on the buttocks of the unaware. Anxious about Jack he looked round the room. He hoped he was all right but doubted it somehow. John had himself spent the preceding hour in consultation with his psychiatric nurse about his medication. The Voices who had been surprisingly restrained during the meeting now burst noisily back into his head like adolescents tumbling into a room, each determined to seize the remote control first. They were all there, the Academic, the Bastard, the Tempter and, bringing up the rear, the Jester. They ignored me completely. The first to speak was the Academic.

'*Let me see,*' he said as if working his way down a checklist. John instinctively lowered his head towards his shoulder as if to hear more clearly the conversation about to be conducted inside his brain. '*I know what he said in there but I'm decidedly anxious about the side effects. We can't afford to get things wrong again. Akinesia, akathisia, you had that before, John. Remember? You spent days crossing and uncrossing your legs ...* '

John slapped the palm of his hand against his ear as if to empty it of water.

'*Like a tart waiting in a queue*,' suggested the Bastard. '*All tights and stilettos. Don't forget, what was it? Yes, the "oculogyric crisis" when your eyes started turning of their own accord. You frightened a few folk then didn't you, John? And then they started to pop out; you looked like a frog in a vice. Do you remember how that young girl ran screaming down the street? Happy days ...* '

The Academic grunted in agreement. '*And then all that pacing and shuffling. Not to mention the dysphonia that played havoc with your larynx and temporarily robbed you of the power of speech*.'

'*He had nothing of interest to say anyway*,' continued the Bastard. '*And by the time the symptoms had worn off you had decided you quite liked not speaking. You're a big fat hairy fraud, John. Not worth bothering with. You know what? I miss the old days when you suffered from TD. What's it stand for, Academic?*'

'*Tardive Dyskinesia. A disorder of the central nervous system that causes abnormal, uncontrollable, disfiguring, and embarrassing movements ...* '

John tightened his grip on the arm of the settee and shook his head from side to side as if this simple motion might dislodge the Voices. Sometimes he pictured them asleep hanging from his neurotransmitters like malevolent bats in a cave.

The Bastard continued, '*Great times! Your tongue lolling about like some idiot child, a lustful lizard, grimacing like Quasimodo in a silent movie. Do you remember when that bus driver refused to open his doors? He just drove off as you pawed the glass, a windae licker. And that barman in the Canny Man who took one look at you and barred you for life! Social inclusion at its best. It was probably the dribbling that clinched it. "I'm sorry sir, we don't serve grotesque salivating salamanders"*.'

'And of course there are the sexual side effects,' continued the Academic oblivious to the interruption.

'Yes! You had lovely breasts for a time, didn't you? Bigger than that wife of yours if I recall.'

John groaned as the Jester seized his chance. *'Not as funny though as that time Kevin got a hard on and frightened the cook! If I remember she ran out of the kitchen. Mick suggested they put his hat over it so as not to cause an affront to public decency. Kevin loved it though. He wandered into the pub convinced he would score. The barman phoned the police who charged him with concealing a dangerous weapon.'*

'Although rare, priapism is distinctly unpleasant,' intoned the Academic. *'If left untreated it can cause serious harm to the penis.'*

'You don't need yours anyway do you, John?' asked the Bastard in a tone of mock innocence.

In a doomed attempt to distract himself from the chatter in his head John turned his attention to the newly installed table-tennis table. He vaguely remembered playing once for money in his previous life. He was totally drunk in Jenny's Pool Emporium. Sarah had just left him. He had evidently vomited over the table, and watched helplessly as the chicken vindaloo morphed into the green baize, before he was thrown out onto the street. *'It was chicken jalfrezi,'* said the Bastard.

John had no appetite for lunch and made his way upstairs to his room again. As he turned onto the last landing he saw that Janet, the volunteer support worker, was trying her utmost to coax Dennis out of his room. 'Come on Dennis, there's nothing to worry about. The men are not cross with you. No one is out to get you. Trust me.' The door opened the merest slither and John saw a single frightened eye fill the small gap. 'It's mince and tatties, your favourite.' Dennis may have caught sight of John standing at a distance but it was enough. The door slammed shut.

Janet continued her cajoling for a while longer before shaking her head and making her way down to the kitchen. Part of John had always wanted to befriend Dennis and tell him things would get better but he knew he would be lying.

John closed the door on his own room and slowly put his arms round himself as if they belonged to someone else who was delighted to see him. He rocked his brother in his arms.

As you may have gathered, I'm John's preferred Voice, the one John chooses when he's well. Isn't that right, John? I'm neutral, allegedly. I call things the way they are which qualifies me for the main chronicler and Narrator of all that follows. You trust me, don't you, John? It's been a hard battle. But for much of the time I rule the roost and call the shots. It helped of course when the psychologist from the Hearing Voices clinic urged John to concentrate on the Voice that approximated most closely to his own inner voice. And of course he chose me. Which is why I don't need italics.

At first the others were furious but, sadly, from both our points of view, they've made a comeback. Did you notice how the Bastard upstaged the Academic earlier? But fair play, I was exhausted. The Bastard is powerful and intrudes whenever he can to harvest the seeds of doubt long planted in John, destroying whatever equanimity is permitted to a man in his forties who hears Voices. If I'm honest I quite admire the Bastard's creativity. Some of the things he comes out with are quite astonishing. That reference to John's impotence was nothing. You should hear him when he gets into his stride.

'Don't patronise me, "I quite admire the bastard's creativity". A pathetic attempt to ingratiate yourself. Piss off.'

Bastard, just remember I have the power. I'm the main custodian of John's story.

'Whatever.'

Exactly. Anyway the reason for John's reconvened meeting with the psychiatric nurse had its origins in a half-hearted suicide attempt the previous day.

When he opened his window I knew it wasn't to welcome fresh air into his life. I tried to point out that he was only two flights up and would just end up injured, but I was outdone by the Bastard who suggested that if he stood on the ledge and then fell head first onto the path he would find peace. All would be still.

Beverley, who had seen him from the street, opened his door, took him in her arms and held him hard, an action probably in contravention of the Home's policy on physical contact with vulnerable adults. All credit to her, she distracted the Bastard long enough for the Tempter to get a word in edgeways. He chipped in, promising the tantalising possibility of better times, although I do wish he wouldn't mention The Book. The Jester too did his best by pointing out that if John caught his foot on the television aerial on his descent he would dangle upside down, clearly visible from the TV lounge. He would give Kevin one hell of a fright. A salivating, inverted Cheshire cat with mad staring eyes would certainly distract him from *Cash in the Attic.*

Eventually his key worker arrived and I know John likes her. She just spoke calmly and offered him choices. Did he want to increase his medication? Would he welcome the respite of the Royal Edinburgh for a few days? The Bastard insisted that The Village of the Mad, aka the Royal Edinburgh Hospital, was indeed John's true spiritual home. The Tempter reminded John of the hospital gardens, making them sound like Fontainebleau or Versailles. The bit about asses' milk was difficult to reconcile with my memory of the hospital bath. Eventually John chose the medication route though I wish he hadn't as it makes me lose my voice and gives the others an unfair advantage.

John made a slight adjustment to the picture that was hanging off-centre on the wall nearest the door. It had always been his favourite image in The Book. He had found the framed print in a charity shop in Great Junction Street and I knew at the time it was an ominous choice. I told him it was a bit clichéd. I told him that every student flat in the seventies had Bruegel's *Hunters in the Snow* on its walls but he wouldn't listen. I told him he should move on from that phase of his life. The Bastard elbowed his way in saying it was a pathetic purchase by a sad loser who had once thought of himself as Renaissance man on the strength of having attended two optional lectures on the History of Art at university.

Three black figures out of breath stare down into the village where tiny skaters frolic on the frozen pond, pulling each other along or dancing together. Children play with spinning tops. Panting dogs sniff at the roots of a tree. In the foreground, villagers are roasting a pig that attracts the attention of the men, but they have a mission. Overhead a strange bird soars towards the distant snow-covered hills ...

John found the *Big Book of Bruegel* at a jumble sale some fifteen years ago. At that time he and Sarah were sleeping in separate rooms. Saturday was the worst day of the week. Without the discipline of the early morning commute he would just lie there trying to work out when it was safe to make coffee without resuming unspoken hostilities.

Queuing at jumble sales was an answer of sorts. At the time he was trying to convince himself that a career in the second-hand book trade would be a viable alternative to teaching history. Apart from anything else, queues were sociable. He enjoyed the banter with the various dealers determined to hoover up the bric-a-brac, records or, in his case, books, before the loyal parishioners and the seriously poor got within a yard of the stalls.

Published in 1936 by Anton Schroll & Co. Vienna, it was bigger than a tabloid newspaper and almost four inches thick, a ridiculously underpriced gem. On taking the book home he made the mistake of trying to share his enthusiasm with Sarah who reacted with a look of withering disdain. Having ascertained from *Book Auction Records* that a copy in similar condition had sold at Dominic Winters for £110 in 1988 he set it aside with a degree of satisfaction.

Shortly afterwards the obsession started. Unable to sleep he would creep downstairs to the dining room and turn the pages with reverential slowness and immerse himself in the cold medieval worlds depicted therein. On one occasion Sarah had caught him staring intently at *The Massacre of the Innocents*. 'Why can't you read pornography like ordinary men?' she asked him.

He tried to explain how the Holy Roman Emperor Rudolf II had fundamentally altered the picture from a tableau of unremitting horror to a harmless pastoral idyll. He pointed out the woman on the left preoccupied with loaves of bread in the snow. Those loaves were originally dead babies. Likewise the calf by the barrel in the foreground, having its throat slit, and the wild boar being lanced below the group of mounted soldiers. That too was a baby. She shook her head and left the room.

In the early years of their marriage Sarah had made allowances for her husband on account of his apparently dysfunctional childhood. He had been in care apparently. In the past she would compliment him on his resilience and determination in surmounting all the odds and becoming a respectable member of the middle classes. But those days were long gone; she could only see his weakness and oddness.

When Sarah was out he would immerse himself in whichever picture best reflected his mood. The comparatively rare moments of pleasure in his life found expression in *The Corn*

Harvest. He would place a forefinger on the hungry peasant emerging from the pathways cut through the corn as if guiding him towards his fellow villagers. Soon this stranger too would be lounging among the ricks spooning gruel into his mouth, oblivious of the heat haze creeping in from the coast.

The Dance of Death would give shape to his darker moods and somehow make them more manageable. He knew there was a hint of *schadenfreude* in his enjoyment of the details, the oddly shaped skeleton with its skinny arms round the hysterical woman in red, more throat slitting, the dead man doubled over with his naked buttocks in the air, the grinning horse with flared nostrils. The influence of Bosch was obvious.

For more innocent escape he would watch intrigued at the urchins relaxing in *Children's Games*; children playing pat a cake, children on piggy back, children riding imaginary steeds, and over by the river three tiny girls who had stretched their skirts into crimson lily pads.

'That's my jotter you've drawn on, weirdo!" John looked up from the pile of marking and saw one of his gum-chewing charges looming over him. The late Friday afternoon classroom felt heavy with a languid heat, adolescent hormones and Brut. 'You're no right in the head, sir. You should have a word with that fat wifey in charge of guidance.' Snorts and sniggers from her wakening peers. John looked down at the open jotter and the three black figures from *The Hunters in the Snow* that, unbeknown to himself, he had drawn on the lined page. He was about to sketch the first of the dogs.

Part of him knew that he was losing his grip. Things were worsening at home. He would retreat early to bed in the spare room leaving Sarah to talk endlessly on the phone to friends, perhaps to her lover, about his latest oddness. All he wanted to do was hide under the bedclothes like a child and summon his recurrent dream. Letting the imagined coldness of the winter scene wash over him, his hand would move down the bed looking for the cold snout of his favourite dog. Sometimes he slept with the window wide open to let in the frozen air.

John became a familiar figure in the university library. Although a graduate of St Andrews he had taken out a general council membership of Edinburgh University. He was having moderate success in convincing himself that his odd obsession with Breugel was a legitimate area of academic interest and one about which he might write in the future. Having taken notes from the History of Art section he moved among the European History shelves.

He was increasingly convinced that the conventional interpretations of the picture were misleading. Clearly the men in the foreground were hunters but what was their quarry? The emaciated fox which one of them dangled served to reinforce the view that they had no motivation beyond putting food into the mouths of their children, and were pausing exhausted to gaze at the frozen lake before returning home, but he was far from convinced.

Despite the turbulent times in which he lived, Bruegel managed to survive the paranoid religious purges of the Inquisition. Moving from Brussels to Antwerp in 1556 he stayed one step ahead of the medieval McCarthyism sweeping the Low Countries. He somehow managed to please his patron Antione Perrenot, Cardinal de Granvelle, while keeping his integrity intact and his true religious affiliation a secret. His paintings are not what they seem. They are crowded with symbols that tell of adherence to different truths. The hunters in the snow are indeed in pursuit of something but their quarry is neither fox nor bear. On what journey have they embarked? What are they seeking?

One late February evening before the library closed, John glanced out of the window and saw that the yellow lights marking out Middle Meadow Walk were virtually obscured by swirling snow. As if summoned by a force he didn't understand, John stood up from his study carousel, ignored his overcoat and walked through the doors into the blizzard. He positioned himself equidistant between George Square and Melville Drive and stood stock-still. If he stared hard enough he would see what they saw, and know where they were going. Shaking with incipient hypothermia he had a sense that a young child was out there somewhere, a young boy.

Sarah collected him from the Royal Infirmary, conveniently close to where he had been found by several drunken students. On leaving the Outpatients Department she could contain her exasperation no longer and pummelled her gloved hands into his face, each blow emphasising a syllable in her invective, 'You useless man, you useless waste of space of a man, you pathetic, sad, weak, mad, incompetent failure!' He offered no resistance. She left him shortly after.

After his career and marriage fell apart John agonised, analysed, apportioned blame, and invoked revenge on all who had harmed him. He waged imaginary conversations with various protagonists, punished at will, felt sorry for himself but always in his own internal voice. This internal voice was indistinguishable from his speaking voice in which he conducted day-to-day business, relationships and transactions. His own voice was soft, educated Edinburgh, middle class. He had been told it was a calming voice; certainly he had used it to great effect in the classroom, pouring vocal oil on potentially troubled waters. His first girlfriend had told him he sounded sexy and begged him to read poetry to her. Keats always worked, if he remembered.

Gradually though, his internal monologues became dialogues in which he was aware of engaging with distinctively different personae. At first he was frightened and felt – rightly as it turned out – that he was going mad. Initially drink helped to restore prominence to his own, albeit slurred and increasingly inarticulate, voice. He blamed the stress of his domestic and professional situations and took disproportionate comfort from the times in the early days when the Voices left him but they always returned and always stayed longer.

Various other Voices arrived unannounced over the years and left just as abruptly. He sometimes hankered after the Girl who was there one morning in his head, teasing him with sexual banter, promising him a good time, urging him to touch himself.

The Old Woman was a strange one. She would regale him with stories of her own dysfunctional childhood in the Bronx. No one else could get a word in, and she would talk over them in an ever louder nasal drawl until they gave up. He had no idea where she came from. Alarmingly he would always smell her before she turned up and took over.

Unwashed, with a patina of garlic, alcohol and subway, she had views on everything and fundamentally trusted nobody. Her bags had always been gone through while she slept in a doorway; other vagrants were always molesting her, 'wanting to get their hands on her purse,' as she put it. She had a soft spot for one of the police who patrolled her territory, 'Pat always looks out for me,' she said. 'Sometimes he slips me a burger.'

What did he think of the current crop? If he was honest he was growing increasingly fond of the Academic, completely lacking in social skills perhaps, and an appalling sense of timing, but driven by an intellectual rigour and an insatiable quest for knowledge. John certainly recognised something here of his own early self. He was haunted though, by the fact that the Academic who lived in his own head had access to knowledge that was significantly beyond what he, himself, knew, or had ever known. Where did it come from? There was of course the possibility that the Academic made up half the things he claimed to know while perfecting the cadences and verbal nuances appropriate to great certainty and insight. He had also read about psychic interpretations of schizophrenia, but that was somewhere he didn't want to go. The idea of Dennis Wheatley and entourage camping in his brain was not an appealing thought.

He felt much more ambivalent about the Tempter. On the one hand he held out hope and blew skilfully on the flames of possibility and redemption, on the other he would dash out the brains of hope against the nearest wall when it suited him.

Although the Bastard could make him physically sick with his plausible accusations, and his ability to rake up ugly little kernels of long-forgotten sins, he felt, at one level, that they deserved one another.

And of course he admired the apparent objectivity of the Narrator and his capacity to endow the mundane with a sort of poetic truth. (I had to say that John.)

FOUR

At breakfast Beverley was her usual breezy self. 'Morning, John, you look smart today. I like you in that cord jacket.'

Sometimes I think she overdoes it. He looks all right for a large man in his late forties with unfashionably long hair but he's not going to be asked to take part in a photo shoot for *Vogue* – I must be careful what I think; I don't want the Tempter to put ideas in his head. John nodded at Beverley and patted his pockets indicating that he was out of cigarettes.

The corner shop was in the next block. Leith Walk was busy with people who in the main didn't hear Voices apart from those of self doubt, worry about work and family; whose fantasy worlds were bound by action replays of Hibs' late equaliser and impossible yearnings for unavailable potential lovers; whose anxiety levels rarely exceeded the fear of being late for work or niggling concerns about the facial mole that in some lights seemed to be getting larger.

John looked carefully at every male face, even those who could not under any circumstances belong to his brother. His scrutiny was habitual. Sometimes he held the gaze of strangers for a millisecond longer than was socially acceptable. Last week someone had asked him 'What are you staring at, you scary bastard?' He avoided confrontation by lowering his eyes and muttering apologies.

He didn't even own a picture of Andy. He would though stare for ages in the mirror at his own face and slightly alter its contours as if he were a *Crimewatch* reconstructed photo fit. Add a moustache, make the cheekbones thinner, recede the hairline, add a hat. What other tricks could time play on flesh over thirty years?

The *Evening News* was invariably a source of promise then disappointment. It seemed that every reader who celebrated a birthday, wedding anniversary, or mitzvah would pay for the publication of a head and shoulders portrait invariably cropped from family holiday snaps.

A month back John had taken the bus to Cramond. He had read that a man called Andy was going to marry a woman called Sylvia after a long engagement. I told him it was pointless but the Tempter urged him on. For an hour he paced nervously up and down the narrow street outside the parish church into which chattering wedding guests wandered. He was grinding a fist into the palm of his hand. I tried to calm him down but nothing worked.

Then his eyes lit up with recognition and he rushed forward as the portly groom stepped out of a black limousine parked on the gravel. The best man reacted as if he was protecting an American president from a potential assassin.

John shrunk as if an air valve in his flesh had been released.

After Jack's failed attempt at self burial the hostel managed to secure a small grant to renovate the garden and Beverley did her utmost to involve the residents in a decision over the best use for the small space. The suggestion box revealed several receipts and a betting slip covered in something unpleasant. A meeting was convened in the garden.

Kevin sneered and suggested that maybe Jack had a point, a residents' graveyard was a practical solution. Someone suggested a bowling green. The idea caught on. Derek said they could enter a local league. Kevin said he wasn't aware of a league the rules of which specified an officially agreed quota of schizophrenics and others with alcohol problems. Beverley, mindful of the last Care Commission report, suggested it might be a good idea to grow vegetables.

'I hate fucking cabbage,' said Mick.

'Language,' said Beverley.

Once the others had returned to the house John picked up the new spade that Beverley had produced as an inducement and walked to the upper part of the garden. More than ever he needed to distract himself from an environment he hated, but to which he was resigned and probably deserved. During his student days he had worked as a labourer earning significantly more than in his short-lived teaching career. He instinctively checked his palms for calluses but there were none.

'Hairy palms?' asked the Jester.

'Certainly a wanker,' sneered the Bastard.

The new blade sliced into the wettish clay, a knife into a cake. Had his brother married? Was he an uncle? *'Some uncle!'* the Bastard chipped in predictably. *'A fat retard with no pals.'* John turned the first sod over. It glistened and a resilient worm pulled itself to safety. Perhaps Andy was searching for him too.

John looked up. He felt that someone was watching him, trying to communicate with him. The Bastard suggested it was the Governor from the children's home wondering which innocent he would take into his study. *'It's your turn, John, you know it is, you deserve it after looking at that magazine.'*

The Tempter butted in. *'It's the young woman you saw in the park yesterday. She really liked you, she knows about your diagnosis and thinks it makes you interesting. She is sometimes unwell herself. Soul mates waiting to meet ... And she knows where Andy is.'*

John looked round the garden. '*There's a man in uniform behind that tree, he's playing with himself,*' said the Bastard.

'*She just wants you to hold her, she's desperate for a kiss and she's brought a bottle of wine with her,*' said the Tempter. John, his unease mounting, stared at the tree and then scoured the sky above the brick wall. Why wouldn't the Voices give him a break, why not just fuck off and leave him alone? If he concentrated on the strange bird circling the garden and excluded all else the Voices might go away. It was probably a crow, perhaps a hundred feet in the air, circling slowly, sometimes gliding, riding the current. As if catching sight of what it had been looking for it climbed above the tenements and flew towards the snow- covered peaks, the tallest of which pushed its dagger-sharp ridge into the hanging belly of the turquoise sky.

FIVE

'It's just a bird,' said Cornelius. 'Probably the same one that has followed us for days now. Satan's own spy.' The men huddled together on the cold ground.

'Keep the faith,' said Balthasar, 'keep the faith.'

'Isn't faith to blame for all this?' asked Cornelius.

Johannes looked into the dark. Adopting the new religion had been easy in the early days. The villagers had received the visiting Anabaptist pastor with the courtesy that tradition demanded. They had broken bread and offered him a floor to sleep on. He had seemed old beyond his years but spoke with a simple, almost hypnotic, conviction about the essential goodness of Christ and the irrelevance of pomp and ritual.

He took care not to trample on the old ways that had provided solace to past generations in harder times. He even spoke fondly of how his own villagers would dress up in their finest clothes to process along the riverbank behind a shaking statue of the Madonna. He described how one year the village simpleton, having been entrusted with holding a cord, started speaking a language no one could recognise, his words sounding like birdsong on a spring evening while his breath had the fragrance of flowers.

'Did I ever tell you why I stopped going to mass?' asked Balthasar.

'Yes,' said Cornelius and Johannes with one voice.

'I was fishing down by the river. The day was hot. I had finished a flagon of best mead and my wife's cake. The line dragged slowly downstream and my eyes closed. After a while a grunting, slavering monster wandered into my dreams. Then the rogue made sighs and little laughs ... ' Having heard the story many times Cornelius shook his head and soundlessly mimed along to the much-rehearsed tale. 'I opened my eyes and saw Father Hoekstra with his cassock round his ankles and his priestly member firmly planted in my neighbour's wife. "On your knees, Balthasar, and pray,' he said, "I'm exorcising a wicked spirit." He was a man after all, I had no problem with that and the woman was bonny. But on Sunday he preached about the seventh commandment. He called us all adulterous sinners for whom the fires of hell would never be sufficiently hot to purge our lustful ways. Legions of devils their faces contorted with sin would be queuing to tear out our innards. I walked out and never returned.'

' ... and never returned,' said Cornelius shaking his head.

'Do you think they're missing us?' asked Johannes, keen to interrupt before Balthasar embarked on another tale.

'Who?'

'The villagers.'

'I hope so,' said Cornelius.

'Perhaps the apprentices have taken over,' suggested Balthasar.

Fathers, anxious about finding work for their sons, frequently petitioned the group to remember them when they next needed a helper. Unsolicited baskets of wine and pancakes were left at their doors. The villagers often assumed the weavers were brothers, and frequently remarked on the facial similarities between them. Perhaps their faces had become similarly lined by staring at the heddles for hours on end and frowning when the warp tangled. Last month they had discussed the possibility that their separate machines, having developed personalities of their own, were now capable of playing tricks and being mischievous.

'Make us a fire,' said Johannes.

Cornelius swept the needles into a pyre with his feet and reached into his smock for the tinder stones. His firemaking was legendary in the village. He would often wander past the homes of the elderly and, at the houses where no smoke rose from the stacks, would knock at the door and offer to raise the fire in the hearth.

True to his reputation, he soon conjured the imps of flame and wisps of smoke. 'Come closer, Johannes. Get some warmth in your bones.'

Johannes reached into his bag and sunk his fingers into a clod of sodden bread; it was all that remained. Expressionless, he showed the wheaten mess to his companions.

Balthasar took the dough and reshaped it and then placed it next to the fire. 'I should have been a baker, not a weaver,' he said.

On the cusp of sleep the men grew silent and preoccupied. Cornelius yearning for Geertje, tried to dismiss the dumb show of possible horrors that his fear acted out for him. How safe was any young woman from the Spanish mercenaries? Would she stay in the loft as agreed? Would curiosity and boredom get the better of her?

Balthasar thought of Wilhelmien. They had not parted well.

Johannes thought of Michel. Why had they snatched him? Why hadn't the stupid boy stayed hidden? But there was still a glimmer of hope. They hadn't found his body broken and tossed aside in the snow. They had seen a set of distinctly smaller footprints alongside the others. And there was the lace. Michel was young and strong, but there had been rumours that the Spanish took boys as slaves to carry food and weapons from plundered village to plundered village. What if they had taken him for other purposes? Dear Christ!

SIX

John woke consumed with anxiety, thinking his heart was going to burst from his chest. The bedclothes were wet with sweat. He didn't fancy breakfast but couldn't stay in the room for a moment longer. Pulling on yesterday's clothes he stepped into the corridor where he was met by the smell of piss from Dennis' room. When he had first stayed in the hostel, John too had been too riddled with fear to step across the threshold. In some ways it had been easier living on the streets.

'*Dennis is an even bigger loser than you*,' said the Bastard. '*He's on his last warning. Beverley told him they wouldn't replace his carpet again. It smells like a shite hole in there. Poor mad sod. No wonder his wife used to beat him up. Why wouldn't you want to beat up such a useless wee runt? You know what the problem is, don't you? He blocks the sink with fag ends and then pisses in it. He's almost as bad as you, John. At least he doesn't whine on about his lost brother all the time. By the way he's dead, you know, don't you? They fished him out of the Clyde a month or so back. Didn't you see the article in the* Mail? *Headless body in river. You're wasting your time.*'

Leave him alone Bastard, he can't take it. Come back later if you must.

'I don't know why you think you should be narrator-in-chief, you're just a voice like me. Delusions of grandeur. You're meant to be objective; all you do is pussyfoot around with your misplaced compassion. What you don't understand is that John and I have a Faustian pact. We deserve each other. The trouble is you haven't got a Helen in your life, have you, John? In fact you've got fuck all in your life. I'll leave you alone just now but I'll be back!'

He's gone John. Are you all right?

Mick was already at the table. He grunted as John sat down but didn't look up. 'They were asking for me yesterday but I gave them the slip. You can't keep a good Communist down. I've cancelled the *Morning Star*, it was just asking for trouble. I'm going to get the *Telegraph* just to confuse them. Porridge. Ye canny whack it. Any luck with your brother yet? He may be in a camp. I'll ask round. Have to be careful though. They don't like too many questions.'

John pushed the egg round his plate. If there was a message in the smear of yoke he couldn't read it.

Paul joined them, his head in Conrad's *Nostromo*, the same dog-eared Penguin that he had been committing to memory for the last year. When he wanted a change he would go back to Rider Haggard's *Nada the Lili*. He would only read books that started with the letter N. 'Someone's been drinking,' he said with the righteous authority of a housemaster. 'I can smell it.'

'What's it got to do with you, Arsehole?' asked Richard. The moment passed and they ate in silence. Richard continued to drum Beethoven's sonata in G with his fingers on the table. According to the gossip he had been a concert pianist who, after his breakdown, worked on the pier at Southend sharing digs with a contortionist and a female impersonator who had eventually robbed and beaten him.

Back in his room, John sat on the edge of his bed, staring at a day that seemed to stretch forever with absolutely no point or ending in sight. He had tidied his room yesterday and had washed his clothes but had derived little pleasure from either task. He heard Janet's voice outside his door. 'Can I come in, John?'

'You OK?' the young support worker asked, sitting next to him. 'Is the new medication working?'

'*You could give her one,*' said the Bastard. John flinched.

'I've been thinking over what you said last time, about your brother. You said he used to get a row at home for not changing his Hearts top. I know it's a long shot but people don't just give up on their favourite team. My Hibee boyfriend says he wants to be buried in his green shirt. Even if your brother moved away he may come back to Edinburgh sometimes to watch a game. You could always wander down Gorgie way on match day.'

Unlike his previous key worker, Janet took his obsession seriously. She had spoken to Social Work who had eventually confirmed the location of the care home where John claimed he had last seen his brother. It was in Ayrshire, now lying derelict. The previous month he had gone back. He had told Beverley that he would be away overnight, he told her he wanted a wee break in Largs and had found a B and B.

Taking the Citylink to Glasgow and another bus to Auchinleck, the Bastard and the Tempter had been waiting in the queue with him. '*They'll take you back,*' said the Bastard, '*and it will start all over again. You're a glutton for punishment and you asked for it with your angelic smile and the curls. And you enjoyed it despite what you say now. You led that man on. You're just rotten to the core.*' The woman with the large message bag changed seats.

'*Don't listen to him,*' said the Tempter. '*You will find a clue, a sign. Your brother will be looking for you as well. You will see him before he sees you. He will laugh and hug you to death. He's a rich man, married with two lovely kids. His wife will welcome you and cook for you. You will sleep in a wonderful bed and stay with them.'*

'*Bollocks! No happy ending for this loser. He'll be arrested for trespass and loitering and the Mental Health Officer will pronounce him mad and dangerous and put him inside the Hilton again. Ward five, your favourite, John. Remember when you first went there. Lying on your bed, feeling sorry for yourself, curled up like a lost baby sucking your thumb. The medication didn't work did it, John? And then the joy of electricity. It certainly beat the joy of sex into a cocked hat. Not that you ever had much of that. And what about that time they got the anaesthetic wrong? You howled and begged. Do you remember that scorching smell? It worked though, didn't it? Lying there like a zombie. Catatonic, isn't that the term?*'

'*If I can interject,*' said the Academic, interjecting. '*Future interventions may not be so barbaric. According to a recent article in the* Guardian *scientists are examining whether computer-generated avatars can help patients with schizophrenia, not that I am endorsing that particular diagnosis for John, I honestly think the jury is out on that one. Nevertheless the idea that avatars, designed by patients, could give a form to voices they may be hearing which can in turn be controlled by therapists who encourage the patient to oppose the voices …*

'*Avatars, my hairy arse,*' said the Bastard.

Noticing his agitation and suspecting drink the bus driver looked at John through his mirror but was soon distracted by an oncoming lorry.

'*Can I sit here?*' asked the Tempter. '*There's no doubt about it; your brother will take you into his firm. You'll share an office and gradually learn the ropes. You'll go out for a drink together.*'

'*He's an alci remember?*' said the Bastard leaning over the seat in front. '*You'll never get out, John. Severe and enduring, isn't that the term? Let's look in that little locker next to your hospital bed ... What have we here? That pathetic picture of your brother, your wallet, your disabled person's bus pass. Soon, when you leave the ward for another failed therapy session that old man with dementia will rob your locker and wipe his arse with the photo.'*

The Jester joined the bus at Kilmarnock and sat next to John. '*Did you hear the one about the Irishman and the egg? Did you hear the one about the talking dog in the bar? Did you hear the one about the man who thought the microwave was a telly?*'

Auchinleck had been bleak and windswept. The woman in the cafe wouldn't serve him. 'No vagrants here,' she told him. 'I'll call the police if you don't get out.'

He had trudged through the scheme on the outskirts of the town where two boys, no older than nine, threw stones and called him 'paedo'. A postman, after giving him a second glance and deciding he was harmless, had given him directions to where he thought the home had been.

He saw the boarded-up building across a field, his heart pounding as he waded through the nettles, cutting himself on the barbed wire. '*Look, there's the Governor,*' said the Bastard. John stared at the boarded-up window.

Moments later the Governor was just yards behind him. He heard him panting; he smelled his onion breath.

SEVEN

Balthasar kicked at the embers, retrieved his stave and looked at his two companions, now wrapped in each others' arms sleeping fretfully. They both looked younger in their sleep, and part of him was loath to wake them into another day of endless futile pursuit, dangers unknown and bone-chilling cold. He would leave them for a moment while he checked on the dogs which were foraging a distance away in the trees. They had found a small dead creature which they were tugging apart, a rat, perhaps, or a squirrel. He waited until nothing remained of the animal and whistled quietly. They bounded towards him. Their barking woke Cornelius and Johannes who stretched, grunted at each other and picked up their staves.

Johannes was still frozen to the core, but yesterday's aching sense of dread had passed. Perhaps, just perhaps, they would find Michel today. Somehow the dawn had managed to fight its way into the forest, its cold talons reaching towards the small knot of men stretching and rubbing their eyes.

'Dongen is an hour's march away. We can beg bread there and ask.' Balthasar remembered the village where he had attended a cousin's wedding.

As they trudged through the pine needles towards the edge of the forest he tried to repress memories of the feasting and dancing that had lasted for two days and nights. He smelled the hog roasting on the spit, so large it needed two men to turn it. The juices had run down the sides of his mouth as he bit into the sweet crackling. At one point the legs on the trestle table improvised from a door had buckled under the weight of sweetmeats, pickled birds, soused eels, pancakes cleverly tiered like newly nailed tiles on a roof, and marzipan cakes. When he lost his balance during the troika his wife had chided him for his drinking.

'Pluck de dach,' he told her. In retrospect, this gentle reminder of life's transience had proved prophetic. His cousin had become unwell within months of the wedding and died soon after. Balthasar felt so hungry he could only assume that his stomach was now consuming itself.

As the forest petered out they emerged into the snow-covered plain of neglected fields, collapsed ricks and tumbled wooden shelters that in safer times were temporary homes to itinerant shepherds and herdsmen. The river meandering towards the horizon had been turned to frozen stone by a vengeful alchemist. Overhead, fat-bellied clouds looked as if one poke from a well-aimed stave would bring down the snow. Balthasar pointed towards the tiny spire which would guide them towards the hamlet. The men walked in silence, the panting of the dogs setting the rhythm for their footsteps. Cornelius consciously distracted himself from his hunger and the cold by concentrating on a problem that had arisen in the days before the invaders smashed their looms. Lately the linen had been too dry and was snapping several times a day. There must be a better way of keeping the warp damp.

Johannes had already surrendered to his own tide of obsessive thoughts. He was to blame for his son's abduction; he could have insisted that he stay hidden until the sign was given. He hadn't been the best of fathers to the boy anyway; he rarely agreed to fish with him, or show him how to change the set on the loom. All those questions he had answered with a dismissive, 'Ask me later.' He had taken his hand to him too often. Michel had complained of ringing in his ears for days after one angry skelp across the head. The boy was always hungry, always asking for food his father couldn't afford.

They had been too old to have a child. The villagers joked and asked if they had heard the rush of angel wings as Gabriel came to deliver the message. 'We were out that day,' he would reply.

The boy's mother had never really recovered. Years before her death she started to fade into her own world. Small devils took her happiness; they hung from the corners of her mouth, they poked her awake at night. He found her once down at the washing place as if turned to stone, her arms rigid and her head bowed. Michel had been howling but she was deaf to his cries. If he was honest he sometimes resented his son and blamed him for changing his life. He deserved to be punished for not embracing God's gift of a young life. Repeatedly watching the devil's dumb show was part of his contrition: Michel dead in a ditch; left to starve in the bottom of a well; his head on a stake to remind a rebellious village about the consequences of dissent. 'My son, my son,' he said. Balthasar placed a comforting arm across his shoulders. Overhead a bird soared.

The signs were not auspicious as they approached the village. Several bundles of clothes had been thrown into the snow-filled ditches. Johannes stooped to pick up a child's toy lying by a style. It was a bone rattle trailing cloth streamers. The lurchers rushed to inspect the carcass of another dog. After sniffing cautiously they slunk back to join the men.

'This is not good,' said Cornelius, stroking the whining animals in turn.

‘The Black Angel has been,’ said Balthasar.

There was more smoke rising from the first few houses than would have been expected at this time in the morning. Thrift normally dictated that fires were only lit in the early evening when the men returned from the fields and a meal had to be cooked.

Balthasar pushed against the door of the first house they came to. It creaked on its hinges and swung open. A black pot lay on its side, its stale contents spilled onto the floor and soaked into the straw mattresses that had been ripped from the alcoves. In the corner of the room a Bible was covered in excrement. A very thin cat rubbed against Cornelius’ leg, scuttling into the darkness when it smelt the dogs.

The men moved warily from house to house where the same tableau was repeated. Fires had been lit in some of the rooms. All clothing and bedding had been swept into the centre of the floor and set alight.

From nowhere, a small ancient woman leaped shrieking and enraged at Johannes. She clawed at his face and neck, cursing in an unfamiliar dialect between banshee wails. She wrapped her legs round his waist pinning him in an embrace of hatred and venom. The nearest dog tugged at her black skirt, ripping a large swathe from the garment. Still she clung on, sinking her fingernails into Johannes’ cheek.

‘We come in peace!’ he shouted, while Cornelius and Balthasar took an arm each and prised her away. She spat at them both until Cornelius clamped his hand across her mouth. She promptly bit into the soft flesh between his thumb and forefinger before she was flung to the floor where she lay stunned, resigned to a fatal retaliation. Cornelius pointed at her. ‘Stay still, harridan! Or the dogs will rip your arms from your body.’ Visibly cowed she looked from one to the other.

'What passed here?' asked Balthasar. The woman pulled herself into a squatting position and rocked soundlessly back and forward on her haunches. Eventually the words came.

'Jan the simpleton saw them coming. He had been trapping birds but returned without his net and cage. He had swallowed his words and stood choking. There was no need for him to speak, his eyes like mad planets said it all. The elders quickly left to order the pastor to ring the church bell. He was still swinging on the rope when they entered the church and cut his throat, tied him upside down like a pig, and hoisted him towards the belfry. By then all of the villagers apart from the elderly had fled. May God hide them in His arms.' She crossed herself and resumed her rocking. 'They chased the old sisters out of their home, beat them with sticks, tore off their clothes and pushed them into the pond.'

'How many were there?' asked Balthasar, 'and was there a child with them?'

'Half a dozen men and yes, there was a child tied to a horse. Poor mite.'

'Was he a thin boy with a raggedy cloak?' asked Johannes, oblivious to the blood streaming from his hand.

The woman said nothing but as she rocked she emitted a long guttural note as if about to keen an ancient psalm. Johannes kicked a pot out of his way as he stepped out of the hovel, his eyes smarting from a flurry of snow running ahead of the gusting wind. There was no horizon, nothing beyond the straggly clump of willow trees huddled together as if supporting themselves through difficult times. If he really concentrated he might, just might, catch sight of his boy, a tiny, distant wisp of life.

EIGHT

The Governor's silhouette morphed into that of the newsreader. The men had been fighting over the TV again. Kevin clenched the remote as if it were all he owned in the world. At one point Richard had tried to unpick his fingers from the black plastic. 'Fuck off!' roared Kevin.

'Fuck off yourself.' They seesawed across the arm of the chair until Kevin poked his finger in Richard's eye. Richard roared and clutched at his face, 'You bastard!'

Paul shouted at the pair of them to be quiet as he couldn't read above the noise, and it was important that he found what happened to the silver. Even Kevin paused and looked at him. 'What silver, bampot?' Paul held *Nostromo* even closer to his face.

Derek stopped loading the dishwasher and rushed upstairs. 'Come on, men,' he said, 'what's going on?' Kevin let go of the remote and sulked in his chair. Richard rubbed his eye and listened to Beethoven's *Moonlight Sonata in C Minor* playing in his head. 'We agreed, men,' said Derek. 'We stick to the rota. It's Tuesday, John gets to choose.' He handed the remote to John who pointed and flicked at the screen with no interest whatsoever.

'The latest score from the Hearts Kilmarnock game at Tynecastlelelelelel ... ' The screen froze.

'Shit,' said Kevin.

'Language,' said Derek. John looked at the television. The Tempter seized his chance and burst into the comparatively open space of John's head. *'It's a message, John. At last, he's getting in touch with you. Janet had a point you know. He's at the game. It makes sense, you told me he loved football and painted his room maroon before he was made to scrub it clean. And the home was in Ayrshire, another reason why he will be there. Don't lose him again. Go now.'* John rose to obey the command. He muttered something to Derek and collected his coat.

Mick saw him leaving. 'Where are you going now? I'm coming with you anyway, can't stand football, the opium of the masses, but I'll no let you go on your own, you're a vulnerable adult.' There was no need for Mick to collect his overcoat; he was always wearing it, 'Just in case.' No one asked any more what particular contingency he was prepared for. The ancient trench coat was his second skin. Incremental layers of grease had turned the original gabardine into a close relative of leather. The belt improvised from a regimental tie – 'a trophy,' he once explained enigmatically to Derek – barely enclosed his considerable girth. Now in his mid sixties Mick had long ago turned his back on notions of recovery and rehabilitation. He had established a modus with his own demons. His prejudices sustained him. He looked after John in subtle ways.

They sat upstairs in the front seat of the bus. The Edinburgh International Festival was in full spate and crowds eddied from the tributaries of Rose and Thistle Streets into the swirling flow of Hanover Street. Most of the revellers were in t-shirts and many wore shorts and, for a rare moment, John's memories came to the fore.

Big Andrew, his emergency foster carer, ignored the seething petulance of his new charge and announced they were going to Tynecastle to watch an evening match. It was January. Fourteen-year-old John resisted but, realising that his self-perceived victim status would only be enhanced, acquiesced. Moments after joining the brigade of men hurrying in overcoats and caps along cold, dark, Gorgie Road, his mood changed completely. Part of a collective frisson of nervous anticipation, he had never known anything like it.

A solitary foot soldier started singing, 'Hearts, Hearts, Glorious Hearts'. The triumphal hymn was taken up by the marching choir. Andrew thrust his open newspaper of chips at John; you couldn't sing, clap and eat at the same time. Andrew then steered him into a public house under a railway bridge. The fug of fags and beer and shouted conversations belonged to the adult world and, for the first time, it was a world that John wanted to join.

The subsequent heavy metallic click of the turnstile was a more profound initiation into adulthood than any subsequent rite of passage, including his first arrest for drunkenness and, indeed, his marriage to Sarah. He snorted at the thought that if his obsession of choice had not been *Hunters in the Snow* it could have been Lowry's *Going to the Match*. He could have spent a long time unpicking the lives of the thin men hurrying to the game. Meanwhile the Tempter moved down the bus and whispered in his ear.

'Getting closer, getting closer, any minute now. What will you say, John, what will your first words be? Shake him by the hand; hold him in a manly embrace as he wipes away the tears. Lead him into the Diggers and buy him that pint you have both dreamed of. He has so much to tell you. How he joined the army. The time in Iraq, the troubles he had settling back into civvy street. The brush with the law. And every waking moment thinking of you.'

The bus stopped at the junction of Dalry and Gorgie, the pre-season game had just finished and the crowd possessed the streets. They got off the bus and walked into the face of the human tide. Mick paused so that he could stand to mock attention inches in front of a policeman's face, as if it was a formal inspection. It was a favourite trick, one that he had borrowed from the press coverage of the Orgreave stand-off during the miners' strike, and one that invariably caused him grief. 'Piss off!' hissed the officer touching the riot stick on his belt.

'*He's somewhere, look at every face, every face,*' squealed the Tempter with the enthusiasm of a Pop Idol wannabe.

'*This is delusional shite!*' said the Bastard from nowhere. '*Step aside Tempter, back in your box. What have we here? A pathetic wreck of a man with his pal rushing into the crowd looking for a brother who is definitely not here, and who is probably dead, or even more likely profoundly indifferent to the annoying sibling he was glad to see the back of years ago ...* '

Look, you pair, a little notice next time you want to intrude please. Where was I ... ?

Yes. John, rocked by the Bastard, lacking the foresight to sidestep the punters flushed with victory and drink, animatedly sharing action replays in their heads. They barged into him and looked angrily at the dossers in their path.

'*Spot on, Narrator, you let your guard slip there, didn't you? That's what you are John, a dosser, plain and simple. Especially the simple bit. And they're not much better. At least you've got an excuse; you're mad after all and live an empty life in a hostel for the deranged. Second thoughts, perhaps you belong here, every one a loser. Not a working-class hero among them, teachers, accountants, lowly civil servants. Put on a football scarf and you will become a man, my son, an honorary member of the proletariat. Three pints before the game, three after, loads of macho banter and back into their empty lives. In fact you definitely belong here.'*

Starting to panic, John knew he had to concentrate and make the Voices go away; he must, must look for his brother, and not listen to the Bastard.

'Stare all you like, John, I'm not going anywhere ... '

'Keep looking, John, he'll be in his early forties, medium height, like yourself, heavily built.'

'Heavily built? You're a bit of a porker, John. In fact look at the pair of you, Tweedledum and his large pal. And don't blame the medication.'

'Ignore him. Just concentrate, concentrate. Make eye contact. Look at that man with the two boys. He's listening to them. A good man. Smiling. It could be him; it could be him. What about those three men eating pies, one of them's laughing, it could be, it could be!'

'I told you, he's probably dead. Murdered I wouldn't wonder. His body found in someone's yard partially eaten by foxes.'

Concentrate John, I'm still here, your favourite Narrator, ignore them, let me tell it the way it is.

The public address system from the stadium stuttered into life for a final announcement aimed at the departing crowd. DON'T FORGET NEXT SATURDAY ... AND I SAW A WOMAN SITTING ON A SCARLET BEAST COVERED IN BLASPHEMOUS NAMES WITH SEVEN HEADS AND HORNS.

The Academic was suddenly alert. *'How interesting! I think we are talking the book of the Apocalypse.'*

Academic, no one's interested.

John stopped in his tracks. Mick was bent double having retrieved a still-burning cigarette from the ground. The crowd identified John as an unmovable object and reformed behind him. He was being tugged back.

Three mounted policeman. *Lothian and Borders* embroidered on the horse blankets. One of the beasts was pawing restlessly at the ground. A small, sharp tug of the reins and it desisted.

NINE

Three soldiers in armour, the Spanish *fleur de lys* embroidered on the horse blankets, one of the beasts pawing restlessly at the ground.

The three men were warming their hands by the fire in the middle of the square. The soldiers glanced at them with disinterest.

'Who do they think they are?' said Cornelius. 'Foreign leeches, Hapsburg whores.'

'Don't start on the whores again, you'll just get yourself excited,' said Johannes.

'Did I ever tell you about that one-legged woman who ravaged me in a pig sty?' asked Balthasar.

'Yes,' said both of his companions.

The dogs sniffed warily at the fire, their coats giving off a pungent smell of wet burning hair. The heat made the travellers gasp. The fiercest flames were consuming the black wooden pews which had been dragged from the church once there was nothing else to loot. Charred pages from a hymn-book flicked themselves over in the draught from the fire, as if Satan was desperate to find a tune that would celebrate his recent success. Black embers swirled in the up draught. A single illuminated letter E came to rest on Johannes' shoulder, an ironic epaulette which he brushed it off with his hand.

Two lumpen gray villagers linked arms and danced in slow motion round the fire, their eyes apparently sightless, their sensibilities blunted by the recent atrocities and endless flagons of sweet mead.

A boy rolled a barrel down over the cobbles. If he beat the end out it would make a house for the night. He would roll it as far as the river where he could lie undisturbed in the freezing night and the stillness, put his thumb in his mouth and pretend it had all been a bad dream from which he would wake in the morning to find himself in his own bed, and hear his mother singing in the kitchen.

A woman was hunched over the black wall of the well as if staring into its depths for something she had dropped. The empty bucket swung gently above her head, a censor. It occurred to Johannes that she might be dead, speared for sport by one of the helmeted soldiers on the far side of the square.

'Fair play but these images are lifted directly from Bruegel. Very reminiscent of The Fight between Carnival and Lent. *There's a well in the centre of the picture although if I remember the woman appears to be drinking. And there are barrels everywhere.'*

Shut up, Academic.

With their hoods obscuring their faces the travellers looked like the itinerant dispossessed peasants that they were. They certainly didn't merit a second glance from the bored Spanish mercenaries. There were thousands of their scavenging ilk roaming aimlessly, ripping the flesh from sheep newly dead in the ditch, begging and threatening when they had to.

'I could kill the two of them,' said Cornelius, 'pull them quickly from their horses and cut their throats.'

'Don't think of it,' said Johannes, 'they might lead us to Michel.' Cornelius nodded.

Having finished looting and pillaging for the day the nearest soldier dug in his spurs and pointed his horse towards the twilight beyond the market town. His companions followed. As the sound of the hooves retreated Balthasar made a sign and the three men and their dogs followed at a discreet distance. There was at least a chance that they might lead them to the camp where Michel's kidnappers were resting for the night.

They trudged in silence past the merchant dwellings with their high arched doorways and steep tiled roofs, snow piled as high as the windows. Visible through the open shutters of a corner house and illuminated by high flaming candles was a ceiling braided in blue plaster ringlets. Inside, a young woman was playing inexpertly on the family spinet and singing of love and loss with an unconvincing vibrato. Cornelius paused to listen and shook his head.

Excited by the strong smell of men and horses the dogs ran ahead with an urgency that obliged Balthasar to whistle them back. Obediently they returned to fret and forage nearer to their masters, their hot breath turning the snow on the leather breeches into droplets of water.

Eventually the houses gave way to open country where a reluctant sun squatted on the horizon, lacking both the energy and motivation to sink any further. The hunters too had no relish for a pursuit through the night. They must rest soon.

Preoccupied, the men crunched through the snow in silence. Balthasar would never admit it but he had been initially reluctant to join the hunt. Wilhelmein had berated him with venom, 'You're an old man of sixty with weak knees. Who is going to look after the looms if all three of you go? You're a fool! The Spanish took Michel, yes, it's hard but hard things happen in this dark country every day. What do you think you will achieve? Will you conquer the Spanish army on your own? The order from Deventer isn't finished. Loom three is broken. You promised to retrieve the dead goat from the well.

Your only daughter is about to give birth, and where will the child's grandfather be? Away chasing phantoms.'

His wife slapped him about the face until he held her wrists and told her he had to go, they were all in it together, and he would be back. In his heart of hearts he knew she was right. The mission was hopeless and the chances of their racked bodies swinging from the Inquisitioner's gallows were considerable, but he had had no choice. He knew he had to act when he found Johannes howling at the moon, shouting at the God who had let his only son be taken into slavery.

Apart from anything else he could not have let Johannes and Cornelius set off without him. They knew nothing of dogs and little of their own country. At least he had fought in a war and survived. That said, the thought of snuggling up against the snuffling body of his increasingly truculent and shrewish wife was not completely unattractive.

Having resigned itself to the inevitable, the sun had finally surrendered and sunk into the earth, granting territorial rights to the full moon. Because of the pale light reflecting off the snow much of the landscape was still visible. A bird shrieked from the eaves of a black-silhouetted barn, the skeleton of an abandoned plough lay with its nose in an adjacent field. Above the field a tall square windmill, its blades stilled, squatted on a trellis of legs that seemed too spindly to support its weight.

Cornelius concentrated on the sensation of his feet pushing into the snow; each step sounding as if he was trampling on the bones of small rodents. With each footfall he was cranking up the tension of the warp on the loom. He was squeezing the last drop of rennin from the taut muslin. Anything to block out the intrusive, insistent, repetitive image of Geertje being discovered by the crusaders. His anger made him stamp deeper, and the veins stand out on his neck. He was marching now at the front of a vast army that was gaining fast on the fleeing enemy; retribution would be swift and brutal. No lives would be spared. No prisoners taken. The carrion crows would gorge until they burst. His country would be free. No man would ever again question his religious beliefs. Every last Catholic bible would be torn apart. Every Spanish flag would burn until the embers scorched the sky ... three smirking soldiers held her down ... every flag would burn ... three smirking soldiers ... every flag ...

One of the dogs pressed against his thigh. Cornelius ruffled its head with a gloved hand.

A shrew scuttled across the crust of snow in front of Johannes who was staring with trepidation at the tapestry being once more unfolded in his head by unseen malevolent spirits. Michel featured in every neatly hand-stitched panel. Here playing boules with his father in the track outside the weaving shed, there playing huckle bones with Lodewyk from the adjacent cottage, then begging his father to re-attach the blade to the end of his stick so that he could rejoin his friends by the pond. Now staggering on stilts, now whirling the whirligig, now swimming with the bladder in the summer river, now beating the holed cooking pot with a wooden ladle. And all the time his father was too busy, too distracted to pay his own son the attention he craved and deserved.

Cornelius reconnected with the weaving problem that sometimes served to distract him from his anger. 'The solution lies with the thickness of the dauble,' he explained to his bemused companions.

'What?' asked Johannes.

'The free spindle rubs all the time. If it were thinner the thread would ease without the constant adjustments that slow everything down.'

'Have you been at the mead again?' asked Balthasar.

'I wish.'

Johannes was now in front of the other two; the path above the frozen river was narrow and, if they walked abreast, their tall staves tangled with the overhanging bushes and released booby traps of snow. The dogs too louped in single file, their snouts inches from the ground as they swept up every vestige of scent from the troops that had recently passed. Sweat and leather, oil from the armour, dung from the horses, meat from the saddle-bags, Spanish wine from leaking holsters.

I'm getting tired, John. Narrating your fantasy is hard. Sometimes the words won't come.

TEN

'Your friendly Bastard here, John, now pull yourself together, get a grip, you're being pathetic again. Your indulgent delusion can't block me out for ever you know. I'm always waiting for you. I'm a very patient Voice. What on earth are you doing wandering through Sighthill with Mick? I'll tell you something, Narrator, your continuity is crap. Is that a little dribble I see on your coat, John? A small slaver? Go on, blame the medication you loser rather than admit you're a mad, slavering lost sod whose life is a train crash. On second thoughts I don't think I can be arsed telling your story. It's boring. What do you think Tempter? You take over.'

'OK, thanks. People turn up in the most unexpected places. Don't they, John? You read about it in the Express *all the time, long-lost cousins meet up after being separated by continents and twenty years, beneath a photo of old folk smiling fondly at the camera, one of them saying, "We won't let it happen again, now we've found each other, we won't leave each other's side." That'll be you, John, with Andy. You're bound to meet up; he's waiting for you somewhere. Keep right on 'til the end of the road ... '*

'For Christ's sake, Tempter, you talk as much shite as him. You're useless. Back in your box. Let me trawl the archives a

while ... John do you remember that time you stole from your brother? Now, don't deny it. You must have been twelve and so Andy was eight. He was in the dormitory next to yours wasn't he? Stop blubbering; you're pathetic. Face up to the past. Get over it. You stole from him, pure and simple. You convinced yourself he had a letter from your equally sad, dysfunctional mother. He told you that she had written to him and not you. So you opened the door quietly and crept into his room at night, put your hand under his pillow and took away the note he had written to himself in big spidery writing, all that mawkish stuff clearly not written by your alcoholic mother. Have you considered the possibility that, like you, your brother was delusional from an early age? He's probably in a locked ward somewhere; it runs in families you know.'

'That's not necessarily true. It's nature versus nurture. Environment versus genetic predisposition ... '

'Academic, you've been warned! Don't you dare interrupt me again. Where was I? Yes, in the morning your brother cried and said someone had stolen his precious note, and what did you do? Nothing, you just shrugged. Did you put your arm round him? Did you buggery! A shit then, and a shit now. I really can't be bothered with any of this.'

'OK another chance for me. John, I've had a thought. He may be living rough. After all, you did. Perhaps he's closer than you think; perhaps he's one of those dossers over there in that building? Can you see them, by the fire on the other side of the pillar?'

Enough. Leave the man alone. He's upset. I'll take over again; I've got my words back.

Mick slouched behind John muttering something about Capitalism and the plight of the homeless. John looked up at the high-rise flats still obstructing the view of the new Napier University building. Their eyes had been gouged out and additional wounds inflicted in their sides. Black plastic sheeting wreathed every other floor. The sign said that the road would be closed in a fortnight for the demolition. Hazard signs and pictures of yellow hard hats were tied to every section of the perimeter wire. All interior fittings, sinks, boilers, window frames, had been stripped out and laid in separate piles, as if by a meticulous serial killer. Admit it, John, I have a gift for description. You are well served by your Narrator ... All right, Academic, what do you want to say? Be quick.

'I *am still preoccupied with the whole question of where we, his Voices, come from. If we were merely repressed aspects of John's psyche it is unlikely that we would so consistently display insight and skills denied to his conscious mind. So where do we come from? Even the Bastard knows things about him that go well beyond repressed or false memory syndrome. So why have we taken up residence in his head? So many questions, so few answers ...* '

Fair point, Academic, but I have a story to tell.

John was still considering the possibility that the Tempter might have been right. There were three figures in the shadows. His brother might be there; it wasn't beyond the realms of possibility. He only wanted to get close enough to see their faces. By following the fence they found the gap the men had used. Checking that the coast was clear Mick prised the wire further apart so that John could climb through. Two small children came up to them, one of them leaning against a bike too big for him. 'Don't go in there, the Council is going to bomb the place soon, all they buildings will come down, clouds of smoke and that. There's bad men in there. I hope they get bombed and all. By the Council.'

'Away and shite!' said Mick.

ELEVEN

'Shush,' said Cornelius, shepherding the dogs and his companions into the shelter of bushes bowed with snow. As their breath hung in the night air he pointed to the lights in the next field where the soldiers had set up camp. Three small braziers equidistant from each other attracted a storm of small insects diving catastrophically into the flames.

Several soldiers wandered through the camp having removed the heavy helmets which lay on the ground with their visors up, a random scattering of small decapitated heads.

A solitary guard wandered round the perimeter, his cocked crossbow pointing towards the snow on the ground. The soldier nearest to the hunters scrunched his shoulders and stretched his head from left to right and back again. Their lances had been stuck in the ground in a clump, a strange tree of weapons. A knot of men crouched before the fire playing cards. They took it in turn to hold their hand toward the flames to distinguish between the clubs and the aces.

As one of the soldiers walked directly towards them, the hunters shrunk back into the darkness. Cornelius gripped his stave, ready to crush the man's skull if he spotted them. The soldier lowered the front of his breeches and relieved himself, sighing as the stream of urine arched towards the hidden men. He said something to himself and wandered back to join the others.

A dozen or so horses fretted and steamed in the improvised pound, pawing at the brown churned snow, unable to settle after the excursions of the day. A boy moved among them wiping them down with a blanket: Michel. Johannes felt as if he had been punched in the stomach, he leapt forward and was hauled back by Balthasar and Cornelius. 'It's my boy, it's my boy!' he shouted, before Balthasar placed his hand across his mouth and forced him to the ground.

'Patience, Johannes, patience. We must plan. Be still. Michel might sleep with the horses. We must wait until the others have returned to their tents, then we may have a chance.'

Johannes rocked on his heels, 'Let me get him now, while he's there.'

'Balthasar's right,' said Cornelius, comforting Johannes. We must wait.'

At intervals Michel appeared at the side of a different horse which he patted and dried with slow gentle movements. Johannes failed to suppress a sigh that consumed every second of one slowly exhaled breath. Sometimes the boy paused and stared into the night, as if listening. Johannes rose on his knees and waved his arm. This time Cornelius restrained him, pulling him back to the ground.

After the interminable ache of an hour or more, during which Johannes sat clenched and tight, the gamblers slouched ever lower towards the dying fire before lying on their sides and resting their heads on their hands. The game was incrementally less compelling than the lure of sleep to which they all eventually succumbed, choosing the residual warmth of the fire to the chill of the tents. There was no sign of Michel; the hunters could only hope that he too was sleeping on the far side of the beasts that were still padding the frozen ground.

Balthasar signalled that Cornelius should crawl towards the enemy. He was the smallest and arguably the fittest of the three. Johannes struggled with the decision but saw the logic behind it.

Balthasar peered through the darkness to check that the dogs were still sleeping as Cornelius edged forward on his elbows. He passed within a man's length of the sleepers curled round the fire, one of whom started in his dreams, grunting words of disagreement before subsiding once more.

The fire had melted the adjacent snow. Cornelius gasped as he dragged his body through the heart-stopping wetness, his swollen clothes making the effort of inching forward almost impossible. He could no longer feel his fingers through the sodden gloves. Trying hard to stop shaking he levered himself towards the horses.

Balthasar held Johannes by the shoulders in a gesture that was part comforting and part restraining. 'My son, my son,' whispered Johannes.

The nearest horse stared into the night, spooked by the invisible presence of a perceived threat. Cornelius stayed motionless but the damage had been done. The horse threw back its head and brayed as if its final moment had come. The other horses attempted to turn in tight circles of panic and bumped into each other, a maelstrom of flank, leg and breath. The soldiers stirred then jolted into violent wakefulness. They added their battle cries to the commotion from the horses and grabbed at the swords piled high near the gray ash. Cornelius leaped to his feet and ran back into the darkness that hid his equally startled companions.

For a moment Johannes couldn't take in what happening. He stood up and reached out to Cornelius who hurled himself into his arms. Balthasar had already roused the sleeping dogs with a sharp whistle and had reached for his stave. The foremost of the pursuers launched himself into the darkness that had swallowed Cornelius. His progress was abruptly halted as his neck was pierced by Balthasar. He gurgled and for a split second Balthasar felt him hanging heavy on the end of the pole as if he had levered a dead sheep from a ditch.

The dogs hurled themselves at the onrushing soldiers and tore at clothes and flesh. Assuming that they were under attack from an entire army of Flemish beggars, the soldiers scrambled to extricate themselves from the unseen devils and ran back to the camp to rouse their companions. In an instant the three hunters and dogs turned and ran into the night knowing they only had minutes before the full force of the Spanish troops would cut them to threads.

They quickly put distance between themselves and their pursuers. As a cloud snuffed out the moon Johannes lost his footing, tumbled down an embankment, and landed on the frozen surface of a river. Balthasar quickly ushered the other two men and dogs onto the ice. Moments later they felt the riverbank shake from the weight of the passing troops.

TWELVE

Mick and John approached the three crouching figures with the exaggerated gait of pantomime villains. The drinkers, clutching cans of Special Brew, looked at the strangers violating their space. The tallest shouted something in a foreign language and kicked at a heap of broken bricks. His two companions picked up pieces of rubble and hurled them at the intruders. 'Asylum seeking bastards!' shouted Mick, momentarily forsaking his Socialist principles. Clutching his bloodied face, John stumbled back to the hole in the fence, ducked through and ran towards the housing scheme. Mick was nowhere to be seen.

John heard the horses pounding in his wake, he heard the disembodied sirens from police cars on the main road, he heard the Spanish cries in his head, he heard one of the small children shouting after him, 'I told you mister, there's bad men in there.' He saw a dog howling at him from a balcony. He saw the red-eyed hounds.

Walking fast helped the nightmare to fade. Perhaps it hadn't happened. The encounter with vagrants on the outskirts of Edinburgh was just a variant on his usual delusions. The evidence was compelling. He had assumed Mick had been with him but Mick was nowhere to be seen. Anyway, where were the Voices? No, none of it had happened. He felt relieved.

After no more than a moment's hesitation during which he pretended to prevaricate, John went into the off-licence in Stenhouse Road and congratulated himself for his subtle impersonation of someone with a genuine choice to make: Bells (too many maudlin New Years that only heralded more of the same), Teachers (a too painful reminder of his short lived career in the classroom), Black and White (a too simplistic view of the world, racial even). By now the Asian shopkeeper had noticed the dried blood on his temple and decided that if he wanted to pay, fine, if he just pocketed the bottle and left, that would be fine too. In the event John paid for a bottle of McKay's (no associations) and left. His joyful anticipation was compounded by an equal measure of crushing guilt and self-loathing.

Paradoxically the best way to dispel these thoughts was to open the bottle and make a start.

The orgasmic hit of spirit on belly made him gasp. He re-aligned his oesophagus with his stomach and poured until he was breathless and blinded by a sun that had appeared from nowhere to hold out promises of holidays and laughter.

That infinitesimal millisecond of euphoria was snuffed out by the fearful realisation that the Bastard would persecute him mercilessly for his weakness. So it proved.

'Look at you, a stupid grin on your face, lurching your way into that bus queue, upsetting that woman. It's a bit like the good old days, isn't it, John. Where shall we start? It's no use getting upset, you should have thought of that before you bought the bottle. At least your Dutch delusions are comparatively harmless and take you away from the past. But it won't go away, will it? Will it? Which video shall we take down from the shelf? How about this one, After Class 2004. *Do you*

recognise that awful looking man in the tweed jacket and the desperate expression? Yes, full marks, sir! It's you, and you are trying to persuade that delightful third year girl from your history class not to tell anyone that she caught you necking a bottle of spirits in the store cupboard at the back of the class, before stuffing your mouth with peppermints. To be honest, John, they probably sacked you because of the peppermint ectoplasm that exuded when you walked – staggered – by. Shall we fast forward?

This is brilliant; I am Christmas Past in the horror movie of your life! That must be your appearance before the General Teaching Council accused of threatening that same nice little girl. Do you remember how angry her parents were? And that time they came round to your house and spoke to your wife. Do you remember your wife? Hang on, she's here somewhere. Yes, there she is, that must be your bedroom. Did you ever have good sex there or were you always a failure at everything? Pull yourself together, it's only a commercial!'

John hauled himself up the hostel steps and searched frantically for the key. The alcohol had made him anxious and paranoid. There was altogether too much stuff in his pocket: letters, anonymous and full of hate, bills unpaid, solicitors' final demands, hundreds of unmarked jotters, articles cut from the papers. Too much stuff. Where was the key?

Somewhere among the court summons, the letter of dismissal, junk mail feet high.

Others had crowded on to the steps. He was jostled by his wife, by his sneering head of department, by the Governor from the Home, the asylum seekers in the condemned building, the Asian shopkeeper reluctant to sell him the drink. The school secretary who told him he was suspended and could he hand in the key, the kids who chased him on their bikes taking it in turn to spit at him, his key worker losing patience, the psychiatrist who never, ever made eye contact with him, the neighbour who sided with his wife, the private detective who ripped him off, the Sheriff's Officer at the door, the class of adolescents chanting at him as he cowered in the book cupboard (he never did order more copies of *The Hitler Years: A guide for schools*), the brown-coated janitor who led him away, the Marchmont neighbours who complained about the shouting, the laughing lads who set his cardboard bed alight under the arches. Underneath the Arches ... I dream my dreams away ... Underneath the arches ... On cobblestones I lay ... Every night you'll find me ... Tired out and worn ...

Beneath the halo of street light he saw his former friends running in slow motion towards him mouthing silent abuse: the paper boy too scared to put the *Evening News* through the letter box in case the psycho got him; Sarah, consumed with disgust and loathing; the fat woman on the ward who cried all the time and wet herself.

The key turned and he slipped inside leaning heavily against the door to keep them all out. Eventually he gave up and curled into a foetal position waiting for the first blow to be struck.

Desperate to eat but conscious that the merest hint of food would make him vomit John pushed the cereal round his bowl.

'Heavy night?' asked Richard, looking up briefly from the sonata he had been tapping out on a napkin.

'Certainly not,' said Beverley, 'John's been dry for a month, haven't you John? A new record, I think.' John couldn't bring himself to correct her.

'Can I tell this next bit?'

By all means, Jester, there has been little light relief so far. You can take over until the end of the chapter.

'Can I drop the italics for a while?'

Just this once ...

'That'll be effing right,' said Kevin, 'I saw you sneaking up to your room with the brown paper poke in your pocket.'

‘A lot of Ps in that sentence,’ said Paul, not looking up from Nostromo.

‘A lot of Ps in Dennis’ room,’ said Kevin.

‘Stop it,’ said Beverley, ‘if you lot didn’t go on at him when he does come down it might help.’

‘If he had a shower some time, that might help,’ retaliated Kevin.

‘Pots and kettles,’ murmured Mick from beneath his black beanie. ‘Watch yourself, Johnnie Boy, they’re spying on you, sending in reports. Your drinking habits are on file now. Lock your door, old son, security will come soon. Your goods and chattels will be confiscated. There will be poundings at the end of your street. You’ll be tagged, curfewed and monitored.’

‘I wish my social security would come soon,’ said Kevin.

‘You owe me,’ said Richard, suddenly interested. ‘I gave you those tabs the other day.’

‘Look,’ said Beverley, ‘if I find out, Kevin, that you’ve been cadging medication from other residents you’ll be in a lot of trouble.’

‘It was fucking aspirin.’

‘Language’, said Beverley.

‘It was aspirin.’

‘And I’m the Prince of Rome,’ said Mick, suddenly fond of the idea he had conjured from nowhere. ‘I shall issue a Bull.’

‘No change there then, it’s always bull with you,’ said Kevin.‘You will all bow to me in St Peter’s Square.’

‘That’s Muslims’ said Kevin. ‘Kissing the ground with their arses in the air. It’s part of ramadamadingdong.’

‘Better than kissing their arses,’ said Mick.‘Like the appeasers.’

Not bad, Jester, not bad.

‘Can I just finish off the chapter as you said?’

Do it in one sentence.

‘Beverley shook her head and left to make the evening meal. John was lost in blackness.’

Fine.

THIRTEEN

The men slept under the arch. By curling around their masters the dogs had lent them their warmth and hot breath. Balthasar wondered for a fleeting second why the end of his stave was red.

'I want this to end,' said Johannes.

'It's because of you we're here,' said Cornelius, immediately regretting what he had said.

'We'll see it through,' said Balthasar, alarmed at Johannes' anguish.

'Pish, shit and holy farts!' said Cornelius, trying to retrieve the situation.

'Shrivelled pope's testicles,' contributed Balthasar, with little enthusiasm for the game.

'The suppurating bowels of Cardinals, and angel dung,' said Johannes, consumed with gratitude for his friends who were risking all for him.

After stretching they conferred briefly and agreed to fight their way through the falling snow and put as many miles as possible between themselves and the soldiers who would inevitably return.

The tumbling white clung to their clothes and faces. It stung their eyes and slid into their mouths, the flakes melting on their tongues. Speech was impossible and each step was heavier then the last. Johannes felt the weight of a young Michel clinging to his leg as had been his wont, obliging his father to walk as if he were completely unaware of the grinning small child holding on for all he was worth.

Through squinting eyes Cornelius glanced at the blizzard and calculated the average space between the falling motes of heavy whiteness, more numerous than heavenly bodies in the firmament. In a previous life he had stood on the threshold of his cottage and stared in awe at a shower of stars that had raked its way across the northern sky. It was clearly a sign of his good fortune and he had offered thanks for the gift of a wife before closing the door, undressing and sliding into bed alongside Geertje.

Balthasar was puzzled at how the dogs managed to keep going even though the snow was deeper than their legs were long. Somehow they still managed to pull themselves forward with a rhythm reminiscent of the new loom recently purchased at great expense from the squinty-faced Westphalian merchant. At intervals the dogs looked behind to check that the men were keeping up.

As the dawn broke the snow assumed a reassuring brightness. Apart from the pain and numbness of the cold the main obstacle to their progress was debilitating hunger. In their haste to escape from the camp Balthasar had left behind the holster of food.

Imperceptibly the snow eased, Cornelius measured once more the average distance between the flakes, a hand span rather than the width of a small bird. The calculation gave him little pleasure. Hunger was making him angry and he improvised an elaborate curse to distract himself.

'May Spanish wombs grow sterile, may their lackey army of lascivious monks choke on their Eucharist.'

'Amen,' said Johannes.

'May the whorish nuns stuffing their bellies on vittles stolen from the mouths of children die of plague. May their tongues turn into rotten salamanders.'

'Amen.'

'May the hideous Duke of Alva's balls be torn from his body by jealous eunuchs ... '

'Where do the jealous eunuchs come from? Are there many of them?' asked Johannes.

'Trust me, they live in the Hapsburg court,' said Cornelius. 'Legions of them.'

'Do you remember the day he passed through the village with his torturers, mercenaries and hangmen?' asked Balthasar. 'The Holy Bible had its own horse festooned in silver cloth. Silver cloth for God's sake!'

Shortly afterwards a consignment of codpieces in a muslin bag and a clutch of tiny pearls had been delivered to the cottage by a smirking retainer. Wilhelmiens's fingers were still bleeding from stitching the woollen stockings that had suddenly become popular with the troops camped in the wood. She had no alternative but to agree to sew the pearls onto the codpieces which she then stuffed with spare cloth. What men they must be. What a shock to their women when they tear off the reinforced cloth to reveal the full glory of their mice-like genitals. He regretted linking Wilhelmien and genitals in the same thought. It had been a long time. Many years, he reflected.

Johannes looked up at the red watery sky. That strange bird was still circling. He too was hungry. When as a boy he had first laboured, repairing dykes, he would enjoy the same meals as his seniors, soup and wine in the fields when dawn broke. At intervals they would stop chewing and listen for the ominous trickle of water from the walls. Then warm spicy beer, black cabbage and rabbit or beef at midday when the sun would warm their backs. There would be more vegetables and wine when they returned to the barn to sing together before they were felled by sleep.

Despite her difficult nature, and no matter what particular grudge she was nursing, Antonia always cooked as if Mary Magdalene herself had knocked at their door and politely asked if she might eat with them as she had changed her ways. Apples, prunes and stronnen all on the same dish.

Johannes wondered if Michel was hungry. He always was. Only last month he had snatched the last piece of rye bread from his father's plate and been beaten for his pains.

A light wind was shaking the sculpted snow from the otherwise skeletal branches overhead. A clump of snow landed on Johannes' neck and found the only gap between flesh and overcoat. He shivered as the unwanted parcel of coldness slithered and dissolved into the warmth of his back.

The white landscape was gradually resolving into discernible shapes which, as they approached, refined themselves further into the outline of dwelling houses smothered in snow, steep white roofs almost touching the ground. Red brick chimney-stacks reassumed their identity as the men approached.

The hamlet was completely unfamiliar to the travellers. 'How far do you think we have come?' asked Balthasar.

'Perhaps twenty leagues, perhaps more, from the village,' suggested Johannes.

It was still early morning and there were few signs of life. Several hens stamped their twig feet on a patch of wet ground that had been protected from the snow by the eave. An icicle, as long as an invader's sword, thawed slowly above a water barrel, the drops bouncing off the surface ice. On a flat stretch of whiteness that may or may not have been the village pond, a small dark figure was attacking the surface with a hammer; each dull strike rang out like a church bell. Several carts lay abandoned in the square, their thin spokes caked in mud and snow, the twin shafts pointing upwards like muskets. A lone woman tugged at a cart lying on its side, its axle clearly broken, its wheel turning in response to the wind that cut through the clothes of the weavers. She strained helplessly against the immovability of the frozen cart, a tug of war long lost.

The dogs, sensing the possibility of food, showed enthusiasm for their new surroundings. Balthasar whistled softly and they moved back into position, one each side of the three men. There were no signs that the Inquisition had passed this way: no gibbet in the square, no corpses propped up against the church doors with tracts stuffed into their mouths. Perhaps the village was too remote to matter; perhaps its turn was still to come.

As they rounded a corner, noise and light spilled from a tavern opposite. Balthasar motioned to the others to stay back while he peered through the window etched with crescent drifts of snow. By looking sideways into the room it was clear that a wedding celebration had endured throughout the night. Johannes and Cornelius wiped their gloves over the glass and looked in at the locals some of whom still had sufficient stamina to dance and carouse. An old man was asleep in the corner, the table in front of him still loaded with untouched food.

'Come on,' said Balthasar who led the way through the half open door.

'Will you welcome strangers who wish only good to the bride and groom, who bring no gifts but their friendship?'

The company froze as the newcomers were appraised.

'Balthasar,' said a wispy-haired skeleton of a man extending a talon in the direction of the second cousin he had not seen in ages. 'Most welcome.'

Several of the guests echoed the gesture. A fat man, unsteady on his feet, embraced them each in turn and made an expansive, inclusive gesture towards the table. Cornelius accepted a pitcher of beer from a young boy relieved to part with the jug which he was about to drop. 'Bless you,' he said, raising two fingers on his left hand in a gesture of insincere benediction while he drained the vessel into his throat with the other.

The two dogs shook their coats sending a fine spray over a young couple who had fallen asleep in each other's arms. Their faces moved towards the unexpected but welcome wet mist and they smiled in their dreams.

Cornelius moved aside to let pass two lads in aprons who were manoeuvring an improvised table made from a gate. It was loaded with bowls of broth. He counted the guests: nineteen in all, not including the late arrivals whose sodden clothes distinguished them from their invited peers.

Johannes noticed a small boy licking a plate, oblivious to his surroundings. Michel had an identical flat brown hat the brim of which almost obscured his entire face. It was his 'hiding hat,' he had once declared to his surprised parents. 'Enjoy your food, son,' he muttered.

'Can I butt in here, Narrator?'

Academic, what is it? I'm in full flow. You're spoiling the story.

'I just wanted to point out the interesting similarity between the scene you describe and Bruegel's Peasant Wedding *which was mentioned in the inventory carried out in 1659 at the Kunsthistorisches Museum in Vienna. I would also like to comment on the oblique reference to Charles V who passed a proclamation, aimed specifically at wedding feasts, on May 22nd, 1546. He stipulated that no gathering was to exceed twenty for fear of insurrection and plotting. The party you describe was clearly keeping within the letter of the law ... Again, the real question is how did these facts got into John's head in the first place? Where does this level of detail come from?'*

Well, if you are determined to distract me, we all know that John studied Dutch history as one of his options, isn't that right, John? Who knows what the unconscious mind tucks away?

'True but ... '

Not now, Academic. Let me get on.

Cornelius abandoned his conversation with one of the senior guests as a bagpiper embarked on a drunken serenade inches from his ear. The peasant pumped the leather bladder under his arm as if he were single-handedly emptying an irrigation canal, his swollen cheeks made him look like a fat child. The noise reminded Cornelius of the pig he had inexpertly slaughtered on St Nicholas' day. Geertje had rushed into the yard at the very moment when the knife had become stuck in the animal's windpipe. She had refused to eat the pig thereafter.

Balthasar's cold bones responded slowly as he tried to keep time with the jig. The words came back to him in snatches and he hummed to fill the gaps. 'The drunken bees of summer ... the dark face of my love ... the red moon of harvest ... '

'You dance well for an old man,' said Cornelius.

'What was that?'

'YOU DANCE WELL FOR ... forget it.' They both grinned and accepted that conversation was simply not an option.

Johannes looked at the guests seated in the centre of the table. 'Which one is the bride?' he discreetly asked his companions.

'The ugly one staring into the middle distance with a wreath in her hair,' suggested Balthasar. The woman in question did look immeasurably sad, as if she was staring into an unwelcoming future. Johannes had frequently seen the same look on Antonia's face. Three stillborn children, the endless arguments over religion, the problem with her brother and, if he were honest, problems with himself.

The dogs were salivating over the remains of a chicken on a Majolica plate decorated with a seascape.

Balthasar was surprised to see a Franciscan monk with heavy brown beard and sword in deep conversation with a young woman, her face largely hidden by a gray cowl ...

'Seen as allies of Luther most of the order had abandoned their cassocks and debauched lifestyles before merging with the general population to avoid persecution by the Spanish Catholics. This man must be either brave or foolish to flaunt his affiliation at such a time.'

Thank you, Academic.

'I don't trust that priest,' said Cornelius. He was soon distracted from a growing sense of unease by a black-toothed wedding guest who jostled him and placed a hand on his shoulder. Incoherent with drink, the intruder tried in vain to persuade his words to form themselves in even a semblance of order. As he swayed he spilt his beer on Cornelius who thought it best to hide his annoyance. After all, they had invited themselves. The man was desperate to communicate some important truth and kept glancing towards the Franciscan. He staggered like a novice sailor in his first storm. He clutched Cornelius' sleeve ever tighter but still struggled to tame his words sufficiently.

Eventually Cornelius extricated himself and moved towards a young woman dancing on her own. 'Do you bide nearby?' he asked, but got no reply. The man failed to notice that his companion had left and continued to frame his mouth in odd shapes, still hopeful that they would eventually enable him to convey meaning. The young woman was so completely oblivious of Cornelius' presence he wondered if he had drunk some potion that rendered him invisible. Eventually, still staring at a point in the middle distance, she took his hands and steered him though a slow motion dance he failed to recognise. She then held him to her breast and hummed a tune close to his ear. She was comely, firm and warm.

Cornelius was gnawed by loss. He just wanted to be home.

Now becoming something of an expert at extricating himself from barely conscious wedding guests, he stepped aside. The woman continued to move with her arms outstretched as if he were still contained within them.

At a sudden sound the drinkers stopped drinking, the dancers were still and the barely conscious opened their eyes. Balthasar's first thought was that the thick snow had avalanched off the roof now warmed by the heat of celebration inside. The double doors of the inn splintered apart, the planks lurched into the room like falling drunks, the bagpipe tune resolved into a consumptive wheeze. A horse and helmeted rider stood in the doorway, the animal reared onto its hind legs, its fore hooves pummelling the air, a pugilist spoiling for a fight. The rider having lowered his lance to clear the lintel now thrust it towards the startled company who slid away from the table as if swept by an invisible arm. Pitchers broke as they met the stone flagstones.

A girl screamed and beat her small fists against the invader's brocaded saddle. 'Spanish whoremasters!' shouted another of the guests, and was promptly kicked in the face by a spurred boot.

Other horses appeared to either side of the first intruder, pushing their heads into the space, nostrils flared, eyes bulging. At the precise moment of the eruption Balthasar and Cornelius were crouching at the back of the room giving food and water to the two dogs. They stayed on their knees and watched events unfold from the edge of the table. 'Stay still,' said Balthasar, 'stay still.'

The Franciscan stood up and grabbed Johannes who was too stunned to react. The monk wrenched the weaver's hood over his head trapping his arms and effectively blinding him in one movement. Cornelius made to move but was held back by Balthasar who could see the crowd of soldiers in the yard.

Resistance would prove fatal. Johannes was manhandled out of the inn and thrown across the back of a riderless horse. His hands were quickly tied. The Franciscan climbed up behind one of the riders and the party swept out of the square.

FOURTEEN

'Hair of the dog,' muttered Mick as he steered John though the early morning crowd at the foot of Leith Walk. 'Trust me,' he said. The odd couple attracted little attention as they walked beneath the overhead posters on which Tom Farmer, The Proclaimers and Uncle Tom Cobley and all declared their undying loyalty to the neighbourhood. 'I lent Sean Connery money once,' said Mick. 'Skinflinted bastard never paid me back. Mind you, I was offered a part in one of they Bond films. After all, I was doing odd jobs at the time and it made sense.'

Once more John concentrated on every passing face. Occasionally the inner mantra, 'Is that him? Is that him?' became an outer mantra.

Jester, do you want a shot?

'*A Pleasure. "What are you saying?'" asked Mick. "Oh aye, your brother. Ken that pub?" he said, pointing at the Victorian splendour of the Central Bar. "I sang there once, it's my voice like, it's pure Tam White, deep ken. The women all loved it. It's like pure gravel. I owe a debt of gratitude to the fags, a blessing in disguise. I had offers, ken. One night after the gig, this boy sidles up, 'Are you free pal?' he asks. 'Who's asking?'*

I says 'Don't say a word,' he says, "it's Princess Anne," ken, her what watches the Scotland rugby, she'd escaped her chaperals and went in search of a bit of rough. I tells they boys I hate they royals and I don't want to catch yon King's evil from shagging a princess. They weren't happy mind. That's when it started, the following, the phone calls with nobody at the other end, my mail was gone through. The persecution. My career suffered, but you ken all that. I've told you before."

'With no warning Mick executed a sharp left and disappeared into a charity shop. It was a while before John noticed that Mick was no longer at his side and retraced his steps. As he crossed the threshold he saw Mick saluting an RAF uniform hanging next to a Bakelite kitchen chair. "Heroes against the fasciste," he declared.

"Watch your language," retorted the shop assistant. Mick raked through the assorted contents of an open suitcase and slipped several pairs of spectacles into his pocket. "Against the dying of the light."

"Put they glasses back. You lot from the hostel are all the same, minky, thieving weirdos."

"Madam," said Mick, "I assume you are in the pay of the Emir."

"A mere what?" snorted the woman. Mick tapped the side of his nose, winked at her and left the shop with John in tow ... '

Nice one, Jester. I'll take over again.

John desperately wanted to go back to the hostel. He must have stared intently at two or three hundred different male faces since they left. All their features had started to merge and he knew it was only a matter of time before the Bastard would start his predictable tirade of wheedling abuse. As if he had accidently rubbed the genie's lamp by the mere act of articulating his anxiety, his nemesis appeared and swatted aside the Jester who was quietly rehearsing an amusing interpolation.

'Come on, John, stop the self-pitying. "Wanting to lie down!" my arse. What a girly thing to want. What a prima donna, it's not a bed at the Intercontinental that you crave, it's that midden at the hostel, or had you forgotten? A second-hand bed. Come to think of it, John, do you ever wonder what happened in that bed before the council bought it? Couples made love in it, spoke fondly to each other, planned the next day, discussed the children, and then fell asleep with their arms round each other. Just what you do in the same bed, eh, John? Saddo. Just you with your picture. Sweet delusions, baby. "Oh Andy, come back to me, I want to talk to you, I want to hear about the missing years." Wanker! No, I want to be in a Bruegel painting and have adventures. Absolute bollocks. Your punishment today for being the saddest person whose head I have ever been in, is to stay with Mick the lefty loony, stay with your self-obsessed paranoid, schizophrenic fellow hostel lodger. Now get in that pub and devil mend you. Not a bad idea that, I'll ask around and see if Old Nick can spare an hour or two and join you for the odd beer. He's all yours, Narrator, I can't be bothered.'

The pub was full at ten o'clock in the morning, its licence justified on the grounds that it catered for the folk on night shift, the nonexistent army of exhausted fish filleters and hard-working posties for whom night was day and vice versa. Mick pushed his way in, past the knot of smokers squinting uncertainly at the daylight. John muttered an apology and followed. A dog lapped at a puddle of beer near a table leg. ''scuse us ladies,' said Mick exploiting a small gap left between two middle-aged women on a bench. 'Come on, John, loads of room. Do you want a drink, ladies?' They both shook their heads and lowered their eyes.

'A half and a half is it, John?' He slouched towards the bar managing to look forwards and sideways at the same time, in case he was being followed by the many agents who defined and proscribed his life. He paused at a boxing poster sellotaped to a pillar advertising a fight between Edinburgh and London and raised his fists at the two protagonists. The women glanced at each other across John but said nothing.

'Pair of slags,' said the Bastard who, along with the other Voices, had been waiting for me to draw breath. *'They might give your cock a feel, John, they do charitable work you know. They get a tax rebate.'*

'Did you hear the one about the horse who went up to the bar?' asked the Jester.

'Eyes open, old son,' said the Tempter. *'He might be here. He probably enjoys a drink just like you; perhaps he works down the docks and pops in here for a wee pint every morning. Is that him reading the* Mail *over there? Could be, you know.'*

John looked at the man lost in the sport pages. He felt nothing. He was sure that he would know when he saw Andy, something in them both would stir. It would be obvious.

There was a younger man holding on to the jukebox as if the floor was experiencing a seismic shift that only he could feel. No, it wasn't him. A man wearing army fatigues emerged from the gents, still doing up his fly.

'It's him, it has to be!' shouted the Tempter, *'Right age, looks a bit like you, a bit thinner but he's in the army, you'd expect that.'*

'Anyway, the barman said to the horse ... '

'He's looking for a rent boy,' said the Bastard. *'It must be him, old habits die hard, John.'*

'We have reason to believe you are associating with known terrorists, we have the evidence, your fingerprints are everywhere ... '

Who are you?

'I can't tell you that, I might have to kill you,' said a Voice, with the patrician tones of the establishment.

'My colleague is right, Official Secrets Act and all that. Very hush hush.'

But you don't live in John's head; you can't speak.

'Of course not, we are assigned to Mick, covert surveillance.'

If you live in Mick's head, go away. You have no connection with John; he belongs to us.

'Not as simple as that I'm afraid. Territorial rights and all that, love and war, know what I mean?'

'Can I say a few words here?' asked the Academic. *'This is fascinating, and very little researched. The accumulation of new Voices for those with the diagnosis is well established, if not understood, but from my reading of the literature Voices do not normally transfer from one hearer to another. The nearest precedent is the Koranic understanding of Djin possession. Muslims believe in both good and bad Djins who can move from one person to another on a whim, but the phenomenon is little understood in Christian-Judaic concepts of schizophrenia.'*

All very well, Academic. But they are not welcome. John's head is ours exclusively. After conferring, the alien Voices returned to their rightful home as Mick, holding a small tray of drinks, sat down between John and the older of the two women.

'Come here often, ladies?' he asked. 'It's not safe ken, eyes everywhere. Do you belong to the collective?' The two women nodded to each other, finished their drinks and left. 'Not very friendly like,' said Mick.

John was feeling tired and increasingly depressed. He didn't want to spend more time with Mick; he had sufficient problems of his own without being recruited as a passive witness in an endless struggle with unseen governmental powers and the forces of reaction generally. Yet for all his challenges Mick was rarely aggressive and made few demands.

At least the hair of the dog seemed to be working. The pounding had stopped and for the time being the Voices were quiet.

Mick was happy enough muttering to himself, engaging with his own demons, too preoccupied to be making any demands on anyone else.

In that moment John wrongly assumed that I had forsaken the narration and that he was at liberty to pursue his own thoughts. It seemed unfair to disabuse him as he tentatively savoured the silence in his own head. He genuinely thought he was taking stock. Or, put another way, judging himself harshly. Not realising that I was recording all the while, John reflected on how listening to the unrelenting parliament of Voices in his own head had robbed him of the capacity to think uninterrupted. He basically agreed with the Bastard's assessment. By any criteria he was a total failure. The debit side of his life was overwhelming: a failed marriage, a failed career. In addition he had a drink habit brought on by the need to drown out the people who had decided to squat in his head; the travellers who had set up camp in defiance of byelaws and indeed natural justice; cognitive parasites living off his brain, consuming the grey matter.

On the credit side? Well, he was still alive but, as the Bastard never tired of telling him, this was more attributable to his cowardice than any life-embracing decision. With the medication he could lead a comparatively independent life albeit in the hostel. He had sufficient money between his living allowance and disability benefit. So far he had avoided having to surrender all financial responsibility to Beverley under the terms of a Community Order.

He had found professional staff who genuinely seemed to care for him but, then again, they were paid to care, rewarded for empathy. They gained SVQs for demonstrating the right values towards him and adherence to procedures compatible with best practice as defined by the National Care Standards. He had a reputation for gentleness and he knew he was still the unwitting beneficiary of those years spent learning middle-class politeness. He preferred to interpret this as manipulative behaviour that ensured better treatment from those professionals who thought they recognised one of their own. Perhaps Mick was right.

'It's a plot against the working classes,' said Mick, drowning his half pint.

Ignoring this unwanted evidence that Mick was telepathic John resumed his brooding. The bottom line was his unremitting loneliness. Yes, he knew this thought only served to reinforce the Bastard's perception of him as a self-pitying loser. Even when the Voices were quiet or distracted for some reason, they might as well have still been there. He anticipated what they would say if they had been active.

'It's all a conspiracy,' muttered Mick again, with a prescience that was starting to become unnerving.

Ignoring the possibility that Mick, beneath his preoccupations, was subtly attuned to his own thought processes, John continued with his own increasingly painful introspection. Perhaps he needed to punish himself periodically with this intense scrutiny of his negligible worth.

There was still the issue with his brother. One of his many therapists had encouraged him to let go of the obsession suggesting it was a displacement activity subconsciously calculated to distract him from his present challenges, a sort of vicarious search for his own self.

Then there was the Bruegel thing. He understood that what had started as an obsession had escalated into a delusion that sucked him in, yet, if he was honest, he had no wish to forsake that part of himself. In a peculiar way he felt kinship with the people in his delusionary world.

'It's loyalty,' said Mick.

Momentarily startled, John realised that I had in fact never been away. All the while I had been sitting quietly on the sidelines of his brain painstakingly chronicling his thoughts.

I must give you some more background. I mentioned earlier how that psychologist from Dundee had encouraged John to differentiate between the Voices in his head and make a choice. That was the moment when he chose me. Since then he has on occasions admitted that his life seems more manageable when I shape it. From his point of view I am an unknown, essentially non-malevolent persona. Certainly in the past the Jester too was generally welcome although nowadays John rarely finds solace in his inappropriate and often surreal humour. Talk of the devil ... Hi Jester.

'A young man in a black hoodie sidled up to the pair of them, "Hi boys, can I interest you in some bacon? Finest smoked back. A bit like that stuff you can buy in Tesco's."

"Aye, very like," said his pal.

Sensing a possible sale the boy with the bacon chanced his luck, "I've wifey's knickers as well, not to mention dog food for your pet ... Pal for your pal if you ken what I mean. And some of they scratch cards. A new life beckons. Beckons with bacon," he continued.

"Scratch yourselves a new future. A coin will do, just rub it along the card and all your wishes will come true. Like Christmas or a break-in at Poundies."

"Free enterprise in the black market," said Mick, running an appreciative finger along the packet of bacon. "The inevitable consequence of exploitation."

"Aye whatever. Are you wanting the bacon? And don't forget the knickers, wear them yourselves; we're an equal opps employer ken, no prejudice against trannies and all they perverted folk. After all my dad's a mason, and he lives in Leith mind. Just slip them on under your togs, feel that silk against your legs, and dream, boys, dream."'

Enough, Jester. Small doses remember?

'You dirty wee shites,' said Mick, suddenly roused. Then fearing that he might miss out on a genuine bargain with the bacon tried a different approach. 'Is bartering out of the question? How about a few tabs that'll take you to places you've never been. Here, John, give the lads that pack of fluoxetine you got from Boots yesterday.'

Because John had been distracted by the snail traces from his own reflections and had not heard a word of the recent exchange he put his hand in his pocket and pulled out the antipsychotics in their blue blister packaging. The nearest lad snatched it from him ...

... At a sudden sound the drinkers stopped drinking, the dancers were still and the barely conscious opened their eyes. Balthasar's first thought was that the thick snow had avalanched off the roof now warmed by the heat of celebration inside. The double door of the inn had been splintered apart, the planks lurched into the room like falling drunks, the bagpipe tune resolved into a single note, a consumptive wheeze. A horse and helmeted rider stood in the doorway, the animal reared onto its hind legs, its fore hooves pummelling the air, a pugilist spoiling for a fight.

The bigger of the two plain clothes policemen put a hand on John's shoulder, 'You are not obliged to say anything but anything you do say will be noted down and may be used in evidence.' John was bundled into the patrol car outside.

He felt claustrophobic. He asked the driver to stop. Ignored, he shouted. This time the car slowed and pulled over. One of the officers climbed into the back, grabbed him by the lapels and told him, 'Shut the fuck up!'

FIFTEEN

Johannes vomited the wedding sweetmeats down the horse's flank. His head bounced off the animal's flesh as it gathered speed and left the village.

After the first few miles his head felt as if it had been pummelled by a bully with fists the size of hams. His cowl slipped down affording him a blurred upside down view of the snow-covered ground between the horse's legs. He vaguely heard intermittent Spanish voices as if they were checking their whereabouts.

After an hour's relentless pounding, during which his eyes clouded over and he longed for death's release, the party slowed and the horse was led down a steep slope or embankment. The stiff ice-covered rushes suggested they were attempting to cross a frozen river. After picking its way over boulder-sized lumps of ice the horse stopped and the sound of rushing water drowned out all else. The beast was reluctant to wade through the thawed channel in the middle. Johannes heard angry shouts, and felt the impact of a stave smacked hard against the animal's flank. It brayed its shock and pain before tentatively entering. The water rose as high as Johannes's face, burning burned his skin and, for a moment, stopping his heart. He retched and choked on the cold air in between the periods of immersion. Time itself become sluggish and half frozen before the horse picked its way up the opposite bank. Gasping, shaking, and cold to the marrow, Johannes felt a blind panic. He could not endure more of this. He wanted to die.

On the other side, the party rested. Johannes' body started to shake in rhythm with the frozen horse. For sport, one of the men pretended to wipe his dripping nose with his 'kerchief then, laughing, slapped him hard across the cheek. The pain barely registered. He could tell that the men were eating and drinking. He heard the loud bragging voices, one of their number started speaking in a high pathetic voice, perhaps a cruel imitation of a female victim pleading for her life. The others guffawed.

The journey resumed and gradually Johannes lost consciousness.

When he was eventually hauled off the horse Johannes' legs crumpled under him. Two soldiers hauled him upright by the armpits.

The building in front of him stood alone in a bleak landscape. Three stories high at the front and two at the back, it sloped towards a field from which smoke was rising. Johannes thought he could hear a woman wailing, but perhaps not. It may have been the wind. All of the windows were barred apart from the one at the top of the building that was open to the weather: two square dark holes from which bodies could easily be encouraged to fall. A thick rope swung in the aperture. A merchant's home hastily converted, thought Johannes once his world stopped spinning. The trees in the immediate vicinity had been cut down, presumably to prevent curious onlookers from approaching undetected. From the one remaining tree hung a faded red inn sign, depicting a boar and a crudely drawn angel. The two soldiers guarding the entrance made an effort to straighten themselves as the party swept into the building.

Johannes' feet dragged on the ground as his captors rushed him inside, uniforms dripping on the black and white chequered floor. A thin stream of wax flowed uninterrupted from the chandelier. The oak furniture had a solidity that suggested it had been liberated from a church, a suspicion confirmed by the presence of the framed pictures of saints in various states of gloomy martyrdom: pieced by thorns, flailed by scourges. A fireplace bigger than a horse dominated the room, with a single skull positioned on crimson cloth at the centre of a functionary's desk. A dark figure watched the play unfold from the vantage point of a minstrel's gallery.

The custody sergeant barely looked up, 'Name?' he asked.

'Johannes Pakesoon.'

'Speak up'

'Johannes Pakesoon.'

'By the grace of God, the holy apostolic church and our king Philip II you are required to submit yourself to examination upon the charge that in defiance of natural justice, and in contradiction of the teachings of Jesus Christ Our Saviour you, Johannes Pakesoon, have embraced heretical views which, if proven, will require that you be taken from this place and broken on the wheel. Do you understand?

Johannes could only concentrate on the large black wart that protruded from the interrogator's cheek, that could at any moment burst out of his face and spit bile over all present. Instinctively the official quickly touched the carbuncle before proceeding. The small man, whose frock coat was adorned with a ruff of such size that it threatened to devour his entire head, waited patiently, pen poised.

'Do you accept that infant baptism is a false baptism. One has to be saved in order to be baptised?'

Johannes stared. 'Write the witness in agreement,' instructed the official.

'Do you believe that God does not unconditionally reprobate people to Hell. Rather, God's Manifested Wrath is conditional, and the condition is of not being in Christ. God elects only people who are in Christ? Witness in agreement.'

'Look, son, one of our officers saw you handing over the drugs. I don't care if it is prescribed medication. They should close that hostel down, burn it, fumigate it and stop the vermin from returning. Mental illness, psychosis, it's all bollocks. It's all words to disguise the fact that you are a load of filthy drunken wasters who spend all their benefits on drink and drugs.' The veins stood out on his neck. John cowered, frightened lest he would be hit again.

'And there's no point you remaining silent, what do you think this is, the IR fucking A?'

'This is wonderful!' declared the Bastard. *'I couldn't have put it better myself! You've had it coming to you, John, haven't you? This is my territory, stand aside, Narrator.'*

Bastard, back off, he's struggling enough as it is. Where is your compassion?

'So, where shall we begin? Whatever happened to your mother, John? Remember her? You know she tried to give you away don't you? No? You didn't hear? It is bizarre really, a gipsy woman came to the door selling clothes pegs and your mum said she could have you. You couldn't make it up could you? No? You don't believe me? Suit yourself ...

'Ah, the joy of flicking through the family album. Memory lane! No, it's not a lane. It's an alley next to the pub; it's where she left you both. Poor mites frozen and cold in the pram. I almost feel sorry for you myself. She woke up the following morning, probably not on her own, what do you think, John? A new man next to her? Smoking together in bed, him with

a string vest and a smirk and then she says, "My God, where are my boys?" She leaps up, and runs out of the flat wearing a towel. Lady Godiva with manky hair. Good news though, you were still there, no one had noticed. And what's more, you had a new guardian angel; a big bastard crow was staring at the pair of you. Perhaps it was a black dove, cooing away. That sounds better, not any old bird waiting to peck your brother's eyes out. A happy ending then wasn't it, all things considered?

'And what about the time when you blamed your brother for raking through the kitchen bin for food and it was you all the time. She leathered him and you just watched. And now you want to find him again, touching really. It would break your heart. Yes, it all comes back to me now, do you mind the week before, he got a row for eating the dog's food, and you had encouraged him. Winalot wasn't it? Pretty ironic don't you think?'

'Look pal,' said the policeman, 'I don't care if you just sit there and say nothing. No skin off my nose.' He stopped turning his roller ball pen over on the desk and glanced at John. Clearly the man was not well. For a moment looking into his eyes the sergeant felt something like compassion, a distinctly unfamiliar emotion. Six hours to go and then home to the new house in Bonnyrigg. He really must get the patio sorted before the weekend.

SIXTEEN

Inquisitor Goya glanced at the high window, through which shone a symmetrical shaft of light suffused with dust motes. Sometimes he really couldn't be bothered. Being a circuit administrator wasn't all it was cracked up to be. He dipped the quill into the monogrammed well and pretended to write. Instead, he sketched a rough outline of his wife's face on the blotter, capturing her high cheekbones and enigmatic eyes. She had been cold to him the night before, accused him of being a fanatic, telling him he had changed. She was probably right. Remembering what he should be doing, he resumed from memory. 'Do you believe that Faith in Christ should be a living faith, faith which is confirmed in the fruits of Spirit. People who are living a sinful life, without true repentance, will end in Hell. Living in sin and occasionally falling in sin are not the same thing. All children of God can fall in sin because of our weaknesses, but they do not live in sin?' He realised he was declaiming ever louder, and to increasing effect, as he settled back into the role of righteous and passionate Inquisitor. Pausing for effect he could see the court official looking at him with an expression, part admiration, part terror. By way of a climax to his party piece he pointed his pen at Johannes and roared, 'Witness in agreement!'

The black wart burst, the black stuff spurted into Johannes' eyes. Blinded, he fell to the floor, to be dragged unconscious from the court and thrown into the back of the building.

A junior officer took John's arm, led him into the station cell and slammed the door after him.

Cornelius tore himself free from Balthasar, picking up a tankard from the floor and hurling it towards the departing soldiers. 'Shit filled heretics, Satan's whores!' This last word was swallowed by snow gusting into the room.

A young girl, possibly the bride, sobbed. The two dogs, sensing something amiss, growled before turning their attention to the copious amounts of food spilt on the floor. The piper inspected his instrument. Trodden on during the fracas, it looked ruined beyond repair, a swan with a broken neck. 'Don't worry, don't worry,' he said, as if consoling an injured child.

An elderly man spat in the direction of the space previously occupied by the door. The father of the bride, a dignified man in green hose, approached Balthasar and the brooding Cornelius. He placed an arm on each of them to show there was no resentment against the uninvited guests who had inadvertently turned a joyous occasion into a calamitous one.

'It's not your fault. Don't blame yourselves. We all agreed to an act of defiance to mark my daughter's wedding. We met and voted to ignore the curfew. This is our life, these are our children.' The other guests moved closer and nodded. 'We knew they might come. Their spies haunt the hedgeways and listen in the taverns. They blackmail the weak, and frighten the strong.' He moved closer to the doorway and peered into the blizzard. 'We gave victuals to two young men from the next village. They were to scour the horizon for intruders. If they raised the alarm all music, laughter and merriment would cease on the instant, all fires would be doused and candles extinguished. They will be lying somewhere, their blood draining into the snow.'

From the back of the room a drunken peasant emerged from his self-induced catatonic state. He embarked on a bawdy song that included frequent references to a bull's pizzle before the woman standing nearest to him slapped him across his face, instantly returning him to his previous state of oblivion.

'Your friend will be taken to Gravenvezel where he will be tortured and killed unless you buy his freedom,' explained the bride's father. Others nodded their agreement with this analysis.

'We have no money,' said Cornelius. Balthasar shrugged and tapped his pockets in a gesture of futility.

After a moment's silence the young bride and her new husband approached from the back of the room. The other guests moved aside respectfully. The woman took Cornelius's clenched fist, gently opened it and folded it again around a coin. 'If you take this,' she said, 'we will forever associate this day with giving hope to strangers. The memory will erase that of the Spanish mercenaries who subjugate us and destroy our happiness.' The murmurs of agreement that initially filled the room like penitents' whispered prayers grew louder and more insistent until they erupted into a shout of defiance.

The assembled guests crowded forward to embrace the two men who were overwhelmed by their generosity. The old man led them to the doorway, wiped the stinging snow from his eyes and pointed towards the east. 'Four leagues, maybe more,' he said. As they stood there a young girl approached and handed Balthasar an improvised parcel of food rescued from the upturned table.

'Bless you, bless you,' said Cornelius holding her hand with such fervour that the girl became embarrassed and turned back into the assembled mass of well-wishers. The dogs too were patted and spoken to encouragingly.

John stared at the black and white chequered tiles on the floor of the police cell, which was suddenly crawling with large flies, bloated bluebottles, fat larvae squeezing themselves out of their pupae. His feet were barely visible under the squirming mass of putrefying insects. The smell belonged to the charnel house; to murder victims left in ditches, to fetid putrid wounds.

'*Brilliant,*' said the Bastard.

SEVENTEEN

There were others in Johannes' cell. A father and son slept in the corner with their mouths open. A young man, whose clothes were soaked with urine, banged his head against the wall repeating a phrase that Johannes could not make out. A peasant woman with the nose of an eagle and metal teeth was stamping the straw at intervals, cackling with satisfaction whenever she crushed one of the darting cockroaches. She picked up their smudged remains and dropped them into her mouth as if they were oysters.

Noticing Johannes, she approached with the shy demeanour of a young child and opened her hand, offering a tiny black carcass. Johannes shook his head whereupon the woman grew immeasurably sad and shrank into a corner.

An emaciated but dignified figure, wearing the remnants of what may have been a Pastor's cloak, walked slowly towards Johannes and placed an arm round his shoulder.

'Welcome,' he said.

He was strangely familiar but Johannes could not place him. 'This is our mansion, maybe God has others for us but ... ' His gesture encompassed the whole space. Johannes glanced at the wattled walls, stained with what he hoped was not human blood.

Messages were scratched at head height, mainly dates and names; there were simple prayers too, begging notes to a God who for reasons best known to himself was now indifferent to the petitioners' persecution. Perhaps, after a short flirtation with Luther, God had reverted to Catholicism. This was the same God who had allowed Michel to be taken. Feeling his anger rise, Johannes distracted himself by reading the more secular messages: simple ill-spelt declarations of love to wives, mistresses, children.

'Maria blyf my trou.'

'Mother, hold me.'

'I strayed from the path. Forgive me'

A wall of missives destined never to be read by those to whom they were dedicated, most unbearable were those urging family members and friends to remember the writer after his death. There were drawings too: a dog, a small hut and, etched in red, an image of the wheel upon which the draughtsman would in all probability have been strapped and broken. Johannes was not, at that moment, strong enough to face his own nightmare apprehensions concerning Michel.

The man who had embraced him earlier was still watching. Johannes remembered where he had seen him before. He was the hedge preacher who had first sown the seed of doubt about the old religion in the hearts of the small community.

The weavers and their families had gathered under the branches of the large tree outside the village. It was a hot day and the shelter was welcome. Frenzied crickets almost drowned out the deferential conversations. They spread cloths on the ground and shared rye bread, cheese and wine. Children ran among their elders playing tig, the village dogs did likewise, young lovers stole kisses and said secret things. Expectation grew until the preacher appeared. The jostling crowd parted respectfully as he was ushered towards a knoll at the foot of a large oak.

'We're moving through the oeuvre now. St John the Baptist's Fast Day Sermon *from the Budapest Museum of Fine Arts if I'm not mistaken.'*

Probably, Academic, but it doesn't matter.

Antonia was quickly won over. She had only reluctantly agreed to accompany husband and son after complaining about the foolishness of leaving the looms to hear the latest fanatic. Standing in the shadow of the oak, screwing up the corner of her apron and squinting into the preacher's sunlit face, in that instant she was wooed, won and ravished by his openness, honesty and warmth. He reminded her of her father, she said. His voice soared into the branches and his eyes lit up as he declaimed the joys of salvation, conjuring the vision of an eternity untainted by fear, illness or death. At one point, just as his rhetoric strove to encompass the rapture and ecstasy of union with God, a neighbour's child tumbled from a tree amid a flurry of leaves and small branches. Even that was turned by the preacher to his advantage as he built in references to fallen angels and predestination. In quieter moments the old women at the back strained to hear, interrupting proceedings with 'What did he say?' They were hushed by those standing further forward equally eager not to miss a word.

They walked back through the fields, in the early evening, in the warm glow of the setting sun and were, quite simply, happy. Michel skipped ahead eager for his supper. The following day Antonia lapsed into her sorrows.

There was a barred window on the far wall. Curious, Johannes moved towards it until the pastor stood in front of him and blocked his way. Johannes moved him aside and grasped each of the two metal bars.

Smoke from numerous small fires hung in the air, the cloying, choking smell made Johannes pull the front of his smock over his nose. The landscape was battle scarred and burning, the few remaining trees blackened. In one of them a tiny naked figure hid in the charred and hollow trunk. On the horizon an elongated corpse hung from a gallows beneath which small figures watched without interest. A man on his knees, head bowed, was being beaten by a tall thin figure with a long cane. Victims were herded towards the open doors of a box-like container. The dead, already dressed only in white shifts, were being ravaged by dogs and further stripped by rapacious looters.

'It's The Triumph of Death, *the Prado, Madrid.'*

Shh! I'm getting into my stride now. A cart overloaded with corpses and skulls trundles through the market place of the dead, dying, mutilated and desecrated. The bone-thin nag straining under its burden is urged on by the flail wielded by the skeleton-in-chief who struggles to hold a lantern with his spare arm. An open coffin, already occupied, straddles another white clad corpse rocking as if on a fulcrum. A body has plunged head first into a crater of cess and rain. Its legs wave at the sky in slow motion. In the distance the battle still rages; a frieze of lances, broadswords and cudgels is visible above a pall of smoke and flame. A raven picks at the flesh; a dog sifts through the bones. On the distant gray sea an arc of lost souls floats towards oblivion. On the deck tiny figures with oval mouths crowd together, their arms trapped at their sides. A beacon lit with human eyes sinks into the water. Strange black dragonflies hover; emaciated s oldiers press their shields against the insistent army of the dead.

'For God's sake, Narrator, get a grip. This is overwritten, self-indulgent shite!'

I'm sorry, but the Academic is right. This is an accurate depiction of *The Triumph of Death*. Each detail is lifted directly from the canvas. Remember, John would stare for hours at this painting. Isn't that right, John?

'Big hairy deal. It's crap and you know it'.

Go on, if you don't believe me look it up, I'll even give you the link www.museodelprado.es/.../the-triumph-of-death

'Don't be stupid. And don't sulk. Pathetic!'

I'm not sulking.

'You are!'

Where was I? An impotent militiaman tugs at his sword which refuses to leave the scabbard. A terrified harlequin hides under the table still set for a feast. Insect figures without eyes smile at everything and nothing. A bogie man in black silhouette rails at his dying flock. Two skeletons tug at bell ropes. Thighbones mark the hour on the clock. A girning wraith empties gray bladders from a wicker hamper. A torso, half man, half frog struggles to remove a cage from its head in which frets a small bird. High above the burning ground spindly cartwheels, nailed to the tops of charred poles like carnival hats, hang heavy with tortured, limp carcases. In the foreground an oblivious youth plays the mandolin to woo his lover.

I'm sorry, John. I'm struggling now. I'm not sulking. I just need to lie down...

'About time. After all, this is my territory. When all is said and done, this is an accurate representation of your soul; isn't that right, John? A wonderful metaphor for the essential sickness that characterises your whole being, the same sickness that made you neglect your brother in the home, that drove your mother away in the first place, and drove your wife into someone else's arms. Isn't that right, John? Do you think they're having sex even as we speak? She can't get enough, especially after living with you with your pathetic cock and lack of appetite ... '

'Jester, stop pushing! All right, go ahead. I can't be arsed anyway.'

'There were funny moments though weren't there, John? Do you remember when you fell in love with that naked mannequin in Debenhams? You caressed her cold plastic

breasts and averted your gaze from her smooth and rounded pubic area. You tore a dress from an adjacent clothes rail and, covering her modesty, swept her up in your arms and steered her out of the shop. You have to admit, it was amusing. "We are meant for each other," you explained to the security guard on the door. "Ours is a marriage made in heaven." The man was so astonished he did nothing. Then you tried to pay her fare on the number 44. "Get aff ma bus!" said the driver ... '

From an academic perspective the pair of you are contributing nothing.

'*I was only trying...* ' explained the Jester, upset at being interrupted.

'*I'm sure you were ... the research is certainly interesting. All that the Narrator describes is indeed taken from the picture he mentions. Some experts suspect that our old friend Bosch may have had something to do with it. But undeniably it is this picture that is referred to in the estate of Philip van Valckenisse,* Triumphe vanden Doot, van Bruegel. *All of the traditional elements of the medieval Dance of Death are there, the skeleton riding a miserable nag, a burning landscape, it's all there. Well done. There you are, Narrator, I've done my best to provide a sense of perspective, if you'll forgive the pun. I'm sure you've got your breath back by now. I think you should take over again, after all, even from an academic point of view, you are very good ...* '

Flatterer.

The pastor moved Johannes away from the barred window and ushered him towards the heap of blood-stained straw.

EIGHTEEN

John huddled, foetal-like, under the single blanket in the cell until the panic attack subsided and his body unclenched, his hyperventilation mutating into laboured breathing. He felt cold from a film of sweat. He knew he must become grounded so tried to concentrate on the detail of his surroundings. Pale green painted walls, a lavatory pan with no seat, a wooden bench the length of the wall, a light bulb encased in a mesh of protective wire, the small spy hole in the door and the untouched meal on its tray on the floor.

At the very moment he teetered on the cusp of deep sleep, the Tempter popped up and woke him.

'Stay vigilant, John. He might be here you know. Like you, he could have fallen on hard times, the wrong side of the law. He might be in the next cell, thinking about you. Imagine that, after all this time the pair of you separated by a thin wall, neither knowing the other was just inches away.'

Lacking the energy to resist, John pulled himself upright and listened intently for sounds of sleeping from the adjacent cell. Nothing, only the dull buzz of the lighting and the occasional ping from the radiator.

'Still, next time,' said the Tempter.

Still clutching the coin, Cornelius attempted to fasten his coat at the neck. The buttonhole proved elusive. 'Spanish sodomites!' he shouted, stamping on the ground. 'Catholic catamites, Lucifer's lepers. Bastards!' He was shushed by the wind-shaking trees. Knowing that his friend's anger had to run its course, Balthasar turned to chastise the dogs who were understandably reluctant to forsake the warmth of the inn and pad once more into the snow.

'We can be there at dawn,' said Cornelius.

The wind tore at their faces as they set off in the direction indicated by the father of the bride. Although it was only mid-afternoon the weak sun had already given up the pretence of holding any real shape or purpose in the sky, its residual light was shredded across the white bleakness.

Balthasar thought of home. He found himself hankering for the tedium and repetitiveness of the loom, and glanced down at his gloves. What had happened to his weavers' hands, softened by the lanolin?

He stood on the stone flags of their kitchen and moved towards Wilhelmien who initially resisted and pushed him away before responding, albeit grudgingly, to his kiss. He checked the logs in the hearth, stirring the broth as he always did.

Cornelius punched his stick into the grinning face of the first soldier to force his way over the threshold of the inn. He derived great satisfaction from toppling the next Spaniard from his horse and smashing his elbow into the gap beneath the visor. He spat at his victim and pissed into his face as he squirmed on the ground. As the chill wind snapped him out of his reverie he thought of Johannes. There was no guarantee he had been taken to the Dieventoren, he might already be dead, beaten and killed by the soldiers to keep themselves warm and stave off the boredom of their long journey back to the barracks.

'Keep the faith,' said Balthasar.

The sluggish water seeping from the dykes gradually solidified into frozen ropes. Elsewhere globular icicles hung like forsaken weapons. The dogs growled as they floundered through the drifts. The only navigational aids were the setting sun and the intermittent smudge of a church spire that would briefly emerge on the horizon before being hidden again by flurries of snow.

A clump of snow would, now and then, drape itself round their faces like a cold flannel, at other times single playful flakes wandered into their open mouths. They passed a pond which held the frozen shapes of two ducks, perfectly upright, rendered immobile at the very moment when the already heavy water froze.

The dogs stopped and turned their snouts upwards. Correctly interpreting the gesture, the two men nudged the animals into the hedgerow to let pass several horses and their riders which had emerged without warning.

'Walloon mercenaries,' muttered Balthasar, correctly identifying the red coats. The snarling dogs spooked the last horse in the procession. The frightened beast reared and teetered and, for a moment, Cornelius' face was inches away from a flailing spur as its owner reined his horse down and threw a curse at the two peasants. They were too busy to stop and interrogate them. Having fulfilled their quota for the investigators, their imperative was to get to camp as soon as possible and share details of the women they had manhandled at the previous village. Cornelius brushed himself down and waved his fist at the departing group. 'We're going the right way,' commented Balthasar. 'At least they have trampled a path for us.'

The path meandered across the smothered fields towards a windmill. Men and dogs approached cautiously. Its sails were still, each blade thick with snow, their rough hewn sides black with wetness. It was a redundant engine. A sinister wooden sarcophagus balancing improbably on a rick of beams that looked as if it had been abandoned in a hurry. Several sacks had spilled their contents onto the ground, hempen stomachs split for pleasure. A sodden bonnet lay at the foot of the ladder.

While the dogs nosed round the spilled grain for the rich scent of vermin, Balthasar tentatively stepped onto the first rung and pulled himself upwards. As his head reached floor level a crossbow bolt was pushed against his forehead. He looked up carefully and saw it was being held by a small, elderly man with the physique of a bird.

'God's peace,' said Balthasar, maintaining eye contact despite his obvious discomfort. The man lowered his weapon and used it to beckon him inside. 'My companion too?' The man nodded.

Cornelius choked as he too emerged into the musky stinking interior of the mill. Their host, a tiny, wiry figure with the eyes of a madman, pushed them both against the far wall with a strength that belied his size. Balthasar and Cornelius looked at each other as the man put a hand up to each of their throats. 'We come in peace,' mouthed Balthasar.

Satisfied, the man released his grip and motioned for them to sit down on the line of stuffed sacks that divided the available space.

NINETEEN: The Miller's Tale

'Excellent!' said the Academic. *'The interpolated tale has a long and respectful literary history. Mind you, judging by the title we can't deny Chaucer's influence.'*

Quiet! Why do you keep interrupting the narrative, sometimes I think you're just showing off.

'I just thought ... '

Well, don't. What did Hamlet say? 'Every thought quartered hast ever three parts coward ... ' See it's easy to be clever for the sake of it.

'They came last week,' said the emaciated Miller, rubbing his brow with the blackened fingers of one hand. 'They found nothing. I saw them approach and brought inside the rancid food which I keep for such occasions. The fat maggots swarmed,' he added gleefully. 'They clutched their noses and muffled themselves with their cloaks as they gagged at the stench. "For Christ's sake, old man," said their leader, "you should be put to death for smelling like that. Is this a mill or a charnel house? Do you collect the dead from the fields and hide them here?" He chuckled as he relived the moment of deception. "He kicked the legs from under me, spat, and made his way back down the ladder. And look what they missed, boys, look what they missed.' He pulled back the curtain at the back of the room and showed the printing press.

The wooden frame was nearly the height of a man. Cornelius touched it. 'Lovely wood,' he said.

'I left with the other printers in '56. Over fifty of us from all over Brabant made our way to Antwerp. The whole guild. Each of us with a bag of lead type, all emptied in haste from the frames before the raiders came. At first it was just the books. What bonfires, boys! Who would have thought bibles would have burned like that. "The Lord your God is a consuming fire ... Who among us shall dwell with the devouring fire? ... Who among us shall dwell with everlasting burnings?" He scampered through the confined space, skipping past the flames of his memory. 'Spitting words and spines, precious prints of saints, martyrs, angels, prophets, gold lettering painstakingly applied, now curling in the fire. Each village square was alive with fire.

'The solders would return from the raids with armfuls of bibles, testaments, homilies, imprecations, incantations, prayers for the dead, sermons, commandments. What a lot of holy words, all sacrificed to Satan, and then they demanded to know where the printers lived. Dragged screaming and struggling from their families and hearths, they too were thrust into the flames until their hot blood mingled with the molten lead running in white streams from the fire. My apprentice was spared for their sport. They stripped him naked and covered him with his own vat of ink. He roared like a blackamoor, the children screamed and ran away. The soldiers were so busy holding their sides and laughing they forgot to kill him. For three days and nights he hid in the wood and then came home, a shaking black Beelzebub. By then nothing remained, just the embers blowing on the wind. All God's words scattered into the hedgerows, and into the river. Who knows, distant peoples may have snatched at a passing word, as at a butterfly, and taken it to heart.' He mimed plucking the burned scraps from the air and then focussed with glee on an imaginary half page. Cornelius and Balthasar stared at the bizarre pantomime being acted by their insane host.

'We couldn't stay, not after that. The pedlar agreed to spread the word though all the parishes and so it came to pass that the printers' army arrived in Antwerp. At first the sea beggars who had agreed to take us to England thought our bags held gold but, no, it was lead, enough to sink their ships they said, and demanded more ducats. They made us sleep on deck, each man curled round his precious bag of type.

'One night Leviathan himself came to the boat and swept his hand across the deck dragging one of our number over the side. He went to his death still holding his bag close to his chest. Think of his business now, boys, printing tracts under the salty waves. Sending his words out on every new tide to wash up on the shores of foreign lands and convert the heathens.' Delighted with his own conceit, he cackled and smacked Cornelius on the shoulder.

'England was cold. The people were cold. Not understanding our tongue, they would shout at us. Their children would laugh at our clothes and throw stones until we gave them letters, single carved nuggets of lead. The children cupped them in their hands like injured sparrows and took them home to their parents who soon arrived demanding their own pieces. They gave us beer; we gave them letters. It worked well.

'When we saw the farmer squeezing whey to make English cheese we gave him money for his press. Soon we had a barn where the carpenters fashioned the rollers. The women scoured the hedgerows for berries, nuts and leaves, crushing them between stones. Soon their cauldron boiled with dark, dark ink. We tipped the letters on the ground and made our alphabets, but we had a problem. The children's favourite letter was the S, but we had given too many of them away.' He drew a huge S in the air, his elbow emphasising the shape like a painter with his brush. 'They would offer their puppets, skittles, pickup sticks, rats' skulls, lizard skins anything for the precious S; the snake letter that would ward off witches and bogymen. They would hide the magic letter in amulets; the young boys wooed the girls with a single S. So, what could we do? The only solution, said the elders, was to use the letter f ... And God bleffed them and God faid unto them, Be fruitful and multiply, and replenif the earth, and fubdue it: and have dominion over the fifh of the fea.' The lunatic miller threw back his head and roared. Balthasar was transfixed by the man's epiglottis waggling in his black mouth.

'*Absolute nonsense,*' said the Academic.

'*Fooled you all!*' said the Jester. '*Sometimes I take over the story without anyone noticing. The Narrator was getting bored so I seized my chance when he nodded off.*'

Don't kid yourself. I chose to let you in. Where was I ... ?

Eventually the miller became calm again. 'Soon we were printing hundreds, then thousands of tracts a day. Each week one of us would make his way to the dark shore and wait for the boatman who, for guilder, would take the bundles back over the sea. All seemed well until one of the boys playing on the rocks found a floating tide of sodden paper. We had been betrayed by the boatman. When he next arrived to take his cargo we slit his throat and left him among the slimy pools along the stony beach. It was clear that one of us must make the journey with the tracts ... '

TWENTY

'Your gaffer's here,' said the policeman. John's head was a jumble of words, snatches of dialogue and a strange aching sense of something important but not fully remembered.

'What on earth have you been up to?' asked Derek. 'Selling drugs? I don't think so,' he continued for the benefit of the custody sergeant as much as for John. 'Mick wandered in and said that you had been snatched by Nicaraguan death squads, then it was the Nazis, I think the Stasi also had a hand in your abduction, not to mention aliens with neo-fascist tendencies. Even Postman Pat seemed to be part of a global conspiracy to remove you from the streets. And here you are, alive and in one piece. You look a bit rough, haven't been beaten up have you?' He glanced towards the sergeant who raised an eyebrow. When the formalities were complete Derek led John back towards the hostel.

'Another fine mess you've got yourself in, Olly,' said the Jester, in a cod American accent. '*Did you see that hairy mole on that copper's cheek? Come on, John, cheer yourself up, you've only been arrested and charged with supplying illegal drugs, it's not the end of the world is it?'*

'Perhaps your brother has joined the police,' said the Tempter, *'Did your brother have a mole?'*

'Pathetic,' said the Bastard. *'What pleasures remain in the day for you John? There must be a lot for you to look forward to. Let's see, the over-concerned interrogation from Beverley, and your key worker. All that misplaced professional sympathy. I imagine that dippit social worker will put in an appearance and in his usual patronising way talk you through the consequences of your actions. You won't say a word, will you? A big boy, unable to talk, unable to look people in the eye. You don't talk, John, because I am your real Voice. I talk; you listen. It's quite simple. Who would listen to you anyway? You're just a boring shite. That's why your wife left, not forgetting the other small matter of your drink induced impotence ...*

'Do you remember that time in the staff room when you had a semblance of a life? What were you talking about? I can't remember; I wasn't listening either. That colleague from the maths department pretended to fall asleep, it soon spread, everyone there was pretending to snore. Good fun, wasn't it?

'Ah, life at the hostel! A community of the mad and the lost. Limbo lives passing the time before they die. Yet it's home, isn't it, John? Home, sweet home. Come to think of it, aren't these very words crocheted and framed in the downstairs toilet? You don't like that, John, do you? Reminds you of being in care. You still are, if you think of it. It's an odd word "care", isn't it? Basically no one cares, not about you, not about your brother – let's not forget for a moment your favourite obsession. You don't even care about yourself which says it all really. Do I care about you? Well now, that's an interesting question. Perhaps I do, perhaps that's why I have chosen to live in your head. There again, this could be my punishment. Trapped in the stinking cell of your brain.'

Most of what the Bastard said proved to be prophetic. Beverley was indeed concerned and put her arm around John when Derek led him into her office. Overwhelmed by sadness and guilt, John let himself be rocked. 'It's ok,' she said, 'it's ok.'

The social worker turned up as predicted. He leant back on his chair like a bored school kid. He chewed the end of his pen as if he had not eaten for days. 'We can't go on like this, can we, John? You're better off here than in prison, don't you think?' John nodded. Eventually Janet joined them and asked John if he was hungry. He shook his head but made clear that he wanted to be on his own for a while. 'In your room or in the lounge?' she said. 'Kevin's there but he's sleeping.'

Kevin's head lolled sideways against the cushion, his mouth was open and his rigid right hand was pointing the remote at the blaring TV. The unctuous game show host wallowed in the applause and laughter as the wide-eyed contestants radiated disbelief at their good fortune at having been chosen in the first place. The couple hugged each other, and then sought consolation in each other's arms when a tentative answer was met with a klaxon signalling failure. They left the stage to be replaced by an identical pair. He was a joiner with his own business, his favourite food was curry, she was a hairdresser and they met at a funfair in Skegness. Bells rang, gongs sounded, pound notes cascaded into a chest. The air was punched. Manly hugs and back slappings were bestowed on the male contestant by the host.

'*That could be you, John,*' said the Tempter. '*You must enter; they'll give you the number at the end of the show. Nothing easier. Then you could afford to pay a private detective to find Andy. No stone unturned, know what I mean?*' His voice was reasonableness personified. '*It could be the start of great things. A holiday together, your own house. It can happen.*'

'*From an academic perspective and speaking statistically, if one were to devote several years of one's life to applying to appear on game shows, there is only a miniscule chance of winning a modest sum. Even then the odds of getting past the initial screening are remote but, it must be acknowledged, not as great as winning the lottery. According to a recent article in the* Guardian's g2 *the chances of winning the jackpot in America's multistate Powerball lottery is so tiny that a person driving ten miles to buy a ticket is sixteen times more likely to be killed in a car accident en route.'*

'Absolute bollocks. No, to be fair, a game show for psychotic alcoholics could catch on. Lots of folk would want to laugh at the dafties. The Americans would like it. You would each be asked to describe, and possibly act out, your favourite delusion. You're right, Tempter, John would win hands down with that guff about looking for his son in some cold painting. Excellent plan. It gets better, at the end of each episode you get to decide who should be executed. Live of course. Well ... until he's dead.'

'Did you hear the one about the lunatic who ravished the laundrette assistants and then ran away, NUT SCREWS WASHERS AND BOLTS said the headline!'

'Everyone's heard it, Jester. We don't need jokes to make us laugh, just look at this failure here. How funny is he? See what I mean?'

If you lot have finished ...

Adverts followed for stair lifts, health care insurance, dog food and mattresses that retain the sleeper's shape perhaps forever. After several false starts Kevin's snoring reached a snarling crescendo that catapulted him back into wakefulness. He looked around startled before focussing on John.

'Lifted were you? I can't stand sharing my living space with criminal scum. I'm going to ask for a move to supported accommodation. I've had it up to here with this place. Criminals and folk no right in the head. Remember I was the original Bisto Kid, I had a future. They wouldn't have stood for this at ICI ... '

John decided that his room, even if it reminded him of the cell he had just left, was the preferred option. On the stair he met Mick, who grunted conspiratorially and offered his hand.

Paul was waiting for him on the top landing. 'I've found him,' he shouted, ushering John through the door. 'Watch where you stand!' John looked down and saw that every square inch of the floor was covered with index cards, utterly symmetrical, all facing the same way, all impeccably covered in neat copperplate handwriting.

'He's there somewhere,' said Paul. He saw the confusion on John's face. 'Your brother,' he explained, exasperated. 'He's here, it's just a puzzle and I can't quite see him.' He put his hand up to his head and pressed hard against his brow.' He's here, somewhere on one of these eight thousand, two hundred and twenty-seven cards. I've committed half of them to memory but it's difficult. I'm getting tired. I have to get back to *Nostromo*. It's taken me forty-four hours and seventeen minutes to look at all the phone books in the library. They asked me to leave and I hadn't finished. It was very annoying. I had only got as far as Walthamstow; there was a long way to go. Why couldn't they let me stay? I had a feeling about Wycombe.'

'*Autism*,' said the Academic. '*An unusual bedfellow with schizophrenia but not without precedent. Treatment predictably is compounded by the fact that the patient rarely gains sufficient insight to question the reality of the delusions. He experienced them, therefore, they happened. As simple as that.*'

'*You never know*,' said the Tempter, '*there might be method to his madness. He's got a sharp brain.*'

'*A card sharp, by the look of it*,' said the Jester.

John nodded his appreciation to Paul and returned to his own room. His heart was rocking against its chest cavity wall. Perhaps the membrane of thin cartilage would tear asunder and he would be free.

TWENTY-ONE

He woke from dreams of his brother variously falling in slow motion from a high rise flat, sinking into a desolate bog recreated from black and white newsreel footage of the Moors Murders; as a grown man in pyjamas sucking his thumb in a bedsit, staring up at the tiny bright circle of sky from the bottom of a well-borrowed from a story book.

He pulled his pillow over his head and briefly considered the logistics of self-smothering. Pushing his face into the sheet he breathed in. Choking, he moved his face into the air. Somewhere, he knew, the Bastard was smirking. As he relieved himself in the sink he caught sight of an index card that had been pushed under the door. *3, Farrington Road, Newcastle NE5 8GE.*

'You've got to go. At last, progress. A breakthrough. Paul knows things that others don't. It's just a couple of hours away by train. Two trains an hour. You have to. At last!'

John waited for the Bastard to belittle the Tempter's enthusiasm, but he could only hear the Jester quietly singing Blaydon Races in a silly Geordie accent.

The *Big Issue* seller on Waverley Steps looked at him as if he was about to steal his pitch. The woman queuing in front of him at the ticket office tut tutted to her pal and the clerk spoke to him very slowly and loudly.

As he stared at the phalanx of train details on the electronic board the letters and numbers on the digitalised display reconfigured themselves in front of his eyes. 8.10 TO PLYMOUTH CALLING AT DUNBAR NEWCASTLE YORK DARLINGTON LEEDS CHESTERFIELD TAMWORTH DERBY BIRMINGHAM NEW STREET CHELTENHAM SPA morphed into TRULY THIS IS THE HOUR WHEN YOUR SEARCH WILL YIELD FRUIT PRAISE THE LORD BE MINDFUL OF THE PASSAGE OF TIME.

'You're sitting in my seat, pal.' John stared back at the square-necked man with tattooed arms that could have belonged to a Maori warrior. He had staked out his territory by plonking down four cans of Special Brew on the table in front of John who avoided eye contact and moved to the next carriage.

'Granddad, you sit there.' John glanced at the man being steered to the seat next to him by a large woman who then turned her attention to several squalling children for whom Attention Deficit Hyperactive Disorder was a shared badge of honour.

'You'll never be a grandfather.'

John half smiled. For a moment he thought the Bastard had missed the train.

'That old boy's got furry ears,' commented the Jester.

They were all here.

'He's probably a dirty hobbit. He'll be a werewolf before Durham.'

"It's a complaint associated with an overactive thyroid,' suggested the Academic.

'Or wanking in your youth,' said the Jester, *'look at his palms.'*

'A total myth,' said the Academic.

Granddad looked blankly at the man opposite him.

Reluctant to wake the miller, Cornelius and Balthasar eased themselves down the ladder and stretched in the half-light. Balthasar strode towards the sleeping dogs curled round one of the pillars supporting the mill. The hounds shook off the husks sticking to their coats and sniffed at the damp breeches of their masters. The miller had directed them to the frozen river which would take them close to the regional courthouse and prison where they hoped to find Johannes.

A fresh smattering of snow prevented them from sliding on the ice which they knew, despite creaking under their weight like the timbers of a man-of-war, was as thick as a human thigh.

'He never finished his tale.'

'What?' asked Balthasar, whose thoughts were leagues away.

'His story, the miller. What happened on his journey home? Did he smuggle the tracts into the country? Was he caught?' Cornelius kicked a small branch lying on the ice then watched it skid and spin its way over the frozen surface.

'Well, who knows? It's the same for all of us if you think about it. We never live to see how our story ends ... few stories end happily anyway.' (As Narrator I could not possibly comment.)

'There will be a reckoning,' said Cornelius. 'The fires of vengeance will roast their hearts.'

Balthasar thought of Johannes. What if they arrived too late to save him, or worse, before the process is complete? What if the grinning interrogators accepted the piece of wedding gold in exchange for his still living but half-broken body? How could they carry him home with crushed bones and stretched tissues? In his mind's eye he saw them laying Johannes' half-crucified body in front of a cold hearth.

To distract themselves from their respective thoughts, the travellers paused briefly alongside a semi-submerged coracle frozen into the ice. The oars stuck out of it like arms pointing at the pink sky. A single boot thick with frost nestled incongruously in the prow. On the near bank several willow trees bowed obsequiously under the weight of snow like petrified petitioners. Balthasar blew on his threadbare mittens and stamped his feet.

The train slowed on the approach to Morpeth giving John a clear view of the fluorescent graffiti that adorned a wooden fence. The purple and yellow tags and regally flourished initials spelt a secret message for John. KEEP THE FAITH – HE IS THERE – YOU WILL KNOW HIM BY HIS DEEDS.

'Do you shave the top of your head, granddad?' asked one of the ADHD kids.

'He shines it with boot polish,' confirmed his brother.

As granddad had irritated the guard by failing to locate his rail pass, his impatient daughter rested her bosoms on the table and riffled though his pockets. She quickly sorted through a lifetime of passes, old warrants, identity cards and sundry envelopes before grumpily thrusting a small plastic folder at the guard.

'I was made redundant on Tuesday,' a passenger shared with the whole carriage through the medium of his mobile phone. 'You've received my CV ... Yes ... Yes ... I used to wear jeans and t-shirt on the shop floor so that's not a problem ... In fact I'm going to Leeds now for an interview. What's your name? Ok, Roger, that's great ... '

'And you thought you *were mad,'* exclaimed the Jester. John looked at a woman standing further down the carriage in bridal headdress surrounded by her hen party acolytes.

'She's got the wrong aisle. At least she chose Virgin Trains. All train guards can marry folk you know. But the vows are

only valid for the duration of the journey. You can always get off at Haymarket, know what I mean?'

The women shrieked as the inflatable male doll her friends had stowed in the overhead luggage rack idly dangled a leg.

'Remember your wedding, John?' chipped in the Bastard. '*You left a spare seat at the top table for your brother. Even then you were obsessed. Everyone kept asking "Where's Banquo?"'*

The Jester pointed out that a small light was flashing in the woman's veil, so her husband could tell which way up she was in the dark but John had already resigned himself to the Bastard's tirade.

'It was like rentacrowd wasn't it John? No living relatives, and no pals, just vague acquaintances from university days. And so much for your best man. He was the first to forsake you when you became mad, wasn't he? Not a peep out of him ever again. Funny that, no one wanted to know did they? "Always been a bit odd," they said. "Inevitable really. You could see the signs. He didn't deserve her."'

John concentrated on the canal through the window, staring at the green water and the faded bricks in the arch of the bridge. He was powerless.

'And what a wedding night. Too drunk to perform. Sick in the bed too, if I remember. The hotel charged you for cleaning the duvet.'

John knew the only way to still the Voice was to give it what it wanted. If he just embraced his essential worthlessness and consummate failure ... (*An ironically apt phrase*, said the Bastard) ... then he would be left alone.

Even granddad noticed that the man opposite seemed to be weeping.

Johannes looked up as the priest stood in the doorway flanked by henchmen wearing masks. He disdainfully picked his way over the fetid straw and crossed himself with two podgy fingers. The father and son shrank against the wall; the pastor too instinctively moved backwards.

'*In nomine patri et fili spiritu sancte.* You have placed yourselves beyond the pale of Christ's salvation. Your putrefying vileness will drip down the hot walls of hell. Your deaths will be slow and protracted so that in full consciousness of your own turpitude and spiritual decay you can contemplate your imminent lingering death on the scaffold, the rack and the wheel. Your flesh will be ignored by the carrion; your putrid organs will rot and your scattered bones will turn to foul smelling dust. Amen.' The priest yawned. Sometimes religion and death were so boring.

It was not the imminence of his own death that disturbed Johannes, rather the knowledge that he would slip into that dark night without ever seeing Michel, without ever seeing his son alive again or, indeed, knowing what his fate had been. He looked at the sneering cleric whose fingers were hovering round his nostrils to protect them from the smell of the dispossessed, and walked purposefully towards him. The henchmen moved to restrain him and each seized one of his arms but not before Johannes' face was within inches of the priest's. The startled cleric was trapped in a protracted moment between disbelief and fear. He saw something in the older man's eyes and shrank backwards. 'You first, Anabaptist!' he shrieked. The guards bustled Johannes through the door that opened onto the plain of Golgotha.

TWENTY-TWO

Newcastle station was busy and, for a moment, the echoing announcements drowned out the Voices. He accidently knocked against a woman who turned and swore at him. The vacuum thump of a newly arrived train startled him as he felt himself being flattened up against a billboard extolling the benefits of the Halifax Building Society.

He entered the Centurion Bar but, despite ducking and diving between various punters lined up at the bar, failed to get served. Increasingly agitated he pushed his way into a gap that instantly closed with the consequence that he spilled the drinks of two men jealously guarding their easy access to the next pint. One of them sprang from his stool as if scalded, brushed the beer from his jacket and turned towards John. The barman noticed and without any hint of ambiguity indicated the door towards which John was propelled.

He showed Paul's card to the taxi driver. 'You're five years too late, mate, they demolished that street years ago. It's a supermarket now.'

Johannes stared at the killing field that lay before him. Fires burning at regular intervals were being fed with the clothes and possessions of the dead by bored troops who stirred the embers with staves. A black figure on horseback supervised proceedings, chiding or encouraging as he deemed necessary. A servant wrote in a large tally book at his side with an oversized quill. Someone had to record last minute confessions and retractions, not to mention the curses and imprecations that would be punished with an even more painful death. He crossed out the last entry and wrote over it muttering beneath his breath, 'So much work, so little time.'

A red semmit was refusing to burn and Johannes couldn't stop himself wondering which material was proving so resistant to the flames. The Antwerp merchants would certainly be interested if they could produce a batch. In the foreground a body was being taken down from a gibbet, its limbs still pliable, its arms draping themselves round the shoulders of its rescuer as if in gratitude, its eyes open. The soldiers instinctively riffled though the pockets of the corpse before loading it on the already overburdened cart. The nag in its yoke seemed unnaturally small, withered and diminished by its human load. Johannes looked away.

'*Not this again.*'

Quiet!

A single magpie perched on the crossbeam of the scaffold, its head jerking as if it was interested in the proceedings. One for sorrow, thought Johannes. The two soldiers holding his arms handed him over to an adjutant whose job it was to bind prisoners' hands behind their backs as part of the efficient progress to execution and oblivion. He had prepared well for his duties; several equally sized pieces of hempen rope lay side by side on his table, improvised from provision boxes on which Spanish writing was legible. As the ropes cut into his wrists Johannes looked at the watery sky. Was Michel looking at the same clouds thinking about his father?

'My son, my son.'

'Save your prayers,' said the ropeman. 'No one's listening. There's no place for Christ here, but you can see Lucifer if you look hard enough. That might just be him over there, that old fellow licking his lips and rubbing his hands. No wonder, a good haul today and no mistake.' He gave a final tug on the cords and patted Johannes as if acknowledging another job well done.

The magpie took flight in slow motion into the smoke. As he followed its flight, Johannes saw on the far horizon the grave diggers, their ritual movements of raised and plunging spades resembling one of the new pumping engines powered by human treadmills installed near his village.

On the return journey the Voices chattered and boomed in his head. The carriage was full of them. He thought he could see them standing on the seats ahead, craning to locate him. The Bastard was manoeuvring the drinks trolley down the aisle. *'Have a drink, John, celebrate another glorious, ignominious failure. I can only offer you a can of Strongbow or Carling Special. Nothing else left I'm afraid. I've got a tikka masala sandwich if you want. Demolished five years ago, would you believe it. Perhaps Andy died there, John, have you thought of that? He's probably under the foundations of that supermarket. They'll find his skeleton sometime in the next century. An archaeological dig will speculate over the identity of the desiccated pile of bones wrapped round a fading picture of you. Like that Richard III they found in a car park. Sure you don't want the sandwich?'*

'I must say,' said the Academic, *'this is all very interesting. You realise the figure dressed in black was probably the Duke of Alba appointed by Philip II to oversee the persecution of the Calvins and Anabaptists?'*

'Not to worry,' said the Tempter, *'one of Paul's cards will come up trumps, next time.'*

'The detail of the magpie is equally fascinating. Bruegel used the bird as a symbol of his own paranoia.'

'Did you hear the one about the magpie that went into a pub and asked for a pint of black and tan?'

The Voices shouted louder to make themselves heard over the train tannoy. WILL PASSENGERS LEAVING THE TRAIN AT DUNBAR REMEMBER TO LOOK ROUND FOR ANY PERSONAL POSSESSIONS THEY MAY HAVE LEFT. THE LORD HIGH EXECUTIONER IS MAKING HIS WAY DOWN THE CARRIAGE PREPARE TO DIE.

'Are you losing it, John? Is it a real crisis this time?'

THANK YOU FOR AGREEING TO TRAVEL WITH VIRGIN TRAINS ON YOUR LAST JOURNEY EVER BEFORE YOU ARE ANNIHILATED BY THE FORCES OF RETRIBUTION.

'This is it, John, here you go!'

'Ah, delusions of reference as first identified by Dijkman in his monogram Ten Types of Psychotic Disorder *published by Yale University Press in 1938. A seminal work.'*

'Brace yourself, John, here he comes!'

'Don't worry, John, things will work out, your brother might be in the next carriage.'

'Christ, John, here he is!'

The figure on the black horse burst through the door at the end of the carriage. Flames shot through the visor eyeholes. Decapitated heads hung by their sinews from the saddle. Balthasar was there, Beverley, Paul, Antonia. The stench of death filled the carriage. With a blood harrowing cry Alba forced his horse into the space occupied by John's body. Horseflesh, breath and saliva. John's trousers were soaked in an instant as his bladder emptied.

Aided by the passengers not rendered immobile by shock, the train guard finally extricated himself from John's grasp and reached for his mobile phone. Within moments the buffet car staff arrived to restrain John, already beyond further struggle as he prepared himself for his inevitable death at the hands of the Spanish commander.

The Bastard smirked as the police who had been waiting for the train in Waverley station snapped the handcuffs on each wrist and led him away.

TWENTY-THREE

They soon caught up with the tiny figure tugging a sledge loaded with twigs and branches. It was not apparent whether it was a child or an age-shrunken adult. 'Is the courthouse near?' asked Balthasar, while the dogs sniffed at the haul of wood. The old woman, for such it was, stared straight ahead and muttered something that seemed to have no connection with Balthasar's question. After dismissing her invisible inner gossips with a few well-chosen words she turned her face towards Balthasar, who saw that she was blind. The angle of her head made her resemble a caged bird craning towards a source of food. He dug into his tunic and took out a small quince, given to him by one of the wedding guests, which he pressed into the woman's hand. She stood stock still, fingering the fruit through the worn fingers of her mittens and looked up completely puzzled. 'God's peace, woman,' he said.

The increasing frequency of frozen buttresses of water hanging from the riverbank suggested the likely approach of a village or town. A half-built wooden pump had fallen into one of the frozen channels. As if demonstrating its superior strength, a scarecrow maintained its outstretched arms while straining under thick, perfectly symmetrical muscles of snow.

'Do you think the problem is with the heddles?' asked Cornelius.

'What?' asked Balthasar, trying hard to catch up despite not having been party to the previous stages in his friend's inner discourse.

'If the ridges could be bevelled then the rate of flow would increase without snagging.'

'Surely the warp threads would build up at the point.'

'True,' conceded Cornelius.

Both men were now concentrating on a low blanket of dark smoke sitting just above the horizon to their right.

'Not long now,' said Balthasar.

John stood between the two policemen at the reception desk of the Royal Edinburgh Hospital.

'Answers to the name of John,' said the taller of the two. 'I think he lives in a hostel in Leith. We've met him before. Creating a commotion on the London train. Risk to himself and others, as the manual says, so he's all yours.' A cursory nod to the nurse and they turned and left. At least he hadn't damaged the car, nor had he been sick, nor had he wanted to talk shite at them. Could have been worse.

'Do you know where you are, John?' the nurse asked with the patronising tones of an infant teacher consoling a small child who had got lost on the way back from the toilet and arrived in tears in the wrong classroom. John nodded.

'It's John McPake isn't it; you've been here before, haven't you? I'm Mary MacDonald, do you remember me, John? Is there anyone you would like us to contact? Wife, sister, brother?' John flinched. 'You've got an Advanced Statement haven't you, John? We'll look it out once the doctor has spoken to you. All right? Do you want a cup of tea? You wait in here,' she said, guiding her new charge into a smaller room with windows on all sides so that he could be observed more easily.

'Home sweet home,' said the Bastard. *'Not much of a reception party though. They might have managed some bunting, the odd banner, don't you think? Welcome home, John, to the house of the truly, irredeemably mad.'*

'You never can tell,' said the Tempter, *'your brother might be here, stranger things happen. Unwell like yourself and compulsorily detained. They'll certainly put you in the same ward.'*

'Statistically unlikely,' said the Academic, *'although the instances of two siblings receiving a diagnosis of psychosis are ten times greater than the prevalence rates in the population at large.'*

'Rejoice, you are going to meet up with all your old pals, windae lickers, schizos, the catatonically depressed who, like you, never speak, preferring to hug their knees and rock backwards and forwards. Those enjoying florid, manic episodes, all those Sons of God, Virgin Marys, the occasional Ayatollah, and the saddos who just cry all the time. A fair bit of incontinence, don't you think? Wards awash with the piss of the lost. Happy days, John. Remember to lock your things in the bedside cabinet. A lot of thieving bastards around here. I blame the addicts, what do you think, Academic?'

'Drug- and alcohol-induced psychosis is a well-documented phenomenon; the symptoms tend to disappear when the substance leaves the system. More interesting was Nurse MacDonald's reference to the Advanced Statement. Things are clearly changing after the belated implementation of the Mental Health (Care and Treatment) (Scotland) Act 2003. It is now incumbent on the psychiatrist to treat patients in accordance with any written and witnessed statement of preferred intervention compiled when the patient is in remission from the illness.'

'Shut up, Academic, you are just boring.'

'Did you hear the one about the mental patient who was congratulated for saving a pal on the ward who was trying to

drown himself in the bath. Sadly he went back to the ward where he was found dead with a rope round his neck. The saviour explained, "Oh no, he didn't kill himself, I hung him up to dry."'

'Good one, Jester! Like that, John?'

'There's better ... Hello. Welcome to the Psychiatric Hotline.

If you are obsessive-compulsive, please press 1 repeatedly.

If you are co-dependent, please ask someone to press 2.

If you have multiple personalities, please press 3, 4, 5, and 6.

If you are paranoid-delusional, we know who you are and what you want. Just stay on the line so we can trace the call.

If you are schizophrenic, listen carefully and a little voice will tell you what number to press.

If you are manic-depressive, it doesn't matter which number you press. No one will answer.

If you are anxious, just start pressing numbers at random.

If you are phobic, don't press anything.

If you are anal retentive, please hold.'

'Brilliant, Jester. You certainly press my buttons. What about yours, John? Come now, no need to be upset.'

John said nothing to the psychiatrist who seemed admirably tolerant of silence. When asked if he felt drowned out by the Voices, he nodded. When asked if life in the hostel was manageable he made a seesaw gesture with his hands and his interlocutor smiled. When asked about the place of alcohol in his life he looked at the ground. When asked about suicidal ideation he shrugged, confirming that he frequently thought of ending his life. When asked if he had decided on a preferred method he nodded once and looked out of the window into the hospital grounds where a middle-aged couple were arguing. The man eventually stormed off leaving his partner, transfixed, next to the roses. She put a hand to her face. When asked if he still thought obsessively about his brother he stared back intently in case the psychiatrist knew something. A single bird pecked on the windowsill.

The Voices convened their own case conference. As principle Narrator I agreed to take meticulous notes, verbatim if I could keep up.

'Lock him up, throw away the key. Let him rot beyond the pale of his own making. Give him false hope through the transitory respite of medication and then fry what little brain remains with ECT.'

'I believe that laughter therapy produces results. Let me tell him jokes until he wets himself.'

'We must keep his spirits up by giving him hope, I can dangle a few teasing possibilities before him, come up with the odd sign that his brother is alive and well. You know, the occasional message from the TV, the odd ambiguous headline in the Evening News.'

'And then dash his hopes, trample on them, strangle them at birth. Let him howl at the moon; let him languish in the special purgatory reserved for losers. And then, after an appropriate period of time, kill him. I will be his anointed executioner, I know which lever, which finely tuned, subtle, decisive insult will open the trapdoor. What I will say is my secret and mine alone. Something more terrible than he has ever imagined. Something that will destroy what vestigial self-esteem remains.'

John was led to Ward 5 by the charge nurse, a burly man who had a word for every patient they passed in the corridor. 'All right, Joe?' 'Looking smart, Mary.' 'The Hearts lost again.' 'Watch that tray, health and safety! Remember?'

Three of the four beds were occupied but no one was awake. The mound under the sheets of the bed nearest the window was particularly small, hardly big enough to cover a human being.

'They're admitting pets now,' said the Jester. *'It's all these depressed black dogs. I blame Churchill myself. Even gerbils*

have mental health problems these days, gerbilmania I think they call it. Lemmings are the worst of all, desperate to kill themselves. I blame Cliff Richard.'

The Bastard managed to smile sardonically but said nothing.

'They had a cow in here the other day, hoof rot and udderly depressed. And a horse tortured by self-hatred, almost nagged itself to death.'

'That could be him,' said the Tempter, '*in the corner fast asleep*'. Tired and unable to resist, John stopped at the bed he was passing and pulled back the covers before the nurse firmly intervened. An elderly man with startled eyes and tousled gray hair stared uncomprehendingly before lapsing back onto the pillow.

A nurse approached his bed with a syringe so large she could barely lift it. She eventually hoisted it above her head like a huntsman aiming at a single strange bird flying high. As she pushed the huge piston plunger a noxious opaque liquid leaked from its tip and splashed onto the floor. John cowered.

There had been a delay, a backlog, a jam. Requessen's lackey had been furious and smacked his sword round the neck of the soldier who had only been trying to explain that the carters could not cope with the numbers of the dead. As a consequence the corpses were now intruding into the execution space and making things very awkward.

With his hands still roped together Johannes had been returned to the waiting shed. He could make out three or four other figures cowering on the far side but felt no inclination to join them. If it was his last night on earth he wanted to remain focussed; he had a lot of reflection to undertake, a lot of memories to sort.

To an extent, Michel had been adopted by the village and Johannes had benefited from the unspoken division of labour undertaken by his neighbours. Michel would wander into their homes and was fed, allowed to play with the dogs, collect the eggs. They would take him to the harvest where he played among the ricks, always failing to catch the mice scurrying through the stubble, and was put in charge of the wine, staggering under the weight of the flagon when summoned by the men to the field.

One late evening beneath a bright moon Maurits had carried the exhausted boy home in his arms and gently handed him over. Although fast asleep Michel was clutching a reed whistle made for him by one of the labourers.

Not wanting to confront a related memory, Johannes looked into the gloom of the holding shed where one of his unknown companions was talking in his sleep in a high-pitched voice, spouting syllables and single words with a fluency which belied their nonsensical content. Johannes ground his fist into the palm of his other hand. 'Come on, come on,' he told himself and then surrendered to the long-repressed flow of recollection that tumbled like seawater over a breeched dyke.

Only reluctantly had he let Kenaut the sorcerer woman over the threshold. The nearest apothecary was several days' ride away. Less than a year later they came for her in the night and hanged her as a witch. She was essentially harmless, a simple soul who meant well and spent most waking hours gathering rue and rosemary from the riverbank. She was endlessly teased by the young men in the village. Johannes had always given her bread when she arrived at the door offering blessings and faded herbs. Antonia had always disapproved. She was beyond disapproval now. There had been no alternative but to light the room with burning faggots. The smoke clung to the ceiling in folds and to an extent hid the sweet smell of disease that had become all too familiar in the village.

Kenaut and the pastor had made an odd couple at the bedside. Despite his tender years Michel knew full well what was happening. He spent the whole day running fast in ever-tighter circles in the yard as if by making himself dizzy and kicking up the dust he might faint and then wake to find his mother back baking bread and scolding him. He emitted a high-pitched whine as he birled mindlessly, the memory of which made Johannes flinch. His exorcism was only partially complete; there was more.

Witnessed by a single crow, Cornelius and Balthasar dug the grave and lowered her in.

Johannes noted with ironic satisfaction that he had, in fact, found the courage to face the second worst event of his life. The man at the end of the shed exhaled unevenly as if his chest was being pressed at regular intervals by a large force. An intimation of what lay ahead thought Johannes.

He steadied himself to put his fingers into the deepest wound of all, the abduction of his son. He couldn't do it. The best he could manage was to cling to the same far-fetched hopes that had sustained him on his shared journey from the village to imminent execution in a strange landscape. Perhaps his captors would treat Michel well, perhaps he would escape, perhaps he would be adopted by a kind patron, apprenticed even, and perhaps someday he might even mourn the father who had given his life to find him. All hope was suddenly extinguished as he saw Michel's open jaws trapped in mid-scream.

TWENTY-FOUR

The ECT room was full: various technicians, the anaesthetist, the psychiatrist of course, the nurse who had settled John onto the ward and several medical students for whom this was a completely new experience.

'*What did the condemned man have for his last meal?*' asked the Bastard in a Southern drawl. '*No word from the Governor yet? No last minute reprieve? No pleas in mitigation? No new evidence? But he's facing reselection isn't he? Doesn't want to be seen as weak. Not in this state. Is* Fox News *ready to rock and roll? The crowd outside's getting restless. Are the witnesses ready to be taken in, remember to give the widow the best seat? She's looking forward to a good fry. Eyeballs popping out, that sort of thing, the smell of burning flesh. Closure really, isn't it? Do you want the chaplain, John? It would pass the time.*'

'*A controversial but effective treatment,*' intoned the Academic. '*Pioneered in Switzerland in the 1930s. Arguably preferable to the Darwin chair used in the 1800s. Patients would be strapped into a chair that was then rotated at speed until blood oozed from the mouth, ears and nose. Surprisingly, many successful cures were attributed to this method.*'

'Fancy that, John, a dervish whirl on the carousel for the mad? You wouldn't want to get blood and snot on all these nice people though ... '

'In the 1940s, doctors Kennedy and Anchel reported in the Psychiatric Quarterly *that they considered a patient sufficiently regressed when he wet and soiled or acted and talked like a child of four ... '*

'Happy times, get the nappies out ... '

By 1942 85% of all psychiatric institutions in the United States used some form of shock treatment for psychosis, depression, mania and homosexuality ... '

'That sounds better, Gay Boy ... '

John sought comfort in the eyes of the ward sister who had monitored him since his arrival. He wanted her to hold his hand but the straps had already been tightened.

Diddums ... You're regressing already and it hasn't started yet.

John wanted to scream, to smash his own head, pummel his skull, gouge out his eyes, anything to silence the alien Voices that had pushed him to the edges of his own consciousness, uninvited squatters, invaders, life-sucking parasites. He pushed hard against the straps restraining his wrists.

The IV drips were attached with the minimum of fuss.

'This is good, up until the 1950s before the use of muscle relaxants and anaesthesia 20% of patients suffered compression fractures of the spine ... '

John was reluctant to open his eyes in case the sunshine went. His whole consciousness was suffused with light. He listened but heard no Voices apart from mine. He felt warm and could watch the progress of the motes on his inner eye as they floated airily in the light. He was back in bed with his wife in the early days of their marriage, lying half awake just happy to be in each other's presence. Soon the clock radio would come on. Soon the cockerel from the Van Erst's would throw back its head and announce the day. They lay spooned together his hand resting between her legs with no urgent sexual intent, just an intimacy full of promise.

It was Sunday, no reason to get up, no real plans, a walk perhaps and some essay marking later. It was the Sabbath; the church bell from Crousen Village had started up its early competition with their own. Although the pastor forbade work he would nevertheless inspect the dye batch put down last night. He waited for the *Observer* to drop through the letterbox and the inevitable cajoling, affectionate debate about who would retrieve it and bring it back to bed. He realised his legs were trapped under the weight of the cat that slept with them despite his protests, 'Him or me,' he had tried once but then accepted that the decision was unlikely to go in his favour. He heard the hounds moving in the yard below. He would take them with him when he and Balthasar went to look at the far dyke. He was hungry, scrambled eggs probably. Was he hungry, oaten meal or bread? He searched his head in case there was anything he should be worrying about. The car needed its MOT, and the central heating had been making odd noises; apart from that all was well. The pivot on the far loom had become inextricably slack and he had better make a small leather harness for Michel's sledge if he was to keep his promise of taking him to the banks of the Eisel. He remembered the previous evening's argument about his drinking after the football. He remembered Antonia falling out with him, saying he was too hard on Michel, he was only a boy. A cloud passed in front of the sun. He was in hospital. He was in a shed waiting for his execution.

TWENTY-FIVE

As Cornelius and Balthasar got closer to the town their progress along the frozen river was made ever more difficult by the increasing number of barges, coracles and flat bottomed punts semi-submerged in the ice, abandoned until spring. The usual detritus of rural commerce, wooden boxes and staves had also been thrown onto the river despite the absence of flowing water to carry it downstream. Domestic waste too, vegetable peelings, bones and broken implements sat on top of the snow.

The remains of a small fire on the deck of one of the boats was further evidence of villagers being evicted from their homes by the occupying Catholic troops. The dogs sniffed at the charred rodent heads lying on the ice where they had been tossed by the hungry squatters. In the middle of the river a crude bull's-eye had been etched onto the ice, and the adjacent snow swept clear so that men could launch the rough-hewed curling stones to claim victory and the pooled prize money of farthings.

'Did I tell you about the time when I took the stone weight from the mill, fitted a handle and beat the whole village on the ice?' asked Balthasar.

'Yes,' said his two companions.

'Did I mention the prize money?'

'Yes.'

Balthasar stumbled as he climbed onto the bank where the willow trees had been reduced to a skeletal state, all branches stripped by frozen hands for kindling and fence repairs. Cornelius hauled him up by the armpits. 'It's my age,' said the older man brushing the snow from his coat.

The village was quiet and subdued, its life blood sucked out by fear and unwelcome proximity to the Inquisition headquarters in its midst. In the square a few peasants, long immune to harassment and abuse from bored soldiers, went through the motions of selling small items of clothing, crude mittens, heavy shawls, and simple food, mainly bread and grain, from improvised stalls. The hounds growled at each other as they tugged at a bone that had fallen from a trestle table. A hunchbacked man sat on the cold ground hammering a nail into a broken stool rescued from the river. The sound of the pounding echoed round the square. His eyes were closed; he had been hammering the same long-sunken nail since daybreak.

A line of shackled prisoners was being herded down the side of the square by several men on horseback. Their cowled charges muttered prayers as they passed, raising their hands as if to bless themselves before being impeded by the weight of the chains.

'Hieronymus!' Cornelius recognised the cloth merchant who would visit their village in the autumn to bargain over the bales. 'You still owe me money!'

Recognition glimmered for a moment in the prisoner's eyes before his chains were tugged by the more vigilant of his captors. His mouth moved as if chewing tough meat. His half tongue, a legacy from torture, fought with his palate to frame words. Cornelius watched helplessly as the despairing man lolled his head and dribbled more wetness down his cloak.

'Leave him,' said Balthasar. 'We can do nothing for him. We can't save everyone.'

'Why not? Why do our people just accept this? Why do they lick the boots that kick them? We will rise again.' Cornelius shook his fist at the soldiers whose attention he was now attracting. Balthasar made a conciliatory gesture at the soldiers and shrugged as if to say, 'Excuse my friend, he's mad.'

The two soldiers guarding the courthouse moved to intercept the weavers now approaching with a confidence they did not feel. Having tied the dogs to the outer fence Balthasar pressed his chest into the crossed pikes barring his way. He moved the outer one aside and said, 'We have business with the Commissary.' Grudgingly, the soldiers relented and let them enter.

'Your purpose?' asked the figure hunched at an ornate desk on which rested several ink wells and a selection of quills.

'We bring tangible evidence of the contrition and true repentance of our brother Johannes Pakesoon,' said Balthasar. Cornelius produced the wedding coin and placed it on the desk. The official glanced round nervously and when he was certain that there were no witnesses to the transaction he covered the coin with his hand, drew it towards him and feeling its weight muttered, 'God loves a sinner.'

Johannes knew that he was next. Once the cold light seeped through the cracks and under the door of the holding shed his companions assumed identities. The first to be hauled out was a man of a similar age with a wound disfiguring the left side of his face. He offered no resistance when the soldiers came to bind his hands and take him away. The silence hung heavily in the room until it was broken by a single strangled cry which could have been defiance, resignation, acceptance, or simple terror.

The next was an elderly woman who walked slowly towards the guards when they returned. She offered her hands for tying and let herself be led towards the door through which the fires Johannes had glanced the previous day were still burning. The door slammed shut but there was no cry.

In the moments that followed Johannes tried to savour the sensation of living: the blood pounding in his chest, his breathing, which he tried to make more regular, the small pangs of hunger and fear in his stomach. He concentrated on the small noises that penetrated from the outside, the incongruous chatter of the executioners, even a small burst of laughter. A bird cry somewhere. As the door opened for a final time his stoicism collapsed before an overwhelming sense of having failed Michel, and awareness of his own imminent oblivion.

TWENTY-SIX

The other Voices had stopped. Apart from me, John was untroubled by the rat pack of personae who lodged in his consciousness. Respite was temporary but welcome all the same. His tongue felt too big for his mouth, swollen and sore after the guard had slipped during the ECT. He couldn't remember anything of the train journey and fretted lest he had lashed out at any innocent passengers who had the misfortune to be his travelling companions that day. He looked at his knuckles and saw no scratches or other evidence that he had fought against his perceived transgressors. His wrists were still red from the handcuffs.

'Do you fancy a walk?' asked Derek who had told Beverley he would get John out of the ward for an hour or two. This despite the fact his shift had just finished and his girlfriend was waiting for him in the Asda car park.

John put his face up to the fine drizzle that smothered the hospital gardens and reread the array of white signs that pointed to the different wards, supplies, family rooms, chapel and morgue. He thought he heard the Bastard muttering in his ear, 'Only a matter of time,' but no, he was merely anticipating what the Bastard would have said had he been active and not recovering from 200 volts of electricity. It occurred to him that the Bastard might as well be there if his absence was only filled by him imagining what the vindictive Voice might have said. The circle had been squared.

Derek gossiped harmlessly about the other residents. 'Cracking new cook,' he said. 'Mick was convinced she was a poisoner and insisted I taste his macaroni cheese. Dennis came out of his room and chatted with the others, he was OK. Beverley brought in the remains of her son's birthday cake. Grand.'

They left the grounds and walked up Morningside Road towards Bruntsfield. Derek bought a paper from the *Big Issue* seller outside of the bank. They recognised each other. 'How's it goin', pal?' asked the vendor. 'Still working at the hostel? Am getting ma life together. How's it hangin', John, still lookin' for yer brither?' He abandoned his enquiry having caught the eye of a possible punter. '*Big Issue,* sir? Great articles ... suit yersel, sir, have a guid day ... wanker.'

John's instinctive reaction to *Big Issue* sellers was one of respect and envy. When he was homeless, his head had been too chaotic to embrace the status afforded by vest, badge and supply of magazines. *Big Issue* sellers were on the way back; they had turned corners and re-engaged with a world of supply and demand, of financial transactions, negotiations and moral certainties. 'We can't accept charity, you have to buy a magazine.'

John's aspirations had extended no further than securing the thin strip of pavement that abutted the hot air grill from the old Waverley Hotel. His bulk had helped. He looked large and scary. Rivals for the pitch invariably slunk away muttering until, one night, he was wakened by a hand on the shoulder. The touch was too gentle, too tentative to be the police. 'Is it you, Mr McPake?'

The young street worker had been one of his former pupils. She hid her astonishment and passed no judgement with no hint of how are the mighty fallen. She had played Nancy in the school production of *Olive*r that he directed. With her hand still on his shoulder she sang softly, 'Consider yourself, at home, consider yourself one of the family,' and laughed at the unintentional irony of the words. It was she who had arranged for a mental health assessment and smoothed the way for him to move into the hostel. He owed her a lot, and hoped her life had turned out well.

They were soon marooned in a sea of kids liberated from Boroughmuir High School and caught up in a miasma of chewing gum, aftershave and perfume exuded by the hormone-fuelled tide which swept through them as if they didn't exist. The wave solidified outside a cafe that had tried in vain to protect its profits by limiting the number of school children who could be admitted at any one time. The surreal jabber of half-insults and inane banter evoked an acute sense of loss in John. He had been a good teacher. He had boundless energy, the kids loved his lessons, and he knew they did. For some reason he heard himself talking to a concerned couple at a parents' evening about a child he couldn't remember from Adam. 'A good lad, distracted sometimes, needs to stick in now with the prelims coming up.' The parents hung on his every sainted word. 'He mustn't be afraid to ask if he doesn't understand.'

And now? The sheer impact of his wasted life left him literally unbalanced. He clutched at Derek who looked at him anxiously. The overwhelming sapping sense of loss made him panic. Pointless, illness-ridden nothingness. A mockery. Everything thrown away.

'*Welcome back*,' said the Bastard.

That evening John found himself mindlessly reading one of the notices near the nurses' station: Waste Management Segregation. Several subtle distinctions were strictly drawn

SANPRO WASTE – specific sites only – Non-infected waste eg continence products, catheter drainage bags (empty); SHARPS CLINICAL WASTE – Needles, syringes, blades, IV cannulae (Placenta packs must be disposed of in a dedicated rigid container); YELLOW STREAM CLINICAL WASTE – Human tissue and recognisable body parts, highly infectious waste – ORANGE STREAM CLINICAL WASTE – items with blood or body tissue waste eg dressings soiled with blood or body fluids.

'*Gives you hope doesn't it?*' said the Bastard. '*You come in because you're mad, next thing you know they've lopped off vital parts and stuffed them in a bag. Recycling probably. Lots of folk would like new bits, not yours though. Be honest what could you give, a ruined liver? An ear perhaps. There is after all a precedent; who's the boy cut off his ear to spite his face? You could give them your cock, good as new, one careful owner.*'

John grimaced and looked through the glass panels on the door down the corridor which evidently led to both the dental surgery, the chapel and the Pimms Ward.

'*That'll be number 7,*' said the Jester. '*Just next to the McEwan's ward and the Bulmers ward. Sponsorship you know.*'

'*A quick game of darts, a few beers, no harm done,*' said the Tempter. '*Help you relax, make a few friends ...* '

Johannes looked down on himself with curiosity and detachment. There was something biblical over the way the soldiers cast lots over his clothing once it had been torn from his body. Comparatively useless he would have thought, but perhaps they were worth a few coppers in the paupers' market.

He watched dispassionately from on high as the small figure below was roughly strapped to a wheel which had previously been attached to a lumbering hay wagon. Bizarrely he anticipated the strange rush of vertigo at the moment when his body, its legs broken and bent, would be hoisted into the sky on top of the poles, one more mast in a macabre fleet lurching towards an unseen horizon. The ropes hung loosely from the pole as the soldiers strained to anchor it in the small stone-lined hole before it could be hoisted upwards. He wondered if conversation would be possible between the dying as they lay together a tree's length above the ground. They would have to shout above the wind, he thought.

One of the criminals who hung there hurled insults at him: Aren't you the Christ? Save yourself and us! He thought it was Luke the evangelist but he couldn't be sure.

He witnessed the functionary scurrying up to one of the soldiers and placing a restraining arm on his shoulder. After some explanation the soldier nodded and efficiently cut though the ropes binding him to the wheel. Johannes watched with curiosity as he saw himself being hurried back into the building where he had been tried.

In a side room he was reunited with Balthasar and Cornelius. The older man could not hold back his tears. 'Look at you, look at you!' was all he could say. Trapped somewhere between anger and joy Cornelius punched Johannes in the shoulder and ground his fist into his stained shirt. They clasped each other, three figures entwined in solidarity and love. They quickly left the building in case someone had a change of plan.

Johannes put a hand in each of the dog's mouths. They growled with pleasure as he tugged playfully against their teeth. Balthasar raised a flagon of water to his lips. Not vinegar, thought Johannes. Cornelius handed back the clothes that had, as an afterthought, been tossed into the room before they left. Johannes steadied himself against the fence as he climbed into someone else's breeches.

'While waiting for you,' said Balthasar, 'we spoke to one of the guards, a small runt of a man who said he had only been obeying orders ... ' Cornelius snorted. We asked what was going on. He said he couldn't possibly tell us. After biting on the guilder we gave him he found the courage to gab. He said the Spanish are massing their forces near Antwerp. They believe the sea beggars will soon attack. It was our coward's considered opinion that any available labour was being shepherded to the coast to build fortifications and lay mines. If Michel is still alive he's probably travelling north.'

'Come on, lads,' said Johannes, 'there's a boy to be found.'

TWENTY-SEVEN

John eased himself back into the routine of hostel life. The cook was an improvement although Paul was not coping with the change and would stare at her suspiciously from behind his copy of *Nostromo*. Kevin snorted dismissively when their paths crossed on the stair.

John's CPN, a brusque but compassionate woman in her late forties, appeared more frequently than usual to check that he was taking his medication. Mick studiously avoided her. He seemed in danger of losing weight such was the strength of his conviction that he was still being progressively poisoned by conspirators of various hues, all united by their hatred of Communism.

'Can you lend me the price of a fish supper?' he asked John in the dining room, but didn't take the consequent apologetic shake of the head too personally. 'Got to you as well, have they?'

It was Derek in one of their chats who suggested that John might want to make a start on the garden. Any initial enthusiasm shown by his fellow residents had quickly dissipated once it was apparent that some hard effort was needed. 'Exploitation of the masses,' said Mick, 'Ivan Denisovich all over again.'

In the interval during John's stay in the Royal Edinburgh, giant hogweed had been discovered in the garden, to the dismay of a Council official who toyed with the idea of cordoning off most of Leith until the pestilence could be rooted out and burned. By way of a compromise a small area had been roped off as if it were a police crime scene, which Mick thought it was. 'There's one of us missing,' he said, 'buried in the garden. Mark my words the Hague war crimes tribunal will be here soon.'

'No,' said Kevin, 'Fred West's moved in.'

'Il faut cultiver le jardin,' intoned the Academic. '*Work as the panacea for life's ills.*'

'Even if your left buttock has been lopped off by a Bulgar soldier,' quipped the Jester, showing a surprising erudition and familiarity with *Candide* thought John, who could only assume that the Academic had been secretly holding tutorials for the other Voices.

The ground was initially resistant to the spade which had to be levered backwards and forwards before John could make any impression. Eventually the sucking clay let itself be prised out of the ground and turned over.

John had not gardened since he was encouraged to do so by the second or third foster carer who came into his life, a well-intentioned taciturn man with an allotment on the outskirts of Lanark. When alone with John he would share homilies that testified to God's infinite goodness, and the importance of repressing all thoughts that were not conducive to treating one's body like a temple. John had failed to understand the metaphor, and had tried to identify similarities between his gangly adolescent frame and the sort of pillared buildings he had seen in *The Children's Encyclopaedia*.

The tenement flat where he had briefly lived with his wife in Tollcross had a shared back green and neither of them had felt sufficiently pioneering to tame the communal weeds or justify their intervention to the neighbours.

After the first dozen or so spadefuls had been prised from the earth, he stretched and looked back at the three-story building that was his home, as the Bastard delighted in reminding him. He thought he caught sight of a curtain flickering in Dennis' room but no face appeared. A slow lizard of water leaking from the rhone pipe had turned the stonework green. A window was thrown open in the adjacent property and he heard someone coughing as smoke was exhaled from the narrow opening.

Perhaps if he really concentrated on the effort of digging he could keep the Voices at bay.

'*You can't keep me out,*' said the Bastard.

'*It's dark in here, I can't read,*' said the Academic.

'*Black as a whore's armpit,*' said the Jester.

John's thoughts were at least partially his own. He should go back to Register House. Janet had accompanied him before and had explained to the slightly disapproving librarian that they needed to trace an Andy McPake.

The initial search had proven fruitless but had to be abandoned in any case once the Bastard started laughing like a hyena every time John thought they might be getting somewhere. Eventually he had been reduced to holding the sides of his head and pushing his thumbs into his temples. Christina had helped him onto a passing bus where to the acute annoyance of the driver and the other customers he refused to relinquish his grip on the stair handrail, preventing other passengers from getting off. He should try again, next time he would search records of all marriages in Scotland in the last decade.

He stooped to pick out two white objects from the hole opened up by the last upturned sod, one was a plastic fork planted in fond memory of either McDonalds or KFC, the other was the bowl of a clay pipe. He turned it over in his hand and tried to envisage who smoked it before dropping in to the ground. It was probably Victorian but was quite possibly much, much older. Overhead, the bird soared.

'We need money, we must find work,' said Cornelius.

'We must find Michel,' retorted Johannes.

'I know that, for the love of Christ! But we must eat.'

The men trudged on in moody silence.

It was Balthasar who suggested that they join the gang of hired labour. The men were working to stem the flow of cold sluggish water leaking into a field from a partially collapsed dyke.

'We have to,' he said, 'you can see the dogs' ribs.'

The turquoise sky was streaked with slivers of cloud and a long line of geese climbed ever higher towards warmer climes: a thin arrowhead of birds following a single speck. Cornelius shivered and Johannes patted the foremost hound.

The foreman, a dour man in a greatcoat with oddly bulging pockets quickly agreed a rate for three days' labour and the weavers were directed to the far corner of the field where the black pumping engine was barely turning.

As they approached, the two incumbents of the treadmill emerged exhausted, clung briefly to each other, groaned in unison and fell to their knees on the sodden ground, too tired to acknowledge their replacements. One was an old man with a distended belly and red face, the other a slim boy shaking with fatigue and ague.

Having secured the dogs, Balthasar entered first and climbed to the bar some fifteen feet from the ground while the other two stopped the wheel from turning. Then Cornelius held the structure steady until Johannes had taken up his position just behind the older man. On the count of three they trod down on the slats and slowly the contraption turned.

They soon established a rhythm and fell into a companionable silence, broken only by the creaking wheel and the regular plash of water dropping from the wooden blades.

An hour or so into their journey to nowhere, when their limbs were beginning to ache and hunger was making its presence known, Balthasar started singing the song of Halewyn:

'BUT FIRST LAY OFF MAER TREKT UIT UW
OPPERST KLEED
WANT MAEGDENBLOED DAT SPREIDT ZOO BREED
ZOOT U BESPREIDE, HET WARE MY LEED ... '

Academic, have you any idea what it is about?

'Let me think, those lines are easy, But first lay off your upper robe/for maiden's blood it spreads so far/if it stained you, it would be my grief.

'An interesting choice. The situation is complex; Lord Halewyn, a possible antecedent for Bluebeard has the uncanny knack of entrancing beautiful young women with a single glance. Not being the nicest of chaps he invariably leads them to their death. However on this occasion his latest conquest is allowed to choose the manner of her death. Despite being in a field of gallows she asks to be beheaded but suggests that her captor first removes his shirt to protect it from her blood. A very clever ruse. The very moment the shirt is over his head, thereby blinding him, she seizes her chance and lops off his head instead. There are of course many different versions.'

Thank you.

As Balthasar sang, Cornelius transposed the squat black figure of Alba onto the torso of Halewyn and savoured the moment when the maiden, on behalf of the entire subjugated country, swung her axe at the tyrant's head. As her first blow missed he himself nobly offered to help. He flexed his arm muscle against the restraining bar in the treadmill as he hacked and hacked again at the ogre.

For his part Balthasar projected his daughter into the song and wished her well, and wondered if she had had her baby yet. He hoped he would see the child but held out no great hope.

Johannes found the song with its evocation of the killing field too close to his recent experience and, before jerking his attention elsewhere, imagined Michel being asked to choose the method of his death. 'Make it quick, Mister! Make it quick.'

TWENTY-EIGHT

John hummed under his breath as he sweated in the garden. His own physical effort brought various related images to mind including, bizarrely, a chain gang including George Clooney in *O Brother where art thou?*

'*Excellent!*' shouted the Bastard, who had been quiet for too long. John redoubled his efforts and thrust his spade into the clay with as much strength as he could muster, jarring his wrist against the handle.

'*Perfect. Criminals chained together. Loads of adventures. Right up your street, John, it would make a change from that Dutch shite. All you need are a few hobos and a passing train. Of course, there is one essential difference. Everett and Delmar find Pete alive and well, whereas your sainted brother is dead.*

'*Anyway let's talk about pleasanter topics. Yes, the cinema. Do you remember the time when you and Sarah were trying to make a go of things? You were both trying to come to terms with her affair, remember? It was you, magnanimous, broad-minded as ever, who suggested you go the Filmhouse. Yes, that's right, some explicit art house film. Wild close up bonking from the moment the curtain opened, a couple wildly, physically obsessed with each other, consumed with passion beyond your wildest dreams ... '*

John tore into the earth hurling sods and clods in every direction. A substantial hole opened up as the spade hacked great lumps out of the ground.

'Could be a grave. Could be yours. Could be Andy's. Give it a try, perhaps Jack's had the right idea all along.'

A patina of earth sprayed against the kitchen window alerting Derek who was quickly at John's side.

'It's all right, it's all right. Let go of the spade. Come inside, come on.'

John stood rigid, obliging Derek to unpick his fingers from the handle before leading him back inside and up to his room. 'It was starting to rain anyway,' he said.

Derek eventually left after saying the same kind, gently encouraging things which, as always, made matters worse. John felt undeserving of any kindness and was impervious to all of Derek's well-intentioned messages of hope. He had no real belief in his own recovery. He could not see a life outwith the hostel, unless he included intermittent stays in the Hilton.

John stood at his window and looked out onto the wet street. A few people hurried past holding their collars up to their necks to keep out the cold dribble of rain. He ran his hand over the glass to wipe off the fat viscous drops which were obscuring his view, but succeeded only in clearing the thin veneer of mist made by his own breath.

The tenements opposite were absorbing the wetness and turning even greyer; a dog with its head down skirted round the puddles forming in the road; a mother grabbed the toddler who was serenely oblivious to the rain and marched towards the communal stair door, a small boy under one arm, his red trike under the other. The boy struggled and wriggled but got nowhere against overwhelming force.

A man walked past holding his briefcase over his head with one hand which he soon swapped for his other as the water ran down his upturned sleeve. John caught sight of Jack on the pavement gesticulating and shouting something at him as he turned to enter the hostel.

John saw himself on a similar street some fifteen years back. The same rain, different challenges. Had he stayed arguing any longer it would have ended badly; he had never hit anyone in his life, but the torrent of accusations – many of them with a basis in truth – was unsupportable. He remembered wondering if all marriages ended in the same way or if they all had their own imprint of unique awfulness. Didn't Tolstoy have a view on that?

The rain on that occasion had seemed particularly invasive and cold as he had left without a coat. He had no idea where he was going but, even then, recognised an element of self-pity as he cast himself in the role of the victim, misunderstood and cast out of his own home. He made his way round to a friend's house. More of a former colleague than a friend, if he was honest. Either way it was someone would who let him rail and rant and put a spin on events that would absolve him from at least some of the blame.

The strange continuity of rain moved him to a different wet street. Leven Street, where he had climbed at least four feet up a lamp post to get a better view of the audience pouring out from the King's Theatre. He knew his wife had gone there with her new man, but all he could see were umbrellas like Roman shields raised to protect the troops from attack from above. There could have been numerous adulterous couples scurrying beneath the shuffling black scarab but he couldn't see them. It was probably just as well. What would he have done or said?

John knew that the Bastard was hovering in his head, somewhere in the frontal lobe, waiting to deliver a killer blow with a perspective on his failed marriage that would take his breath away with some appallingly accurate insight. For some reason he was keeping his powder dry, as if the fear of what he might say was in itself sufficient to disconcert John who, in any case, was doing a sufficiently impressive job of making himself miserable. Just now he did not need any additional prompting. The Bastard had made his presence known but felt no need to speak

The third panel in the rain-soaked triptych showed John and his wife in a small wood next to their rented Catalan cottage. The holiday had been booked for a long while and, absurdly, both parties thought it would be very grown up to go away together and, for a fortnight, park their animosity and bitterness. After all they had been together for a significant period of time, during much of which they had apparently liked each other.

John had suggested they go to the wood to make love, he had even added, with what he hoped was a hint of poignant irony, 'Perhaps for the last time.' Sarah had reluctantly agreed through a combination of residual but diminishing affection, genuine concern for John's mental health and a degree of guilt. The deed itself had been quick and perfunctory. In the short time they had lain together the rain had percolated through the trees, dampened their spirits and irrevocably extinguished their marriage.

'A guy goes to a psychiatrist, "Doc, I keep having these alternating recurrent dreams. First I'm a tepee; then I'm a wigwam. It's driving me crazy. What's wrong with me?" The doctor replies: "It's very simple. You're too tents."'

'Not really funny is it, John?' said the Bastard with mock sympathy. *'In fact, it is about time to end all this pain, all this disappointment. You can't go on like this, it isn't sustainable … '*

'Unsustainable,' echoed the Tempter.

John was disconcerted at this apparent alliance between the two Voices. In perfect harmony they chanted together, *'End it now. End it now, end it now!'*

TWENTY-NINE

After three days spent alternately powering the treadmill or snatching sleep inside the cramped structure, the men set off across the field to find the dyke-reeve and claim their wages.

'I feel I've been trampled by horses,' said Balthasar, bent double against the driving rain.

'Danced on by wild bears,' contributed Johannes.

'Shredded by Lucifer's sharpened hooves,' shouted Cornelius.

The wind heavy with musket balls of rain pitted the earth and stung their eyes. Their boots let in the melting sludge that was already mingling with the clay, making each step a challenge. Johannes muttered as the sucking ground refused to let go of his left leg, clinging to him like an aggrieved lover. A sharp pain twisted into his knee and he paused, breathing heavily with his hands on his thighs. 'You two go on,' he said, 'I'll catch you up.'

Wet and shivering, Cornelius and Balthasar located the paymaster in a wooden shack, built to protect him from the worst excesses of the weather while his men toiled outside in demonic conditions. They stooped to enter through the flap which provided the only outlet for the smoke from the fire that was crackling and spitting in the centre of the small room.

The dyke-reeve was bent over a ledger, but as he didn't look up from his calculations, they could only see the top of his leather skullcap. 'You agreed three days, you have only worked two.' He stared at a black spot that had appeared on the page of his ledger, tutted and reached for the blotter. 'Three days, not a minute less.' A spiral of smoke uncoiled itself from the fire like a malicious genie spoiling for a fight and sought out Cornelius' eyes. Rubbing them he walked closer to the reeve and brought his fist down on the ledger, smudging the latest entry.

'We have slept for two nights in your wooden wheel; we have worked three days. Our bones ache and our stomachs are empty.'

'You owe me one more day and if you defile my records with your peasant hands I will pay you nothing.'

Cornelius lurched forward, picked up the open book and made to hurl it into the fire. Balthasar put himself between his friend and the flames while two henchmen holding picks entered through the flap. They were the same age as Cornelius but built like executioners who had feasted on the fat of others. One held the shaft of his pick across Balthasar's throat while the other struck Cornelius in the stomach.

Feeling distinctly sorry for himself Johannes had only managed to limp slowly towards the hut. As he paused to catch his breath he saw the henchmen enter and heard the commotion. Turning his back to the wind and looking towards the treadmill he put two fingers to his mouth and whistled for the dogs.

For the smallest moment the first hound, its eyes red from hunger, stood trembling in the entrance, tossing out silver tapeworms of saliva. It then leaped, clamping its jaws round the thigh of the nearest assailant, growling as it worked away at the flesh until it tore loose. The second dog hurled itself at his companion who tumbled, terrified, into the fire under the beast's weight. Cornelius punched the dyke-reeve repeatedly until he spat teeth and blood. Balthasar sought out the silk purse from around the reeve's waist and emptied it of money.

Holding the injured Johannes between them, the trio and the panting dogs hobbled as quickly as they could towards the edge of the sodden field. Glancing back they could see the black flames from the shed and hear the confusion.

The gale redoubled its ferocity. The wind tasted of the salt it had skimmed from the sea and black gulls were funnelled inland faster than they had ever flown, utterly powerless before the tempest, their wings swept back against their bodies like missiles in a siege. They instinctively ducked as scraps of tinder wood, berries and tangles of vegetation, passed overhead. Conversation was impossible. The slouching dogs looked skinnier with their wet matted coats flattened against their flanks, smaller and less powerful somehow, diminished and intimidated by a stronger power.

The numbing cold masked the pain in Johannes' knee. He was only aware that it would not work as it had done before. Cornelius too could no longer distinguish the pain in his knuckles from the overwhelming discomfort of the storm.

Johannes felt panic as he strove to picture Michel in his mind's eye. Fearful that his son's image would fade he had, for days, obsessively tested his memory to see if it would still deliver intact the image of his son, enacting this ritual at every crossroad on their journey, every night before he slept and, more recently, after every dozen rotations of the wheel. Horrified he felt that the rain was distorting his son's features leaving him to snatch at the remaining details of Michel's face before they too were washed away. Then the wind would take over and scour Michel's features, progressively rubbing out his eyes, his smile; drowning out the sound of his voice and his laughter.

THIRTY

'End it now, end it now!'

John woke in a sweat from a nightmare in which his brother was staggering, clearly unwell, towards the edge of Platform 4 at Haymarket Station. The tannoy had warned passengers to stand clear as the next train was not stopping. He lay in the darkness and, outside, heard a wheelie bin being blown down the street. Downstairs he heard two of the men talking angrily in the lounge, their voices menacing and querulous. Next door, Jack was shouting in his sleep something about his mother.

As he lay there John listened impotently to the conversation raging in his head. The Voices were all speaking at once and he could only distinguish the occasional phrase:

'The time has come, a good man really, no hope, no respite, it needs serious consideration, needs must, what about breakfast, body and soul together, a statement really, stands to reason, we've tried, inevitable, quality of life, free will, end game, respite care, only eternity, over in a millisecond, paramedics of course ... '

The Voices were again conducting their own case conference about him. He felt excluded from the process, waiting outside for a decision, for a verdict to be handed down. When they sensed he was listening the Voices became quieter but no less urgent. The whisperings became a sibilant crescendo flooding his consciousness, dragging him helpless in its wake. He let himself be forced out of bed, into his clothes and onto the street.

He had no idea where he was going, he just had to walk fast and distract himself from not only the Voices but a mounting sense of dread. At the end of his last stay at the Hilton his therapist had reminded him about the importance of mindfulness approaches. He tried to bring awareness to the process of walking. Left leg, right leg, calves tightening then relaxing, each arm a slow piston, aware too of a small nagging ache in his right thigh. He was also suddenly aware of a completely alien Voice.

'Watch out for snipers!'

What are you doing here?

'We met before, in the pub, I belong to Mick, but I'm getting fed up with him, I want a new head. They have you in your sights on the high rises, Special Forces.'

'Mindfulness is a way of being grounded, of living in the moment, borrowed from Eastern cultures and increasingly embedded in mainstream approaches,' explained the Academic. John stared intently through the window of a shoe repairer and key cutter. If he concentrated completely on what he saw then the Voices would lose control.

Hundreds, perhaps thousands of golden freshly minted template keys hung on hooks along the back wall, symmetrical and neat.

'A key to a new life,' said the Tempter not wanting to be silenced by a therapeutic practice in which he had little faith. *'One door opens ... '*

'But all your doors close,' said the Bastard. *'Slammed in your face then boarded up. Or locked behind you. Prison cell, forensic ward. Happy days.'*

John quickly moved to the window of the travel agents

next door hoping to sidestep the Voices, give them the slip. He must concentrate, focus on the now.

MARCO POLO CRUISE FROM LEITH NORTH CAPE & LAND OF THE MIDNIGHT SUN 10 NIGHTS WAS £1069 N0W £855.

'You need a break John, could be the making of you. Meet a nice widow, a bit older but you know ... '

'Cruises for losers ... step up the gangplank, be piped aboard by Satan, and rearrange the deck chairs on your own disaster.'

'Trading Standards and the ombudsman are relentlessly pursuing travel agents who mislead the public ... '

John left the windows and concentrated instead on the pavement in front of him. Within moments he was hit by a blind man's stick sweeping a path ahead of him. John muttered an apology and stepped aside. Two more blind men followed in his wake, all were listening to headphones and mouthing along to unheard tunes.

'Ah, the blind leading ... they might of course be blind bakers.'

'Join them, John, join the cripples, ally yourself with the deformed, team up with the mad, do the disability conga down Great Junction Street, hold their waists.'

'It is reminiscent of Bruegel's painting The Parable of the Blind *in the National Museum of Naples. The parable can be found in the gospels ... from memory, "let them alone: they are blind guides. And if the blind guide the blind, both shall fall into a pit" St Matthew, 15, 14.'*

'Come on, John! Your very own shitty pit is waiting ... pity shit ... '

He broke into a run. He was surrendering, capitulating, giving up. The Voices had broken him. He was lost. It was all simply intolerable, beyond bearing.

The Academic grew anxious and stuttered, *'They say that people who think of suicide don't want to kill themselves, they just want the pain to end ... '*

'FASTER, FASTER JOHN, FASTER, ALMOST THERE!'

He reached the bridge that spanned the Water of Leith, climbed onto the parapet and stood with his arms outstretched. A young woman with a baby in a pushchair on the towpath put her hand to her mouth. The last thing he noticed, in an extended moment of luscious and serene calm, was the sight of a child's silver scooter nesting in the branches of a tree where it had been thrown from the bridge.

'GO JOHN! GO JOHN GO! DO IT NOW! DO IT FOR YOUR BROTHER!'

Up on his toes, aware of the wind in his face he leaned forward.

PART TWO

THIRTY-ONE

At first they didn't notice the rise in the water. Their boots and breeches were soaked; their eyes tightened against the wind but remained sufficiently focussed on the disappearing horizon to pick their way over the sodden debris. The three men had also failed to notice that they were dragging their legs against a small tide. It was Balthasar who, wondering why the dogs were lagging behind, looked back and saw the younger animal struggling to keep its head above the water. He got Cornelius' and Johannes' attention.

'Something's happening,' he said. They looked beneath the hanging clouds towards the blurred line where the sky met the sea. The dyke had been replaced by a tumbling bolster of water gathering momentum as they gazed.

'Jesus wept!' said Johannes.

The roar was audible beneath the wind. The landscape between them and the coast was changing rapidly as the tide blotted out any residual greenness and gobbled up everything in its path, small wooden farm buildings, cattle, whole hedges.

'*A not infrequent occurrence*,' said the Academic. '*Worst was the All Saints Flood, or Allerheiligenvloed of 1570. Tens of thousands of people became homeless; livestock was lost in huge numbers. Winter stocks were destroyed. The sea wall collapsed the entire length between ... and ... Do you know, I can't remember! Anyway there is a fine drawing of the Scheldt flood by Hans Moser... '*

'Mother of God,' said Cornelius. 'The sea wall has gone.' For a moment they could do nothing but watch the ambling predator rolling up the fields beneath an increasingly black sky.

They dropped their staves and ran further ahead of the dogs. Not daring to look behind, they were half braced when the tide struck them. Instantly lifted off their feet and driven upwards they danced like marionettes in the hands of a drunken showman, tossed head over heels by the ferocious surge.

Johannes caught his breath moments before his total immersion. Silence and darkness. He was vaguely aware of some sort of forward momentum as his lungs struggled to be freed from his chest and, in that infinitesimal sliver of time, felt totally and inexplicably calm. He burst into the fresh air, gulped and went under again.

At the last moment before the water struck Cornelius turned towards his enemy who instantly punched him in the stomach and knocked him off his feet. His fists remained clenched as he was sucked under.

Balthasar was searching his limited field of vision for the dogs before he was hit on the head by a passing branch and lost consciousness.

THIRTY-TWO

'So a Dutchman saved you,' said Beverley. 'At the very moment of tipping forward you were suddenly wrapped in the arms of a complete stranger who gripped you tightly and slowly lowered you back down to earth. This large man smelt of dogs ... '

John nodded and looked at the work surface in the kitchen. The Formica was badly scorched. The conversation should have been taking place in Beverley's office but the CPN was talking to an especially petrified Dennis about him forfeiting his tenancy unless he stopped peeing in the corner of his room. 'And how was he dressed, this Dutchman? Was he wearing clogs?'

'Just a Dutch cap,' suggested the Jester, *'safer that way.'*

'Special forces,' said Mick who wandered into the kitchen scratching his armpit.

'Enough Mick,' said Beverley, 'Have you cleaned your room yet?'

'Ever hear of Dutch courage?' continued the Jester.

'Didn't work though, did it? You failed cowardly shite ... ' contributed the Bastard.

'Alcohol plays a part in over 80% of suicide attempts.'

Thank you, Academic.

'*Was it a Flying Dutchman, did he swoop low over the parapet and sweep you up in his arms?*' asked the Bastard.

'You may not be so lucky next time,' said Beverley, 'The Dutchman might be busy, you know, planting his bulbs.' She knew that sarcasm was not the therapeutic intervention of choice but she was tired. The fire alarm had gone off during the night and she had been summoned at four in the morning to confirm that no one had burned to death.

'*It is crucial not to collude with the delusion,*' chided the Academic.' *You could say, "I know the Dutch man was real for you, but not for anyone else who was passing."*'

'Anyway, we're all glad you're OK.'

'*Oh no we're not,*' muttered the Bastard.

'*Oh yes, we are,*' retorted the Jester.

'I think you should go and sit quietly somewhere and we'll chat later.'

John spent the next eighteen hours on the settee in the TV room, sleeping through Oprah Winfrey, *Antiques Roadshow*, two films, several news bulletins, a satirical review and a documentary on Ontario. Before she went off shift, Beverley tried to rouse him but, eventually, decided that the most charitable option was to leave him there.

In every nightmare he was falling from high buildings, from a variety of bridges, tumbling down lift shafts, and on one occasion from the top of a crane swaying above the high rises in Leith. He became one of the anonymous jumpers from the Twin Towers, falling in slow motion towards the Manhattan sidewalk, apparently contented, or at least momentarily resigned, already in the foetal position, his body about to add one more nightmare crump to the soundtrack of screams and sirens.

Invariably every dream ended just before he hit the pavement, the water or whatever surface was waiting to erase his consciousness. Every time his descent would be halted inches before the impact and, on every occasion, felt utterly cheated, as if denied a sexual climax after hours of foreplay.

'You'd be so lucky,' said the Bastard.

He went for breakfast not because he was hungry but because he clung to the unlikely hope that if he sneaked from his room and crept down the stairs he might leave the Voices sleeping. Stepping high like a pantomime villain, he avoided the creaking step on the second landing. His ploy failed.

'Ever put your finger in a dyke?' one of them asked. John wasn't certain if it was the Bastard or the Jester. He didn't actually care.

Kevin sidled up and pushed a postcard under the edge of John's plate. 'You're popular,' he said.

John glanced at the nondescript seaside scene and then turned it over.

SEE YOU ON THE BEACH, ANDY

He dropped his spoon laden with cornflakes. Mick leaned over and read the card. 'Looks genuine,' he said. 'Difficult to say without forensic examination but, you know, it could be him.'

The Tempter thought it was his birthday.

'Of course it's him. It's the sign you've been waiting for. Rejoice! All will be well. Good times ahead.'

'Nice one Tempter,' murmured the Bastard who, on occasions, saw the Tempter as a kindred soul more than capable of destroying John through hope alone.

'Tell you what,' said Mick, 'let's walk to Porti, have a look round, ken what I mean?' He tapped the side of his nose. 'Have to avoid the roads, not safe, spies everywhere, lookouts, snitches, stool pigeons, turncoats.' Clearly on a roll he added for good measure, 'third columnists, traitors.'

True to his word, Mick walked fast and close to the buildings in Constitution Street. He tugged his beanie down over his forehead and led the way to the docks while John struggled to keep up. He couldn't face another day in the hostel and Mick's suggestion made as much sense as anything ever did. Mick glanced towards the Alan Breck tavern, 'A good man,' he said, without elaborating.

The security guard at the entrance to the Port of Leith Docks, utterly engrossed in the silicone enhanced beauty pouting at him from the pages of the *Sun*, failed to notice them ducking under the barrier and making their way round a Liberia registered freighter, past the towering stack of sea and weather-beaten containers, pallets and coils of wire as thick as an arm. The two men soon faced a mountain of scrap metal which, viewed from its foothills, blocked out the sky.

Until that moment John had honestly believed that he had given the Voices the slip. Where he was standing or where he was going, or in whose company were matters of total irrelevance. Space was opening up in his head. Until the ambush.

'Climb it, John, climb it. It's a challenge, solve it and you find Andy. Climb it, climb it, climb it, climb it, you cowardly bastard. Climb it!'

Powerless to challenge or resist, John scrabbled at the foot of the hill. He dug his hands into the metal shavings and pulled them out covered in blood. He hauled himself higher up. His feet started to slide down but he clambered upwards holding onto the twisted sharp edges of old engines and machinery inwards. Mick looked at him from below, 'For fuck's sake!'

John slid down a car bonnet but managed to halt his descent by clutching at a metal pole protruding at right angles to the rest of the heap. Blood pouring from a wound in his cheek ran into his mouth. He was face to face with a gearbox, but someone or something was tugging at his leg. Muttering, Mick hauled at his companion.

Standing once more on the cinder path Mick brushed him down and wiped his face with the sleeve of his coat. 'No harm done,' he said. 'Christ, I could do with a drink. Let's get under cover,' he said sitting on the sea wall before turning and dropping onto the metre-wide ledge that ran along the top of the sloping sea defences. John did likewise.

Once he was certain that he could not be seen from the path Mick pointed towards Inchcolm Island, 'Great country, Scotland. The coast of Fife. See all they wee houses? That's Dalgety Bay, and over there the Bass Rock, and in between is Portibelli, where, if you recall, we might find you brother.'

The lens in John's head shifted radically. He saw himself from a mile up in the sky, a tiny black figure with a speck next to him moving slowly at the edge of a vast sea. In the space between his viewpoint and the ground gulls fought over scraps scavenged from the adjacent landfill. The sea was punctuated with commas of white foam and sterner exclamation marks where the tide rippled over wooden groynes.

'You're no very talkative the day,' said Mick, 'but that's fine, I ken how it is. That hostel'll drive you mad, if you're no mad when you sign up, and let's face it, most of us are mad as hatters. I just don't trust that Kevin. I think he's in the pay of the enemy.'

John zoomed back to earth, his face still hurting. He hadn't the remotest idea what Mick had been talking about but welcomed his company nonetheless.

As they walked, single file along the ledge, they were followed on the other side of the wall by the angular intestines of a petrochemical plant emitting steam, then a warehouse and a huge white storage sphere. 'It's for listening to ordinary folks' conversations,' said Mick, without looking up. The ledge was smeared in green algae.

With no warning, Mick threw himself down on the concrete ledge, 'Get down for fuck's sake! Enemy fire!' John crouched and then lay on the ground; he had no idea of what made sense and what didn't; of what constituted ordinary behaviour or what didn't. He just wanted to find his brother who would make everything all right again. In the meantime it was easier to do what he was told.

'Three o'clock! Man down!' shouted Mick. 'Small arms!' He slowly raised his head and looked out to sea. 'The Hummer's on fire!' he said pointing in the general direction of an innocuous dredger on the horizon. He removed his hat and held it to his chest. John hadn't realised until then that Mick had hair. 'IED. Filled with nails and excrement to infect the wounds. They're all young boys.' As Mick sobbed inconsolably, John held him and rocked him in his arms. Nothing made any sense. Nothing.

THIRTY-THREE: Mick's Tale

'I lost my boy in the war,' said Mick. 'Afghanistan, Helmand Province. We weren't close before he went like. He'd left home, living on the streets, cadging from his auntie. I wanted a reconciliation, ken, but it never happened. We'd fell out over money; he says I stole his brew money but I didn't; it was his mother but she was no well herself, ken. She was drinking; we were all drinking ken. A family hobby. We could have represented Scotland at drinking. Anyways, Ruth, that was my wife, ken, says that if we didn't pay the Man his pals would break my arms. "Don't talk to me about interest. Just a one off," she says, "I promise, Mick. Let's get the man out of our lives. Just once, let's borrow the boy's brew. He's been saving. It's under his bed." I said over my dead body, I think she quite liked the sound of that. I said I would meet with the Man and explain things ken. So I phoned the big Man and we did meet on the waste ground behind the shops at Wester Hailes. I was all masterful on the phone like, "No tools," I said, "just you and me to work out an agreement ken, an amicable solution to suit everybody."

'We met all right. High Noon. Just me and the bandits. Ten

of them ken. I said "Come on pal, we agreed, man to man," but he just hit me. And the others just joined in, kicking my ribs like it was a cup final. Then they carried me down to the canal like a bag of tatties and on the count of three hurled me in. It was rank ken, but no deep. I could just stand in the water. And the blood was streaming down my face. There was a wee boy fishing under the bridge with his pal. They took one look and fled home to their mammies.

'I walked home, dripping and droukit ken. Folk in the street thought I had pished myself. "Minging bastard!" they said but that was nothing compared to what Ruth said when I got home. I stood wringing wet on the mat, like some monster from the deep, weeds in my pocket, and humming something rank. "Jesus wept!" she said and crossed herself lest the priest was passing.

'Anyways, his mother took his money to pay the Man and our boy left home. He didn't rant or that, just left with a bag of clothes and his X-box. Just as well his mother hadn't found it, it would have been sold. We missed him ken, there was this gap at home. Nobody to fall out with, just ourselves but it wasn't the same. His mother kept drinking as if she was training for the drink Olympics. Held every four years, by the way, but always in Scotland, like the Eurovision Song Contest, the winners always play host. No other bugger gets a shot. But she was different ken, no arguing, no nagging which was good for a while ken. She just sat and drank and never said anything.' Mick paused, looked up and flapped his hand at a gull that evidently felt territorial about this particular section of the coastal defences. John lifted his foot from the cloying slime spewing from a cracked overflow pipe.

'Thank Christ for that,' said the Bastard. *'Have you ever listened to such self-indulgence in your life, John? I almost feel sorry for you having to listen to that. But you haven't been listening, have you? Too self-absorbed to pay attention*

to anyone but yourself and your own sorry life. Come to think of it you two deserve each other, both barking mad and seriously deluded. If I'm honest I prefer that Dutch shite you conjure from nowhere to this. Watch your step!'

The Bastard's warning came too late as John lost his footing, tumbled down the side of the concrete pyramid and slipped into the sea.

Balthasar was cartwheeled by the complex, feuding currents, curled like a foetus, a human kernel, an aimless projectile joining the submerged armada of junk and detritus, logs, branches, planks, earth, pots, tools, livestock, whatever the foraging waves could uproot and dislodge.

The sensation of drowning was not unpleasant once the fight for breath had ceased. He was being sucked towards the dark centre of something. Once beyond resistance there was an exhilarating aspect to the tumbling journey. He saw faces, some more clearly than others. Wilhelmein flashed into view and then was gone. He was sure the outstretched hand belonged to his daughter. Was that a glimpse of her unborn child? For some reason the gargoyles from the local church put in an appearance, girning and pouting at his plight. His neighbour was waving a fist. What had he done to offend him? Nothing that he was aware of. The streaming bubbles configured themselves into the face of the woman he had briefly lusted after in his youth. She was an early victim of the smallpox that swept though his village decades ago. She was smiling at him; he was sure she was.

Johannes's journey was equally transformative. From the first moment of unconsciousness he saw Michel just ahead of him, urging him onwards, beckoning, their fingers almost touching before they were separated again. What was his son saying, what words were being shaped by his mouth? Tell me, son, tell me!

THIRTY-FOUR

The shock of the water emptied John's body of air. He looked up at Mick who was clambering down the slope with a surprising dexterity. 'No chopper,' he said 'Give us your hand.' John was vaguely aware of his coat floating around him on the calm sea.

'*Very like the pre-Raphaelite depiction of Ophelia*,' suggested the Academic.

'*What?*' asked the Bastard with a tone of hostile incredulity.

'We'll have you out in no time,' said Mick, who had managed to grip John round the wrist. 'Loads of bodies floating,' he explained, 'hundreds of them, all from the same ship. Argie bastards. Iron Lady, my arse, drinking gin with that dipso Dennis, no understanding of the common man.'

No need to say anything, Academic, even I can tell that he's got his wars mixed up.

Eventually John hauled himself back onto the lower path, shivering as the water cascaded from his clothes. A stray black dog appeared from nowhere and sniffed at his legs, 'Get to ... ,' said Mick, almost succeeding in kicking the beast into the sea.

With their arms round each other, the two men tottered towards the point where the sea wall gave way to a snatch of beach. 'Stay there, pal,' said Mick sitting John down on an upturned pram on the foreshore while he strode off into the undergrowth of weed and rubbish that proliferated between the sea and the road.

Mick returned with armfuls of driftwood which he dumped in front of John. He snapped an orange box into lengths of kindling over which he sprinkled the contents of his cigarette lighter, expertly fanning the flames and moving the wood around until it caught. He stood back, hands on hips, and surveyed the small fire with satisfaction.

'I was talking,' he said, resuming the earlier monologue, 'about my boy.'

'I can't take any more of this,' said the Bastard. John was inclined to agree as he squeezed water from his sleeves. He had to admit that the fire was impressive. Mick had unsuspected talents – at the back of his mind John vaguely remembered a history of arson. Kevin had crept into the office one day when Beverley's back was turned and read all of the residents' files. Ever since he had used his stolen knowledge and illicit insights to great effect.

'Behave!' interjected the Academic. *'Oral history at its best. Just listen for a change'*

'Except not a word of it's true, a figment of a dysfunctional mind. It's all made up. Claptrap. Much more of this and I'm going to live in someone else's head.' John perked up at the thought.

'We didn't ken he'd joined the army. We thought he'd gone to live with his uncle in Dundee. We used to look at yon Basset place on telly as the coffins came home. Hairy bikers and wee wifies united in grief and all that. No for a moment did we think our Kevin was in Afghanistan.'

'This is so much shite!'

Quiet!

'Anyways, we got the knock on the door. The whole slow motion bit, his mother in a silent scream, me wanting to lamp the man standing there in his shiny uniform, commiserations, sympathy, all that patter. It was as if I could see this mist creeping up the close, a cold creeping mist, just furling up the drive. Except it wasn't just the close, it was my heart. It was gripped in this dark mist, its fingers dug deep. And you ken what, Johnnie boy, it's still there.' He beat his chest for effect and stared at the fire.

'I couldn't go in his room. Football posters, next to a picture of a woman with big breasts. It's not been touched since. A shrine. That's why I understand about your brother. It's the mist ken.'

John nodded and nodded again, and again. His chin moving ever faster towards his chest in a hypnotic rhythm. Mick looked at him strangely, 'Are you ok?'

'Of course he's not ok, are you John? The merest mention of your pathetic brother and you're off, isn't that right?'

John dug his thumbnail into the side of his forefinger until it started to bleed. At least the pain was starting to drown out the Bastard.

'Ouch! It's not that easy. I'll be back. I'll be back.'

'That's when the head got bad,' said Mick. 'It had not been the best before, ken, but after his death things deteriorated. First it was his voice. My son, ken. I heard gun fire too. IEDs, they improvised roadside things. Then it was loads of voices speaking Arab, mocking like. I seen the doctor, shock and bereavement he said. It'll pass, but it didn't. And then they Arab bastards started to come after me. I heard them at night. Laughing in the corner of the room as they ate their rations. His mother couldn't stand it any more so she left me. They soldiers live in the hostel now ken. But it's not just the Arabs, there's a dark conspiracy going on and nobody but me kens it. Have you heard their Voices, John?'

'Ha! A good question,' said the Bastard, at the very moment when John stopped pressing his thumbnail into his finger. *'You*

see, you've lots in common with Mick. You both hear foreign voices, the difference is Mick only lives with a few Afghanistan veterans, pensioned off no doubt. Whereas you live in an entire world, a full-scale imaginary menagerie of weird foreigners. Have you heard the voices? I love it! Is the Pope a Catholic?'

'I think you'll find he's an Argentinian, but the one before him was German and the one before him ... '

'Academic, I'm losing patience with you!'

The wind had caught the flames which shot out in great tongues towards the sea. Mick dragged two creosote soaked planks from the undergrowth and added them to the pyre. Unbeknown to John several errant sparks leaped onto his coat and smouldered until they took a hold. Mick noticed the small fist of flame on his companion's chest, 'Christ!' he said beating out the flames with his hands. ''You look like the Sacred Heart in my missus' church!'

'Well look at that, a visiting card from hell,' said the Bastard, *'it's waiting for you, not long now!'*

THIRTY-FIVE

When he woke, Johannes was staring at a dead mouse inches from his face. He lifted his hand and stroked the animal with his forefinger before engaging once more with his surroundings. He was on a small knoll surrounded by water that seemed to stretch forever.

When he got to his feet he saw that this particular infinity was more proscribed than had been initially apparent. After watching the water draining from his breeches and spouting from his coat, he surveyed the changed landscape. The mass of water bore a resemblance to the Schelde in full spate. Several islands had sprung up. At one point a track rose from the water and climbed onto an isolated finger of land where a windmill stood untouched by the torrent, its blades turning furiously, inhabited by a mad miller determined to harvest the wind and grind corn for the devil.

He saw a black drowned horse sweep by, its head upturned and its eyes open. It was followed by several small trees floating in a straight line as if striving to recreate the symmetry they had known in dryer times. Water was eddying either side of a farm building, the red tiled roof of which poked above the surface. A blue bonnet with a white band floated past, as if its anxious owner was running along the bottom of the riverbed.

As Johannes scoured the horizon for his friends he heard a groaning to his left. Balthasar was lying face down into the edge of the water. He ran towards him and hoisted him by the armpits onto dryer land. 'By Nicholas' blood, you're still alive.'

'Only just, only just,' said Balthasar, coughing while clutching at the arm proffered to haul him up the embankment.

'Where's Cornelius?'

'I don't know, I can't see him.'

The two men stood back to back and shouted Cornelius' name but their voices were swallowed by the wind and driving rain. The last time Johannes heard the pastor preach in the depth of the forest he had told the assembled to close their eyes and listen to the wind as it crept among the trees and scuttled the leaves. 'Hear the groans of the damned,' he said, 'listen to their plaintive lamentations as they are dragged towards the land of the dead; hearken as they howl at their own misfortune; hearken to the gnashing of teeth and rending of clothes.' Michel had hidden his head in his father's coat. Even Antonia had looked uneasy.

'He'll be safe somewhere,' said Johannes who was far from convinced yet unable or unwilling to entertain the thought that Cornelius might have drowned.

They shaded their eyes from the squall and continued to shout but heard nothing apart from the elements. They stared bleakly at each other. 'We can't stay here, we must search,' said Johannes, staring through unfocussed eyes at the passing flotsam: planks, staves, the halters from a cart, a fence, something that could have been a gibbet, fish boxes, a cat, a fisherman's coracle.

The coracle, itself half submerged, was heading towards their spit of land. Balthasar saw it at the same moment and waded into the water to intercept it as it flowed past. Together they dragged the coracle onto the bank and turned it over. Balthasar pointed out a hole just beneath the middle point. He turned back towards the water, knelt down and dragged out a handful of vegetation that he twisted and forced into the small aperture. 'It will do for a while,' he said, already on the lookout for a branch that could be stripped and used as an oar.

Johannes balanced himself in the middle of the unstable craft while Balthasar stood behind and dipped the improvised oar into the fast flowing waters. The tiny one-man boat, woven from rushes and covered in animal skin, almost sank under the combined weight of the two men.

They knew they were moving away from the sea but, otherwise, had no idea where they were headed. Johannes, feeling sick, shivered. He surrendered to his worst thoughts. Needles in haystacks, a goose chase as wild as they get, cold and wet and miles from home, at the mercy of a raging torrent and a flimsy vessel. All this and a missing friend, probably drowned and a missing son, probably ...

The coracle lurched and drank in the water as Balthasar shouted something and pointed ahead. Johannes was startled to see a pair of legs hanging from a tree in the middle of the flood. Bizarrely he was reminded of the crudely drawn cartoons on the broadsheets passed on by the itinerant pedlars who risked their lives by lampooning the Spanish.

The wriggling legs with their thin calves clearly belonged to Cornelius.

Both men, elated beyond words, roared with laughter. 'Having fun, Cornelius?'

'Look! A chicken stuck up a chimney.'

'Useless clods of dung!'

'You should take up dancing.'

'Treacherous spawn of Lucifer.'

‘Shapely calves to make a maiden swoon.’

‘Pair of shits!’

Balthasar steered the craft under the overhanging branches of the tree while Johannes grabbed hold of Cornelius’ legs. He fell into the water, momentarily disappeared and then resurfaced spluttering, clinging to the outside of the frail boat as it was swept onwards by the tide.

Using branches as oars, Balthasar and Cornelius managed to steer themselves out of the main flood which lost momentum as the invading sea reached a rapprochement with the newly conquered lands. The brown water had become sluggish under the weight of soil and clay it had gouged from the fields. Storm clouds retreated towards the far horizon.

Caught in a small eddy, the coracle moved of its own accord towards a field that marked the start of higher land. They waded ashore and looked back at the swathe of new sea interrupted by the occasional roof and stubborn tree. Whole hamlets, small holdings tended for years by the same families, meticulously cultivated patterns of land, intricate patterns of ditches and irrigation channels all wiped away: all history, all labour, all colour eradicated.

For a moment the three men lay on the wet earth laughing and punching each other.

‘The dogs,’ said Balthasar. The others looked out over the water as if they could conceivably catch sight of the beasts swimming towards them. No one spoke.

‘I saw Michel,’ said Johannes quietly, ‘in the water, at least in my mind’s eye. Just before I passed out. He was holding out his hand to me, urging me on.’

‘It was a sign,’ said Cornelius, ‘definitely a sign. We must continue.’

Balthasar drew their attention to a thin spiral of smoke rising from the copse of trees at the top of the field above which a solitary bird circled. It signalled the prospect of food and warmth.

Seeing a knot of men sprawled on the ground made Johannes think of the post-harvest feasts he had known at home. He half expected to see the village women dispensing beer and cheese from wicker baskets to their tired spouses.

At their approach the nearest of the men sprang to his feet and gripped the stave lying next to him. The others followed. Within seconds the new arrivals had been surrounded by at least twenty men exuding a stench of alcohol and damp clothes.

Cornelius grabbed the end of the stave that had been poked into his stomach then released his grip once he saw how heavily the odds were stacked against him. Johannes noticed three women with shaven heads, nuns, apparently holding hands round a tree. He looked again and saw that they were tied together.

'What is it with effing nuns?' Mick asked John who was staring out to sea. At first John had not the slightest clue what Mick was on about then briefly considered the bizarre possibility that his companion had been eavesdropping on his own delusion. He shook his head.

'The worst are they nuns that train wee girls in the Legion of Mary, I ken because my mother was a member so she said, only eight year old ken. They would dress in black and visit dying folk. Kneel down by the bed, hands thegether, praying for the no-quite-dead soul shiting himself in bed. I'm telling you son, if I wake one morning and see all they wee praying bitches lined up by my bed, I'm out of there.'

THIRTY-SIX

'Speak!' shouted one of the men, 'and if your tongues are tainted with Spanish sweetmeats they will be ripped from your throats and burnt in front of you!'

'We are Dutchmen looking for my son who was taken by Philip's men. We are simple weavers and wish you no harm.'

The mood of the group changed. Disappointment was palpable as the staves were lowered and their leader made a grandiose gesture inviting them to join the party.

'And we,' he said, 'are a dishonourable party of sea beggars, geuzen if you will. A parcel of rogues. Vagabonds, looters and pillagers by appointment to His Royal Majesty William the Silent. We came ashore for sport but apparently the sea was missing us and set off in pursuit. One minute we were minding our business quietly ransacking St Michael's Abbey, the next running for our lives. We lost three men but there are three of you. You look fit, ideal replacements really. Though you, sir, look a bit old for the chase,' he said, staring at Balthasar.

Balthasar bridled.

'Very well,' said the leader. 'Roll up your sleeve.'

'What?' asked an incredulous Balthasar.

'Your best arm, come now. If you beat me, all three of you

will join us, indeed if you beat me you can choose which nun you wish to have sport with.' He glanced back towards the terrified women playing ring-a-roses round the tree. 'My personal recommendation would be the tall one; she knows a trick or two. If you lose, well ... ' He had already rolled up his own sleeve and was resting his elbow on a tree stump that was being used as a table. He was flexing his fingers. Shaking his head, Balthasar did as he had been told and knelt down opposite his opponent. After a moment they locked their hands together.

'This is fascinating!'

Academic, this is not the time to interrupt.

'Arm wrestling can be traced all the way back to ancient Egypt where a painting depicting a type of arm wrestling was found in an Egyptian tomb dating to about 2000 BC. There's more to it than meets the eye. Although technique and overall arm strength are the two biggest factors, there are others: the length of the wrestler's arm, muscle and arm density, hand grip size, wrist endurance and flexibility, reaction time.'

'It's all crap!'

Will you both just let me get on and tell the story?

'Well, it is, isn't it? They've survived the Inquisition, then a flood and now their very lives depend on the outcome of an arm wrestling encounter between a geriatric weaver and a sea-begging megalomaniac. It actually sea-beggars belief ... It's bad enough having to listen to a lunatic rabbiting on about the war on Portobello beach ... '

Let *me* tell the story. I want to find out what happens if you don't.

Balthasar stared into his opponent's eyes and watched as the sweat broke out on his brow. He detected the merest hint of a tremor in the younger man's arm. He had him for sure. He forced his hand no more than one inch closer to the surface of the rough hewed tree stump but then had to concede the ground won. Back on the vertical they fought until Balthasar felt as if the sinews in his bicep would burst. What was the expression in the man's eyes? Uncertainty, bravado, vulnerability, tiredness? He couldn't tell but his opponent broke the stare first.

Balthasar used the instant to force a tiny advantage once more. His opponent's face was clenched and tight, his eyes now closed but whatever mental image he was conjuring imbued him with sufficient additional strength to force Balthasar's hand almost to the horizontal.

'Come on, old man, come on!' shouted Cornelius whose own face was now within inches of the sea beggar's. Noticing that the other crew-members were about to drag him away, Johannes restrained his friend. Cornelius let himself be moved back to the edge of the jeering crowd, from where he stared at Balthasar's opponent with undisguised hatred.

Sensing that he had nothing to lose, Balthasar summoned power from somewhere and slowly, inexorably, his muscles in spasm, he re-established the triangle of arms, the white knuckled fists forming the apex. Stalemate! Both men were totally and equally unyielding. Balthasar became aware of the other men shouting encouragement. Both sides were bellowing as if at a cockfight in a darkened inn yard. He could pick out Cornelius' voice above the others and hoped he might somehow suck in the power that was being projected across the space between them. Aware as never before of his own muscle and bone, and feeling suddenly invincible, he forced his enemy's hand down onto the table. For a moment he didn't release his grip as if the effort to unclench his fingers was simply beyond him.

His opponent roared with laughter as if he had intended to lose. 'Too bad, no more throat-cutting today. We sail at dusk.'

'We are weavers, not seamen. We will take our leave.'

'You don't understand do you?' said the Leader, rubbing his bicep. 'If you attempt to leave you are spies for Spain, simple as that. We will kill you. The alternative is to accept a commission with the geuzen and serve your country.' He stood close to Balthasar, his eyes dull, unfocussed, his leather skullcap clinging to his head. He was bouncing slightly on his heels as if ready to attack at a moment's notice.

'We are following the Spanish to Zuid-Holland to find my son. The rumours say there will be sieges and battles there that will shape our nation,' said Johannes.

The Leader clapped his hands together. 'Our route exactly!' His men laughed. 'For the sake of argument I will assume you to be people of good name and fame.'

'Remarkably accurate!' proclaimed the Academic unable to contain himself. *'When the sea beggars or watergeuzen as the Dutch called them were eventually persuaded to forsake their life of pillage and plunder by William of Orange and join the cause, he issued letters of marquee which specified among other stipulations that no persons were to be received on board, either as soldiers or sailors, save folk of good name and fame.'*

'Academic, take a hike. Sometimes you are as sad as the lost deluded soul whose head you live in. Whoever said a little learning is a dangerous thing had a point.'

Cut it out both of you. There is a story to be told.

'Oooh, get you. Suit yourself. You're a shite storyteller anyway. Call yourself a Narrator, it's all strained metaphors, hopelessly overwritten and, essentially, it's nonsense ... '

The men jostled the new conscripts. One of them, a short man with beaked nose fingered Johannes' coat. 'Nice cloth, nice cloth.' He muttered. His companion insinuated his hand into Johannes' pocket and, undetected, removed a small knife. He recoiled in mock horror waving the weapon. 'Armed to the teeth. A Spanish blade I wager!'

Cornelius meanwhile had attracted the unwanted attention of a small man who had grabbed his sleeve and sniffed. Cornelius jerked away in disgust. 'Careful now,' said the Leader, 'you don't want to upset Ulriche, our own blind soothsayer.' Ulriche raised his sightless eyes towards the leader and flared his nostrils as if drinking in his words through his nose.

'If you cross Ulriche he will sniff you out, like a hound he will track you down, he will smell you in the midden, he will find your scent in water, and then he will rip out your own eyes. He recruits, you understand, for the King of Darkness. There are many young brides in Madrid and Valencia who stare in horror at their husband's empty sockets.' Ulriche nodded enthusiastically.

'We will join you and labour on your ship in exchange for free passage,' said Johannes. The Leader repeated his earlier exaggerated mocking bow and ordered his men to strike the camp. Smouldering logs were kicked out of the fire. The busy sparks spiralled upwards and then died. A man went to untie the three nuns from around the tree and jerked them, still chained together in a line. 'Call me Holy Father!' he shouted. 'Yes, Holy Father!' they chorused in terror. Satisfied, he grunted as if his newly acquired dogs were finally learning obedience.

Several of the men struggled to lift the studded chests on to their shoulders. Cornelius was reminded of the box crammed with bedding and curtains gifted to him and his new bride by the elders of the village. It had remained virtually unopened in a corner of their bedroom. 'Wait until we get a big house,' Geertje would say. 'Or when we fall on hard times.'

He was distracted by laughter and looked towards where one of the men was staggering under the weight of an enormous cross presumably looted from St Michael's Abbey. His fellow beggars flailed him with imaginary whips while shouting 'Release Barabbas!'

Eventually he was relieved of his solitary burden that was then shared between four men who either took an end or the cross length as if hurrying to get an imminent crucifixion over and done with.

Balthasar shivered as the wind blew in from the adjacent flooded land. 'This too is meant,' he said, more to reassure himself than the others. Cornelius and Johannes nodded grimly.

The walk to the coast took under an hour. On several occasions the Leader paused and called Ulriche to the front of the party. Everyone watched as he raised his nose in the air, puckering his nostrils before pointing with great certainty in a particular direction.

They marched until their eyes were smarting with the salt whipped off the spume. As they clambered through the ferny undergrowth they disturbed a nest of gulls which erupted into a flurry of wings, web and feather. One of the birds brushed against Johannes' cheek. He raised his arm to protect himself but the bird redoubled its fury and attached its yellow beak to his sleeve. Cornelius came to his aid and quickly smacked the squawking bird into the undergrowth where it lay stunned.

They eventually came to a gully at the bottom of which a two-masted ship, flying the Lion of Nassau flag of orange, white and blue, rocked on its anchor. The men improvised a human chain down the side of the sloping bank and passed down the crates, chests, barrels, crowbars, the spoils of their ecclesiastical looting and what supplies remained. The nuns were treated in similar fashion and were manhandled towards the vessel below. Most of the men attempted to kiss or grope the frightened women before roughly passing them to the next link in the lecherous chain.

Johannes stumbled down the last few feet and plunged to his knees in the frozen edge of the sea. He had seen enough rain, floodwater and sea to last him a lifetime, and was overcome with bleakness. Unsteadily he hauled himself back onto the lichen-smeared rock and made his way to the split log that stretched from the shore to the ship. Balthasar and Cornelius had already stepped over the gunnel and onto the deck where they were jeered by the crew who had stayed aboard. Balthasar counted some forty men altogether. Most were dressed in black sacking breeches and jerkins stained with shiny patches which could have been tar or spittle. They smelled of latrines.

The weavers progressively backed away from the menacing phalanx of men, several of whom moved slowly towards them with daggers drawn.

THIRTY-SEVEN

'Do you remember that song by the effing singing nun, "Dominique, nique, nique" or some rubbish like that. They shouldn't be singing on Top of the Pops, *ken, they should be praying for lost souls like us.*

'Most of them are crabbit, twisted wee women, and so ugly ken. Brides of Christ, I don't think so! It's not right; all they frustrated women living in the same home. No men. All salivating over the parish priest when he comes to say mass. Most of them are lessies anyway. Christ has no chance!

'And don't mention that thrawn sleikit old crone, Mother Teresa. A wee twisted midget, with no concern for the livin; she couldn't move for all they papal medals round her neck, weighed down she was. Humpybackit.'

Jester, did I say you could take over?

'Sorry boss, I thought you were getting tired and I just slipped in there.'

Well, just slip out again!

'Nobel Peace Prize, my arse!'

The two men wandered further along the beach in the direction of Portobello and the fun fair closed for the season.

'She also won the Pope John XXIII Peace Prize in 1971 and the Nehru Prize for the promotion of international peace and understanding in 1972 ... '

At a word from the Leader the crew desisted and returned grudgingly to their duties. The Leader then ordered one of the sailors, a thin man whose face was covered with bulbous carbuncles, to show the three new arrivals their quarters.

Their guide led the way below deck and along a sloping dark passage that smelt of fungus and bodies. Cornelius hit his head against a beam that bisected the increasingly narrow space. He swore and felt for wetness. Carbuncle stopped. 'Fresh straw, lads,' he said, 'you must be favoured guests, but remember you have to earn your passage.' Chuckling, he left them and retraced his steps to the thin aperture of light that showed the upper rungs of the ladder down which they had climbed. Water dripped from every knothole.

As their eyes adjusted to the dark the men could make out other shapes resting on both sides of the narrow corridor. One of the shapes put its leg out and guffawed as Johannes stumbled. Other shapes were quick to join in the mocking chorus. Eyes shone in the darkness.

'Is this hell?' muttered Balthasar. 'Are these men or demons?'

'I preferred the flood,' said Cornelius, leading the way back to the hatch.

The light was fading and the sky heavy with sagging black clouds, the sea air welcome after the rancid stench below.

There was much activity on deck. Serpent ropes uncoiled, spun by an unseen sorcerer. The men watched as the crew worked to a pattern the shape of which was not immediately apparent. Cornelius was minded of a dumb show he had watched when strolling players had visited the village and, without recourse to language, had conjured the death of Abel and his subsequent redemption.

Ropes were fed through hands at a rate that should have shredded flesh from bone, but the crew seemed immune. Balthasar looked overhead where the main sail shrugged, a surly giant reluctantly waking from a deep sleep. Wooden crossbeams groaned as pressure was applied from taut ropes. Johannes glanced at the lattice-work of rigging that enveloped the ship like an old lady whose face was swaddled with a cloth to alleviate toothache. Small figures, silhouetted against the setting sun, clambered towards the crow's nest.

'Idle weaver scum,' said the Leader. 'We don't deal with cloth and buttons here. Get to work.' He ushered them to the gunnel and demonstrated how to close the gun ports, a necessary precaution as the ship lurched into life and wind fought with tide.

Cornelius worked on his own while the other two developed a rhythm, each pushing the heavy oak shutters from opposite sides. The movement and the degree of effort was exactly that required when the loom had to be repositioned. For a moment Johannes saw Michel at his side, plying him with questions as he strained to fix a problem that could, if handled badly, jeopardise the day's labour.

Blind Ulriche stood stock still at the centre of the hubbub, his face slightly raised towards the breeze, which he smelt as if savouring a decaying fruit.

Cornelius was the first to hear another sound mingling with the wind. He paused for a moment and motioned to the others to listen. The crew were singing.

LET GO THE ROPES, UNFURL THE SAILS,
AND LET US BE OFF TO SEA,
WERE WE EVEN LORDS ASHORE
OUR HEARTS WOULD LIE WITH THEE

'Let me just say the sea shanty has an honourable lineage. For many centuries sea-faring folk have often improvised verses

lacking either explicit or continuous themes. The rhythm of the song quoted above suggests a Long-drag or Halyard shanty, both of which were devised to synchronise with the job of hauling on halyards to hoist topsail or topgallant yards.'

Academic, I appreciate your enthusiasm but increasingly you are getting in the way of the story. No, Bastard, back to sleep! I do not need a contribution from you, not now.

'Can't stop me, I live in this head, same as you. Anyway, I'm getting pissed off listening to a tale about pirates. Why don't they sing "Yo-ho-ho and a Bottle of Rum", and be done with it. It's all rubbish.'

'Sorry to butt in again but Fifteen Men on a Dead Man's Chest *was made up by Robert Louis Stevenson in 1883. Although it was subsequently expanded in a poem titled* Derelict *by Young E. Allison and published in the* Louisville Courier-Journal *in 1891, there is absolutely no evidence for its existence in the 16th century ... '*

Both of you, behave! You consistently compromise the momentum of the narrative.

'Sorry ... '

'Pair of losers ... '

When the gun ports had all been closed the three men rested their backs against the gunnel. The other crew did likewise. As the ship was now well underway, riding the swell towards the open sea, most of the men were stood down. Johannes smiled ruefully at his companions.

'God's will,' said Balthasar.

'God's will,' echoed Cornelius in his best priest's voice before grinning. His mirth was infectious and the others joined in until they were convulsed, tears running down their faces. Even Ulriche moved his face towards the sounds of joy that had their origins in the absurdity of the recent days, overwhelming relief at still being alive, and an irresistible sense that all was not lost.

THIRTY-EIGHT

While Mick continued to mutter to himself about the irredeemable evil of nuns John looked at the forlorn beach. The tide was out and it was difficult to see where the sand ended and the water began. There was an indistinct blur of wetness through which two dogs scampered in a pointless gull hunt. The birds flapped towards the distant waves and merged into a haze of spray and faltering daylight. The wooden groynes sank deeper into the sand the closer they got to the sea, like the rib cage from the carcass of a sunken hulk.

Minutes earlier he had been able to make out the tiny silhouette of a two-masted ship on the horizon but that too had disappeared behind the encroaching murk of dusk. A memory had been stirred but he couldn't tie it down. It felt like an itch in his head that he couldn't quite scratch. The Voices tried to help him. The Jester was first up.

'Come on, sir, dirty postcards, loads of them, bums and tits, sir, don't show the missus, ooh aah!' John stared at a non-existent wodge of saucy seaside cards from the 1950s. Striped bathing costumes, breasts merging into beach balls, pouting lips, silly captions. Huge arses and ice creams.

The Bastard swatted the Jester to one side. *'John, you came here to bury something once, what was it? Some shameful secret, a dirty magazine stolen from the corner shop, someone's pet you killed out of wickedness ... '*

John flinched then relaxed as the more welcome urbane cadences of the Academic gradually grew in volume and prominence.

'I've been looking through the archives and, although the evidence is a little ambiguous, I think you were brought here when you were much younger. A holiday, the sun was shining. You got a little burned and were eventually caked in calamine lotion then placed behind the collapsible wind shield. The only surviving photos from that day have been damaged; it's impossible to tell who was with you.'

'Probably your brother,' interjected the Tempter while the Academic marshalled his thoughts.

'They Christian Brothers were just as bad as the nuns,' commented Mick unhelpfully. 'I was held off the ground by one of they Catholic hooligans, he lifted me by the lug, it's not been the same since.' He held out the lobe of his left ear for John's inspection.

'There's a lot of work been done on false memory syndrome; you have to be on your guard.'

Despite the Academic's warning, John focussed on the shade of a particular memory until it became less blurred. He did remember the ache of sunburn and had a sense of a large woman bending over him. There was a man too, though at a distance. He was smoking and looking out towards the sea. He had hated the feel of sand between his toes. One of the grown ups, probably the woman, had chided him and told him to take off his sandals. Who were these people? Foster parents perhaps, the latest in a long line.

He strained to look round the edges of the sepia photograph that he was desperate to restore to its original condition. Was his brother there? Could he see him in his peripheral vision? He tilted the photo. Could he hear him shouting as he played at the water's edge? He put the print close to his ear but could hear nothing. Then the clouds came in and obscured the memory. The large woman faded first, then her male companion. The pain from the sunburn subsided and John was aware once more of Mick ranting at his side. Aware too that he had wandered into a stream of dubious-looking water gushing from another outlet pipe and making a slurry mess of the sand. Mick was cursing, mincing on tiptoe as he edged his way across the flow. 'For fuck's sake,' he said, 'as if life's no bad enough.' He glanced up and pointed towards the Mecca amusement arcade. 'Look, son, the promised land, an oasis of light and hope.'

John followed in Mick's wake as he swept into the arcade, pushing both swing doors simultaneously as if he were an emperor paying a surprise visit to his errant people. He glanced at the significant list of prohibitions in the foyer, NO FISH AND CHIPS NO DOGS NO SKATEBOARDS. 'Fascist bastards!' He grasped the loaded shove ha'penny machine between outspread arms and, summoning strength well beyond his frame, shook it. The precariously balanced avalanche of ten pence coins proved remarkably resistant. 'Glued thegether,' he pronounced, transferring his interest to a cage crammed with smiling toy kangaroos beneath an industrial-sized grabber. 'And they say I suffer from psychotic episodes.'

John was disconcerted by the barrage of neon, invitations to kill the freak, make a fortune, and test his strength in a booth dominated by a smiling Mohammed Ali. A nightmare ceramic toddler was suspended by a wire from an air balloon next to several garish full-sized horses frozen in mid prance.

'It's a trial,' said the Tempter. *'Keep your wits and you will find him.'*

'Join the losers!' said the Bastard, obliging John to look at the other punters, all of whom were clad in identical beige raincoats. Each was patiently feeding the residue of their benefits payment into lucky slots while the proprietor lorded it in his own perspex cage fortified by towers of two-penny coins.

He was tugged by another memory which he knew was going to be unpleasant once it materialised but he lacked the strength to let it go, whatever form it was about to assume. It already held him in its thrall. His mounting anxiety centred on one of the male figures hunched over a slot machine.

'It's him,' said the Tempter. *'By his deeds will you know him.'* Something was not right. John knew it wasn't his brother. It was someone else. Unable to stop himself, he reached out and touched the man on the shoulder. The unkempt man in his sixties turned and stared. His lip curled as he appraised the stranger at his back. He muttered something and returned to his game. John felt diminished.

'Well now,' said the Bastard. *'Interesting or what? Let me think. Could it be the Superintendent? Could it be your father? Now there's a thought. Some nightmare figure from your past. Someone who rightly despised you for the runt that you were.'*

'Amusement arcades,' said the Academic loudly, determined to distract John and rescue him from the dark place that had momentarily claimed him, *'developed out of penny arcades from the nineteenth century. Initially popular were the bagatelle machines which combined elements of billiards with modern pinball. Of course the Victorians were attracted to What the Butler Saw, not to mention the unfortunately named Pussy Shooter.'*

'Your sort of game, I would have thought, seems perfect for a sexual deviant with a fear of women and unresolved anger issues,' quipped the Bastard.

'Survive the trial, and you will find HIM,' persisted the Tempter.

'My favourite is the Cochon Electriser developed in France in 1898 which administered electric shocks. You turn the handle on the pig's belly and receive a shock. If you can withstand the maximum charge the pig's eyes light up.'

'Now that's familiar, isn't it, John. A bit like the Royal Edinburgh. Did your eyes light up last time? Did they?'

John grabbed his head with both hands.

'You can't squeeze us out, John.'

He blundered his way back through the double doors, into the fresh air and the dying light where a square woman in a headscarf was scattering bread for the gulls. He concentrated hard on their demonic squawking hoping to drown out the Voices. To an extent he succeeded as his protagonists' banter merged into white noise somewhere in the back of his brain. The woman looked at him oddly. A moment later Mick emerged from the arcade propelled by the proprietor's boot. As he regained his balance he swung his leg at the gulls scattering them. 'Wee scavenging bastards!' he shouted. 'And you, you old witch, get to ... '

Mick waited until the muttering woman had waddled off and the gulls had flown to forage elsewhere before stooping to pick up the abandoned crusts.

'Good bread, wasted on they birds,' he ventured before stuffing his mouth with his recycled spoils like a hamster preparing to hibernate. 'You want some?' John shook his head.

'Eat when you can, my son. An army marches on its stomach.' The two men walked along the promenade in an ostensibly companionable silence that masked their radically different internal worlds.

THIRTY-NINE

Unable to sleep, Johannes disentangled his limbs for those of his companions. The ship seemed to creak even louder in the dark as his head rubbed against a beam in a rhythm dictated by the swell. The snoring from the rest of the crew brought to mind his neighbour's pigs foraging hard against the wattle fence that enclosed his own ground. Antonia, convinced that the beasts were eating her cabbages, had insisted that he build the fence. Johannes tried in vain to explain that he had on several occasions chased Klaas the simpleton off the patch, his arms loaded with vegetables. No, it was the pigs. Michel had sided with his father but had been slapped for his pains.

Johannes stretched and moved his head from side to side. 'Soon, my son. Soon.'

One of the waterguezen was in the grip of a nightmare. The man alternately simpered, shouted and then spoke incomprehensibly in the voice of a small child. Someone else complained and threw a drinking vessel in his direction but it missed its target, clattering against the hull. The sleeper continued to act out all parts in his internal mummers' play, now the angel, now the ogre.

Treading as carefully as he could over the sleeping bodies Johannes made slow progress towards the single shaft of moonlight that illuminated the ladder leading to the hatch. One of the sleepers touched his leg as if coaxing a reluctant lover back into bed.

On the deck, Johannes gasped with the shock of cold air and the bilious sensation of the stars rising and dipping under the horizon as the ship rode the waves, the silhouette of the motionless watchman on the prow. A single cloud slit the moon for an instant, a mercenary's knife dragged silently across a white face.

When he was a child, his own father had taught him to recognise the stars. He told him how the hunter's bow always pointed towards the mortally wounded swan diving head first through the firmament, and how the twins could never be separated despite the best efforts of the jealous gods. The dancers too had been thrust into perpetual exile for violating the Sabbath while the bootmaker's last tumbled towards the earth. Despite years of trying Johannes had never been able to locate the corners of the weaver's loom that his father swore fixed the edges of the sky and stopped it crashing to earth. The explanation was always the same, only the most favoured of Guild members were allowed to see God's own loom.

Eager to exorcise the sleep from his limbs, Johannes worked his way towards the fo'c'sle by holding onto the rope strung the length of the deck, his stomach lurching in time with the swell which seemed to be growing stronger.

When the plague visited his village during his parents' time most of the young men fled to the coast to find work on the fishing boats laden with their silver hauls of elvers and mackerel. Johannes chose to stay and face the skeletal reaper culling the hearts out of home and family. He was less disturbed by the nocturnal psalm of widows' cries than the siren calls of the deep ocean. The notion propagated by the parish priest that Christ was a fisher of men provoked a nightmare of dripping bodies hooked through the lip being hauled ashore by a statue with a bleeding heart. He was tasting some of that fear again as the vessel plummeted ever deeper into dark troughs.

Candlelight danced on the planks beneath the partially open fo'c'sle door. Johannes approached and peered through the gap. The three semi-naked nuns stirred uneasily on a red bed of plundered rugs. The Leader, his back to the door, ran his hands through a tumbling cascade of amber beads, kissing with the ardour of a penitent.

Johannes backed away.

The ship woke with the dawn. Several crew members bedraggled by sleep and discomfort emerged from the hatch and went to their allotted stations. Eventually Balthasar and Cornelius appeared and greeted their companion. 'I hate the sea,' mumbled Cornelius, stretching his arms above his head before bringing them down and wrapping them round his sides. 'It's as cold as the devil's arse.'

'You would think the devil's arse would be roasting,' said Balthasar, gazing across the expanse of sea visible when the ship was borne upwards on a crest.

'It can't be far to Utrecht,' said Johannes. 'Dry land and wages to buy bread. God willing we will find Michel.'

Their musings were interrupted by a voice from above. Looking up they saw a geuzen shouting angrily at them from a tiny platform halfway up the main mast.

'You lazy Dutch turds! Get up here now, cowardly pig shaggers!' His gestures left them in no doubt that he expected them to join him on his elevated perch. Sighing, Cornelius took the lead and started the ascent. The hempen ladder swung violently until he was facing the opposite direction, meanwhile the twisted grip dug deep into his palms.

Balthasar steadied the ladder and started to climb. By the

time Johannes joined them they were being buffeted by a malevolent wind, determined to hurl them back onto the deck. Eventually they joined their taskmaster on his platform when his pustulated face identified him as their earlier guide to life below deck. All three stood shaking, their arms intertwined round the mast. With the dexterity of a small goat, their tormentor lowered himself onto the spar that ran from the platform and with his legs dangling, pulled himself towards the tip that rose and dipped. By violently jerking his neck and cursing he made clear that he expected his reluctant apprentices to follow.

Johannes glanced down at the distant sea and felt a terror he had not experienced since he realised that the Spanish had abducted his son but, from somewhere, found a strength that made a mockery of his position. Emboldened by whatever power had taken control of his limbs, he led the way and moved arm over arm towards the carbuncled smirking sailor wallowing in his power. Cornelius and Balthasar followed.

Their task was to release the sail furled beneath the spar. Cornelius kicked out, only to snag the canvas on Balthasar's legs. The older man felt his strength draining as he thrashed like a drowning man. In an instant the sail was free and swelling, harvesting the wind. Feeling the sail bucking and billowing beneath them the men shared a frisson of pleasure.

Back on deck and distinctly unsteady on their legs the companions rested against a cannon that alternately had the sky and the sea in its sights as the ship soared and plunged.

'We should be in Rotterdam by now,' said Cornelius, looking anxiously at the dipping horizon. His comment had been overheard by Ulriche who had been standing motionless, his beak-like nose pointing into the wind. For no apparent reason he turned and faced the opposite direction. The gesture disconcerted Cornelius, who interpreted it as confirmation of his growing suspicion that they were travelling westwards.

Balthasar got the attention of a sailor struggling under the weight of an enormous barrel balanced on one shoulder. 'Where are we headed?' he asked.

'England,' replied the man without breaking his stride. Before he could reply the ship was seized by a wall of water and pitched towards the sky. The men were torn from the cannon and thrown like inn skittles in the direction of the fo'c'sle, where they landed on top of each other. The vessel continued to climb, prow foremost, clawing its way up the side of the wave. There was no horizon, just rushing water. They were soon joined by the barrel that travelled towards them as if catapulted by a siege engine, hurling itself against the now closed door where it disintegrated in a flurry of staves and thick black liquid. The terrified screams of the nuns echoed the screech of the gale and, for a moment, all motion ceased as the ship balanced on the crest, a tiny wren held motionless on a zephyr. Then the plummeting descent: the wooden bones, sinews and knuckles of the ship snapped and creaked and men were thrown back along the deck along with ropes, sails and the contents of a tool chest torn from its moorings.

FORTY

Chris Evans filled the dining room with false jollity. The jingles, catch phrases, bantering weather forecasters and surreal titbits of tabloid news provided the aural wallpaper as the residents trooped in. Out of habit John took his seat close to the fireplace. He felt distinctively queasy and had no appetite. Mick pulled his beanie even further down over his eyes, as if restricting his own field of vision would somehow make him less visible to others; a known toddlers' trick.

'The conquering hero returns,' shouted Kevin as half of Dennis' face appeared round the dining room door.

'The spectre at the feast,' contributed Mick.' The half face instantly disappeared.

'Come on, boys,' said Derek. 'It's hard enough for Dennis without you all staring.'

'Come and sit here, Dennis,' said Jack.

'That's my seat!' shouted Paul, barely looking up from his book as he entered. 'My seat.' He swept in and sat down with the pouting petulance of a teenager. Muttering to himself, he spooned sufficient sugar into his cup to displace any residual liquid and then stared intently at page 127, paragraph three, of *Nostromo*.

Dennis returned to his room.

'Any sign of that brother of yours?' Kevin wheedled.' What with that postcard and all.'

John shook his head.

'Just missed him,' said Mick. 'Close mind, we were on his tail but they kept him moving, yon arcade at Porti's in the hands of the tartan mafia. Masons ken, capitalist bastards taking the pennies from poor folk. John's brother had no chance in there. They moved him on, probably rotting in some jail with Jihadi suspects. Guantanamo Bay most like. Orange jump suits. He's been tangoed, mark my words.'

John stared at him blankly.

'*Home sweet home*,' said the Bastard, the first Voice of the day. Most days John was woken by the Voices, invariably bored by the hours wasted while he slept, eager to re-engage, chatter and bitch among themselves. He had long since abandoned the hope that one day he would wake and discover that all of his unwanted house guests had packed and gone and his thoughts were his own. Luxuriating in the silence, he would wander round the house plumping up cushions and collecting the half empty wine glasses abandoned by the virtual lodgers who had left in a hurry. There would be no one waiting to criticise, make fun or pontificate.

'*Bad times, eh, John?*' said the Bastard who had been listening all the while. John knew his tone of sympathetic complicity did not auger well, and he was on guard. '*Better now, isn't it, enjoying a breakfast surrounded by some of the least functional human beings on the planet. Cornflakes with the truly flaky, toast with the toxically mad ... eggs made from scrambled brains ...* '

Before he could get into his stride an alarm sounded, Beverley's door opened and she ran up the stairs where Derek was shouting for help. All of the residents poured out of the dining room except Paul who looked up unconcerned before sipping his tea and committing another paragraph to memory. Several cups spilled onto the tablecloth. The door to Dennis' room was open. Dennis was hanging from the ceiling with Derek draped round his legs.

'He's still alive,' said Derek, straining to take the weight off the light cord. Linda the cook, who had conveniently joined the rush upstairs holding a kitchen knife, pushed her way though and climbed onto the chair that Beverley had placed alongside Derek. Linda swore under her breath and hacked at the cord until the last fibres gave way. Derek fell backwards underneath Dennis' body to the stained carpet where they lay like lovers whose exertions had exhausted them. As if horrified by what it was witnessing, Dennis' budgie squawked hysterically from its cage on the mantelpiece. Kevin flicked his middle finger in its general direction.

The residents were silent apart from Mick who muttered something about enemies of the people hiding in the room. Surprisingly, Kevin was lost for anything cruel to say. Paul, who had finally abandoned *Nostromo,* was visibly distressed.

John moved into the room, knelt down and touched Dennis' legs with a gesture of inexpressible tenderness.

'As if you care!' said the Bastard.' *There but for fortune ... Dennis was a useless cretin anyway ...* '

Shut up! Shut up! I'm telling the story and do not need your poisoned observations.

John untied Dennis' shoes, pulled them gently from his feet and laid them side-by-side.

Derek moved Dennis into the recovery position, talking to him all the while, 'Come on Dennis, come on Dennis.'

'*Why is it that the recovery and the foetal position are similar?*' mused the Academic.

The noise emanating from Dennis' throat proved not to be a death rattle despite Kevin's enthusiastic interpretation of the sound. He gradually recovered and tried to sit up. John helped him into a more upright position and left his hand on his shoulder while Beverley fled downstairs to phone for an ambulance.

John walked back to his room, climbed fully clothed into bed and pulled the covers over his head. Any residual interest in the day had been dissipated. Despite only just having risen he wanted to sleep again. As he reinhaled his own warm breath he kept seeing Dennis' bulging, terrified eyes. It was only a matter of days since he too had literally stood on the edge, on the bridge at the foot of Great Junction Street, only to fall into the arms of a large Dutchman.

FORTY-ONE

Several of the crew had been hit by flying cargo and lay injured on the deck. Part of the foremast had snapped and lay like a felled tree in a tangle of sail and rope. The Leader eventually emerged from his lair and moved among the men, administering strong drink and words of encouragement. Eventually, most recovered sufficiently to stagger back to their posts. The swell had abated but was still sufficiently strong to make the three weavers retch over the side.

'This may be God's will,' said Balthasar, wiping his mouth with his sleeve, 'but I think the devil got the upper hand there. I saw him sitting, black and naked, on the top of that wave, grinning at us.'

'Why are we going to England?' asked Johannes, ignoring the possibility that his companion had actually seen the Prince of Darkness. 'Michel is still in the land of his birth. He has not been taken over the sea.'

Cornelius patted Johannes' arm. 'Soon we will find him. The geuzen take their plunder to England, when merchants flock to the coast and haggle over riches stolen from monasteries. They need food and water as well.' He glanced back along the deck where the water barrels had been tethered;

only one seemed intact. He drew his companion's attention to something happening on the opposite gunnel.

The Leader was giving orders to four crewmen who were lifting a weight onto the side of the ship; two trailing arms identified it as a body. The extent of their struggle suggested the body was that of the fat sailor who spent most of his time skulking near the cannons. Curious and concerned, they crossed the deck and leaned over the edge in time to see the huge corpse hit the boiling sea. For a moment his outstretched arm was visible in what might have been a final salute, a gesture of defiance or a terrified signal for help before he sank beneath the waves. The Leader shrugged and directed the men to remove the broken spar that had felled him.

The companions too were deployed clearing the decks and carrying out simple repairs. Soon bored with hurling splintered staves and shutters overboard Balthasar moved to the foot of the main mast where the deck was piled high with rigging and seaweed. He beckoned the others to join him. Because of their life's work they instinctively understood the nature of the challenge and set to disentangle the mesh of rope swamping the ship. The Leader, noticing that they had given up on their allotted tasks, moved towards them angrily.

'Do what you were told!' he shouted, grabbing Johannes. He paused. 'Weavers ... ' he said, looking with a dawning admiration at the dexterity of the men whose fingers moved to a pattern that was collectively understood. Without another word he left them, strode along the deck and ducked into the fo'c'sle, presumably to console the naked nuns and find a way to distract them from their prayers to Our Lady of the Sea.

The men smiled as they once more enjoyed the pleasure of working together on a shared task. Cornelius started singing under his breath, the tune that one of them would always start in the past when the work was going well and the looms had settled into their own rhythm.

Johannes disentangled a small fish from the ropes. 'Here you are, Antonia,' he said under his breath, 'supper, and give some to the boy.'

Cornelius took the fish and turned it over in the palm of his hand, running a finger along its scales. 'One moment in the depths of the sea, the next flying through the sky like a bird.'

'Lucky not to have been eaten by the devil,' said Johannes, glancing slyly at Balthasar.

'Devils don't eat fish on Fridays,' said Balthasar, enjoying the jest at his own expense.

Feeling the need to stretch his legs and relieve himself Cornelius moved away from the others and along to the small gate that opened onto the sea. He undid his breeches and altered his stance as he realised that he was pissing into the wind. Not for the first time, he thought. On his way back he looked into the only barrel that had survived the storm, and saw several apples lying on the bottom. Intending to take one for himself, and one for each of his companions, he leaned into the barrel but couldn't quite reach the fruit. He readjusted his weight on the edge, pivoted briefly and then lowered himself head first into the musky interior.

'Top him before we see the white cliffs,' said a voice that Cornelius recognised as belonging to the carbuncled sailor.

'Hit him over the head with an empty bailer.'

Jester, I've warned you before! You spoil everything.

'This is fascinating. Jim Hawkins in the apple barrel on the Hispaniola *listened to talk of mutiny. Of course there is a fine line between* homage à Stevenson, *pastiche, parody and plagiarism ... '*

'It's all shite if you ask me ... '

No one is asking you, Bastard. There is a story to be told. Back off!

The men were arguing among themselves.

'Throw him overboard with his fornicating nuns.'

'Leave the nuns. The crew will want their new loyalty rewarded.'

'I could do with a good nun now ... but I'm still poxed from that Amsterdam whorehouse.'

'Stick his head down a cannon and roger him with the powder lance.'

'Hang his arse from the nest and let the gulls peck his eyes out.'

'Drag him under the boat, let the barnacles shave his face.'

The men's spirits picked up as they concocted incrementally more lugubrious punishments for the Leader. Eventually they hauled themselves back to their feet, spat in the barrel and wandered off to resume whatever duties they had temporarily abandoned. Cornelius waited until he could hear them no more, stuffed the remaining apples into his jerkin, wiped the spittle from his face and climbed out of his hiding place.

His companions were pleased to see him return. 'Thought you'd been tempted into the deep by one of those sirens,' said Johannes.

'Or were shagging a mermaid,' contributed Balthasar. 'Slippery creatures, mermaids.'

'What would Geertje say if I went home with a mermaid?'

'She could get a little one in the pot, invite the village round. Use her scales for pearls.'

'Anyway you'd stink of fish,' said Balthasar, between bites of his apple.

Grinning, the men applied themselves once more to untangling the ropes. It was Cornelius who was the first to notice Ulriche standing stock-still and pointing towards the sea.

FORTY-TWO

A distant freight train rumbled somewhere in the distance. Normally the sound comforted John. As a child during the time of his incarceration he would hide under the false security of the blankets and listen to a faraway locomotive struggling over the moor. He associated the sound with escape, the possibility of travelling far away from his then life. He would project himself into the cab, having befriended the driver who, in contravention of all railway protocol, had helped him aboard. The few illuminated metres of track quickly converged to an apex that was sucked inexorably into the night as the train hurtled into unknown lands.

At other times like his hero Jan from Ian Serraillier's *The Silver Sword,* he would position himself under a goods wagon between the screaming axles, frozen rigid, a human icicle destined to thaw in a better place. Tonight the sound of the distant train offered no respite or comfort. In any case it had gone now; all he could hear was the blood coursing through his temples.

He leaned out of bed fumbling for the light switch. As he stretched, his cheek came to rest on the bedside table inches away from the *Good News Bible*. It hadn't been there before.

Some Holy Joe must have sneaked into his unlocked room. It was in ugly leather binding with the texture of old skin. He had no time for either Testament. The Bible featured as an intrusive prop in the dimly remembered tableau of abuse and misery that sometimes played in his head, a symbol of power, chastisement and spurious justification for a raft of sins. As he fingered the silver-painted edge he knew what was coming.

'Ah, the, Bible, John ... Well now, what a discovery!' The Bastard slapped his own head as the enormity of the connection dawned on him. *'You ARE Bible John. You murdered those women in Glasgow, didn't you?*

John was stunned, completely unprepared for this new line of attack. If he lay there and waited patiently perhaps one of the other less malignant Voices would intervene or at least distract the Bastard. Where were they?

'Followed them home from the bingo, lured them up an alley, all the while savouring the delicious smell of perfume and fear. The twist of the knife, their final breath, a prolonged letting go, a surrender, tainted with peppermint to hide the fags.'

Where were the other Voices?

'An impressive lineage, Jack of course, the Master, then Neilson, Myra Hindley, Fred West, and now, you!'

'Could be a sign ... ' Rarely had the Tempter put in a more welcome appearance. *'You know, things written in the Bible and all that. What do you think? Worth a try?'*

Powerless to resist, although he did so with a sinking heart, John half sat up in bed and, opening the Bible at random, stabbed his finger at a page.

'And they said everyone to his fellow. Come, let us cast lots, that we may know for whose cause this evil is upon us. So they cast lots, and the lot fell on Jonah.'

'Oh well,' said the Tempter.

'Told you, told you!' screeched the Bastard. *'Evil, pure evil!'*

'A classic oxymoron,' chipped in the Academic, who was

not normally available for comment during the night.

'Keep reading, keep reading, there's still a chance,' prompted the Tempter.

'So they took up Jonah, and cast him forth into the sea: and the sea ceased from her raging.

'Then the men feared the Lord exceedingly, and offered a sacrifice unto the Lord, and made vows.

'Now the Lord had prepared a great fish to swallow up Jonah. And Jonah was in the belly of the fish three days and three nights.'

'Count your blessings, you could be eaten by a bloody great whale,' smirked the Bastard triumphantly. *'Yes, life's looking up isn't it, John?'*

'Hang on a minute,' interrupted the Academic, gradually warming to the topic in hand. *'Herman Melville quotes Bishop Jebb who suggested that Jonah merely lodged temporarily in some part of the whale's mouth which, if I remember correctly, he said was big enough to accommodate a couple of whist tables. He also cites a German exegetic who believed that Jonah must have taken refuge in the floating body of a dead whale just as the French soldiers during the Russian campaign turned their dead horses into tents.'*

'A bit like living here,' commented the Jester.

For some reason the Voices started mumbling and then faded altogether, leaving John alone. He switched off the light, turned to face the opposite wall and tried to sleep, considering the implications of living in a whale's belly. At least it would be warm and he might feel safely cocooned. There might be something exhilarating about the motion of the whale as it dived through the raging sea. A child on his first roller coaster, aware of his stomach and unusual physical sensations for the first time, something akin to a prematurely early sexual wakening at the hands of the Commandant. The whale's belly became a prison with hot, pulsating walls. It was pitch dark and stank of rottenness.

FORTY-THREE

The sea assumed a brown hue that for Johannes evoked the ploughed fields of home with seagulls a feature of both. Because of the unusual light they seemed whiter than usual as they flew towards each other, banking away at the last moment. As Johannes leaned over the wooden rail a large gull came within an arm's length and by flying into the wind moved in exact harmony with the ship.

He had never believed in angels, even in the old days when they poked their wings into every aspect of Church business. Cast in stone and clinging to the pulpit, hanging round the edges of every painted crucifixion, fawning on saints, consoling martyrs pierced by thorns. He had jested to Antonia just before Michel's birth that he would not welcome any holier-than-thou Gabriel turning up with an announcement. She had tutted and crossed herself at his blasphemy. Johannes had always far preferred the imps and swollen-headed trolls who danced attendance on Beelzebub.

He felt that by reaching out he could grab the angel bird, hang onto its talons and be flown to wherever Michel was being held. Like Icarus, in a way, he wanted to fly close to his son before being consumed by his love for him. Was he in service, servitude or slavery? Had he resisted his persecutors who stripped the clothes off his back and beaten him until he bled? Had he escaped only to sleep in rodent-ridden hedgerows, a prey to every passing beak-faced beggar, avaricious mountebank and snivelling charlatan?

As Cornelius stared at the brown sea he tried to work out which combinations of dyes would best capture the exact colour of the waves. Ochre for certain, a pinch of sulphur, and if he could lay his hands on them perhaps sea urchin hearts and cuttle fish. He would make a secret batch and then surprise Geertje with the sheer beauty of the coat he would weave for her. She would be grateful, put her finger to her lips and lead him to the alcove opposite the glowing stove ... He sighed, dredged the phlegm from the back of his throat and blew it into the sea.

Balthasar drew the attention of the others to the fact that they were no longer alone. A small flotilla of similar ships was slowly materialising from the heaving waves. As one craft disappeared into a brown trough another was thrown upwards to straddle the adjacent crest. Several of the crew emerged from below decks to point excitedly, waving exaggeratedly as if unfurling sluggish flags for the benefit of acquaintances on the new ships.

'Victory for the village of Zutphen!' shouted one of the geuzen though cupped hands into the wind.

'The wives of Zutphen are whores and sluts!' came the muffled reply.

Some made to drink out of imaginary tankards while the carbuncled one gripped his breeches and made bucking, taunting gestures signifying his carnal intent once ashore. Balthasar shook his head, pitying whatever Dover wife would soon find herself press-ganged into unwanted close proximity with the suppurating face.

It was Johannes who was the first to notice the whale, a hill of glistening flesh rising from the spume. Water spouted into the air from the front of the beast, shot upwards as if escaping from a rathole in a dyke. At its zenith the spout slowed and opened into petals that fell heavily back into the sea.

By now the others had noticed, and panic spread among the crew. Sailors collided with each other as they ran away from the monster, bigger than the ship, contentedly flicking its tail in their direction. One of the nuns emerged from her captivity and rushed to see what the commotion was before fleeing, screaming back into the sanctuary of the fo'c'sle. She was knocked out of the way by the Leader who was pulling the buckle tight on his belt. 'The barrel!' he shouted. Eventually several of his crew moved towards the empty barrel into which Balthasar had fallen earlier. Groaning and cursing they wheeled it towards the edge then hoisted it over into the sea where it bobbed towards the monster.

'Well blow me down with a feather!' said the Academic.

'Particularly nasty weather ... ' retorted the Jester.

I'll knock you both down with a stick if you interrupt like that again. Apart from anything else you gave me a terrible fright and I've lost the thread of what I was trying to say. This is a moment of some tension if I say it myself.

'But don't you see? We have changed pictures again. This is word for word, you know what I mean, taken from The Storm at Sea *which is also in the Kunsthistorisches museum in Vienna. Brueghel shows how sailors toss a barrel over the edge to placate or otherwise distract the whale that is following them. In 1921 M.J. Friedlander suggested that the artist may have been illustrating a proverb. This notion was subsequently confirmed by L. Burchard who wrote "Fleeing ship, whale and barrel are the three elements which together form an emblem that can be interpreted from the following passage in Zedler's Universal-Lexikon*: If the whale plays with a barrel that has been thrown at him and gives the ship time to escape, then

he represents the man who misses his true good for the sake of futile trifles."'

This has nothing to do with the narrative. You are only concerned with flaunting your own erudition. What you say is of no interest to anyone. Sometimes I think you are worse than the Bastard.

'Leave me out of this. I haven't said a thing. There's actually no need. It is all utterly pointless, hopelessly episodic, lacking structure or interest. In fact, bollocks!'

Eventually, curiosity proved stronger than cowardice, and the crew reappeared in time to see the leviathan flick the barrel into the air with its tail before diving under the ship to the hurrahs and cheers of the geuzen.

The flotilla of small ships which moments earlier had filled the entire horizon on the port side had been smudged out by the stealthily advancing mist.

The Leader started issuing orders with an earnestness that suggested that there were other dangers more substantial to be faced. The weavers were despatched below decks to bring drinking water for the crew. Unwilling to lose face by asking where the water was stored Balthasar led the way into the dark maze of small rooms. A rat scuttled over his foot and skittered into the bowels of the ship. By leaning in and feeling the contents of the first chamber they realised it housed the weapons and powder. Balthasar felt the blade of an axe hanging at waist level. Next to it were ranged cutlasses, rapiers, dirks, muskets and a heap of powder horns nestling like a pyre of small animals.

The musky smell of the next chamber betrayed the presence of the ship's provisions. As their eyesight adjusted to the darkness they could make out silhouettes that were either hanging sides of salt beef or exhausted torture victims. Cornelius picked up the flat carcass of a dried fish, put it to his nose and threw it down again in disgust. 'Mother of God!'

They soon located a rack of stoneware flagons, but removing the corks revealed the contents to be vinegar. Sniffing the acrid vapour Balthasar saw the image painted on the old church wall of the soldiers offering vinegar to Christ on Gethsemane. He had always thought that must have been one insult too many, the final spite that made him cry out to his Father in despair.

FORTY-FOUR: Blindman's Tale

Mick visibly paled as he moved his hat away from his eyes to better read the price on Tesco's finest two-litre bottle of cider. 'Robbing bastards! I really enjoy your scintillating banter. Can't get a word in once you start ... yak, yak ... like some old wifey. Pass us yon bottle of Domestos. The lavvy on the stair's humming. Some clarty bugger doesn't bother. I think it's Jack. No house trained. Cleans round the bend. That'll be for us then. Round the effing bend.'

The next small room was piled to the low ceiling with sacks of cheese and biscuits. Beneath the overwhelming stench, subtler memories could be sniffed; for Balthasar it was the slippery cheese wrapped with bread in the chequered cloth that lay in the shade of the bushes at the edge of the field. For two weeks each summer weavers, bakers and tinkers became harvesters. Lying on the stubble at midday was an art but once positioned correctly the sharp stubs of corn could massage the muscles along the spine. Eating on your back was also an art as the sweat would run into eyes already painful from squinting at the sun.

For Johannes it recalled the shard of disappointment he felt when Michel at the age of four first wrinkled his nose at the cheese on his plate. 'It smells like sick,' he protested, pushing the plate aside before feeling the weight of his father's hand. Thinking back now he realised what his son had meant.

For Cornelius it evoked early bachelor years spent consuming prodigious amounts of weebled cheese, sluiced down with equally startling quantities of beer, both of which were a necessary precursor to bouts of bare knuckle fighting in the inn yard.

The ship rocked as the whale passed underneath. After steadying themselves the three men covered their noses and passed onto the final compartment where the water was stored. After a brief discussion the men repositioned themselves along the dark constricted passageway and passed the flagons from one to the other and then into the unknown hand dangling through the hatch. The rhythm was familiar from scooping mud out of flooded ditches in winter, and flailing the vegetation that threatened to overwhelm their cottages during the late summer months. Eventually the Leader shouted for them to stop.

'Let's rest awhile,' said Cornelius, whose head ached. In full agreement Johannes and Balthasar moved towards him. Cornelius meanwhile was feeling in the dark for the next doorway. When his hands eventually flapped into a void he moved carefully into the space which, he suggested, might be the sail store. They followed him into the chamber and made themselves comfortable on rolled bails of rough textured canvass.

After a shared exhalation of breath they heard an unearthly high-pitched singing. Staring into the dark they realised that someone was coming along the narrow passage.

'It's Blindman,' said Balthasar, who had noticed earlier that the sightless crewman would often stand stock still and emit a whine, as if incanting a psalm in a foreign tongue or lisping angrily at a demon.

'Weavers, you are shirking?' he wheedled. 'You have a choice; you can be broken at sea, or broken on the land. Though blind to the things seen by ordinary men, I hold the sights that no one else could bear. I am the custodian of all wickedness. I have toiled for the Grand Inquisitor, I have burst eyes from their sockets at his behest, I have snapped the heads from children.'

'In the holy name of Christ!' shouted Cornelius, moving to within inches of Blindman's face. 'Get out of here! Take your poison elsewhere.'

Blindman hummed, as if listening intently to orders from another place.

Johannes grabbed his arm and attempted to force him back along the passage. Blindman stood firm.

'If you meddle with me then you will hear nothing of your son. You will not see Michel again.' He rocked on his heels and resumed his unearthly keening.' Johannes stepped away shocked, unable to absorb what he had heard.

'Tell me, tell me,' he said quietly, all the anger in his voice doused, replaced by a pleading desperation. 'What do you know?'

'I'll pluck your vile tongue from your head if you say another word!' said Cornelius.

Johannes held him back. 'Let him speak' he said.

For what seemed like a long time Blindman's humming was accompanied by the sound of the ship stretching its wooden bones in response to the swell.

Blindman nodded sharply. 'Very well. My mother was a soldier's whore. She followed the camp through Dettingham and Veirholm; raped and enslaved she hoisted her linen for farthings, fucked for bread and favours. She squatted and squeezed me from her womb over a ditch by the road and held me under the fetid water before limping back to join the troops. My young skull burst from the water screaming for the breast and the sweet milk of revenge until the rats fled from the ditch, unable to stand the noise. A passing witch, whose own child had been stolen before her aborted drowning, heard my cries. Thrusting her arms into the slime, she pulled me into the world for a second time. After spitting on her 'kerchief, she wiped the blood and mud from my face and was smitten. Such a beautiful child. Soon I was melting hearts as she tugged at the coats of strangers begging for money. "For the child, not you," said the gentry.

'As I grew she tired of me. No longer a beautiful baby, no longer a changeling infant left by an angel who would melt indifferent hearts and loosen purse strings. Just an urchin like many, many more. One night she soaked my bread with laudanum, forced it into my mouth and held my jaws until I choked. Her lover roped me across his horse. Long we rode into the bleak night before he untied me, kicked my arse and left me in the fields. Like a dog I howled at the moon and drank at the pond, and saw a face smiling at me from the depths of the water. Behind the face the demons danced. I was the Chosen One, I would wreak havoc on the earth. I was the emissary of God himself. That night I suckled on cattle that gave their teats willingly to one such as I.

'On rising, I stole a poacher's pelts from a drying pole and tied them like a lady's shawl, prancing and preening across frozen earth that was all mine, beneath the sun that I owned. After stealing from a sleeping tinker, catching and selling birds from hedgerows, and robbing other children of their fancy toys I made my entry into Antwerp. My city. My time.'

'Where's Michel?' shouted Johannes in exasperation.

Unhappy at having his story interrupted Blindman became silent. Through the criss-crossed shafts of light leaking from knotholes in the timber, the weavers saw that Blindman was once again completely still.

'Tell us in your own time,' pleaded Balthasar, aware that the strange figure might abandon his tale if they annoyed him. He did know things. He just might know something about Michel.

'Strange times for a boy. A score of naked Anabaptists were running through the street beating their chests and shouting about the Lord. In pursuit were the guards competing to see who would be the first to plant his pike in a holy man's hairy arse.' Blindman paused and chuckled. 'I knew then where to go.

'The fat parish priest looked both ways up the street to see if I was a stooge but then let me in to his house. I was his boy, and his alone. I was to be his companion and plaything.

'As I grew to be tall and strong for my age things changed. I became his master and he became my dog, but he needed me to protect him from the Lutherans who wanted to string up his carcass that it might be eaten by beasts. Happy to oblige, I broke the neck of a preacher who made the mistake of knocking at the door and left his body for all to see. Word must have travelled. During the night an emissary rattled his golden-headed cane against the window and said I now worked in the employ of his most Gracious Lordship.' He chuckled again.

'And so it came to pass. With my talents I soon rose to be high executioner and torturer to the Inquisition. I knew tricks. I could make grown men weep, but I also had compassion. Even apostates deserve a say in the manner of their death. Henceforth their choice was either beheading or being burned alive. Much simpler. In any case the soldiers had long complained at having to plunder faggots from farmyards, and uproot trees to make their pyres. It was a hard, messy business driving the stakes into the frozen ground and tying up stupid folk who pled and wept for their unfinished lives, their fat-faced children and their soon-to-be-grieving spouses. As an act of kindness, some said weakness, I insisted that strong liquor be dispensed to the souls while they waited strapped to the stake, their mouths puckering up like small birds craving the liquid that would make the pain easier to bear, but it didn't of course. One, perhaps two mouthfuls, and then feed the rest to the young hungry flames licking at their taut calves. The stink of burning leather, damp cloth – they always wet themselves you see – and flesh was never pleasant. So beheading was my decree. That was more of a sport. The soldiers kept a tally of heads separated from bodies. One or two kept the scalps and used them as 'kerchiefs.'

The weavers shrank closer to each other as Blindman paused a second time.

'Nothing lasts. One night when the moon, for shame, would not show its face the rebels poisoned the dogs and slit the throats of Alva's honest men. Unable to sleep, I had earlier fled along the byway taking only a beggar's coat and stave.

'After travelling for two nights and a day Christ himself found me and smote me to the ground in his righteous anger. The pain from my burning eye sockets taught me that God in his infinite wisdom had struck me blind. Praised be His name, and from my darkness he gave me new sight – I could see into the souls of men, I could foresee events as yet undisclosed. I knew when this man would die, when that woman would give birth. In villages they feted me as the prophet, as the soothsayer whose arrival had long been foretold. I placed my hands on the heads of children and wished them long lives. I blessed the young corn in the fields that it might grow and bring riches. I denounced the thief in their midst and shamed the adulterer wallowing in his mess.

'Soon my prowess, my inestimable gifts, came to the attention of William's men and I threw in my lot with this honourable crew of sea beggars whom I serve with the gifts of prophesy and foreboding in equal measure.'

He threw back his head and howled with unbridled raucous laughter that echoed round the confined space below decks.

'Where is Michel?' asked Johannes, with mixed anger and despair.

The laughter stopped instantly. 'Leyden,' replied Blindman, turning on his heel and shuffling off along the dark corridor. Johannes made to pursue him but was held back by Balthasar.

'Let him go,' he said. 'The foul creature will not say more.'

'A blow to the throat might change his mind,' suggested Cornelius.

'No,' said Johannes. 'You are right. Let him go. Michel is in Leyden. We will find him.'

In desperate need of fresh air, Johannes clambered through the hatch and went to the side of the ship. Although he could not see the vessels of his fellow countrymen, he sensed their presence somewhere in the sea fog.

FORTY-FIVE

'Let me understand,' said the Bastard, in a convincing tone of reasonableness. *'I'm losing the plot here. One of your other Voices, the boring one, is essentially dictating a story inside your head which includes a character who is a paranoid schizophrenic with delusions albeit placed in an historic context. You're madder than I thought, my friend.'*

' Disagree,' chipped in the Academic.

'Who cares a flying fart what you think?'

'On three counts. The tradition of the interpolated tale in picaresque narrative is well established. The Narrator is to be congratulated on his skill and knowledge of literary tradition.'

Thank you.

'It has to be said, the facts, as far as we know them, are historically accurate. It is true that in Catholic countries the Anabaptists were, as a rule, executed by burning at the stake whereas in Zwinglian states generally by beheading or drowning.'

'Zwinglian? Jesus wept!'

'On the third count I think that some of your assumptions about John's underlying diagnosis can be questioned. A slavish adherence to the categories defined in the latest version of the

Diagnostic and Statistical Manual of Mental Disorders *is unhelpful. I think that Dissociative Identity Disorder should remain firmly on the agenda.'*

'Speaking personally,' said the Jester *'I far prefer the Spanish Inquisition sketch in Monty Python where Cardinal Biggles places the old woman in the comfy chair and attempts to torture her with a cushion ... '*

Mick paused at the foot of Leith Walk and wiped his brow. John put the bag of Domestos and ten cans of Tennants onto the pavement. A bald man with spectacles, and a cardigan knitted by his mother before she went off him, thrust a leaflet into Mick's hand.

'God-bothering bastards! Don't speak to me about God's essential goodness. You should try living with a diagnosis of schizofuckingphrenia in a hostel for the damned and demented. It makes Calvary an easy place.'

The bald man backed off and hid behind a large placard proclaiming that we are all loved equally. His associate, a woman who had embraced premature old age as a welcome respite from the trials and disappointments of being in her late twenties, turned up the volume on the cassette player. *Jesus Wants me for a Sunbeam* fought a losing battle with the *Red Flag* as Mick bellowed in the woman's face, making her cover her nose and visibly shrink into the background.

'Easy to mock,' said the Tempter, as John put his own newly acquired leaflet in his pocket. *'Perhaps he did die for your sins.'*

'You don't know the half of them,' interjected the Bastard.

The ten-year-old John knelt on the cushion in the confessional. 'God bless me for I have sinned ... ' Even then the idea of three Hail Marys magically wiping clean the debilitating emotional impact of endless lustful thoughts rang false somehow. 'On your own or with others?' asked the priest enthusiastically.

'Fat chance,' commented the Bastard, intruding unwanted into an already unpleasant memory.

Where was his brother in that memory? Had John taken him to the chapel or was he waiting outside for his turn? He couldn't see him. The failure to visualise Andy felt like a betrayal.

Within a microsecond of that last thought being shaped in words John knew what would follow.

'Yes, old son, you're gradually erasing all trace from your memory. Finish the job, airbrush him from your consciousness. You might as well just kill him off. Ah, we're on to something here! It all falls into place now! That's precisely what you did isn't it. Fratricide!'

To drown out the Voice John moved closer to the loud-speaker elevated to face height on an improvised stand. The tactic worked as his head soon rocked with holy decibels. He could hear nothing but God's own white noise. The woman approached and, her bravery nurtured by a perceived insult to her own private deity, tried to shoo John away.

The Tempter tried to console him. *'Don't worry, John, don't worry, all will be well. Ignore the messengers, listen to the message.'*

John and Mick were both slumped in the sitting room when Beverley came through to remind them about the house meeting. Self-consciously, John wiped the dribble from his chin, a constant unwanted reminder of his new medication, and stood up from the armchair. His legs ached and his head was awash with fading images of somewhere he couldn't quite remember, and snatches of dialogue that meant little. Mick was reluctant to relinquish his grip on the remote and, in a pointless demonstration of power, flicked from *Flog it* to the snooker and back again. It occurred to him that the vases on either side of the fireplace might just be worth a bob or two.

They wouldn't be missed.

'A sham of democracy and consultation,' he muttered as Beverley aimed a friendly slap at the side of his head.

'Come on, you old Communist, move your arse.'

Paul was already in his place on the opposite side of the dining table directly facing the door. His book was resting on the cruet set. Page 241 was proving difficult to memorise, his lips moved and his brow creased under the strain. The frequency of gerunds in the third paragraph grated somehow.

Janet joined the group, smiled, and inadvertently irritated Mick by telling him he looked well.

'I'm not well, slow poisoning ... '

'You look good too, John.' John smiled briefly and looked away.

Kevin ostentatiously moved his chair away from Mick then flapped at the air in front of his nose, 'You're humming. Had a wee drink have we?'

'Mind your own fucking business!'

'Language!' said Derek.

'Mick's stinking, Miss,' said Kevin in the high-pitched voice of a snitching schoolboy.

'You're not the finest example of personal hygiene yourself,' said Beverley, who then glanced anxiously at Mick to gauge the likely degree of retaliation but Mick had already been reclaimed by his own demons. He was shaking his head in disagreement with whoever was taunting him from a different place.

'Where's Dennis?' asked Kevin brightly. 'He could teach us how to play hangman ... there's a noose loose in the hoose the nicht ... ' He then snorted from the corner where he was rocking on the back legs of his chair.

'It's your last warning,' said Beverley. 'Just remember the conditions that were put on your tenancy last time. Sit on a chair properly, Kevin. If you break it again, you pay for it.

Right. The house meeting is officially convened. Just to remind you all what we decided last time. We agreed to keep the sitting room tidier, and there has been an improvement, so thank you. Paul, you were a bit anxious when we had that temporary cook at lunch times who never managed to make your toast the way you liked it. Well, I'm able to tell you that, for some unfathomable reason, Linda likes working here and has no intention of leaving.'

'Great,' said Paul, without looking up from the irritating pattern of gerunds. 'It was always too dry.'

'Kevin has already made an unkind reference to Dennis but I want to say something about last week.' With the exception of Kevin who smirked in anticipation of what was to come, the men grew still. All of them had attempted suicide, most of them on several occasions, to escape their own tyrannous cacophony of Voices.

'Dennis struggles with people, you know that. He gets frightened. He has panic attacks.'

'He's on a list, his card's marked.'

'Quiet, Mick. You must be kind to him. If you see him looking round his door, have a word.'

'There's a smell of piss by his door.'

'We all know he has a problem, Kevin. It doesn't help if you go on at him.'

'I've tried three times now,' said Paul with the resigned disappointment of someone describing a failed hunt for bargains at a sale. 'Drowning proved difficult. Logically a man should be able to hold his head under water and keep it there, but it didn't happen. I don't know why.' He finally gave up on the gerunds and turned the page. 'Jumping from the North Bridge should have worked too. When I stood there in the wind I could hear people down below shouting for me to jump. Some of them were holding up their phones to take photos. I felt encouraged. They understood what it was like.

They wanted me to jump, but there was a net and it caught me.'

'Poor bloody fisherman,' said Kevin as Derek made a threatening gesture at him.

'I went to Haymarket Station. I knew that between the 10.34 to Glasgow Queen Street and the 10.45 Cross Country to Motherwell, East Coast Line, they always let through empty rolling stock going back to the shed. They would always announce that the next train would not stop and tell the passengers to stand back from the edge of the platform. I waited for it but it didn't come ... it didn't come.' His voice trailed away and he gave his full attention to the challenges of the new page.

Beverley eventually broke the silence. 'We must all look out for each other and if you think one of the residents is at risk you must tell someone. Is that clear? Are there any other issues you want to raise?'

'I would like to know,' said Kevin, innocently, 'if John found his brother, what with him sending a postcard saying that he was waiting for him at the seaside. I'm just curious, that's all.'

John looked down and shook his head.

'Right, that's all,' said Beverley. 'Apart from next week's menus and remember to keep the sitting room tidy. Oh, I meant to say John, your CPN's here to see you.'

On occasions Rosa Durkin could barely conceal her frustration with John. Part of her genuinely liked the large vulnerable man sitting in front of her. She liked the way he would always wear a knotted woollen scarf as if it were a badge of his former life and status. Nevertheless the phrase blood from a stone came to mind. Over the months she had become increasingly adept at interpreting his sophisticated repertoire of smiles, nods, shrugs and if she were very lucky, and the moon was blue, occasional shy words signifying agreement with her suggested course of action or changes to his drug regime.

Janet would invariably make herself available for these meetings, changing her shifts if necessary. She acted as interpreter of John's silences and all three parties accepted that in some strange way she did indeed speak his mind.

'John's doing OK but there was an incident last week wasn't there, John?' He looked down at the stained carpet where he noticed a beige-coloured resident's file lying on the floor. Beverley will go ballistic when she finds it missing, he thought.

'Yes, I heard,' said the CPN, consulting her notes. 'Who was it saved you before you fell?' John looked at her blankly.

'Tell her the truth, tell her the truth,' hissed the Bastard so loudly that John visibly flinched. *'Tell her you were saved by the Flying Dutchman, you mad sod. He just happened to be shopping in Great Junction Street, straight off a cruise ship that had docked in Leith from Amsterdam. Tell her the ship left Holland four hundred years ago. She'll love that. You'll be back in the Hilton before your feet touch the ground.'*

'Just a passerby,' said Janet, sensing John's confusion.

'And are you getting any relief from the Voices?'

'No. *We are all present, if not very correct. At your service, ma'am,'* said the Academic. John thought he could hear him clicking his heels as he continued.

'I'm keeping abreast of recent research into psychosis. I'm especially intrigued by the findings emerging from the Bethlem and Maudsley Hospitals based on mind-mapping techniques. The imaging seems to demonstrate that when patients experience auditory hallucinations activity is increased in Broca's area, that part of the brain which we normally use to generate our own inner "mental" speech, strongly suggesting that voices are essentially self-generated in the same way that most of us would say the words of a poem or a prayer silently to ourselves.'

'Total bollocks,' said the Bastard.

'Sorry,' said Rosa, 'did you say something?' John shook his head.

'Don't you dare suggest that I don't exist! You self-serving, toadying bookworm.'

'But the research says ... '

'Up yours!'

John was aware that the normally supportive and insightful Janet was looking shocked. Surely he had not repeated out loud what he had just heard in his head? Mortified he covered his mouth with his hand.

'A touch of the old Tourettes today?' asked Rosa. She instantly regretted the question that should have been confined to the notes she was scribbling. 'Any word from your brother?'

John looked as if he was fit to burst.

'No word yet but still looking, still looking,' said Janet who was growing increasingly anxious on John's behalf.

'Tell them about the latest note,' said the Tempter urgently. *'It's a real breakthrough after all these false starts. This time it will be different.'*

The Bastard snorted but didn't see the point of saying anything. It was all so stupid; he didn't need to waste his breath.

Janet placed a consoling arm on his shoulder. 'Probably enough for today, what do you think?' she asked, in a tone which made apparent it was a statement not a question.

With the meeting concluded, John went through to the lounge. There was no one there apart from Derek leaning forward from the settee pressing both thumbs into a small console while staring hard at his laptop on the table. Almost unable to breathe with anger John felt the pain of his blood pounding in his temples. It was an unfamiliar and deeply unpleasant sensation. He felt frightened by the intensity of his feelings and quite, quite powerless.

'Hi John, how'd it go?' asked Derek, without raising his eyes from the small screen where a naval battle was being fought. Without waiting for an answer, he sighed noisily as a man-of-war disappeared into a jagged-edged cartoon of pink smoke. Martial music filled the room. 'You should try this, John, you saw *Pirates of the Caribbean* at Christmas didn't you?'

FORTY-SIX

The man-of-war materialised from nowhere, cleaving a path through the mist on the starboard side. Johannes choked on the smoke. 'Lucifer's furnace!' he spluttered, eyes smarting and ears ringing with the sound of cannon fire. Moving his arms in front of his face as if swimming through the black haze, he saw that Balthasar was standing next to him, stock still, as if in shock. Cornelius was gripping the handrail and staring at the wooden hulk looming out of the mist.

Armed with grappling irons and muskets the geuzen were ready for the impact when it came. A squat sailor had dropped his weapon and was staunching a wound in his forearm, cursing all the while, but mesmerised by the dark moving wall of timber towering like a giant's shadow over a frightened child.

Within seconds they were thrown from their feet as the Spanish monster sliced into their flimsy vessel, lifting it, skewered, on its prow. The horizon toppled onto itself and, for a moment, the two ships groaned like elderly lovers trying to extricate themselves from a routine coupling. The deck splintered and the sea rose to engulf them along with the first wave of men who hurled themselves into their midst, howling and hacking at everything and everyone in their way.

Johannes grasped at a pike that appeared inches from his throat, wrestling until its owner toppled backwards over the gunnels, a small devil tumbling headfirst down the margins of an illuminated manuscript. Johannes' hands were bleeding profusely.

Cornelius waited until his chosen victim swung against the side of the ship on a thick rope before jabbing his elbow into the man's face. The stricken invader relinquished his grip and fell soundlessly into the water.

Balthasar was being chased round the topsy-turvy deck by a small madman determined to strangle his quarry with his bare hands. The madman tripped on a trailing rope and was kicked in the head for his pains by a passing crewman.

Johannes, still sucking on his bleeding hand, watched as the Leader sliced the heavy air with his cutlass before thrusting it neatly through his opponent's windpipe. For several moments the two enacted a slow motion dance at sword's length until the Leader extracted his bloody weapon from the man's throat.

A knot of men floundering on the swamped deck attempted to swivel a small cannon towards the man-of-war. One of the beggars, who had been protecting a burning taper in his cupped hands as if it were a sacred flame, approached.

'Move your arse, dumb shit!'

The celebrant placed the taper against the powder hole and was instantly killed by the resulting explosion and blowback. The hot cannon flew through the air and effectively cut one of the enemy sailors in half. Meanwhile, a gaping orifice had appeared in the side of the man-of-war. Once the smoke cleared from the edges of the charred hole a gaggle of beggars seized their chance and jumped into the open maul, slaughtering the stunned enemy sailors staggering towards them.

As he struggled to keep his balance on the violently tipping ship, Johannes found himself staring at the crow's nest where Blindman stood motionless and serene. He moved his head slowly in one direction and then the next as if directing the battle from his perch. One tilt of the head coincided with a Spanish sailor losing his footing whereupon he was promptly decapitated by a sea beggar. Another tilt and an enemy clutched his eye and sank to his knees. Blindman nodded in the direction of the Dutch flotilla emerging from the mist.

'Hang on,' said Derek, 'something's happening. Over there!' He zoomed in on a corner of the screen and, pressing furiously on the console, fired several small puffs of smoke at a figure disappearing behind the capstan. 'Bugger!' he said as the figure reappeared further along the deck.

Like a bird in the mouth of a dog the sea beggars' craft was being routinely ducked into the sea in the hope that it would eventually give up and drown. The man-of-war's mainsail had become partially detached and billowed over the smaller vessel. Johannes struggled against the canvas shroud. Unbidden, he saw an image of Michel, much younger, trapped under the blanket in his parents' bed.

Once free of the sail he surveyed the many bodies strewn across the deck. Some were groaning; someone else called on his mother. The carnage had ceased and the only men still standing were his fellow beggars. To his relief Cornelius was nearby on his knees and holding his head, but was uninjured as far as Johannes could tell. Balthasar meanwhile was offering water to one of the fallen.

Johannes looked out to sea and saw that the man-of-war was now completely encircled by the flotilla of small Dutch ships that had thrown off the cloak of mist and joined the fray. 'We're not alone. Christ has not forsaken us!' shouted a geuzen, his face a mess of blood.

The man-of-war now resembled a wounded deer surrounded by a pack of curs. Balthasar felt a fleeting pang of loss as the drowned hounds came to mind. Men were now swarming up the sides of the galleon, their shouts ringing out above the creaking of wood and the suck of the waves which still tugged at their own stricken ship.

The three men reached out to each other just as the invading sea covered their knees and the shock of cold water made them cry out.

'Sons of whores and bitches!' shouted Cornelius.

'Hold fast to one another,' urged Balthasar. They waded in a strange dance for a few moments before surrendering to the inevitable. Their vessel detached itself from the man-of-war and gracefully sank, leaving the weavers floating alongside clothing, barrels, drinking vessels, doors, gun port covers, splinters of wood torn loose by cannon fire, and the semi-submerged bodies of their dead fellow beggars and newly acquired enemies.

Several of the beggars were hanging on to floating spars with one arm while waving with the other. They were encouraged in their efforts by their compatriots, now in complete command of the captured man-of-war and peering down at them.

The survivors grabbed the ropes hanging over the side and were hauled upwards to accompanying cheers.

'God be thanked!' spluttered Johannes.

'Fishers of men,' said Balthasar, accepting two outstretched hands.

Once all were on board the collective mood changed. In the aftermath of the battle some of the crew sat silently on the deck, others still jabbed excitedly at each other as if unable to curb the urge to kill and maim. A sailor retched over the side either from a stomach wound or his inability to digest the horror he had just witnessed. Someone else was quietly humming a tune that Johannes recognised as the lullaby that Antonia used to sing to Michel before she sank into her dark soundless world.

The Leader was going from man to man mock punching them on the chest, holding them by the shoulders to shake them from their private reveries, or putting a consoling or congratulatory arm around them. Many of the crew were strangers to him from the other boats but all were embraced and thanked. He turned his attention to the gaggle of prisoners staring blankly at the dark sea.

The order soon came. 'Overboard with every last son of a fornicating Spanish whore!' The more powerful geuzen easily manhandled the terrified captives and hurled them like sacks of corn over the low wooden balustrade. One of them, a terrified young lad made eye contact with Johannes for the instant before he was upturned and pitched overboard.

Johannes moved towards him. The other sailors lined the gunnels to mock the flailing, drowning men. Johannes looked on horrified as the young lad sank beneath the boiling water. 'In Christ's name!' he shouted, before Balthasar motioned him to step away.

'Choose your battles,' he cautioned. 'Save your strength for Leyden. Save your anger for those who are holding Michel.' Johannes grudgingly saw the wisdom in the older man's words.

Shouts of joy preceded the appearance back on deck of three sailors who were tugging behind them a bound wooden chest. Those able to move quickly gathered round as the Leader attacked the lock with an axe.

As the lock sprang the lid was raised to reveal layer on layer of clothes and finery. The Leader sank to his knees and brought out armfuls of uniforms, dress coats and plumed hats that he tossed to his men like a demented saint dispensing largesse to the poor. 'Satan's vestments! Lucifer's hose. Dress for the wedding, boys!'

At the bottom of the chest were several women's dresses of silk and velvet. 'Where are the nuns?' shouted the Leader, whereupon the three unfortunate women, who had survived the battle unscathed, were produced from the back of the crowd.

'Put these on, ladies, tonight we dine like the kings of Spain!'

Balthasar struggled to tie his newly acquired red breeches which did not quite match his girth, Cornelius stood resplendent in an overlong woollen coat while Johannes roared with laughter as he pulled on a jacket that had previously belonged to a member of his Spanish Majesty's Grand Army. 'Bring me the roasted balls of an Anabaptist!' he shouted.

A stumpy barrel and a fistful of tankards had been carried up from below deck by one of the sailors. Once the barrel had been spiked the rum was dispensed to the crew.

'This is ringing a bell ... yes, the sea beggars did have a notable success when they outmanoeuvred the Spanish fleet off Enckhuysen, sank the greater part of it and captured the admiral's flagship, and Bossu himself ... but that was in 1573, I'm getting increasingly uncertain about your chronology, Narrator ... '

Quiet!

The Leader could barely contain his pleasure in the size of his capture. William himself would soon hear and rush to congratulate all involved, while saving the highest praise for the Courageous Leader who had masterminded the whole operation. Preening himself, and wallowing in anticipated fame, conveniently distracted the Heroic Leader from the truth that no one in the sea beggars' fleet knew how to sail a ship of such size. Already the vessel was wandering across the waves in a listless undirected manner. Rising to the challenge he gave the order that the ship was to be searched deck by deck in the hope that skulking somewhere in the bulwarks they might find a skilled navigator.

The weavers were dispatched to search the lower deck.

Below decks the men ducked between the crew's hammocks swinging with the motion of the waves. All were empty. Balthasar poked each one from underneath just to make sure. Towards the end of their search his fist met resistance. There was someone in the hammock.

FORTY-SEVEN

When he put his hand in his pocket the next morning, John found the crumpled leaflet that had been given to him by the Holy Joe on the street. He smoothed it out with the back of his hand.

'What's that?' Mick asked, already bored by children's television. John passed over the piece of paper.

A TOWN BUILT ON A HILL CANNOT BE HIDDEN.
TRUST THE LORD

'Don't trust any lord,' said Mick. After a small diatribe against the ills of monarchy and privilege in general he looked up. 'It's from the Sermon on the Mount. A fine socialist tract.' He then looked into the middle distance.

HOU HAPPIE THE PUIR AT IS HUMMLE AFORE GOD,
FOR THEIRS IS THE KINGDOM O HEAVEN!
HOU HAPPIE THE DOWFF AN DOWIE,
FOR THEY WILL BE COMFORTIT!
HOW HAPPIE THE DOUCE AN CANNIE,
'FOR THEY WILL FAA THE YIRD!

I don't believe in the God shite but the words are grand. The line you've got there comes later: A toun biggit on a hill-tap canna be holdit.'

'Lorimer's translation of The New Testament in Scots, *published in 1983 by Southside Press if my memory serves me right,'* said the Academic, genuinely impressed by Mick's unexpected erudition.

'Who cares?' mumbled the Bastard.

'It's a sign, it's a sign!' said the Tempter. *'False starts are inevitable. He wasn't at the seaside. We were too late, he had moved on.'*

'Moved on my arse, he's dead.'

'It's Arthur's Seat! You'll meet him on Arthur's Seat.'

'And probably Uncle Tom Cobley and King Arthur himself surrounded by his Court at Camelot, somewhere under Salisbury Crags.'

'No no, I think you're wrong there,' interjected the Academic. *'Malory identified Winchester as the original location, though John Leland in 1542 made a case for Cadbury Castle in Somerset. Colchester is probably the frontrunner at the moment, and as for Tom Cobley ... '*

'Who cares a shit!'

'Mark my words, he's on Arthur's Seat,' persisted the Tempter.

'This is doubly interesting, John,' intoned the Academic. *'The sermon on the Mount was held as the most important passage in the Bible by those self-same Anabaptists that take up so much of your time in your other world. For the early believers the sermon provided the moral framework for their system of ethics which was essentially non-violent. Indeed they were vehemently opposed to war in all its forms.'*

'Get a life!' sneered the Bastard.

Mick was saying something but John couldn't concentrate, distracted by the argument raging in his head. He stared at the screen that was changing rapidly as Mick flipped between channels. A purple lion with a yellow mane was driving a toy train though an alien landscape peopled by ballerinas apparently pirouetting on rotating toilet rolls.

'I pity the kids today,' sighed Mick.

A Batman clone was driving a skidoo at great speed round skyscrapers with white pizza boxes piled precariously on his pillion. It wasn't going to end well. A perfect ethnic mix of cartoon firemen stood alongside their sparkling red vehicle.

'Political correctness,' said Mick, 'What's wrong with Captain Pugwash? Seaman Stains, Roger the cabin boy, you couldn't make it up.'

Mick's beanie had nodded several times in response to John's mentioning a trip up Arthur's Seat. 'Tramping stills the mind,' he said.

The odd couple attracted not a glance from the early morning joggers, many of whom were, in any case, running away from their own tormentors, analysing things said the night before or practising the fine words that would later in the day make their bosses see the error of their ways.

Mick shot a warning glance at the two swans that had wandered onto the path running alongside the lower loch. 'Vicious bastards, the swan and the midge,' he muttered.

'Mythic creatures,' commented the Academic, already out of breath from the pace of the walk. *'As a symbol in alchemy the swan was neither masculine nor feminine, but rather symbolised hermaphoditism.'*

'That would suit you fine, John,' suggested the Jester who was enjoying the misty morning. *'You could just turn over and have sex with yourself.'*

'Shut up the pair of you,' said the Bastard.

'Don't listen to them, John, "Today's the day you will find him. A town built on a hill cannot be hidden. Trust the Lord."'

'For God's sake!'

'Exactly,' retorted the Tempter, who did not normally dare challenge the Bastard. John wondered if this was significant. Perhaps today would be different. A breakthrough at last.

Mick, fully engaged with his own Voices, gestured dismissively with his right arm that smacked into the midriff of a lycra-clad woman overtaking at speed. 'Oy!' she shouted.

'Oy, yourself!' replied Mick, annoyed at being distracted from a debate with Mussolini's henchman. The woman thought briefly of giving Mick a piece of her mind but, deciding he might be dangerous, ran to catch up with her companion.

John glanced across the busy road to where a small knot of women were practising Tai Chi. Before she left him, Sarah went through a martial arts phase that seemingly involved aping 'a snake creeping down' among other exotic practices. Who this snake was and what it was creeping down he never found out.

'Simple,' said the Bastard, eager to corrupt a comparatively harmless memory. '*You were both the snake and the creep.*'

Mick's muttering increased in volume the closer they got to Holyrood Palace. The policeman on duty in the car park seemed to take exception to being called a useless tree-hugging tosser by the dishevelled heckler on the path opposite, equally resenting the accusation that he was a toadying royalist parasite. John sensibly steered his companion onto the start of Pilgrim's Way that signalled the ascent to the crags. The sheer effort of walking up hill stopped Mick's increasingly belligerent rant. The policeman shook his head and went back to directing the queue waiting to park.

Despite the comparatively early hour people kept appearing through the mist on their way down the path. What was the woman in business suit and high heels doing on Arthur's Seat? She and her equally well-dressed male companion strode past as if slightly annoyed at their inability to locate the office water fountain. A mother-earth figure emerged with numerous small children in tow all equipped with sufficient equipment to survive a nuclear winter. An elderly man with a walking stick; perhaps he too was looking for someone.

Two large black dogs preceded by their slightly unearthly panting were next. There was no sign of their owner. Hounds, thought John, disconcerted.

'*Refugees from the city on the hill*,' suggested the Tempter. '*A tableau of people from your brother's life. We are getting close. The young smart couple are his immediate neighbours, the woman and the kids live down the road. He helped that old man off the bus the other day. Kind, your brother.*'

John was experiencing a growing sense of unease. It was all delusional projection, he knew that, but he could not let go of the residual hope that this time it would be different.

'More things in heaven and earth ... ' contributed Mick as if bizarrely attuned to John's unspoken appraisal of the likelihood of the Tempter speaking the truth.

BEWARE FALLING ROCKS

said a sign at the foot of the crags.

'*You could be stoned*,' said the Bastard, viciously. '*Buried up to your neck while your accusers each step forward with their chosen rock. Death to the infidel, death to the idolater, death to the adulterous whore! But Sarah wasn't the only unfaithful one. Was she, John? And then the first rock hits you on the temple ... Then nothing.*'

'The rest is silence,' said Mick.

'DO NOT CLIMB THE CRAGS HISTORIC SCOTLAND
WILL TAKE NO RESPONSIBILITY FOR
ANY INJURIES

'Give it a go, give it a go, give it a go,' urged the Tempter. *'He'll be waiting for you at the summit. Taste the ecstatic joy as he recognises you.'*

'Keep right on 'til the end of the road,' sang Mick at the top of his voice.

The Bastard had to chip in. The opportunity to oversee the oblivion of his host was too great. He could always move on, find another head. *'The Tempter's right, John. One hand over the other, easy, ignore the wind starting up, it will come to nothing. Climb towards your brother!'*

'Climb towards your brother,' echoed the Tempter, delighted to have an ally for a change. John left the path and moved towards the foot of the cliff.

'I could do with a pish,' said Mick, opening his fly.

The Voices stopped. It was as if Mick possessed the power to swat them away. They would be back, even stronger, even louder, John knew that, but for the moment he was content to lean his forehead against the cold rock, hearing the wind in his ears and Mick contentedly relieving himself.

John turned back to the path as the mist retreated before the breeze. The multitude of church spires gradually revealed the buildings beneath. He noted the minaret of the mosque next to the university buildings.

He had enjoyed his time at uni. He had met Sarah at a party; it was love at first sight. He had always suspected that his own love-making was more enthusiastic than accomplished but she had not minded, at least not in the early days. He stopped half way through the memory, bracing himself for the Bastard to make some utterly scathing and derogatory comment. Surprisingly, all of the Voices remained silent.

He remembered that he had heard his first Voice in those far-off days. He had been in the stack room at the library searching for an elusive volume. Probably stolen, he had decided. The Voice was posh English and the content seemed random and inconsequential. It was something about washing lines and pigs. He had looked round the edges of the stack in case some of his mates were playing tricks on him but there was no one there. Although disconcerted, he had decided that he was suffering from lack of sleep and thought no more about it. He did not discuss it with Sarah in case it served to confirm what he thought was her growing conviction, that he was interesting but decidedly odd.

They had married months before graduation, much to the disapproval of Sarah's parents. He recalled resting his hand ostentatiously on the table during his next tutorial waiting desperately for someone to notice and marvel at his wedding ring. No one said anything, but it didn't matter. They were utterly immersed in each other, Siamese twins whose togetherness progressively alienated them from former friends whom they decided were jealous of their love. He realised subsequently that they were fearful this inward facing exclusivity was unsustainable. They were not wrong.

Meanwhile, Mick's mood had shifted from the paranoid to the unashamedly megalomaniacal. He stood with his arms outstretched to encompass the entire panorama of Victorian tenements, public parks, football stadia, warehouses, cathedrals, the Forth estuary and the hills of Fife.

'It's all mine! You are my people,' he shouted. 'I will rule you fairly in accordance with the principles on Marx and Engels. No poverty, no exploitation, no fear, and no religion!' He threw his head back and roared with a laugh that started as an expression of harmless exuberance before mutating into something decidedly sinister, more the demented roar of an ogre about to devour innocent children. He looked at John sheepishly and pulled his beanie over his eyes.

They walked on until the path almost met the road once more. John took the lead and veered to the left where it wound between the Crags and Arthur's Seat, the top of which was still not visible. He sighed. The Voices were back; it had been too good to last. The Jester, taking his cue from Mick, contributed the refrain '*Tho' you're tired and weary still journey on,*' in a rough approximation of Harry Lauder on helium. John was far from amused.

'As he approached the swire at the head of the dell – that little delightful verge from which in one moment the eastern limits and shores of Lothian arise on the view – as he approached it, I say, and a little space from the height, he beheld, to his astonishment, a bright halo in the cloud of haze, that rose in a semicircle over his head like a pale rainbow ... '

Sorry? What's going on here? Academic, why have you butted in and taken over the narrative?

'Don't you see what's happening?'

All that's happened is that you are intruding into the story. Why do you need to be the centre of attention?

'Exactly, a pathetic attention seeking ploy ... '

Bastard, be quiet, let him explain himself.

'Just let me read on, all will become clear ... "he was struck motionless at the view of the lovely vision; for it so happened that he had never seen the same appearance before, though common at early morn. But he soon perceived the cause of the phenomenon, and that it proceeded from the rays of the sun from a pure unclouded morning sky striking upon this dense vapour that refracted them."'

Ok, very clever. James Hogg.

'Well done, well done ...Confessions of a Justified Sinner, *a sadly neglected Scottish classic published anonymously in 1824. If I remember correctly, the full title is* The Private Memoirs and Confessions of a Justified Sinner: Written by himself: With a detail of curious facts and other evidence by the editor.'

I still don't see the point.

'You will, you will. Let me read on.'

Very well.

'"*George did admire this halo of glory...*" Why George? It could just as easily be John, don't you see?'

Not really.

'*Just listen! "... which still grew wider, and less defined, as he approached the surface, of the cloud. But, to his utter amazement and utter delight, he found, on reaching the top of Arthur's Seat, that this sublunary rainbow, this terrestrial glory, was spread in its most vivid hues beneath his feet. Still he could not perceive the body of the sun, although the light behind him was dazzling; but the cloud of haze lying in that deep dell that separated the hill from the rocks of Salisbury, and the dull shadow of the hill mingling with the cloud made the dell a pit of darkness. On that shadowy cloud was the lovely rainbow formed, spreading itself on a horizontal plain, and having a slight and brilliant shade of all the colours of the heavenly bow, but all of them paler and less defined."*'

I'm getting bored ... I might have to ask the Bastard to have a word with you.

'"*He seated himself on the pinnacle of the rocky precipice, a little within the top of the hill to the westward, and, with a light and buoyant heart, viewed the beauties of the morning, and inhaled its salubrious breeze. 'Here,' thought he, 'I can converse with nature without disturbance, and without being intruded on by any appalling or obnoxious visitor.' The idea of his brother's ...* "'

All right I'm getting it now.

'Shhh! "*The idea of his brother's dark and malevolent looks coming at that moment across his mind, he turned his eyes instinctively to the right, to the point where that unwelcome guest was wont to make his appearance. Gracious Heaven! What an apparition was there presented to his view! He saw, delineated in the cloud, the shoulders, arms and features of a human being of the most dreadful aspect. The face was the face of his brother ...!"'*

Ahh...

'"*but dilated to twenty times the natural size. Its dark eyes gleamed on him through the mist, while every furrow of its hideous brow frowned deep as the ravines on the brow of the hill. George [John] started, and his hair stood up in bristles as he gazed on this horrible monster. He saw every line and every feature of the face distinctly as it gazed on him with an intensity that was hardly brookable. Its eyes were fixed on him, in the same way as those of some carnivorous animal fixed on its prey; and yet there were fear and trembling in these unearthly feature, as plainly depicted as murderous malice. The giant apparition seemed sometimes to be cowering down as in terror, so that nothing but his brow and eyes were seen; still these never turned one moment from their object – again it rose imperceptively up, and began to approach with great caution and, as it neared, the dimensions of its form lessoned, still continuing, however, far above the natural size.*

"*[John] conceived it to be a spirit. He could conceive it to be nothing else; and he took it for some horrid demon by which he was haunted, that had assumed the features of his brother in every lineament, but, in taking on itself the human form, had miscalculated dreadfully on the size, and presented itself \to him in a blown-up, dilated frame of embodied air, exhaled from the caverns of death or the regions of devouring fire. He was further confirmed in the belief that it was a malignant spirit on perceiving that it approached him across the front of a precipice, where there was not footing for thing of mortal frame, Still, what with terror and astonishment, he continued riveted to the spot, till it approached, as he deemed, to within two yards of him; and then, perceiving that it was setting itself to make a violent spring on him, he started to his feet and fled distractedly in the opposite direction, keeping* *his eye cast behind him lest he had been seized in that dangerous place. But the very first bolt he made in his flight he came into contact with a real body of flesh and blood, and that with such violence that both went down among some scragged rocks, and John rolled over the other. The being called out 'Murder' and ... "'*

'I'm not your brother! Leave me alone!'

Mick looked genuinely startled as he extricated himself from John's grip. 'Calm yourself, pal. It's ok. It's probably that new medication. You've had one of they episodes. Let's go back eh?'

John was shivering heavily as he let himself be led back onto the path.

'It's ok, pal,' said Mick.

John looked over the cityscape towards the Forth. Beneath the hazy horizon he could just make out the smudges of several small ships. He felt consumed with sadness. He desperately wanted something but didn't know what it was.

So, Academic, what was all that stuff about?

'Who knows? More reflection needed.'

FORTY-EIGHT:
Gerda's Tale

There was someone in the hammock.

'I'm sorry but hammocks were not widely used in the navy until ... '

Shut up!

'I was just saying ... '

There was someone in the hammock. Johannes felt the warm weight as he pushed the canvas upwards. There followed a long expiration of breath. Johannes shook the tight web and a gaunt face appeared over the edge. 'Go away, I'm tired,' said a woman's voice in Dutch.

'You are one of us,' said Balthasar. Slowly the figure lowered itself onto the deck next to the three strangers. She scratched her head and appraised them. 'Ah, my countrymen,' she observed with a resigned bitterness. 'But you are still men. Spanish, Dutch, what does it matter? Just get it over with. I want to go back to sleep.'

'We will not harm you,' said Balthasar. 'What are you doing here?'

'Do you have any liquor?' she asked. Her hands dug deep into her clothes as she pursued a vicious itch marauding up and down her slight frame. Cornelius moved forward and offered her his leather flagon. She snatched it from him, emptied its contents down her throat and sat on one of the sacks littering the floor. Furiously scratching her head, releasing a shower of dead skin, she looked down and spoke almost inaudibly. The men moved closer.

'I am Gerda, woman of sorrows,' she said. 'Listen to my tale and learn ... Pedro, Pedro,' she muttered, 'never in all my days had I been so bewitched by one man. I had only known him for hours although I had waited all my life for him. When we kissed he sucked up my soul and made it his own. He was small, smaller than my oldest child. Black eyes and so sad.

'We lay that night in the cornfield. He beat down the stalks and made our bed. He placed his tunic on the ground and I heard his teeth chattering in the dark. I held my new child in my arms and smothered him in the warmth of my breasts.

'Later he pointed at the black sky and named all of the stars in his own tongue and I told him the names we knew them by. We tried each other's names and laughed before we put our tongues to better use. The field mice fled beneath our weight while the owl kept watch.

'When the red dawn broke the colour was not that of a new day threatening storms but of fires from the town. The smell of burning homes swept through the chill fields. He rose, held me in his arms, spoke soft words and without glancing back walked through the corn towards the pall of smoke on the horizon. I followed at a distance, howling all the while, spitting hate at the God who was leading him back to war.

'On the edge of the town the buildings smouldered, charred black beams pointed up where the roofs had been. Women clung to each other as their lamentations rose like a psalm. Sobbing children rubbed soot from their eyes and dogs sniffed at the clothes of the dead.

'I watched my Spanish boy join a group of men who were

hurrying towards the docks, following them downhill, keeping in the shadow of the carts loaded with plunder. Several of the horses rebelled against their yokes and reared spilling barrels and trunks and fine clothes dragged from merchant cellars. The Spanish drivers beat the horses with staves until they staggered back onto their feet.

'Soon I saw snaking lines of men waiting for their turn. Eagerly they stepped into one of the small skiffs that would ferry them back to the large ships beyond the harbour walls. My boy joined a line and was cuffed for his pains, but I would not leave him, of that there was no doubt.

'I turned into one of the alleys where a man's body was propped against a wall, his face still wet with blood and not yet coated with the wax of death. The dead man leered at me as if he knew what I was about to do. I easily stripped him of his clothes as his heavy rag doll limbs were still soft. Stepping into his breeches, tightening his tunic across my chest, stepping into his large braided shoes and joining the shuffling line I boarded the same ship as my love.

'It was easy to hide in the confusion of shouting and laughter. I made my way, excited, below decks, hid in a far corner and with beating heart noticed how I now smelt like a man.'

'This is reminiscent of the 19th-century folk song, Polly Oliver, *how does it go? ... "As sweet Polly Oliver lay musing in bed / A sudden strange fancy came into her head. / 'Nor father nor mother shall make me false prove, / I'll list as a soldier, and follow my love...* "'

Shut up!

'So early next morning she softly arose, / And dressed up in her dead brother's clothes, / She cut her hair close, and she stained her face brown, / And went for a soldier to fair London Town ... "'

I'm not telling you again. Shut up!

'Benjamin Britten also wrote an arrangement ... '

'I lay stiff and aching in my dark corner. The movement of the ship made me ill; I had to choke on the bile that rose in my throat with every storm lest the sound of my retching led to discovery.

'After two days I could wait no longer, I had to find my boy. I made my way to the quarters where the men were asleep. I knew which was he, and placed my hand over his mouth until he woke. His alarm faded in an instant and he become transfixed with joy. Rising, as if still wrapped in a dream, beautiful beyond understanding, he took my hand and led me into the fresh night air. I pointed at the stars and whispered "Grote Beer". With his mouth on mine we swayed with the swell. Never had he known a dream so sweet.

'Neither of us noticed the watchman who climbed down from his perch, crept towards us and held up his lantern.

'"Sodomites!" he shouted and, like a living thing, the ship awoke. My boy stood petrified as a multitude of angry men appeared from nowhere and jostled us. Someone grabbed him by the throat and forced him backwards over the rail. As others held his legs off the deck, I forced my way into their midst and tore open my tunic letting them see my breasts. They soon forgot my boy and turned their attention to me. With a roar of excitement and lust they dragged me below the decks where I was unclothed by a hundred willing hands.'

'This is more like it! This is what we want!'

Shut up Bastard!

'I caught a glimpse of my boy being held back by two men who wanted him to watch. They poured liquor down my throat and I lost consciousness.

'When I woke I knew the world was a different place. The men were leaning against the bulkheads but no one spoke, and no one looked at me. Someone spat tobacco and coughed. I searched in vain for the face of my boy but he wasn't there. I knew in an instant that he had hurled himself into the sea unable to shake off the nightmare that had strangled his sweet dream. One of the men gave me his coat and laid me down on the straw. Without a word they returned to their sleeping places leaving me shaking with fear and shame.

'They left me alone after that. On occasions one or two of them brought me food and asked if they could lie with me. I gave them what they wanted. Nothing mattered. My life was already spent.'

Gerda wearily pulled herself into the hammock and sighing turned her back to the weavers.

'You must come with us,' said Johannes, gently patting her shoulder. 'When we land, come with us.'

Having failed to find a timid navigator hiding in the bowels of the hull, the great Leader took it on himself to steer his one-sailed, wounded ship. The flotilla followed the grey coast towards Gravenzande. England would wait. Above the thin line of land the clouds dropped rain on the smoke rising from remote farms and cottages. Balthasar screwed up his eyes, hoping the smoke was from innocent bonfires.

Cornelius too looked at the trails of smoke on the horizon and tapped his fingers ever more aggressively on the ship's rail. Cottages were burning on the horizon.

Johannes sat apart from the others, his head in his hands on a coiled rope in the middle of the deck. The rest of the crew, excited at the prospect of being greeted as heroes on their return, either busied themselves with very little or just gave up the pretence of working and chatted idly. 'Cheer up, weaver,' said one of them. 'Soon back with the wife. Get your leg over and forget about us poor sea beggars fighting for your country.' His mates laughed. Johannes smiled wanly. Swatting aside a seagull threatening to steal the bread from his hand, he saw Blindman walking slowly towards him. Johannes believed his thoughts must have been stolen by the unpleasant creature gliding over the deck, his head moving imperceptibly from side to side, a supercilious grin on his face.

'Your son,' he said, 'is not well.'

Johannes leaped to his feet and made as if to strangle the odd figure smirking at him. He thought better of it. 'What do you know?' he asked.

'Skin and bones. Almost beyond hunger now. He calls for you and his mother in his sleep.'

'What do you mean?' Johannes shouted into the man's face, his fists clenched. Blindman paused for a moment as if deliberating whether to continue or not. Sensing that he might have silenced his only source of hope, Johannes relented and begged, 'Please say more.'

'Your son was brave. He forsook his new masters and found a way through the great walls into the city. Only a dog or a small child could squirm through the pipe meant for shit, but even the shit was drying up as the people starved. A single rat eaten by a family doesn't make much shit.'

'Stop the riddles!' shouted Johannes into Blindman's face.

'Patience,' he replied, after another agonising pause. 'The bodies are piled high in the square. Mothers drag their children to the heap. Nothing stirs. The birds no longer visit. If they land in the square they will be caught and cooked. Do you see that walking skeleton there with the net? Never has the town bird catcher been so important. There are no dogs. No cats. No sound.' He paused and smiled. 'Look,' he said pointing into the middle distance, 'that man is boiling the leather from his boots. See, his wife and child are waiting. That must be the mayor, thin like the others but strong. He has a word for everyone as he moves slowly through the square. We need more like him.'

'Where is Michel?' asked Johannes, suddenly aware of the absurdity and pain of trying to see through a blind man's eyes.

The seer paused as if he was searching through each building, opening doors looking for a child. He grunted periodically as if disappointed that the child he found under blankets was not the one he was looking for. 'Ah,' he said after an interval. 'There he is!'

'Where?' demanded Johannes gripping the sleeve of Blindman who froze and waited until Johannes relinquished his grip. 'There in the corner. Look.' Johannes stared wildly round him.

'How interesting,' he said.

'What?' Johannes pleaded.

Blindman chuckled. 'That house belongs to the guild master. You see, he knows he is a weaver's son, but so frail, so tired. Look at his ribs.'

'My son, my son,' wailed Johannes, clutching for words. As he tried to master the choking panic that had robbed him of speech, they were jostled apart by a fat crewman running to join his fellows along the port side. By the time Johannes had recovered his balance Blindman was nowhere to be seen.

'I've got it!' said the Academic excitedly. *'There was a moment when the outcome of the Dutch Eighty Years' war hung in the balance. William the Silent decided to risk everything, his people, his land, by attempting to relieve the siege of Leyden. Quite simply the fate of a new nation depended on the outcome ... But hang on a minute, something's wrong here, I smell a rat ... Narrator, there's a problem, back to the drawing board, I'm afraid.'*

What do you mean?

'I felt there was something wrong with the chronology before, but it's all to buggery now, the whole story's gone to hell in a handcart. If my memory serves me right The Hunters in the Snow *was painted in 1565 and the Seige of Leyden took place in 1574! You're not telling me that our Dutch friends have been wandering about the countryside for nine years!'*

Just piss off Academic, piss off!

'*What's all this?*' said the Bastard, suddenly interested. '*Is that you swearing, Narrator? Tut, tut. That's my job. What happened to the tone of neutral objectivity? You're losing the plot.*'

'*My point exactly!*'

Look, it has a sort of truth that transcends mere detail.

'*Sort of truth, my arse!*'

Just piss off the pair of you!

'*Tetchy!*'

I feel undermined; I'm not going to carry on.

'*Diddums ...*'

'*Ignore the Bastard, Narrator, don't sulk. As an academic of repute I have a responsibility to point out error. Listen, apart from that, it is really not bad at all. Please keep going.*'

Are you sure?

'*Yes!*'

I'll try. Rotterdam dock was awash with people, no that doesn't work. I'm flustered, the words won't flow ... Rotterdam dock was teeming with small figures, all of whom were shouting and waving bonnets. Urchins clambered onto the half-constructed ships propped against the sea walls to get a better view. Apprentices paused on their ladders, calking pots in hand, and waved their brushes at the returning fleet. OK, we're up and running again.

Several coracles in the harbour entrance had been capsized by the wake from the captured man-of-war. The smaller pirate vessels snuggled against the captured prize with the urgency of suckling puppies. In the excitement many of their oars had not been retracted and clashed above the water like battlefield lances.

A youth jumped into the frozen water from a barrel on the quay and swam towards the nearest sea beggars' craft and the safety of the many hands offering to pull him aboard. Coals glowed in the dockside braziers. The returning heroes would soon have the grease from roasted chickens running into their beards, and the arms of their women folk around their waists.

In their eagerness to get ashore the men jumped or stepped from one boat to another until they could haul themselves up one of the many ropes that had been lowered to them.

The three weavers stood on dry land and watched the turmoil of lovers meeting. Small women in best smocks were lifted off their feet by burly partners. Tiny children threaded their way through the sea of adult legs to get closer to the fathers who had been away so long. Heads were ruffled and kisses taken. Balthasar instinctively looked for Wilhelmien though he knew she wasn't there. Cornelius looked for Geertje. Johannes studied the crowd looking for boys of Michel's age.

FORTY-NINE

'Another postcard for you, John,' said Janet, as she distributed the mail around the breakfast table. She couldn't help noticing that Jack had another letter from a lawyer's office in London and made an unhelpful connection in her head with the new version of *Great Expectations* currently being serialised on television. Paul seized his envelope containing *Word Search Weekly* and tore it open. There was nothing for Dennis, there never was.

Janet noticed that John was shaking to such an extent that the crockery was rattling in the box on the middle place mat. He was holding a postcard at arm's length. 'What's up?' she asked, taking the postcard and reading it. In that moment her concern for John overrode her normally instinctive respect for residents' confidentiality.

Kevin snatched the postcard from her. 'YOU WILL FIND ME AMONG THE DEAD MEN,' he read. 'That's it then, John, your brother must be dead.'

Mick growled and Jack handed the postcard back to John who left the table and went into the kitchen.

'Dead and gone. Dead and buried. I told you so. Dead as a doornail,' said the Bastard.

'A strange expression,' mused the Academic, *'featuring in*

both The Vision of Piers Plowman *and in* Henry IV. *There are of course other similies with the same meaning: dead as mutton, dead as a stone. Dead as a herring is another odd one. Although it is true that by the time most people see a herring it has long been both dead and preserved.'*

'*Herrings?*' asked the Bastard.

'*There is the view that the term has its origins in carpentry. If you hammer a nail through a piece of timber and then flatten the end over on the inside so it cannot be removed (a technique called clinching I believe), the nail is considered dead as it can't be used again.*'

'*Quiet!*' said the Bastard. '*Poor, poor John, a dead brother eh? All alone in the world now. Perhaps you should join him, what do you think? Get back to that bridge. You know what they say, if at first you don't succeed, try, try again. That big Dutchman is probably away by now.*'

'*Think of the peace,*' chipped in the Tempter, again an unexpected recruit to the Bastard's cause. '*Endless sleep, rest forever. An end to pain and disappointment.*'

'*The bourne from which no traveller returns,*' interjected the Academic.

'*Who would want to return to this poxy life? Especially when your brother's dead, and you don't have anyone in the world who cares for you ...* '

'Among the dead men, doesn't necessarily mean he's dead himself,' said Mick. He had left the breakfast table and walked slowly up to John who was staring through the window at a bird high in the sky. He put his hand round his shoulder. 'Loads of folk visit graveyards ken. People like the peace and quiet, they go to eat their lunch away from the noise. Graveyards these days are places of refuge and contemplation.'

'*Don't listen to him,*' hissed the Bastard, annoyed that his perfect pitch for suicide had been compromised by a real voice from outside of John's head.

‘I’m not busy the day. Let’s go and see,’ said Mick.

‘He’s right John,’ added the Tempter. *‘He might be there. You’re due a break.’*

‘“STRICTLY NOT PERMITTED,” recited Mick outside the gates of Easter Road cemetery “Scattering or partial burial of ashes. Planting of plants, shrubs, roses, etc. Children without a parent or guardian. Any unauthorised persons or vehicles. Erection of monuments or stone vases. Artificial wreaths or glass of any kind.” Don’t let them see that stone vase you’re carrying, John, for Christ’s sake.’

John had already left Mick and was working his way methodically along the first line of gravestones close to the perimeter wall, quickly scanning the details of the interred. He was helped by the Academic who had assumed a sonorous tone appropriate to the surroundings. *‘Mary Mullins 87, John Bogie 27, Paul Turner 6 months, much missed ... the beloved wife, daughter, husband, brother ... No, not yours, he was 59.’*

‘Faster, faster!’ urged the Bastard. John responded and started running between the stones. The Academic also tried to read faster, *‘Ivy Douglas, housewife, 80 ... hang on, May McDonald, no Mary McDonald, look I can’t do this! Joseph somebody, 42 ... former policeman, Ivandl, no, Ivelleli, Italian I think, no probably Lithuanian ... ’*

‘Faster, faster, no time to lose!’

‘72 years old, John somebody ... died giving birth, no, not John, Harriet ... 27, no, the stone’s chipped, 29 ... I CAN’T DO THIS!’

‘More haste ... ’ said the Bastard.

‘Keep looking, keep looking,’ implored the Tempter. *‘Don’t give up now. Try the ones in the corner. There’s someone there, I’m telling you!’*

John kept his eyes on the far corner of the graveyard where the Tempter had made him look. As far as possible he took the most direct path, walking over graves, knocking over vases of utterly dead flowers. For a fleeting second he eyeballed a stone angel before veering to the right.

'Careful, son,' said Mick, picking up the desiccated flowers and putting them back in their equally faded receptacles.

The Tempter had been right, there was someone there. John caught sight of a male figure lying neatly on a grave some two rows further in. From this angle only his boots and jeans were visible. He clambered over the intervening plots and stood, heart pounding above the recumbent figure.

'It's him, it's him!' shrieked the Tempter with the enthusiasm of an excited child, *'After all these years!'*

John could barely look at the figure lying with his arms neatly folded across his chest.

'Jesus Christ, Jack, what are you doing here? Get up, you fool,' said Mick, helping him to his feet. 'You'll catch your death ... no, that's no quite what I mean ... '

Despite his disappointment, John too felt sympathy for his hostel mate.

'It's peaceful here, it's where I get to think,' said Jack, exhibiting defensiveness and embarrassment in equal measure. 'I get to look at the sky, and prepare myself ... '

'What for? Ah, don't tell me' said Mick. 'Get yourself home, have a lie down in your bed, not a poxy grave, the time'll come for that soon enough.' Mick instantly regretted the last observation, and muttered something consoling to Jack who was already walking slowly, shoulders hunched towards the cemetery entrance.

'You couldn't make it up!' commented the Bastard, a sardonic observer of the farce as it unfolded. *'A small trip round the asylum garden of remembrance, chained together by your shared sadness and delusional states.'*

What do you mean, you couldn't make it up? As Narrator, I resent that. I am the objective recorder of John's inner and outer lives. I also strive, in case you hadn't noticed, to give equal weight to all of the Voices, yours included, and mine for that matter, who live in John's head.

'But are YOU making it up?' butted in the Academic. *'We are dealing here with profound issues of the existence of a reality separate from those who observe and record it.'*

It's my story, right!

'My point exactly. Isn't it meant to be John's story?'

'It could have been his brother,' intervened the Tempter sensing trouble and increasingly disconcerted by the new direction the narrative seemed to be taking. *'You've got to hold the hope, isn't that what they all say, John?'*

'MY WIFE IS DEAD / AND HERE SHE LIES / NOBODY LAUGHS / AND NOBODY CRIES / WHERE SHE IS GONE TO / AND HOW SHE FARES / NOBODY KNOWS / AND NOBODY CARES'

Jester, shut up!

'TEARS CANNOT RESTORE HER / THEREFORE I WEEP'

This is neither the time not the place!

'I just wanted ... '

Well, don't bother.

'You look shattered, old son,' said Mick. Near the entrance he patted the stone on which he sat and John joined him. 'I got Linda to make us some pieces,' he explained offering a wodge of Mother's Pride to his companion.

'In the name of the wee man!' said Mick, 'Would you look at that?'

The horse-drawn cortege was preceded by a single figure in a long black coat and top hat. The horses with black plumes strapped to their heads pawed at the gravel. The coffin itself was scarcely visible though the glass-sided carriage, obscured by a sign made from flowers that proclaimed, MOTHER.

'Gangsters,' muttered Mick. 'Drug dealers, pimps, money launderers, people traffickers ... ' His muttered litany attracted the attention of two burly men hiding behind sunglasses. Mick touched his beanie in respectful acknowledgment of their grief.

'*All the rage these days*,' explained the Academic. '*Themed funerals. Many options. Motor cycle hearses are increasingly popular. Harley Paulson, a Cafe Racer Triumph or maybe a Suzuki Hayabusa. For a little extra the principle mourner gets to ride pillion. There are other more alternative possibilities, a hearse, flatbed lorry, decorated bus, a simple horse and cart, vintage fire engines ...* '

The other Voices were strangely quiet, as if taken aback by the Academic's breadth of knowledge and the visions he was conjuring. John too found himself making theoretical choices for his own funeral.

Taking advantage of the unexpected silence, the Academic continued. '*Mind you, horse-drawn affairs are less popular after that accident in Ipswich a few years back. The horses struck a bollard and careered into parked cars, the carriage flipped over in the street, spilling the old dear into the gutter. All hell broke loose ...* '

FIFTY

The horse slipped on the lamp oil that had been oozing undetected from a large flask on the quayside. The revellers scrambled to escape the cart as it toppled towards them. 'Mind yourself,' said Balthasar, pushing his fellow weavers out of harm's way. The distressed horse fought against the yoke that was now twisting into its neck. The momentum of falling from the cart and the subsequent impact with the ground served to burst open the bales and free them from the hempen ties on which their previous shape had depended. Filigrees of straw cascaded over all and sundry. When the dust settled the weapons were clearly visible. Muskets, flintlocks, arquebuses, and daggers. A small boy who emerged from a heap of straw clutching a cross bow as big as himself was soon squealing under the impact of his mother's hand against his cheek. His friends, not constrained by a parental presence, chased the myriad shot balls running across the cobbles.

Several geuzen emerged from the tavern opposite the tumbled cart. One of their number was holding up his breeches with one hand while trying to extricate himself with the other from the young woman whose body he had been exploring moment's earlier. The weavers too helped to gather up the weapons; many lives had already been lost in their procurement. When they had been safely stowed they trooped back into the tavern with their new comrades.

Two drunks, presumably woodsmen in their previous lives, faced each other with locked arms and mimed sawing the table in half. A tiny man struggled to hold the enormous breasts of his new life companion, one in each hand as if he might drop them at any moment. A geuzen stripped to the waist gargled his ale in tune to a song half remembered from his childhood. His companion slapped him on the back and the contents of his mouth arched onto the floor. A party of four men took turns to rise from an adjacent table with the regularity of a pumping engine to propose toasts.

'To William!'

'William!'

'To my neighbour's wife!'

'I'm your neighbour, you horny bastard!'

'To horny bastards everywhere!'

'Horny bastards!'

An older man slumped in a corner picked at a scab on his arm and muttered. The weavers gave up trying to speak as all words were drowned out by the cacophony of competing songs, bawdy, maudlin, patriotic, and interweaved snatches of sea shanty.

'UP HER ARSE, UP HER ARSE ... FAREWELL MY LOVELY ... GOD'S CHOSEN WILL NEVER KNOW DEATH ... UP HER ARSE ... NEVER KNOW DEATH ... FAREWELL ... ARSE ... 'KNOW DEATH ... ARSE ...

Three stout Wallenders stood looking down at the top of a barrel, then simultaneously opening their fists, dropped their chosen cockroaches onto the wood. The race started badly, two of the stunned insects landed on their backs and had to be turned.

'Come on, you beauty!' urged the nearest roach trainer. His breath propelled the black thoroughbred towards the middle of the barrel.

'Cheating turd!'

Offended, the accused slammed his fist onto the wood obliterating the rival insects, and then defiantly rubbed the black smudges into his stubble.

'UP HER ARSE ... FAREWELL... GOD'S CHOSEN ...
MY LOVELY ... NEVER KNOW DEATH ...

Other beggars arm wrestled, fought, swore, spat, sang, becoming sentimental and belligerent by turns. One was standing on a table, progressively removing items of clothing to a tune only he could hear. Another, having lapsed into a coma, snored loudly into the face of his new female acquaintance. A fat man had fallen asleep while playing a penny whistle. The instrument responded faithfully to each long breath.

A stray chicken ran the gauntlet of legs and boots.

A small man whose head was dissected by a stained bandage spoke to the shade of a Spaniard he had disembowelled days before. 'It wasn't personal, you know that. It could have been you ripping my guts out. You shouldn't have come to our country. How old are you? Sixteen, same age as my boy ... ' He wiped his eyes and went back to his drink.

Two elderly brothers stared at each other, their faces inches apart. Maudlin reminiscence had suddenly flared into acrimonious recriminations over a long-buried childhood slight. 'You did, you did, you did!'

'It wasn't me, you fool, it was our sister.'

A candle jammed into the wall guttered and dribbled hot tallow onto the face of the sleeping man still playing the whistle. He jerked awake. 'Do that again and I'll rip your bollocks off and make you eat them!' Nobody paid any attention. He morosely picked the wax from his beard.

The weavers sat together. 'My belly's not right; I think I'm still on the ship.' Balthasar lurched and steadied himself against a table.

'Look at these hands.' Cornelius rubbed the calluses that had recently appeared on his lower finger joints.

'Geertje won't thank you for rubbing her buttocks with those,' said Balthasar.

Johannes' pleasure in the moment lasted until he felt hot breath on his neck. He turned to face Blindman who, as if deprived of both sight and speech, mouthed a word of two syllables and then laughed soundlessly.

FIFTY-ONE

'Let's try one more,' said Mick, leading the way up Easter Road. 'Let's face it, your brother's not a jaikie skulking in a shite cemetery like that scabby Council tip. If he's anything like you, he's got more class.'

John followed in his wake without the faintest idea where he was being led. He had surrendered all volition. There was no room left in his head for himself and his own thoughts. The Voices had commandeered every corner of his brain. The best he could do was listen impotently as his personal parasites gossiped, bitched and argued among themselves.

'Another goose chase.'

'I don't know, flying geese could be a sign.'

'A sign, my arse!'

'I've always been fascinated by the myth that humming birds migrate on the back of geese. Difficult to accept really as humming birds would not survive flying at 20,000 feet which is the altitude preferred by Canada Geese.'

'Can't you take a sabbatical for a while or do something useful like educating the ignorant forces of darkness who live in Mick's head?'

The Academic ignored the insult but thought it wise to change tack. *'It's true, you know.'*

'What is?' asked the Bastard.

'The sea beggars became expert at smuggling arms into the coastal villages, right under Alva's nose. And by all accounts, and judging by contemporary portraits, his nose was very large indeed. Perhaps it grew as a result of all the lies and false promises he made to the Dutch nobility.' Hugely amused by his own joke the Academic started to honk and guffaw. The Jester shook his head.

Refusing to acknowledge the existence of pedestrian crossings Mick launched himself, and John, into the full stream of traffic turning from Princes Street into the top of Leith Walk. 'Effing green men telling me what to do, when to cross the road, I think not!'

The Carlton Cemetery was altogether a more sombre, impressive affair. A slice of 18th century Edinburgh left untouched, a vast *memento mori* barely noticed by the scuttle of lawyers and uncivil servants preoccupied with their meeting scheduled to start in five minutes in St Andrews House.

Mick paused beneath the smoke-black obelisk that had pride of place in the cemetery. 'Rich bastard.' Tumbling down the slope at odd angles were the open family vaults, sepulchres to forgotten merchants and erstwhile worthies. John looked at the tomb nearest the outside wall. The cracked lintel squatted on two wind- and vandal-eroded columns. There was nothing inside except Special Brew cans and an improvised cardboard bed.

'He might have stayed there last night,' suggested the Tempter, unhelpfully. *'Safe spot away from the gay bashers on the hill over there.'* John looked up at the pagoda folly on Carlton Hill. *'Perhaps we should come back when it's dark. Wait for him.'*

'Aye, he's probably gay like you, a pair of sibling shirt lifters.'

'Look at this one,' called Mick. 'WILLIAM RAEBURN PERFUMER died 24th March 1812. I bet he's humming now.'

John moved to the adjacent vault. Again it was completely empty apart from a matrix of used orange syringes scattered on the ground.

'Perhaps he's got a habit,' said the Tempter. *'Broken home, raised in care. It happens, you know.'*

The back wall featured a single graffitied heart pierced by an arrow with initials.

'Romeo and Juliet on heroin,' suggested the Tempter. *'Perhaps he died in his lover's arms. Worse ways to go you know. It would make a good Fringe play. Perhaps you could write the script John. You could dedicate it to your brother.'*

The Bastard snorted, amused that the Tempter seemed to have usurped his role. He was, though, only an amateur with no concept of how to cause real pain.

'I think you've been here before, John. Yes, it's coming back to me now. Didn't you bring Sarah here in the early days when you were students? You had a few in the Abbotsford. Remember now? You came up here and suggested a knee trembler in one of these vaults. She looked at you as if you were mad. She wasn't far wrong was she? She ran away saying she never wanted to see you again. You ran after her, the length of Princes Street, shouting at her, urging her to stop and talk to you. You couldn't catch her. Odd that. She was always the better athlete. Eventually you knocked over an old lady, sent her tumbling. Her skirts in the air, her messages all over the pavement. Not best pleased, if I remember. You went for another drink on your own. That barman refused to serve you a third pint and you went home, sobbing. You've always had an impressive capacity for self-pity.

'Sarah stayed out that night, didn't she? Do you remember, she was oddly contrite when she turned up at your flat the following day? You knew she had been with someone else, but neither of you mentioned it. The writing was on the wall though, wasn't it?'

Leave him alone, Bastard; it's unnecessary.

'Look, you're just the Narrator, an objective chronicler of all that is said, allegedly. You have no right to censure other Voices. I think you're getting too fond of John, altogether too protective.'

Mick was standing in front of the statue of David Hume, saluting.

'Yes, yes,' said the Bastard sarcastically, *'move the story on, change the focus just when we're getting somewhere.'*

It's my story!

'We've had this discussion before' said the Academic. *'It's John's story.'*

'Some man that Davy,' Mick said. John joined him. 'A major figure in the Scottish enlightenment ... No time for they Rationalists. He preferred passion, desire was the thing with him.'

The Academic also sensed that John needed to be distracted from the corrosive memory skilfully conjured by the Bastard. *'A key figure in epistemology, metaphysics, ethics, political philosophy and classical economics.'*

John mimed the words as if there was solace and respite to be gleaned from concentrating on the terms, each one a mindless prayer on a rosary. He was also feeling exhausted.

As they left the cemetery he felt the desperate need to be somewhere else. He was being tugged away and, after the smallest moment of hesitation, surrendered to the familiar lure.

When they returned to the hostel Jack was in crisis. He was being held in Beverley's arms.

'There's no love in the world,' he moaned. 'No love.'

'Of course there is,' said Beverley, less than convinced as she cradled her man-baby. 'We all love you.'

'No, we don't,' said Paul, who was passing. 'We are fellow residents, I am your friend but I don't love you.'

Jack moaned louder.

FIFTY-TWO

'What are you saying? What are you saying?' shouted Johannes, drawing back his clenched fist.

Blindman moved his head slowly in the direction of a knot of soldiers who were sufficiently sober to string words together. Johannes lowered his fist and strained to hear their conversation. The men were talking of the Prince. Some said he had died of the plague in Rotterdam. Some said his heart had broken on hearing of his brother, Louis' death. Others in the tavern claimed that the Prince had rallied and was about to send his army to Leyden. Johannes joined in the discussion.

'Leyden you say.'

'Two months they've held out,' explained one of the younger sailors, whose voice had barely broken. 'Those who still live are eating the hooves and skin of horses. The pigeons carrying messages of hope are eaten before they can fly home with news but someone still has the strength to send rockets from the tower. Every night the stars erupt. We must go there. I will strangle Valdez with my bare hands, and then make every Spanish mercenary choke on the chicken they stuff into their faces.' He put his hands round the neck of an imaginary enemy as he spoke and made a clicking sound, an approximation of a skull separating from a vertebra.

'There is a plan,' said his older companion. 'The Prince has given orders that the sluices be opened and the dykes breached. He himself supervised the destruction of the barriers on either side of Capelle. Believe me, the waters will carry us to the very gates of Leyden.'

'There are seven thousand foreign troops in Rynland, all approaches are completely sealed,' said the Academic, excitedly. *'Some of the burghers want to sign the truce.'*

Shhh. Listen to the men.

'I've seen the devil's own boat,' explained the young lad. 'It's in the dock, we passed it as we sailed in. Two galleys made into one with wheels so that it can be hauled over the dykes.'

'It'll never work.'

'Have faith. They say Valdes' mistress is Dutch. She stopped him from invading the town. We can get there.'

Johannes got the attention of the others and signed for them to listen. 'Michel,' he said by way of explanation.

'The challenges are twofold,' said the Academic, increasingly frustrated that only his fellow Voices and John could hear him. *'The plague is striking down those still capable of standing, and the brewers have selfishly insisted on using all available corn which means the citizens are left with inedible malt. Furthermore the citizens are hiding their dead so they can still claim their allowance of old flesh.'*

Shhh.

'The waters are flowing. Haven't you seen the farmers outside dragging all they own on carts? Their women stoop under their burdens. They have sacrificed their livelihood, their cattle, their orchards, so we can rise as a nation.'

The idea resonated with Cornelius.

'The displaced peasants are being hired to breach the dykes after they have been secured. The barges have been requisitioned and are ready to sail.'

'*Yes, yes,*' said the Academic. '*Several hundred praams have been collected. Seventy galleys have been equipped with small cannon and seven or eight arquebusiers ...* '

What?

'*Early muzzle loaded firearms which carried a ball of about 3.5 ounces. Sometimes I'm astounded at how little you know!*'

Behave yourself!

'They need men to row the galleys.'

'Count us in,' said Johannes. Balthasar and Cornelius nodded.

'Tomorrow we sail again!' shouted the lad before he became overwhelmed by his own excitement and the belated impact of the drink he had earlier consumed. He slumped down on the table, rested his head in his arms and yawned.

The weavers made a corner of the tavern floor their own and prepared to sleep. Two of the beggars started to argue drunkenly about the relative stamina of their new mistresses until the others told them to be still.

'What do you think, men?' asked Johannes.

'Our lives are not our own,' said Cornelius. 'We join tomorrow.'

'Do you think they'll take an old man?' whispered Balthasar. 'My arms are not what they were.'

'Old man?' chided Johannes, 'You are strong as an ox. Several ox,' he corrected himself.

'*Oxen,*' said the Academic.

Johannes couldn't sleep. Michel was within reach, he knew it. 'My son, my son,' he said.

'Sorry old man, we don't need you,' said the beggar captain, still wearing his newly captured Spanish Admiral's uniform. 'You two, yes.' Balthasar looked towards the others.

'You take all three or none of us,' said Cornelius. The Admiral grunted and acquiesced.

Sixteen galleys choked the Rotte, forming a bridge across the river. Men clambered from one boat to another looking for unclaimed oars. One of the lead galleys had sprung a leak and was slowly filling with water. Cursing, the new crew abandoned their attempt at bailing and pulled themselves onto a neighbouring boat which, in turn, threatened to capsize under the weight of the extra bodies.

Legions of gulls banked and dipped down again towards the human frenzy. A sack of corn split when it was passed down from the dock. Its contents fell into the choppy water forming a sloppy gruel. A woman with a large pannier basket threw loaves at the men in the boats who competed with each other to catch the freshly baked trophies.

Cornelius argued briefly with a small man who had seated himself in the middle of a three-man bench. Grudgingly he moved aside leaving room for the weavers.

'The two of us will take the strain,' said Johannes. 'Rest when you need, Balthasar.' The older man nodded.

The wait seemed interminable as further supplies were brought aboard and stowed under the benches. Johannes was growing agitated and again resorted to his increasingly habitual mantra of 'Michel, Michel'.

'Patience, we'll find him,' said Balthasar, rubbing his left leg which had gone into a spasm.

Finally, a score or so of heavily armed men stepped onto the boat and threaded their way over the seated oarsmen to occupy every available inch of space in the centre of the shallow craft.

'Frenchies,' said Cornelius, after failing to make any sense of what the men were saying.

'Two companies of French arquebusiers under the command old Boisot himself,' explained the Academic to nobody but his fellow Voices and their landlord.

'Who cares a flying ... ?' asked the Bastard, feeling distinctly marginalised by the unfolding activity.

The sound of cheering from the men in the foremost boats provided the first indication that the sluggish flotilla was starting to move. One by one they peeled away and floated into the tide that moved them slowly downstream. The town-houses gave way to less salubrious dwellings propped up with beams pillaged from the houses that had already succumbed to gravity and neglect. They in turn mutated into rural dwellings and random sheds sheltering both men and beasts.

As there was no need to deploy the oars at this stage the weavers watched the unfolding tableau of open fields. A heron stared at them from a clump of reeds with an inscrutability that reminded Johannes of Blindman, of whom there was now mercifully no sign.

Several women were hanging newly washed clothes on the rushes, while others continued scrubbing garments on the rocks at the water's edge. When they noticed the activity on the water they stood, stretching and rubbing their backs with one hand while waving with the other at the passing boats. One of the younger women raised her skirts in the direction of the men who roared their appreciation at the unexpected sight of large buttocks. For a fleeting moment Cornelius thought he caught a glimpse of Geertje in their midst. Realising that this was not possible he felt instantly lost. The sky had turned dark. He hoped the heavy-bellied clouds were not a portent, but was distracted from his increasingly sombre thoughts by shouts from somewhere in front. They were nearing the sluices that had been opened to flood the countryside and enable the craft to pass unhindered towards Leyden.

'Dig those oars deep!' exhorted the helmsman. 'Plough the waters, harvest your children's future.' The veins stood out on his neck as, facing his crew, he pulled on imaginary oars. Slowly the galleys heaved themselves out of the rocking current and into the shallower, calmer waters that now lay over the fields.

Not appreciating the change in depth the inexperienced weavers continued to raise their shared oar high into the air. It struck the submerged field and the resulting jolt left Balthasar convinced that his shoulder had been wrenched from its socket. 'Jesus wept!' he grimaced, holding the burning joint.

The men behind them protested loudly as their own oar became trapped. Eventually after several collisions the ramshackle beggars' navy spread across the flat plateau of flood that seemed to stretch forever.

'Raise your oars, rest and drift for a while,' came the order. The water was no more than two feet deep and the tilled land with the occasional boulder was clearly visible. No one spoke as they stared at the alien landscape. There was no sound at all apart from the water lapping ever more softly like a child recovering from a crying fit. There was no bird song. Johannes looked round him and experienced a calmness he had not known since they began their quest.

After the pause, the beggar admiral moved along the crowded deck space instructing the men how best to row through the shallows. At first the weavers merely skimmed their oars across the surface but soon found a shared rhythm. Cornelius noticed a man was walking alongside the boat carrying a yoke across his shoulders at each end of which was a bucket. Steadfastly ignoring the passing galleys he muttered to himself while laboriously wading through the flood. His destination was a village knee deep in water just visible from the bow. Initially the crew was too dumbfounded to greet him.

'What's he going to do with the buckets?' asked Cornelius, incredulously.

'You mad sod!' shouted someone, in the nasal accent of Friedland. The bucket man started and grunted as if a boat had just strayed into the peripheral vision of a strange dream from which he couldn't fully wake.

As the dusk settled the galleys floated in single file along what would have been the main track separating the sparse dwellings on either side. The inn sign, showing an angel blowing a trumpet, swung in the breeze. A cat mewed forlornly from a flat roof and a line of ducks, disrupted by the disruptive proximity of the oars, took ungainly flight. Balthasar thought he caught sight of an old woman's face at an upper window but he could not be sure.

Simultaneously the three weavers thought of the village they had abandoned many months previously. Balthasar glimpsed his wife shaking her head as she gossiped with their neighbours, nursing her wrath, keeping it warm for his return.

'What do you think Wilhelmien's up to?' asked Cornelius, reading his friend's mind.

'Moaning about me, "Stupid old sod" or something similar. "My husband is as useless as a teat on a sow, as useless as a blind man picking coloured shells off a beach ... "'

'Don't remind me of him,' said Johannes.

'As useless as ... ' said Cornelius, sensing a game, 'as a dead rat for travelling companion ... '

Johannes thought of Michel starving behind the Leyden walls.

'Well,' continued Balthasar, suspecting that the game was not a good idea. 'Perhaps she got over me. She always had an eye for Theo, the pedlar, perhaps she's run off with him. He's on the donkey, she's in the cart squashed under a mountain of pots and pans ... I never did buy her that pot she wanted ... And Geertje?'

'I don't know,' said Cornelius.

They rowed through the night, their path lit by the red moon and the lanterns that were slung on either side of the barge. Their light reached no further than the tips of the oars that continued to dip and pull through the black and silver water. Each stroke mixed eddies of dark liquid into slivers of moonlight, a witch's restorative potion. Johannes sang under his breath the song that previously helped them to work in rhythm at the loom.

Despite their fatigue his companions joined in. Although the tune was unfamiliar to the rest of the crew, they tentatively sang the chorus, twenty homesick men joined at the heart by a refrain that promised succour in the arms of wives and lovers.

'How's your shoulder?' asked Johannes.

'Fine,' said Balthasar.

As the first rays of dawn bled across the water the militiamen roused themselves from their improvised beds in the stern, brushed down their uniforms and inspected their muskets. They exuded a sense of agitated expectation as they peered forward looking for their first destination, the Landscheiling.

'Well done, Narrator, you've done your homework. As I recall the Landscheiding was the first dyke that needed to be breached if they were to progress to Leyden. The original intention had been to attack under cover of darkness and take the Spanish by storm but the journey took longer than expected.'

Thank you, Academic.

'Why are you thanking him? It's all wordy bollocks.'

You're attention seeking again, Bastard, back off!

FIFTY-THREE

Another day, another postcard, this time with an Edinburgh postmark.

'I'VE GONE OFF THE RAILS.'

Kevin smirked at John's discomfort. 'Is it you sending they cards?' asked Mick. Kevin scowled and went back to shovelling in his porridge.

'Today's magical mystery destination brought to you by Psychotic Travel Incorporated is Waverley Station,' Mick announced. Paul raised *Nostromo* until it hid his eyes.

'If you two are off gadding again, look after your pal, Mick,' urged Beverley.

'Take Dennis with you,' suggested Kevin, malevolently. 'He could do with an outing.'

'And you could do with my fist in your throat!'

'Thank you, Mick, that's enough.'

Two British Rail transport police glanced at John and Mick but decided against having a word. They were off shift in half an hour and now wasn't the time to start hassling dossers. Mick muttered something about the forces of repression and pulled his beanie further down. He dropped ten pence into the open violin case on the ground. Its owner, a Japanese student, looked bemused as he bent over the case to check that his instrument had survived the journey from York on the luggage rack. It must be another custom he didn't understand.

John stood in the middle of the concourse and looked at the faces of each male commuter as they raised their heads towards the electronic timetable. Where was he?

'Do you fancy Paignton for a nice wee break? A few beers, What the Butler Saw, donkey shite on the beach. But I'm telling you, I'm not going to King's Cross. Enemies, ken. Unfinished business. Bad folk. We could always get off at Newcastle. A working-class city. In your face, no pretensions. Perhaps not. You had a bad time in Newcastle a while back didn't you, John? I forgot. Mind that was before I was looking after you.' Mick was drowned out by the Voices arguing loudly with each other.

'You never know, this time he might find him,' said the Tempter, without conviction.

'Statistically unlikely,' said the Academic. *'The last train journey saw him back in hospital. A significant setback if I remember ... I've got his notes somewhere ... '*

'Who cares a monkey's fart anyway? I'm seriously thinking of finding a new head to live in. I'm bored with all of you.'

'How about a joke?' suggested the Jester. *'Did you hear the one ... ?'*

'YES!' shouted the other Voices, surprised that they had made common cause.

'I think it's all a trial, a quest, a sort of game show. If John perseveres then he will find his brother, I'm sure of that. A few false starts are to be expected.'

'And bloody Anneka Rice will drop by in her helicopter to point him out.'

'Trust me, a railway station is just the sort of place he might come to.'

'Bugger it!' said the Bastard. *'Let's have some sport. Come on, John, don't stand like a spare prick at a wedding. Get yourself up that escalator.'*

John did as he was told. It was a moment before Mick realised that he had gone on ahead.

'Where are you going, you daftie?' he shouted, before realising that he had stepped onto the down escalator and was treading water and proving an irritant to the descending commuters whose path he was blocking.

'OK, John, you're completely in my power.'

'I don't think that's fair ... '

'Back to your books and theories, Academic. My man's on a mission. Turn right at the top. Well done, now take the stairs, no ticket check, excellent. Platform 9C. No one about. Off you go.'

The Bastard was right; apart from a couple slumped into each other on a bench the platform was empty. John hated this. While the Voices were at best an irritant and at worst a curse with which he had to live, for most of the time he could still make his own choices, albeit limited. But not now. The Bastard was exercising total control, reducing him to an automaton compelled to follow orders. He was experiencing the strange combination of utter panic and the tiniest frisson of gratitude that he had been relieved of all responsibility.

Mick failed to negotiate the stairs, having slipped and twisted his ankle. He now writhed on the ground, from which vantage point he was hurling abuse at innocent passers-by and, more foolishly, at the transport police who had decided on reflection to keep an eye on him. 'Go on without me!' he shouted in the general direction of platform 9C as he was pulled to his feet by his new minders.

'That's it, John, keep going. Don't stand too close to the edge of the platform. That's right, stay inside the white line. We don't want anything untoward to happen to you. A bit faster though. Just in case the police remember there were two

of you. Good, down the slope, mind that pile of sleepers. Best follow the wall. Safer that way.'

John again did as he was told, walked off the end of the platform and onto the pink gravel. He kept close to the high hedge-lined gray wall that marked the boundary with Princes Street Gardens, walking beneath the sign announcing Waverley Station, well to the side of the gantries supporting the overhead cables. Because he hugged the wall he remained invisible to whoever might have been looking out from the overhanging windows of the signal box. A train passed on the furthest track, its brakes biting as it slowed to enter the station.

'You were a train spotter in your youth, isn't that right, John. Bet you never thought you'd get a chance to walk through a tunnel like the one ahead, did you?'

'From a sociological perspective the much maligned train spotter was an interesting phenomenon of the late fifties, early sixties. There were very few leisure activities available to young boys ... '

'Apart from wanking,' said the Jester, trying to rescue a situation that could get out of control.

'You can't even manage that now, can you, John? If you can't even fancy yourself, who else would?' The Bastard chuckled in admiration of his own gratuitously malignant cleverness.

John faced the black-rounded arch of the first tunnel that led to Haymarket Station. Its darkness was sucking him in.

'In you go John, quite exciting, isn't it?'

John stumbled against the near rail and fell heavily across the track.

'Careful now, we don't want you to hurt yourself ... See there is a light at the end of the tunnel. See it as a game of chance, a sort of Russian roulette. Relax. The odds must be against you meeting an oncoming train. Be strong, give it a go. Feel the adrenaline.'

Whose side was the Tempter on?

'If you see a train approaching take off your red knickers and wave them at the driver. It always works in films,' said the Jester.

'Ho, ho, ho,' laughed the Bastard.

John ran through the puddles that marked the start of the tunnel. He was hoping to outrun the panic attack that already had its hands on his chest. He fell again and lay breathless with his face against the cold rail. Everything smelt of oil.

'You could always put your ear against the line and listen for the hum of an oncoming train. It's possible to pick up trains that are over a mile away,' suggested the Academic.

He stood up. Mercifully the aperture towards which he stumbled did appear to be growing with every step.

'Almost there John, almost there.' The Tempter adopted the tone of someone concerned for a much-loved pain-racked relative on his deathbed.

John rejoined the sunlight moments before the blast from the horn of the approaching train made him scramble off the tracks. He tried to breathe as the carriages did their utmost to drag him in. Surely whoever was controlling him would release him soon.

'Would that be the Fat Controller?' asked the nearly hysterical Jester.

'It's just a three car from Helensburgh. Journey time of two hours three minutes. It alternates with the stopping train to Milngavie,' clarified the Academic. 'Mind you it depends if Scot Rail are implementing their winter timetable yet.'

'Come on, John, left, right, left, right. Not very fit are we? Yes, good plan, keep to the wall, keep safe.'

As he passed under the first of the two footbridges that crossed from Princes Street Gardens a youth pulled himself up onto the parapet and spat expertly at the weirdo lumbering along the track beneath him. He then crossed to the other side of the bridge to gloat at his victim and wave his middle finger. John let the saliva trickle down his face.

The young Asian couple kissing on the second footbridge were completely oblivious as he passed beneath them.

'Keep running, don't stop!'

John ran into the second tunnel on the Castle side which carried incoming traffic from Haymarket. Total blackness, he could see nothing.

'No light at the end of this one, John' said the Bastard, as if it had been John's own decision to plunge into the dark. He banged his head against the tunnel wall and reeled back to stumble again against the railway sleepers beneath the track.

'Of course, the Black Hole of Calcutta was not actually black. The term was common military slang for any prison. Having said that, the 1911 Encyclopaedia describes how 69 men were incarcerated in the Nawab's dungeon which measured 24 x 18 feet. Most died.'

'Thank you, Academic. Don't fancy that do you, John? Count your blessings, at least you're the only one here ... apart from us that is.'

'Still on a sub-continental theme it reminds me more than anything of the Marabar caves in A Passage to India. *What happened to Adela? That's the question ... '*

The train was heard before it was seen. An explosion of noise and then light from the driver's cab. The air was syringed from John's lungs, a brass plunger pulled to the hilt, his bones shaken by a dysfunctional mother at the end of her tether. He was back in a concertinaed version of a recurrent childhood nightmare in which a carefully assembled jigsaw depicting a fairground was mangled by an angry fist. The severed rails of the roller coaster hung in the air as the screaming, candy-flossed carriages plummeted. Disembodied raucous faces burst from the black walls in the House of Horrors and the malevolent stallholders beckoned with ugly fingers.

He tried to lean against the tunnel wall, but it wasn't where he thought. He fell backwards as the train thundered past. John was braced, fists clenched, against the far wall of the navvy's alcove into which he had fallen. Once the echo of the train's two-tone horn had stopped bouncing in the confined space he could hear nothing apart from the blood in his ears. Even the Voices had stopped. Having led John into a situation of extreme danger the Bastard was happy to let things unfold, the Academic had retreated meekly, the Jester had put away his motley while the Tempter knew the time wasn't right.

Panic thumped him in the chest and choked the air from his lungs. He was going to die, as simple as that. He slid down the wet wall and lay in the foetal position, his limbs trembling, his thoughts a turbulent soup of small demons, non sequitors and overwhelming fear.

FIFTY-FOUR

'Watch what you're doing!' shouted Cornelius, as a fat militia man stood on his hand, eager to step from the galley and join his companions as they waded towards the Landscheiding.

Urged by the crews, the soldiers clambered onto the dyke and rushed in both directions with fixed bayonets. Disappointed at meeting no resistance from the Spanish who were scuttling away as fast as they could run along the dyke, they shouted back towards the boats and made beckoning gestures. The galley admiral urged the remaining men to leave their oars and take the pickaxes and shovels that he handed them as they disembarked

Balthasar stepped up to his knees in the cold water. 'I'm too old for this,' he said.

'Come on Granddad,' retorted Cornelius, jabbing him in the behind with a large trenching tool. Johannes paused for the briefest moment on the gunnels before stepping into the water. He took in the whole of the vast sky, the muted sun struggling to muscle aside the entrenched clouds; a single skylark soared upwards. He knew with absolute certainty that Michel was near! In that certainty he joyfully launched himself further away from the edge of the boat than he intended and fell backwards into the water. Cornelius pulled him up. 'No need for the bathhouse now,' he said.

Quickly organised into lines, the crew were set to work digging channels in the dyke to accommodate the explosives being laid by the pioneers. They crouched down and covered their heads when the order was given. The precautions proved inadequate for Balthasar who was hit in the temple by a stone hurled into the air by the explosion. When the dust cleared the others saw him clutching his head. Cornelius staunched the blood and held onto the older man who had staggered into his arms. When satisfied that the cut was superficial Cornelius sat his friend down and offered him water.

'A war wound,' said Johannes.

'You might get a medal,' said Cornelius.

While Balthasar rested, the hundred or so other men lifted the dislodged rocks and passed them down the line. The militia rested on their rifles and passed comment on progress as the breach grew wider.

The workers at the foot of the emerging gulley were working up to their knees in the water now being held back by the thinnest of barriers. When the breakthrough was made the men cheered and worked harder to turn the culvert into a channel through which the fleet might sail.

Soaked to the skin, the first line of workers was hauled up the sides of the dyke to be replaced by their peers. This process continued for several hours. The weavers pulled their weight but were increasingly aware of the taunt that they could only work with their hands and not their muscles. Finally provoked, Cornelius dropped the stone with which he had been struggling and grabbed the legs of the nearest taunter sitting on the dyke.

'You miserable piece of Utrecht shite! Low Country puke! Empty-scrotumed eunuch!' he spluttered, shovelling his struggling adversary into the water. Balthasar and Johannes nodded at each other in unspoken admiration of their friend's capacity for abuse.

'An experiment!' declared Cornelius. 'Let us see if these hands which evidently lack the strength for menial tasks can hold this unruly turd of a man under the water until he drowns!'

The victim's fellow workers, all from the same village, understood the message and, muttering, returned to their duties.

The galleys nearest to the dyke rocked as the Delfland waters finally flowed into Rynland. The raucous cheers startled a line of geese that was floating by. Complaining loudly, the birds took to the skies, flying in a long low line before landing on a quieter stretch of water.

As the men returned to their boats a commotion was apparent further along the dyke. Firmly back behind their oars, the crews could only watch as the troops engaged in hand-to-hand combat. There was a strange unreality about the dumb show where a contingent of Spanish troops could be seen running towards the militiamen. As a boy, Cornelius would squat at the foot of the showman's striped booth and watch delightedly through his fingers as Jan Klaazen gave En Klazien what for.

Balthasar was simply disconcerted watching men killing each other just yards from where he sat, quite unable to intervene. His every sinew strained as he ducked and thrust in physical empathy with the Dutch soldier closest to him. As he looked closer he noticed that the foreigner was no more than fourteen years old. At the moment when the boy was stabbed through the heart by his Dutch enemy, Balthasar wondered if his mother even knew he had enlisted. For a second the two adversaries clutched each other in a passionate embrace before the man extricated himself, and with all his force, hurled the young boy into the water where he lay face down, his blood merging with the current.

'Narrator, you're on top of your game. Despite being forbidden to engage with the enemy by the Admiral, the French

defied orders and engaged in hand-to-hand combat. Because of the proximity to the dyke the fleet could not fire for fear of hitting their own troops. La Garde excused himself by saying, nor without some justice, that in a first encounter like this, it was important to strengthen the confidence of the troops, and not to encourage the delusion that our men were not equal to the Spanish.'

Thank you, Academic. Can I continue?

'Be my guest.'

Word soon spread among the men lying exhausted on the galleys that another dyke lay beyond the present one. The Groeneweg, a full foot higher than the Landscheiding, would also have to be breached. And beyond it lay another. Progress to Leyden would be slow. Johannes' earlier certainty had evaporated. Increasingly he was haunted by the visions of starvation conjured by Blindman. As the stranded cattle lowed in the fading light he heard Michel crying for his father; as the chill night air rolled over the flooded lands he saw his cold son lying on the slabs of the street.

'Boisot has sent for reinforcements. We wait on the dark water until daybreak.' The men groaned as the Admiral, his hand still cupped to his ear, passed on the message shouted by a small red-faced geuzen from the nearest boat.

Johannes's anxiety spread though his limbs. His foot tapped in the bilge. As a consequence his knee knocked against the underside of the shared oar. The agitation woke his companions on either side who had fallen asleep the moment they were in a sitting position.

'What's the matter?' asked Balthasar.

'Michel.'

Balthasar and Cornelius nodded in the dark, unable to conjure any words that would bring comfort to their friend.

The light rain that fell during the night insinuated itself

into the bones of the crew, their jute and animal skin clothing became inexorably heavier. Eventually the great puppeteer took pity on his shivering, waterlogged charges and, one by one, cut their strings until they slumped onto the oars where they slept fitfully.

Through half open eyes Johannes looked at the first flickering of dawn playing on the floodwaters. Around him men stretched and sighed. Cornelius woke muttering nonsensical words that carried nuances of affection, as if reluctantly bidding farewell to a lover obliged to leave before daylight. 'Another day,' said Balthasar, stating the obvious.

'Aye,' agreed Johannes.

Commotion from the neighbouring galleys alerted the crew to the presence of a small armada that had arrived during the night. They had been joined by five companies of Frenchmen and four from Noyelles' regiment of Walloons. Their own craft rocked alarmingly as the crew rushed to the far side to hail the new arrivals. Friendly greetings and insults were traded across the waters. By now the pale sun had sufficient energy to pick out the helmets of the foreign militiamen. After the provisioning boat had completed its rounds, the Admiral tossed loaves and sausages to the crew.

'The new day was a reprise of the previous one,' explained the Academic, bursting enthusiastically into John's head. *'The galleys advanced towards the Groenweg; 600 soldiers disembarked only to find that the dyke was undefended, the weavers again joined the pioneers and stood up to their thighs in water for most of the day manhandling rocks to breach the dyke.'*

Academic, while I appreciate your contributions, please remember that I'm the Narrator.

'Give me a while longer, I'm enjoying this ... Cheers accompanied the first galley to penetrate the new channel. The weavers watched both its progress towards the next obstacle, the

Voorweg, and its speedy return. Word soon passed round the exhausted labourers that the dyke was heavily defended. It appeared that Valdez had dug in with 3000 troops and heavy artillery ... See, this narration stuff is easy ... The mood of early enthusiasm was replaced by the sombre realisation that they would have to stay on the Groeneweg until yet more reinforcements could be raised. It could be five more days until they reached Leyden.'

'The suspense is killing me ... '

'Bastard, why do you always turn up and spoil things?' asked the Academic.

'I was getting bored in that tunnel, he's started wetting himself, I ask you! He's less keen on train spotting now, I can assure you of that! Like John, I prefer it here although it is rather damp, I'm getting a bit fed up with the gray skies and there is something undeniably tedious about these Dutch boys ... '

'He won't last five more days,' said Johannes, 'Five days!'

'Excellent plan! Keep him in the tunnel for five more days ... '

Both of you, just shut up! Where was I?

Yes. 'He won't last five more days,' said Johannes. 'Five days!'

'You don't know that,' chided Cornelius.

'He's a strong boy,' added Balthasar. 'Don't distress yourself. All will be well,' he added without conviction.

Pleased to be back on dry land the weavers watched idly as the same peasant who had passed on information about the dykes threw a final armful of wood onto the fire. He was grinning foolishly, wallowing in his new role as camp provider. The men cheered as the revitalised flames chased each other into the twilight. Johannes' heart sank as the new day's light fell on the face of Blindman. What was he doing on the Groeneweg? The smirk on his face confirmed that he had already located the position of the weavers. After standing stock still for a moment he moved slowly towards them. The other recumbent men changed position to let him pass.

'Why have you returned to threaten our peace?' asked Cornelius, tempted to topple the unwanted visitor into the flames.

Despite the knot in his stomach Johannes knew they had to listen no matter how bad the news.

'Plague,' he whined. 'It has been important to separate those dying of disease from those dying of starvation. The Big Bellies bloated with air and want are starving. Those with apples growing from their groin and armpits, fecund buboes of pus ripe for picking, have the plague. Those with stumbling gait and slurred tongues are vexatious. The apothecaries pull at their hair and stroke their chins as they deliberate; is it the delirium of plague or the craven need for the oblivion of drunkenness? Prisoners fretting under the shadow of the axe now earn coins by dragging the plague-riddled from their homes and throwing them in cellars and pits where they groan and plead.'

'Ah, book me a holiday there,' said the Bastard serenely.

Shut up!

'Where is Michel?' shouted Johannes, pulling himself within inches of Blindman's face. As happened before when challenged, he stood silent and motionless. A small thread of mucus hung from his nose. He let it drip rather than wipe it with his sleeve.

'Please,' begged Johannes.

'All in good time. See the queue forming at the flesher's door?' Blindman pointed a languid hand towards the dawn. 'Outside lie the skins of dogs, thick-haired pelts from the pampered. Thin mean skins peppered by the bites of fleas from pauper lairs. Look, see, there's the brown coat peeled from the night watchman's beast, greased by tiny urchin hands. Inside on the white slab lie their lard-veined and gristled corpses. Of course the dog meat is rationed, a cupped hand of offal for each child, a small leg for each adult; it's only fair ... '

The drowned hounds bounded into Balthasar's head. He glanced across the water as if they might still be swimming, trying to catch up.

'During the night the pelts too will disappear dragged away by phantoms and wraiths who will scrape, boil, chew and choke on the dog leather.'

'Where's Michel?' whispered Johannes.

'Do you see the tower?' asked Blindman. The weavers saw nothing but hazy darkness where the early morning sky and the water blurred together.

'Look harder: St Pancras' tower in the square. If you concentrate on the window openings you will see a small figure climbing slowly from one flight to the next. He rests frequently. He is carrying a taper the flame of which he protects with his hand from the wind that is growing stronger with every step. There! He's made it to the top. Slowly he touches the taper to the snake of powder that winds towards the parapet. It catches; the flame squirts towards the charge. See, the heavens blaze as the volcanic twins, sulphur and saltpetre, embrace in the ecstasy of fire!' Blindman threw out his arms as if to embrace the twins himself.

Bemused, the weavers scoured the sky for any sign of ecstasy, nothing, not even a single star left over from the night.

'You lie!' roared Johannes, rushing at Blindman who stepped aside from the men and sank back into the night.

Cornelius waved his fist in the direction of the disappearing Blindman. 'If you ever come back I'll pluck the dead eyes from your sockets, I'll snap your scrawny neck, and I'll bury a pikestaff up your arse ... next time tell Satan to come himself and not send his stinking messenger!'

Some of the geuzen who were still sleeping twitched as the commotion crept into their fading dreams of home.

'It's all true, at least distinctly plausible,' shrieked the Academic. *'It's a matter of historic record that once the sluices had been opened a messenger penetrated Leyden to give hope to the inhabitants. To acknowledge receipt of the message someone flashed a signal from the tower. The Spanish troops outside were so astonished they fired blindly at the city walls.'*

'I'm really bored now' moaned the Bastard. *'Total nonsense. I want to go back to the tunnel. I want to make real mischief!'*

FIFTY-FIVE

In the tunnel John attracted the attention of several rats. Despite the darkness their eyes were visible as pin pricks of light darting across the rails and over his shoes. On two occasions he hugged the cold stone at the back of the alcove as commuter trains thundered through, inches away. After the second time he was aware of warmth spreading down his thigh. He had wet himself again.

'One of yours I think,' said the young policeman, ushering Mick into the hostel with mock politeness.

'Where did you leave John?' asked Beverley, having taken repossession of Mick and signed for him as if he had been sent by recorded delivery. 'For goodness sake, where is he?'

Mick sank deeper into his seat in the dining room, his eyes completely hidden by his beanie.

'I'm not saying,' he growled.

'In the name of the wee man, why not?'

'I've just been savagely beaten by the fascists.'

'No, you haven't.'

'I have so.'

'According to that officer they gave you tea and a bacon roll which is more than you deserve.'

'Good cop, bad cop routine. I've got bruises.'

'Yes, you fell down the stairs the other night, drunk. Have you forgotten? You asked Janet if she wanted to see your tadger.'

'Fine girl that.'

'Listen to me! Where did you leave John?'

'I'm not saying.'

'What if he's in danger?'

'We're all in danger. Our cards are marked. They listen to our thoughts. They speak to us through the TV. Brainwashed. The forces of darkness, repression and retribution.'

'When was your medication last reviewed?'

'You see, you're just one of them. Administer the chemical cosh. Compliance through drugs. I'll not surrender! You'll not break me.'

'Perhaps you should have a lie down, Mick. I'll talk to you later.'

'I reckon that's your last chance gone then, John. Even your old mucker won't save you. You're a bit stuck old son.'

Come on, Bastard, give him a break.

'No chance. Hang on a minute, another train coming.'

For a fleeting flash of a moment the look in the driver's eyes suggested he had seen some movement in the tunnel. He sounded his horn as the carriages roared past, flickering like slides in an Edwardian magic lantern show.

'Don't let me stop you, John. If you think the honourable thing would be to step out then go for it. It would all be over in a second. Then rest. Peace. Perhaps the next train that passes.'

'He's still alive!' said Johannes.

'What?'

'Michel's in the tower. We'll find him.'

'This is getting silly. Sometimes I lose all patience with you, John. Here I am thinking of your best interests and all you can do is seek some spurious solace in a delusionary world. I really think you should do the honourable thing and step in front of the next Intercity. He's waiting for us. Keep the faith!'

'Research shows that on average train drivers are absent from work after a fatality for at least four months. Post-traumatic stress disorder is predictably common. Arguably if the incident happens in the dark the psychological consequences for the driver will be minimal. He may feel a slight bump, that's all.'

'See, even the Academic agrees with me. The time is right.'

FIFTY-SIX

For five days and five nights the beggars, pioneers and militia whiled away the hours on the Groeneweg. The narrow stretch of land had been progressively abandoned by farmers who had left their poultry to fend for themselves. Initially the soaking crews kicked the birds out of their way or swiped at them with their tools but, as they thawed in front of numerous small fires, the men organised a competition to find who could strangle the most hens in a minute. The indignant birds took evasive action darting between the legs of their would-be captors.

'Come here, you vicious little feathered sod!' A geuzen whose hand was bleeding from fresh scratches bit into the bird's neck and threw its twitching corpse into the air. 'Look, look, the runt has learned to fly after all!' The men cheered and took avoiding action as the dead bird fell among them with a last defiant flurry of feather and beak.

'Poor little thing,' whined another in tones of mock sympathy while holding a petrified foul tightly into his chest. 'Come to Papa. Don't be anxious, pretty thing.'

'It's a hen, it wants cock!' shouted his companion, making as if to lower his breeches.

'It's certainly prettier than your wife!'

' ... and more willing by the looks of it!'

As the dead birds fell from their stranglers' arms they were instantly plucked amid a snowstorm of feathers and windmilling arms. Meanwhile the fires were stoked, the birds were caked in mud and left to roast in the heart of the flames.

'Do you remember the wedding in St Oedenrode village?' asked Balthasar.

'I remember the young maid with the squint,' said Cornelius.

'And you a married man,' chided Johannes.

'Not then I wasn't,' said Cornelius, defensively. 'Her father found us in the barn. He had a squint as well. And a scythe ... '

'Is that how you lost your manhood?' asked Balthasar.

When the geuzen lay sated, clutching their swollen bellies and staring at the stars, two brothers from a village in Friedland moved back along the dyke to inspect the condition of the roosters they had earlier isolated in separate huts. In the morning they proudly announced that a cockfight had been arranged for that evening and that they would manage the betting. Excitement spread through the camp.

'I know loads of jokes about cock fighting.'

Shut up Jester.

'The internet is awash with apologists for the barbaric sport. We are told that practitioners spend untold hours caring for hundreds of birds, studying breeding lines and engaging in complex networks of trade and reciprocity. Many have held quasi-spiritual beliefs, viewing the cockfight in metaphorical, almost Darwinian terms ... '

For goodness sake, Academic.

Johannes felt uneasy. He remembered Michel's aversion to chicken and heard Antonia's ranting condemnation in his ears. At the time he had supported her and forced the white meat into his son's mouth. He had choked and retched before retreating to a corner of the house where he lay sobbing.

Johannes felt a sudden compulsion to make a sacrifice to whichever God was shaping their destiny, Lutheran, Anabaptist or Catholic. A small act of mercy might make all the difference.

Accordingly when the rest of the men were busy reinforcing the breach that had partially collapsed during the night, he walked to the hut and quietly released the birds.

For much of the next day the men could talk of nothing else. Guilder and promissory notes were exchanged. Shortly before sunset a sizeable crowd had gathered as the brothers made their way towards the huts. The beggars were confident that their bird, Boisot, would quickly tear the eyes and throat from Durant, the bird championed by the militia. When the older of the two brothers broke the news that there would not be a fight, the two factions in the crowd howled with dismay before turning on each other.

Champions for each side were quickly identified. Delighted that they would not, after all, be denied blood a score of men at the heart of the crowd linked arms and formed a ring. The two champions, stripped to the waist by their supporters, went through various routines calculated to intimidate their opponent.

The choice of the heart biter to uphold the pride of the sea beggars was unanimous. Representing the militia was the young subaltern who had hurled the Spanish boy soldier into the flooded water. After circling each other the protagonists engaged. As fists connected with skulls the spectators, baying like curs, were soon splattered with blood. The heart-biting beggar pounded at his opponent's eye until it swelled like a ripe quince. When the soldier's eye sunk closer to his cheek the ring broke ranks and a mass brawl erupted. The curdling mass of riot soon attracted the attention of the dyke's more peaceful residents who rushed either to take sides or separate the warring factions.

Only when the commander of the Walloons discharged his arquebus did the fighting subside. As the injured lay on the ground it became apparent that the allies had inflicted more damage on their own than had the Spanish. A sombre mood descended over the camp. Johannes wondered what the gods would think of him now.

'I wonder who released the birds,' mused Cornelius.

Balthasar and one of the pioneers had recognised each other. He was a distant relative of Wilhelmein and the two of them spent many hours reminiscing.

Cornelius coped badly with the inaction and took to walking out along the dyke. On his return from one such excursion he was mistaken for a spy and endured a rigorous altercation with one of the guards. Only when he threatened to disembowel the official with his own pike was he grudgingly allowed to continue.

Johannes, increasingly distressed by the delay, concentrated on whittling pieces of driftwood he had rescued from the flood.

'What's that?' asked Balthasar.

'An ox,' said Johannes who had already carved a small goat, a chicken which was in fact the same size as the goat, and a dog. 'They are for Michel.'

FIFTY-SEVEN

As John stood rigid in the darkness he listened to the Voices reminiscing. It was if they knew that he was about to die and, knowing they would soon be homeless, were attempting something like reconciliation.

'You've gone soft over the years,' said the Bastard. *'You've mellowed; you're not the man you were.'*

'Two thousand years is a long time.'

'Just the twinkling of an eye. We were a great team, and it almost worked. Bread, power and glory. Happy days.'

'"And when the tempter came to him, he said, if thou be the son of God, command that these stones be made of bread." You see, you've got a mention in the Bible.'

'Thank you, Academic. You have your uses.'

'Look, I know we disagree a lot but, do you think, when the time comes and John has gone, that we could reform the group and take to the road again. Perhaps a t-shirt, THE OLD TESTAMENT WILDERNESS TOUR AD 23 ...THE HAYMARKET TUNNEL 2012.'

'We must think about it. Meanwhile there is a job to be finished.'

'John, listen to me.' John was surprised; the Tempter rarely spoke with such authority. He was usually no more than a bit

player wheedling and cajoling around the edges of his head. *'Life has not been good to you. You deserve better. You are a man of many gifts who has been thwarted at every turn. Career, relationships, self-esteem all emptied into the sand.'*

'The desert imagery is good; it provides continuity with the first time.'

Academic, don't distract us. We are nearing the climax. Carry on, Tempter, you are doing very well.

'Thanks, Boss. John, you are essentially blameless. Abandoned by your father, neglected and forsaken by your mother, abused by the system, you nevertheless fought back. You got through university. Heroic really, courage in the face and all that, but then the downward spiral.'

'It's called the cycle of exclusion, it's a paradigm for individual decline, you know, drink problems, dismissal, divorce, homelessness. A vicious circle in layman's terms ... '

John's head was convulsed by a sharp pain. Bizarrely he was convinced that the Bastard had finally punched the Academic.

'My teeth, my teeth!'

'As I was saying, you are the innocent victim of your own life, but we have great powers ... '

'Great powers,' intoned the Bastard.

'You see, John,' said the Tempter, "*we can turn back time and stop at a moment that suits you. We have an extensive catalogue to choose from. Let me turn the pages for you. Do you remember this? If memory serves me right this was just before you went to university. A summer job on that fruit farm. Yes, that's your ladder resting against the tree. And where are you? There you are, lying in the grass during your lunch break, your sleeves rolled up, brown arms. Just enjoying the sun and feeling sated and content in a way you have never known since. You chose the spot carefully to avoid the cluster of fallen plums covered in bloated drunken wasps scarcely able*

to drone in the turgid heat. When you close your eyes all you see are succulent purple Vics hanging ripe for the picking. You are daydreaming about the years to come in the fecund groves of academe. New friends, lots of beautiful intense young women eager to be your lovers. You feel slightly roused. We can take you back there, John, no problem.'

'*No problem at all,*' reiterated the Bastard.

'*We have the power.*'

'*Feel the sun and listen for the Approach.*'

Another screeching train decelerated as it entered the tunnel.

'*Feel the sun, John, and when you're ready, take that one small step.*'

FIFTY-EIGHT

'Jesus' Blood!' shouted Balthasar, above the bombardment. The half cannon on the adjacent corn barge fired the first of its twenty-six-pound balls. The galley was swamped by a small wave generated by the displacement and the crew choked in the smoke drifting across the water. Johannes rammed a finger in each ear as further salvos of hot metal tore through the air towards the Spanish forces dug in either side of the bridge on the Voorweg.

The weavers had no alternative but to wait patiently at their oars as the more experienced geuzen were entrusted with firing and replenishing the smaller cannons attached to the prow of their own vessel. Cornelius extricated himself from the restraining oar to help aboard a soldier staggering through the shallow water dabbing a rag at a wound on his temple.

'Come, old fellow, sit with us. You've done your bit.'

The injured man was followed by his equally dazed and bleeding companions. The cannon they had been firing had wrenched itself from the deck whereupon the splintered planks surrendered. The ship promptly sank to the depth of a man's arm and nestled on the field beneath it. Other boats, similarly split asunder by the vicious recoil from the guns, also slumped into the water. Completely deafened, Balthasar could only watch as the daylight was progressively swallowed by smoke and fire.

As the man-made meteor storm howled and shrieked above them he saw once more the triptych that had frightened him as a child. Dragged to church by his God-fearing parents and unable to follow the sophistry of the Jesuitical sermon, his eyes were irresistibly attracted to the devils and demons tumbling through a red sky into the maul of hell.

The gateway to perdition was depicted as a large mouth with broken metal teeth surmounted by massive protruding nostrils one of which was pierced by a ring. A single mad eye stared from beneath a wooden shutter on which squatted three small crows. In the foreground a grotesque creature had contorted itself until it could stare from beneath its own legs, holding out a begging bowl with a wooden spoon sticking, inexplicably, out of its arse.

'*We've been missing the Bruegel influence. This sounds reminiscent of Dulle Griet or Mad Meg which can be seen at the Musee Mayer van den Bergh in Antwerp. She is a kind of female hell-fiend ...* '

You're showing off again as well as knocking me off my stride.

'*Interestingly, the barrel of a cannon, dating from the time of Philip the Good, in the Friday Market at Ghent, still bears this name ...* '

Enough!

' *... just as Scotch and Irish guns are called "Mad Meg" and "Roaring Meg"...* '

Balthasar looked at Johannes who was similarly transfixed by the battle. 'We'll get there' he said, 'we'll get there.'

No sooner had he consoled his friend than they both heard the order to retreat. Men were still wading and stumbling into the water throwing aside the floating planks and debris in their determination to find a place on one of the boats. Because of the tightly packed nature of the flotilla it was soon apparent that they could not easily escape the Spanish bombardment.

'If you can stand, leave the boats. Take to the water. Push them by hand!' Leading by example the Admiral stepped into the water. Cornelius followed him before howling with pain as his thigh became pincered between the hulls of his own galley and that of a corn barge. Balthasar and Johannes forced their bodies into the gap. 'There's a man trapped here,' shouted Balthasar, veins bulging in his neck.

'Move back!' urged Johannes. Eventually the boats drifted slightly apart allowing Cornelius to free his leg. His companions, with the help of the same villagers who had earlier mocked the strength of the weavers, managed to heave him onto the galley where he lay cursing. 'I'm not going home with one leg,' he said through clenched teeth.

'We can always make you a cart, stick a pike on the font and use you as a weapon,' said Balthasar.

'The retreat was a sombre affair made worse by persistent rumours that, tired of fighting from a distance, the French captains, Durant and Catteville, had given the order for their men to land and engage the enemy from behind the peat stacks on the causeway. Noticing too late that the fleet had retreated they took to the water attempting to wade towards the now distant flotilla. Unable to believe their good fortune the Spanish shot them dead where they floundered ... '

Sometimes, Academic, I think you get all this guff from Wikipedia, but thank you nonetheless.

As they slowly returned to the Landscheiding Johannes felt unremitting dread at the realisation that each laborious pull on the oar was taking him further away from Michel.

'Keep the faith,' said Balthasar.

'Mick, you must tell us. He's your friend, he's at risk.' Beverley had exhausted her entire repertoire of gambits. She had threatened, encouraged, offered inducements. She had tried flattery, collusion with his paranoid delusions, sarcasm even, but he was not for divulging anything about John's whereabouts.

'I'm not a grass. You'll not break me. I've to live with myself when all this has blown over. John's his own man. And you ken what the poet said ... '

Beverley had no idea. Derek too tried his best to persuade Mick that there were genuine concerns over John's safety. They walked down the garden together. Derek glanced into the latest shallow grave that Jack had dug the night before. 'It happened in Croatia,' said Mick. 'It's always the same. "Let's go for a walk," all friendly like. "And by the way, that's where you'll be buried if you don't clype on your pal."'

By suppertime the other residents had also turned against Mick. Without taking his eyes of the third paragraph on page 172 of the Penguin edition of *Nostromo* which was proving particularly difficult to memorise, Paul spoke. 'You're a disgrace Mick.'

'Why don't you say it as it is ... ' muttered Beverley. 'I'm going to bring your silence up at the house meeting.'

'Big fat hairy deal,' retorted Mick. 'I'm bringing up the fact that you poison the atmosphere with reactionary bourgeois literature. Who cares a shite about what happened to the lighthouse keeper on the island on effing Great Isabel?'

'There's no f in Great Isabel,' said Paul, staring ever more intently at the difficult paragraph.

'Well, John,' said the Bastard. *'You made the wrong choice there didn't you? I can't believe that you stepped back in that cowardly way. You had the chance of unending happiness, everlasting content, endless sun but no, you chose to cling to the sad delusion that there you could find hope in your fantasy world. It beggars belief.'*

'*Beggars, sea beggars ...* ' sniggered the Jester.

'We too have limited patience, John. We were trying to help, trying to show you a way out of this tunnel, out of this life of unremitting misery, but do you take it? No. *However I have consulted with your fellow Voices and we have decided that, because we all have your best interest at heart, we will give you one more chance. Remember you owe us big time after all the kindness we have shown you. Don't think for one moment it has been easy living in your head. Over to you, Tempter.'*

'Thanks, Boss. Here's another picture for you, John. I think this was taken even further back; the picture is a bit faded. It's sunny again. Look at the bird, a distant speck in the blue sky resting on a current of warm air. And that's you, see, lying on the cliff top. There's someone next to you. It's Rebecca, isn't it? You met her soon after you left the home. You had taken a few days away from the interim hostel or whatever they called it. Your bikes are lying on the path. The half empty bottle of cider is lying between you. Do you remember how moments earlier Rebecca had almost made herself ill with laughter? You had chased her through the dunes impersonating an owl by blowing on the stretched blade of coarse grass held between your thumbs. Listen. The sea sounds distant but comforting. Every seventh wave is a large one, you explained. She counted to six then made a loud roaring noise like a nursery giant that convulsed the pair of you. A small insect has landed on her cheek and she tries to blow upwards from her mouth to dislodge it. You flick your hand towards it and she smiles. Your eyes are closed now. The sun warm on the lids. It feels as if they are open and that the motes you chase are kites in the sky. Close your eyes, John, we can take you back. We have the power. Listen, listen. The rails are humming. It sounds like a gentle wind eager to embrace you. Step out to meet it. Open wide your arms. Join her, John, she's still waiting for you. Join her!'

FIFTY-NINE

Gerda greeted them like lost friends. 'Boys' she cried, 'what kept you?'

The farm buildings on the Landscheiding had been colonised by the sea beggars and the pioneers who, through idleness, fought, gambled and drank heavily. One of them suggested they should choose a King and Queen of Misrule. Gerda had been unanimously anointed queen and installed on a throne of straw bales in the largest barn. Her sceptre was a hoe, her crown a red handkerchief. Her consort slept, snoring loudly through his mouth. The isolated pair of incisors thereby revealed were the same teeth which, according to new legend, had recently torn out the heart of a Spanish soldier. Having ripped open the man's chest and fixed his teeth on the beating organ, he tugged like a scavenging dog until it finally sprang hot and dripping from its cavity. Finding it tasted bitter he threw it away.

'Boss, can I finish this bit?'

Ok, Jester, go for it.

' ... *As their king was comatose the drunken suitors took turns to approach Her Majesty on their knees in gestures of mock homage. The weavers nodded towards their new queen and watched from a distance as the unruly court conducted its business.*

"She seems to have recovered well from her treatment at sea," mused Johannes.

"We all survive," said Cornelius, equally surprised at the transformation in the now only half-familiar woman with blood red beauty spots etched on each cheek.

"What brings you here, you troll of a man?" asked her majesty.

"I am your child, oh Great Mother, oh wondrous queen, I need to be suckled by you," leered the short man on his knees. His companions snorted.

"Approach, loyal serf, your wish shall be granted." The man grinned and raised both thumbs in the direction of his rowdy supporters. He approached the regal Gerda who suddenly leaped from her throne, grabbed the man by the shoulders and forced his head into her ample bosoms. Unable to extricate himself he squirmed and gasped. Eventually Gerda succeeded in lifting him completely off the ground. The audience howled with laughter as her victim trod in the air, his legs paddling helplessly. Eventually she relented and released her breathless subject who collapsed to the floor, laughter ringing in his ears.

"And what is your wish, humpy backed toad?"

"To serve you, oh great queen," replied her next unctuous supplicant, a small brazier-nosed man weighed down by his hunchback. The courtiers roared insults and threw their hats into the air.

"And how will you do that?" asked the imperious Gerda.

"I will live all my days under your skirts ... I will pleasure my glorious majesty ... "

"Hideous little man!" shrieked Gerda. "Remove his breeches." Eager to carry out the sentence his colleagues happily obliged. Soon the half-naked man ran out of the barn in mock terror with his hands positioned over his crotch. Even Balthasar

thought he might be sick if he laughed any more.

Meanwhile the King, now fully awake, felt able to resume his royal duties.

A grinning ghoul of a man hauled himself off his barrel and approached bowing unctuously. "Your most gracious, fornicating majesty,"

"What is your problem, my son?"

"It's my cock, your majesty,"

"Pray, what is the problem with your cock, snivelling peasant?"

"It is too big, your highness ... it belongs to a horse..."

"A sea horse!" suggested a heckler.

"Then get thee to a stable!" decreed the self-elected king of drink and orgies. His raucous courtiers aimed kicks at the priapic petitioner who covered his cod piece with both hands and fled to the back of the room.

The king then abandoned his all embracing benediction as his stubby hand wrapped itself round a tankard offered in tribute to his sagacity and omnipotence. He drained it as if emptying a pot into a ditch, belched loudly and threw back his head, guffawing with laughter. "Bring me Catholic hearts, bring me the fresh organs of virgins, bring me a cardinal's liver, bring me ... " He snatched at the air as if the words were just out of his reach, "bring me, bring me ... "

"Drink!" shouted his companions who held him down on the trestle and poured ale down his open throat ... '

Thanks Jester.

'No problem Boss, I thought things were getting a little tense.'

'This story telling is simply irrelevant,' interjected an increasingly frustrated and grumpy Academic. *'Anecdotes, spurious humour, character and cameos add nothing to the historic dimensions of this significant episode in Dutch history. Narrator, I insist that you move things along.'*

If you're so clever, Academic, you take over.

'It would be a pleasure.'

The Academic cleared his throat ostentatiously. *'It is a matter of public record that the fleet languished for several days while opinions were sought and decisions made. Eventually a Pieter Wasteel, the late Pensionary of Mechlin, arrived at headquarters. Accompanied by a boat builder who was wholly familiar with the terrain, they proposed an alternative route to Leyden which involved penetrating into Rynland not from Delfland but via Schieland.'*

'For fuck's sake!'

'As I was saying, an exploratory expedition of eight galleys confirmed that the route was feasible whereupon the rest of the fleet followed. The main challenge was manoeuvring the preposterous Noah's Ark, a type of floating fort, through the shallow water. Constructed by coupling two boats together, it could only be propelled by manually turning the wheels that separated the two hulls. Just when they were about to set the monster ship on fire to prevent it falling into enemy hands, it reluctantly floated off the restraining dyke. However, despite some progress the entire fleet was eventually grounded in shallow water quite unable to move. This period of waiting was a period of severe trial to the crews.'

'I know the feeling!'

'The men were consumed with impatience and suffered many hardships. Their tedium was only alleviated by infrequent skirmishes with the enemy and the chance to leave their galleys equipped with gauging rods to locate any deeper channels. So near but so far, they could see Leyden on the horizon.

'His Excellency the Prince of Orange, recently risen from his sick bed, visited the stranded fleet in an attempt to raise morale.'

'I wish someone would raise my morale, I'm utterly, utterly bored.'

Bastard, I'm always reluctant to agree with you but on this occasion ...

'Suit yourselves, jeopardise historical accuracy if you wish, go for the cheap narrative thrill, see if I care what happens to your pathetic weavers ... '

Academic, there's no need to sulk, someone's reading this you know, we have a duty to entertain.

Anyway, the rain started. Balthasar had developed a hacking cough and was shivering involuntarily. Johannes offered him his overcoat but the offer was declined.

'You're just being stubborn,' said Johannes. Balthasar opened his mouth to reply but was overtaken by another coughing fit. Johannes put his coat back on and shook his head. The rain was cold. It dripped from the gunnels and ran along the oars. It dropped from their noses. It flowed in rivulets from their shoes and mingled with the seawater already swilling along the bottom of the galley. Somewhere in the distance thunder growled.

Cornelius took the sleeves of his coat in turn and squeezed the water out of them. The wind blowing from the north-west forced rain into their faces. Through smarting eyes Johannes looked in the direction of Leyden but the earlier sighting must have been an illusion. The intervening distance had been smudged and blurred by the incessant downpour. Beyond the boat he could only see a thin strip of water pock marked and pitted by rain. Perhaps Michel had succumbed to the plague, his loose skin similarly pitted by disease.

SIXTY

'I really don't get you, John. You could have been with Rebecca if you had just taken that tiny step. I can do no more, Bastard, I tried.'

'I know you did, Tempter. Some cases are just intractable. Listen up, John, we have offered you glimpses of your own promised land. It was yours for the taking. You could have felt the sun on your back forever, away from all this. I'm sorry, there's no other way now.

'Face it, you are a blot on the landscape. A mute waster. A scrounger. Someone who lives on disability benefits because he hears Voices. Big deal. Get over it. Have you any idea how much money it costs the State to keep you in that hostel with its small army of support workers, a harassed manager, a cleaner, a cook? And what about the other professionals round the edges of your life? They don't work for nothing you know. The community psychiatric nurse, the intensive home treatment team. Odd definition of home isn't it? Living with weirdos. I know you don't get to choose your family but for goodness sake! Then there's the pharmacist, the psychiatrist, your social worker.

'Oh yes, and let's not forget those other unsung professionals in your life. Yes, you're right. The women of the night in the

docks down the road. We know you go to them, don't deny it. We live with you remember? We are in your head at all times including the times when you negotiate a fee with whatever pox-ridden heroin-addicted whore takes your fancy. What was the last one called? Mary, wasn't it? Yes Mary. A good Catholic name. You saved up your pocket money didn't you? You even put your benefits aside in a special tin. A small boy saving up for a treat. Utterly pathetic. And so you were, by the way. In case you've forgotten. "Hand job, blow job, the full works son, what do you want?" And you said you just wanted to talk. Just talk, my arse. Pretending to be a poor lonely little boy, when the truth of the matter was you realised you couldn't get it up. I seem to remember you blamed the medication, it's your usual excuse.

'By the way, what was your excuse when you were married to that poor unfortunate wife of yours? Can't remember? There's a surprise. Anyway let's not forget that particularly amorous encounter up the alley off Great Junction Street. She ignored you and put her hand down your trousers and eventually found your sad wrinkled little cock. "Hame to yer mammy," were her exact words. What a hero you are. A Lothario. Don Juan. A tragic Byronic figure. The Hugh Heffner of the Hostel who can't even buy a wank.'

A sheet of newspaper, propelled down the tunnel in the residual slipstream from the last train, wrapped itself round John's face. He clawed at it, screwed it up into a tight ball and tossed it into the darkness.

'You shouldn't do that, John, it might have a story about your brother, and now you've ruined everything. Perhaps he'd paid for an advertisement, and you've missed it. No, sorry, I was reading the wrong page. His name is in the obituary column; let me see, " ... after a short illness, greatly missed, no known relatives". There you have it, John. You failed him. He died a lonely death. All he wanted was to see you one

more time. Sad isn't it? I think you should join him. United in death, isn't that what they say?'

'Nice one, Bastard, you've got him this time. He can't go back, not now.'

'I feel uneasy about this whole scenario. According to the legal definition of murder in Scots law ... '

'Shut up, the pair of you! That's it, John, stand in the middle of the track. Legs apart, feet planted firmly. Good boy.'

Cries from unfamiliar birds disturbed the darkness. Johannes shivered. They were the souls of dead soldiers being wrenched through the black night by unseen forces to meet their maker. In his troubled dreams he inspected the long queue waiting at the gates, seeing people from his earlier incarceration. The preacher moved to greet him but his face was missing beneath the cowl. The young boy soldier was being comforted by an older man he didn't recognise. There were widows grieving, their heads buried in dirty shawls. The hunchback from Queen Gerda's court was also there, waiting patiently. The nuns too, still roped together, tried to comfort each other. The Spanish soldier killed by Cornelius stood with his severed head under his arm. At the front of the long queue was not St Peter, resplendent in judge's robes, but Blindman. Johannes woke with a start.

There were people stirring on the galley. Something strange was happening. A line of lights was bobbing through the pitch-black night. There was no noise, just phantom lanterns stretching into the darkness. The crew speculated as to what was happening at the distant garrison. The gloomier among them concluded that reinforcements had arrived from Spain.

'No, it's good' said Johannes. 'It's a sign.'

'Well, it's not the Lenten carnival,' said Balthasar, suddenly aching to be back among friends in his village. For a moment he was with his drunken neighbours planting burning tapers in a ring around the church to exorcise the midnight demons of greed and avarice. 'There are no bells for one thing.'

Cornelius looked dispassionately at the floating bloated body of a Spanish soldier. 'He has a mother somewhere,' said Johannes.

Eventually the lanterns were snuffed out and the darkness filled the gaps left by the pinpricks of light. The crews hunkered down once more in the galley and waited anxiously for the dawn. Somewhere an owl hooted and the rain beat down.

That night Johannes dreamed that he was once again watching the night sky under his own father's warm protective arm. For the first time ever he could clearly see the shape of a huge loom straddling the heavens.

Eventually the night lost its certainty and turned from black to gray. A tired hesitant sun peered through the clouds. Johannes blinked and rubbed his eyes. A change had occurred. There was movement. Something creaked as the galley floated free of the water and, surrendering to the breeze, let itself be blown towards Leyden which lay somewhere over the horizon just beyond the smaller towns of Zouterwou and Lammen.

'The waters have risen!' shouted Cornelius. His excitement was echoed in the cries emanating from across the swollen waters as the fleet eased itself off the fields and the men tasted once more the possibility of success.

'Jesus!' said Johannes.

What's happening here, Academic?

'Well, there's definitely been progress. The previous night under Boisot's leadership the most advanced troops routed the enemy at Zoeterwouck, a small habitation on the outskirts of Leyden. And eventually God understood the guttural prayers being offered up by the Dutch. Happy to oblige, He commanded the rain to double its efforts until the barges lifted themselves from the fields.'

'Jesus!' said Johannes again.

'Mary and Joseph!' said Cornelius.

'Melchior, Casper and me!' shouted Balthasar.

Eager to make the task of the oarsmen easier, the pioneers jumped into the water and put their shoulders to the galleys. Balthasar made eye contact with a large soldier stripped to the waist, heaving the boat forward just feet from where he was straining on his oar.

'Come on old man,' urged the soldier.

The distant garrison rising from the water eventually grew sharp edges and pulled itself upright above the steadily advancing fleet. Johannes stood in the galley and stared at the parapet where something was moving. He shaded his eyes to see better, as if the challenge was an excess of light not a scarcity. It was a small waving figure.

'Michel!' he shouted, jumping into the flood. The other beggars looked at him as if he had taken leave of his sanity. He lost his balance and fell, quickly upright he ploughed towards the garrison with flailing arms.

'Michel, Michel, wait for me!'

Cornelius and Balthasar, knowing they had no alternative but to follow their friend in his lunacy, stepped over the edge.

'Jesus! It's cold,' said Cornelius, running quickly through the water, his knees raised high in a parody of dance. 'Johannes, come back here you madman!'

Glancing up, Johannes saw that the figure was no longer there. He paused, water dripping from his arms. His friends caught up and each placed a consoling hand on his shoulders. 'Don't fret,' said Cornelius, 'just a bad dream.'

As the three figures stood trying to fill their lungs again, Michel appeared at the foot of the garrison wall nearest to them. 'Papa!' he shouted.

John staggered towards the light that was growing stronger with every step. The white aperture widened. He broke into a run, noticing how inconveniently close together the sleepers were.

He emerged from the tunnel a hundred yards from the edge of the platform at Haymarket Station. The commuters mentally rehearsing their ten o'clock presentations shuffled uneasily as he approached along the track. Dishevelled and jacketless, with ominously stained trousers, he was still smiling as several hands hauled him onto the platform and out of the way of the Glasgow Central slow train that was following him along the track, its horn blazing and its driver gesticulating.

Michel virtually disappeared in his father's bear hug of sodden embrace. Johannes held and rocked his son until Cornelius and Balthasar started to fear for the boy. Michel was making small noises that suggested he had not taken a full breath for several minutes.

'They've all gone, last night, I'm the only one left,' he said, passing his hand over his father's face to confirm that he wasn't an apparition.

Cornelius looked up at the deserted battlements and, cupping his hands to his mouth, gave the news to the waiting fleet. His muffled announcement was followed by roars of delight from the galleys. Several hats tossed jubilantly in the air soon bobbed on the water. Eager to test the boy's assertion Cornelius ran up the foreshore and pushed open the wooden gate. He stood in the still courtyard breathing noisily, gazing at the flotsam. The retreating army had, apparently, been petrified by an enemy capable of hauling ships with their teeth.

Kicking a path through the ammunition boxes and personal possessions he moved towards a cauldron suspended above a smouldering fire. Although his first instinct was to ladle the gruel straight into his stomach, something held him back. He paused and thought of his fellow citizens in Leyden less than two miles away, picked up a red greatcoat lying on the ground and folded it carefully round the handles. He staggered back out of the gate towards the beggars as they happily disembarked from the galleys.

'It all happened, it all happened just as you describe it, Narrator. Well done!'

Not now, Academic. This is the climax of the story, don't spoil the celebrations with a parade of facts.

'But, the source is impeccable. If I remember rightly, the Trevelyans in their translation of Fruin's seminal work describe how a small boy keeping watch from the walls of Leyden had noticed flares coming from Lammen. The exhausted and emaciated elders promised him a couple of guilders if he would investigate. Accordingly the boy ran along the path from Kronestein towards Lammen from where he waved his cap to indicate that the Spanish had fled.'

Fine, but I've two stories to tell if you haven't noticed.

'Yes but the other thing is that, according to legend, one of the beggars, a man called Cornelis Joppensz entered the abandoned Spanish encampment and returned with a pot of "hutspot" or hotchpotch. Later that day, the sea beggars crossed the Vliet and entered the city and distributed the food. That's why on October 3rd each year the citizens of Leyden celebrate the relief of their city with a traditional meal of herring and white bread. You couldn't make it up!'

You think?

SIXTY-ONE

Mick acknowledged John's return to the hostel with a nod of his head. Paul refused to look up from his book; just when he thought that chapter 21 had been completely committed to memory, he got muddled.

'The lord and master returns,' said Kevin, with an exaggerated bow from the waist. 'Just when we were enjoying the extra space.' Janet gave him a hug and suggested he should take a bath. 'Ay, ay,' said Kevin with a leer. 'Get her to scrub your back, John, and then your front, your lower front, mind.'

'Shut it!' snapped Janet.

As John stepped out of his clothes and into the bath he knew that something significant had changed, a shift had occurred. Although the Voices had not followed him into the bathroom he knew they were somewhere, biding their time. Nevertheless, for a wonderful moment he felt the intimation of a long-forgotten sensation. He was reluctant to probe either its nature or its origins lest such scrutiny should dispel something that was undeniably pleasant.

While the bath was running Beverley entered and emptied a packet of coloured salts into the water. 'Just this once,' she said, 'and don't you go telling anyone. We've just had our boundaries training.' He ran his hand across the top of the foam that was hiding all of his body apart from his toes. By stroking the bubbles carefully he could sculpt them into smooth contours; his palm felt cool where he had punctured the topmost layer of foam. The glass shower screen that ran half way down the length of the bath was clouded with steam. Using his forefinger he etched the silhouette of a castellated building such as a small child might draw. Beneath it he traced the outline of a small boat and by dabbing at the screen made tiny circles for the heads of the crew. Surprised, he sank further into the water and admired his handiwork.

On Platform 4 at Haymarket station he had grasped the hands offered to him. The train announcements had become indistinguishable from the excited hubbub of Dutch voices grateful beyond imagining that their ordeal was over. The siege had been lifted. The coat placed round his shoulders by the British Rail transport policeman was an embroidered cloak of great beauty.

Wrapped in a towel he carried his clothes back to his room and sat on the bed, feeling sweat pricking his forehead. The bath had perhaps been too hot. Despite knowing that the inquest was about to be convened he felt unusually calm.

'*All rise for the Voices*,' instructed the unseen clerk to the court.

'*John McPake*,' said the Academic with as much authority as he could summon. '*You are charged with abject cowardice and having knowingly chosen not to do the world a favour by committing suicide. How do you plead?*'

After a moment's silence he tutted loudly and instructed the clerk of the court to record that no plea had been entered. He then invited the Prosecutor to speak.

The Bastard rose and walked slowly across the court. After making eye contact with each and every member of the jury he turned to face the judge. '*Your honour, quite simply this sad apology of a man standing in the dock before you is not deserving of the court's sympathy. Having been given the opportunity to attend one of this country's finest universities, having been entrusted with the instruction and nurturing of young minds, he chose instead a self-indulgent life of illness. At one point, if you will pardon the cliché, Your Honour, the world was his oyster. A beautiful and loving wife, a job and home, he, as the song says, "had it all". Instead of thanking God for his good fortune he chose instead to embrace a fantasy world where he could live vicariously. He abdicated all responsibility, abandoned his spouse, failed his charges, disappointed his trusting employers and retreated into a world of delusion where he has wallowed self-indulgently for over a decade. During that time he has contributed nothing to society, becoming what I believe is termed, in common parlance, a scrounger, living off the State, seeking out the company of equally deluded failures. To compound matters he has frequently incurred the displeasure of this country's hard-working constabulary thereby distracting them from the more important task of catching criminals. On one occasion, Your Honour, and it is with a degree of reluctance that I mention such matters, John McPake was arrested for importuning prostitutes in the vicinity of Leith Docks. There can be no excuse, Your Honour, no defence against these most serious of charges, the most heinous of crimes. Although we live in an enlightened country, and are all essentially compassionate people, in this instance we must be mindful of the malignant influence that such people can have on the common weal. We all have a duty to protect young impressionable minds from the human cancer standing, no, slouching, before us today. We have a God-given duty to* decourager les autres, *and indeed to punish the wicked. And make no mistake John McPake falls hook, line and sinker into that category. He is quite simply, a wicked, wicked man and as such is deserving of the highest penalty that this court can impose. In short, Your Honour the prosecution is seeking the death sentence. Justice will only be served when your honour dons the black cap and decrees that this pathetic travesty of a human being be taken from the court to another place and hanged by the neck until he is dead. I rest my case.'*

'Fuck off!'

Uproar. Mayhem. Several jury members put their hands to their faces. The court imploded. The Academic and the Bastard removed their wigs and gowns. They looked round at the Jester, who shrugged, and the Tempter who was equally dumfounded.

'Who said that?' asked the Bastard.

'I can only assume it was John,' said the Academic, genuinely shocked.

'But he never speaks; he's given up since we took over his head.'

'Yes, it was me.' said John. 'Can you hear me well enough? I've been silent too long. Your bullying is over. Are you following me?'

'Yes, but I don't understand,' said the Bastard, confused, *'we live here.'*

'Tenants by default,' echoed the Academic. *'Squatters, if you prefer, though it's a term I don't particularly like ... '*

'Tell me,' said John, 'which bit of "fuck off" causes you difficulty? It's simple; I want you all out of my head and out of my life. Pack your metaphorical bags and go. I'm reclaiming the space.'

'Can I say a few words first?' pleaded the Bastard.

'Only if I choose to let you,' said John. 'I think on balance I might quite enjoy hearing you squirm. Go ahead. You've got three minutes.'

'Well firstly, we've known each other a long time now haven't we? Fifteen years perhaps. All right, it's been something of a love-hate relationship ... '

John snorted.

'All right then, mainly hate, but sometimes we all need to listen to unpalatable truths. We might not always enjoy what we hear but an alternative, perhaps corrective and counter view is necessary if objectivity is to be maintained. You've heard the staff talking at the hostel about notions of "critical friendship", a term that evidently encapsulates the ideal therapeutic relationship between support worker and service user, or resident in this case. Well, I represent the "critical" part of the equation. I said what I said for your own good, John, I did. Apart from anything else I put up with all that delusional shite about the sea beggars. Sorry, but it was nonsense, you must see that for yourself. All that stuff about your brother, it wasn't good for you, there was no point in colluding with the delusion that you might find him one day. It was maudlin, dangerous stuff. It was making you unhappy. I was just trying to help ... '

'One minute ... ' said John.

'Be fair. I may not always have been as tactful as I could have been, and I'm sorry for that. It's just that sometimes, you've got to call things the way they are. Any psychiatrist worth his salt would have done the same. Believe me, it hasn't been easy living all these years in your head. It's not a good place, you know that, but I've always liked you, John. You know that too don't you.'

'Fuck ... off!' said John.

'But I've nowhere to go, you can't ask me to live in Mick's head, I couldn't stand it, and apart from anything else, there's no room. I've always liked you, John, honest ... '

After a long silence the Academic cleared his throat and spoke, '*You and I, John, are university people. We understand each other. We know that the devil is in the detail. We know that knowledge and critical reasoning are the key. Indeed to quote Erasmus ... '*

'If you must, but be quick,' said John.

'Well, as I was saying ... in my defence I have consistently cast light into dark corners; I have provided a theoretical framework for both of your lives. All right, I might get carried away a bit sometimes but it was important not to let the Bastard always get his own way. We both know that he wasn't a man of intellectual rigour or insight. Correct me if I'm wrong but you've always been someone with a thirst for both accuracy and knowledge. I may have got a bit carried away some times but you understand don't you? Knowledge is power, isn't that what they say? Surely I enhanced the quality of your Dutch delusion by proving the overview, ensuring continuity, protecting the truth. I appreciate that you and I never finished our discussion about the relationship between the perhaps forgotten knowledge lodged somewhere in your consciousness and my apparent ability to provide a patina of historic accuracy ... '

For some while John had been trying to get a word in edgeways. Sensing the inevitable the Academic gallantly conceded defeat.' *All right'* he said *'I know, I know ... two words, Fuck and off.'*

After a short interval spent rehearsing his defence the Tempter stepped forward.

'John, I freely admit that recently I've got it wrong. I was powerless to stand up to the Bastard, he made me do it, and you know what he was like. I didn't want you to walk out in front of that train. You know that. In many ways I was the direct opposite of the Academic. You and I know full well that the key to recovery is having and holding hope, in whatever form that might take. Well, that was my function, don't you see? Without me you would have given up ages ago, just thrown in the towel. I kept the hope alive in you. I made you believe that you would find your brother. And let's face it, he's out there somewhere. He's looking for you as well. Think of

your joyful reunion, feel the tears and hear the laughter. Who knows, even as I speak he may be making his way to the hostel. It's going to happen, John, believe me ... The last few days have been an aberration. I wasn't feeling well, it won't happen again, I promise, keep the faith, John, keep the faith ... '

'This man went into a bar ... an Englishman, a Scotsman and an Irishman ... did you hear the one about the old woman on the escalator ... '

The hint of a smile crossed John's face. He had frequently found the Jester genuinely amusing. Even when his jokes were far from funny he had appreciated his capacity to defuse or redirect conversations. The Jester was not a bad Voice, at worst he could be inappropriate but even the concept of appropriateness or otherwise was barely relevant given the mental turbulence he had endured through the years.

John thought ... Sorry, what are you attempting to say on my behalf?

'But I'm the Narrator. I'm the voice who has consistently maintained detachment and objectivity despite the grievous provocations I have endured from the others. It's good to hear you, John, but remember you surrendered all rights to this story ages ago ... and why have you given me quotation marks?'

Because things have changed. It's my story, it's my life, it's my head.

'Yes, fair play but I'm not like the others. It is not easy for a sick man to simultaneously conduct his life and comment on it as well.'

Sorry, a sick man?

'You know what I mean'

Not really.

'I don't mean to cause offence but with the diagnosis and all that. Anyway, think of all the times the other Voices wanted to take over the narrative and I stood up to them. All right, for most of the time apart from when I was exhausted. Did

you really want to live through the Bastard's view of the world? He was poisonous, John, you know that. I kept him at bay as much as any human being, well Voice, could. There again did you want your life to be reduced to a dry academic account, its significance lost in a fog of detail and trivia? I was the umpire in your head, remember that. It wasn't always easy keeping the peace, maintaining a degree of order. Who do you think rationed the contribution from the Tempter? You don't know the half of it. He was always coming up with half-baked suggestions about your brother's whereabouts. He was all right in small doses but I rationed his contribution.'

I understand what you are saying.

'If I had given in to the Jester you would have gone mad. Well, you know what I mean.'

I know what you mean.

'And let's not forget my artistic contribution. Apart from being over-wordy on occasions, I haven't done a bad job. Admittedly I've struggled with the continuity a bit. Even I found it difficult to work out which world you were living in. It hasn't been easy finding language appropriate to 16th-century Holland. Your figurative language is buggered for a kick off. You can't just drop in a simile which depends on the 21st century for its point of reference. It was quite restricting at times.'

Narrator, you've done very well, although I think you'll be struggling to find a publisher. Basically it is time to move on. There are many stories out there waiting to be told by someone with your talent.

'Thanks. I don't suppose there's any chance of a sequel?'

I'm afraid not

SIXTY-TWO: John's Tale

I remember waking in the morning to the extraordinary experience of having space in my head. The curtains in my room remained unclosed. This in itself was unusual. A cherubic cloud moved between the chimneystacks on the tenements opposite. There was nothing metaphoric about the cloud. It was just a cloud. I listened to the silence in my head which made itself manifest like an echo of the white noise associated with tinnitus. Nothing stirred in there. No one spoke. I waited unless the Voices, led astray by the Jester, were playing a macabre game of hide and seek, and would suddenly burst into my consciousness with a loud 'Boo!' If they were hiding they had gone very deep. I waited, reluctant to embrace prematurely the possibility that they had indeed fled. Eventually I spoke out loud. 'OK, where are you? I've slept well, come out and do your worst.' The half door swung on the saloon bar, the tumbleweed bowled down the deserted street but no one stepped out.

In the dining room I nodded at my fellow residents as they went through their daily breakfast ritual. As usual, Paul spilt milk down his cardigan. He had finally got one over on the gerunds and did not want to lose the momentum. Kevin put the toast back on his plate and stared at me. 'You're different,' he said, with a tone that hovered somewhere between a smirk and derision.

'The voices have left him,' said Paul, without glancing up from page 314.

'Something like that,' I said.

'Are you going to talk all through my breakfast?' asked Kevin.

'You've been lulled,' said Mick, tapping the side of his nose, 'into a false sense of security. Mark my words, son, they'll be back soon enough. I ken their tricks. You can't outwit them. Christ, I've tried!'

My mood at that point was somewhere between ecstasy and unadulterated elation. My heart was, quite simply, bursting with joy. I had experienced manic episodes in the past but this felt different somehow. In that moment, holding my cup with a shaking hand, I was paralysed with happiness. If I moved too suddenly I feared that I would shatter the porcelain-thin bubble that had enveloped me. If I stood up from the table the world would go dark again.

'Are you all right, John?' asked Janet.

'Never better,' I replied truthfully. 'I think I'll go for a walk, it's a fine day.'

Mick glanced up from under his beanie as if hoping for an invitation, but I wanted my own company.

As I walked down Broughton Street towards Canonmills I was aware of the complete absence of commentary from the Narrator. My every move was not being tapped out on someone else's laptop. My thoughts were my own; no one was questioning them, casting scorn or making mischief.

I paused at the noticeboard at the entrance to the Botanic Gardens and smiled at the invitation to *Celebrate Life at the Botanics*. Worth a try I thought. *Become a member.* I could if I wanted, no problem. *Study Practical Horticulture at St*

Andrews. I don't think so, thanks very much. I was very conscious that these thoughts remained my own spontaneous internalised reactions, for the first time in a very long while they did not belong to uninvited parasites lodging in my head.

Despite the early hour couples were wandering fondly trying to make sense of the Latin names on plaques at the foot of every exotic tree. I knew what the Bastard would have said had he been there. Something along the lines of 'No loving relationship for you, loser.'

What mattered as I wandered through the gardens, past the ornamental bridge spanning the lily clad pond was the sheer novelty of being liberated, and being happy.

Each door into the nine greenhouses opened automatically when you pushed a button. After a short delay the double doors opened into a world that was markedly different from the one to which I had so recently returned. The wet walkway led between high ferns and fronds that climbed towards the glass roof. The intense smell of damp earth made me catch my breath. Water trickled into a dark grotto carved between lichen-covered rocks. Coins glistened at the bottom of the pond. Huge red flowers burst.

Quite simply what I was experiencing was exactly the elation that must have suffused Johannes' soul as he clutched his son as they wandered through Leyden lapping up the gratitude of the citizens. This awareness didn't alarm me at the time and still doesn't.

Although I still do not fully understand the other world I entered or indeed created, be it psychotic delusion, an intense self-constructed fantasy into which I could escape at times of stress, or simply an experience that defies all explanation, I feel acutely fond of all three weavers and think of them often. Why did the Spanish take Michel to Leyden? Why was his life spared? His captors were hardly renowned for their compassion. How was their journey back to the village? In my mind's eye I saw not the *Hunters in the Snow*, which was the start of this whole thing but Bruegel's *The Corn Harvest* suffused with the heavy languid heat of summer.

Most of the peasants take their hard earned rest while others continue to work bent double as they tie the corn. Did the weavers break their journey a while and accept bread from the woman with the basket in the foreground? There is a small boy at the edge of the picture seated on a rick of corn, drinking a white liquid from his bowl. Is it Michel? If so, where are the others? Come to think of it that might be Johannes and Balthasar next to him. A younger man in a white shirt, clutching a pitcher, emerges from the thin passageway cut through the heart of the cornfield. Perhaps that's Cornelius. Two birds fly low over the field. The crickets ratchet the heat up another notch. The peasant lying full length on the ground snores, loudly drunk with the heat and the aftermath of toil. How will their journey end? Will Antonia shriek with pleasure and disbelief when she catches sight of her men folk coming down the track? Does she drop the wooden gruel basin she was cleaning and run towards Michel, her arms outstretched? I hope so.

SIXTY-THREE: The Exhibition

Come in. Yes, you with a copy of *John McPake and the Sea Beggars* under your arm. You who have travelled with me for three hundred pages. Shall I take your coat? No, it is a bit chilly. Have you been to the Drill Hall before? Nor me, though I know that Stevenson College has used it for their photography exhibitions. But this one is all mine. Remarkable isn't it? I can't even offer you a glass of wine; the official opening isn't until tomorrow. Will I leave you to browse on your own, or will I bore you with a commentary? Ok, serves you right.

Yes, well, that's just my potted biography. 'Born in Belshill in '68. Educated at Aberdeen University, taught at Gracemount High. Dismissed from post in 2000. Eventually lived rough on the streets until diagnosed with schizophrenia ... ' Not a bad CV for an artist is it? It makes me sound interesting, you know, like Orwell in *Down and Out in Paris and London*. Even at the time the psychiatrists couldn't agree. I had more Latin names then a Victorian cabinet of curiosities. ' ... Lived in a hostel managed by the voluntary sector until 2008 when he felt sufficiently well to live independently ... ' again, as you'll appreciate, sufficiently well covers a multitude of interpretations. 'Studied photography at college and won the BP Award in 2010.' I love reading that bit. I know it's immodest but hey!

Enough of this narcissistic claptrap. This is the first snap I took in earnest. It's the folk from the hostel. Bizarre, isn't it. Like a school photo. All we need is for someone to run along the back row to get his picture taken twice. The old boy with the beanie pulled down his face, that's Mick. It was Mick who gave me my first camera. To this day no one knows where he got it. A Nikon 435, nice bit of equipment. It took him ages to agree to stand in line. He's deeply paranoid, an old Communist for whom life is one long conspiracy. 'Photies can be used in evidence,' he told me. 'Don't give them an inch'. I still see Mick sometimes. I love him to bits actually.

See that sleikit man with the supercilious expression, that's Kevin, he caused me a lot of pain. You know all that stuff about my brother, well, I know it was him who sent me the postcards. Wee bastard.

And that's Paul, I've told you about Paul before. He told me straight that he would not look at the camera or say 'cheese' as he had his book to read. He must have memorised it by now.

Do you see that wee man hiding next to Paul? Well that's Dennis, and that's the first time he was ever seen with the other residents, let alone in a photo with them. I was really touched that he left his bedroom for the first time in a blue moon to say goodbye to me. I'd only ever spoken to him before through the narrow crack between his door and the frame. I didn't even know he had a second eye, but there he is. Good on him. I've heard since that the photo opp was something of a turning point for him. After that he would sometimes come down for breakfast. Brilliant isn't it? Sadly, Jack's not in the picture. His death wish finally came true.

And that's Beverley, great woman. She's the manager. She always looked after me, never gave me a row not even when she was dragged out of bed by the police who were returning me, more or less intact, to the hostel. I owe her.

This next sequence is called 'Silence'. I know, some of them are a bit clichéd. *The Meadows at Dawn,* a poor man's Colin Baxter. Likewise *Arthur's Seat,* I had a strange experience at that very spot. Let's face it, I had strange experiences all over the place. I wanted to go back. To be honest I wanted to see if it would all start up again. But no. Nothing. Just a high wind. That one's better. *Mr Heron standing on one leg in the Water of Leith near Stockbridge.* Despite the proximity of the traffic, everything in that moment became still, and utterly silent. And that is what never ceased to astound me in those early days, a life without Voices.

Do I still hear them? I'm often asked that. Let me put it this way, even if I don't hear them as I used to, I still anticipate what they might say if they were there. I have always had an impressive capacity for self-criticism which was the specialism of my least favourite Voice. From that point of view he might as well still be there, except I have much greater control now. Part of my brain has always enjoyed finding out things, I'm probably what they call a theorist. As a result my inner voice often resorts to a parody of what the Academic used to say to me. He was one of the Voices; I didn't mind him too much, although I never ceased to be amazed at sheer range of his knowledge. Does any of this make sense? Am I boring you? Thank you, you're very kind.

I mentioned Mick earlier didn't I? Well this series was taken in the High Street during the Fringe. In all the time I've known Mick I've never seen him without that hat. I'm sure he sleeps in it, it must be mingin'. I still think of that day, actually you couldn't make it up. Just look, there's a geisha girl, next to her is someone with his hand up a squirrel's arse. If you look you'll see that the fellow there has a propeller on his head. And that, unless I'm mistaken, is Adolf Hitler giving out leaflets. I remember Mick shaking his head muttering 'The medication's wearing off,' and then these lads, students, came up to us and tried to guess which show we were in. 'It must be Beckett.' 'No, it's Pinter's *Caretaker.*' 'It's called *Psycho,* and there's no tickets,' growled Mick. It was a great day.

This one, umm, do you recognise it? Yes, well done, close, it's a pastiche of Bruegel's *Hunters in the Snow*. I took it last winter during the cold snap. It's actually Duddingston Loch seen from Holyrood Park. Do you remember, the loch froze over for the first time in a hundred years or something like that? Eventually I persuaded three dog walkers to pose for me on the slope above the loch. They were getting a bit grumpy but I think it worked. And look there, do you see that bird floating in the middle distance? Yes, just like the original. It's the one I won't sell. You know what happened don't you? I've told you before. Yes, my obsession with the Eighty-Years Dutch war and all the times I believed I was living through the Inquisition. I've had lots of discussions with psychiatrists since then. They have suggested all sorts of explanations: a variant on bog standard psychosis, a type of Dissasociative Identity Disorder. I know, I know, in fact as the term came out of my mouth I knew exactly what the Academic would have said. He would have had fun with that one.

It doesn't really matter but the nearest I've found to an explanation that works for me is provided by what's called psychosynthesis. No, I hadn't heard of it either. Evidently some boy, Roberto Assagioli, his name was, a contemporary of both Freud and Jung. He believed in superconscious impulses that we repress at our peril. The trick was, he maintained, to make a bridge to that part of our being where true wisdom is to be found. And I honestly believe that's what happened to me. The delusion, or whatever you want to call it, was not so much a symptom, more a way of connecting with something that would make me better. And so it proved. I've told you all this before, anyway, I honestly believe that the key to my recovery was being able to find, albeit vicariously, hope.

It's difficult to explain ... you know when you wake from a good dream but can't remember any of the detail. Sometimes the afterglow from that dream stays with you all day. You don't know what you are remembering but you feel good somehow, full of hope. That's as close as I can get to explaining why things changed so rapidly for me.

God, I must be trying your patience, you're a good soul. We had better move on before the caretaker switches off all the lights. Yes, there we are, *Tangled Webs*. I took it at the Dovecot Tapestry Workshop in Infirmary Street. It's the strangest thing. Since my delusions, or 'bridges to the superconscious', ended I have developed a fascination with weaving. Yes, I know it's odd. The irony is when I was first detained in the Royal Edinburgh, a few years back mind, an occupational therapist tried to interest me in weaving. It was obviously seen as the ideal therapeutic intervention for the barking mad. Anyway I joined the Dovecot and do you know what the oddest thing is? I instinctively knew what to do. The tutors wouldn't believe me, they obviously thought I had a secret life as a weaver, and you know what? They may not have been far wrong.

That one? That's my sister. See the likeness? Something about the eyes perhaps. Didn't I tell you about her? It's a bit of a long story but basically she turned up out of the blue one day at the Hostel. Beverley, remember the middle-aged woman in the photo? Well she knocked on my door and said I had a visitor. A woman. I asked if it was my new social worker, but she said no, it was someone called McPake. Beverley was obviously anxious on my behalf and offered to chum me down to the dining room where she was waiting. I can honestly say I didn't feel a great deal when I saw her. Just this woman sitting there. 'I'm Lil,' she said. 'Your sister, well half sister.'

To cut a long story short she explained how I had been taken into care days before she was born. 'Mum just couldn't cope,' she said. For the first time in a long while I felt the sensation of total detachment as she spoke; I was somewhere on the ceiling looking interestedly at the expression on her face when I asked her about our brother, Andy. 'What brother?' she asked, 'We haven't got a brother' and in that instant I understood everything. I came down from the ceiling. He too had been an attempt to connect, another bridge with my superconscious or whatever. An imaginary friend, an imaginary brother. A figure conjured from my own needs. A projection if you will. It sounds a bit clichéd but in some way I think it was me I was looking for. I desperately wanted to reconnect with who I had been, more than anything wanted to console that person and tell him things would be all right.

Lil told me that Mum died some ten years back. I noted the fact with sadness but felt no real remorse. I still see Lil on occasions, she's a nurse in Hamilton but, to be honest, she is a bit wary; part of her thinks that beneath this articulate exterior lurks an unreformed axe murderer. That's nurses for you. Anyway.

Just two more if you can stand my monologue for a bit longer. I do like this one. It's Kate. Look at that hair, and that wicked look. We've actually been 'going out' for a few weeks. She's completely off the wall, high maintenance but perhaps part of me needs to look after folk, put something back. Who knows? It doesn't matter. It's working just now and that's all that counts.

This last one? Mmm, it's a bit freaky. At first glance it's just a nice slightly moody shot of a flooded field near Falkirk. I chose black and white. Look at the cows, poor things up to their knees. But the thing is, you see those three shadowy figures in the foreground, they weren't there when I took the shot.

Well look, it's late and you've to get back. Thank you for coming, and thank you for listening to me. Yes, it would be good to have a drink sometime. Can you find your own way out? I'd better switch off the lights. And you. Take care.